600 Letters Home

Cindy Horrell Ramsey

Cindy Horrell Ramsey
Dec 29, 2018

LOGGERHEAD
PRESS

Published by Loggerhead Press

ISBN-13: 978-0692639627
ISBN-10: 0692629624

DEDICATION

This book is dedicated to all service men and women
– past, present and future –
and to the loved ones they leave behind.

Thank you for your sacrifices to secure our freedom.

CONTENTS

ACKNOWLEDGMENTS

The inspiration for this book comes from letters found in the archives of the Battleship NORTH CAROLINA, specifically hundreds donated by former crewmember Paul Wieser. Paul's letters were invaluable for providing gems of knowledge about life during that era – popular songs, favorite movies, thoughts and feelings, and a heartwarming innocence of character.

But this book is a work of fiction. It is not the love story of Paul Wieser and Jean Coddington. Nor is it the love story of my parents, for whom my characters are named.

I am aware that as a sailor in the 5th Division, Roy Harrison sees more and knows more than any one crewmember would have historically seen or known. I ask my readers to focus on Roy's and Evelyn's story of love and sacrifice. For the sacrifice is real. The military events and battles experienced in this novel actually happened to the USS NORTH CAROLINA and her crew.

I love and thank the former crewmembers and their families for welcoming me into their fold since I attended my first crew reunion in the spring of 2001. Thanks to the staff of the Battleship NORTH CAROLINA Memorial in Wilmington, NC, for access and support – especially Museum Services Director Kim Sincox and Curator Mary Ames Booker.

Award winning author Rebecca Lee's positive critiques and feedback encouraged me early in the writing process. Much gratitude to Charlotte Baggett, Debbie Carlton, Patricia Rivenbark, and Ann Beach for reading the manuscript and offering feedback.

I appreciate Denise Kiernan's nonfiction book, *The Girls of Atomic City*, for only after reading that book was I able to develop an intriguing female character who made her own sacrifices and kept her own secrets for the sake of winning the war.

Lastly, I thank my family for always loving and supporting me in this journey to be the best writer that I can be.

PROLOGUE

Simms Hollow, Georgia

December 7, 1941

Chunky hurried out the back, catching the screen door just before it slammed. He could still taste the fried chicken Ma had fixed for lunch. Sundays were the best – a great big meal after church and the afternoon to do what you want before chore time. He grabbed his fishing poles off the porch and headed to the creek. Might catch some trout for supper. Might catch something better.

He'd just settled down on the bank and baited his hook when he heard the dry leaves crunching behind him. He could tell who was coming by the light footsteps, so he just played it cool and tossed his line in the water.

"Mind if I join you?" Evelyn asked.

"Be disappointed if you didn't," Chunky said, barely looking back. He brushed some twigs away beside him and offered her a seat.

"I brought cookies," she said. "And a thermos of milk."

Chunky pulled his legs up and steadied the pole between his knees so his hands were free.

"You make these?" he asked, finishing off his second cookie.

"You're getting to be as good a cook as your Ma."

Evelyn offered the thermos after taking a sip. "Yeah, I did. Ma's been after me to learn how to cook. Figured I better start trying."

Chunky looked at the rim of the thermos where droplets of milk lingered. Evelyn's lips had just touched that same spot. He licked the rim, then took a big gulp. Just about choked. That seemed to be happening more and more these days. She rattled him something awful without even trying.

"You want to fish?" he asked, handing her the extra pole.

"Sure," Evelyn said.

"Need help with the bait?"

"Nah, you know I can do it."

He did know. They had been coming to the creek to fish for years. Evelyn's family owned the farm down a ways from his family. But these days things were different. Evelyn wasn't the scrawny little tomboy who used to follow him and his brother around and aggravate the fool out of them. She wasn't like his sister, staying in the house learning to sew and cook and do the women things. Evelyn was different. She fished and milked cows and rode horses better than the guys.

But then last spring Chunky asked Evelyn to go to the senior prom with him – he didn't have a girlfriend and didn't want to go alone. Thought asking his fishing buddy would work. He remembered standing in the living room waiting for her to come downstairs. He was dressed in a suit with a tie that was just about to strangle him and holding a flower his Ma said he had to get.

He heard her call his name and looked toward the stairs. Every last bit of the air left his lungs. Her braids were gone, replaced by curls the color of a mountain sunset that cascaded across her bare shoulders and down her back. Her jay blue dress sparkled like early morning dew drops. Her emerald eyes glistened with laughter at his jaw-dropped stare.

"You forget I was a girl?" she teased.

"Won't happen again," he said. And it didn't. After that night, holding her hand and dancing close, then that walk down by the river afterwards. Nope, he didn't forget again.

"Don't know what you're thinking about," Evelyn said, breaking his train of thought. "But I like that look in your eyes."

"Want to take a walk?" Chunky asked.

"I got a better idea," Evelyn said. "Could I come over to your house and listen to the radio? The New York Philharmonic Orchestra is playing today, and ours is still broke."

Chunky didn't care much for that kind of music, but Evelyn loved it. She got all dreamy eyed and liked to hold hands, even lay her head on his shoulder when she listened. That was good enough for him.

"You sure your Ma won't care if you come to my house?"

"Well, I am your sister's best friend."

"But she ain't there today."

"Ma don't have to know that," Evelyn said with a shy smile.

The Harrison's sitting room wasn't fancy by any standards, but it was warm and cozy with overstuffed furniture draped in colorful homemade afghans and quilts. Pap had stoked the woodstove right after lunch, and warmth radiated throughout the house.

Chunky knelt down in front of the radio and adjusted the dial until he found the show Evelyn wanted to hear. The couple settled down on the sofa, not so close as to alarm his Ma if she walked through, but close enough that he could reach out and hold her hand under the afghan covering their legs.

After a while Chunky felt his eyelids drooping and had just about nodded off when the elegant music was abruptly interrupted.

"From the NBC newsroom in New York. President Roosevelt said in a statement today that the Japanese have attacked Pearl Harbor in Hawaii from the air. I repeat, the Japanese have attacked Pearl Harbor."

"What does that mean?" Evelyn asked.

"I'll tell you what it means," Chunky's Pap said, standing in the kitchen doorway taking off his coat. "It means we're going to war. Watch my word. We can't stay out of that blamed war no more."

Chunky could feel Evelyn's eyes on him as he stared at the radio. He hated to hurt her with what he was about to say.

"If that happens I gotta go," he said. "I gotta sign up to fight."

1941

DECEMBER

December 15, 1941 (Letter #1)

Dear Evelyn,

I made it to boot camp today. Man, was it a crazy day. We had to take off all our clothes. Then they painted a big red number on my chest with iodine or mercurochrome or something. I was number 62. We went from one line to another. Naked. I'm sure glad that women ain't allowed in our Navy with us guys.

They weighed us and measured us in one line. Then in another they checked our hearts and throats and stuff. Then in another line, we had to get a shot. I don't like needles, so I was sweating bullets, but at least I didn't pass out like that one guy did. Yeah, this really big bulky guy with red hair just keeled right over and hit the floor. Man, was that loud.

He didn't have that red hair very long, and all my brown curls you like so good are gone too. In one line we had to sit in a chair and they shaved it all off. Everybody's head looked the same after that. Well, sort of. You never know how bumpy somebody's head might be when it's covered in hair. Or how many scars they might have. Makes you wonder.

They checked our teeth, too. Reminded me of when Pap would take the livestock to market. Pulled and prodded and poked. Teeth checked. Branded. At least mine was mercurochrome and not a hot iron!

I gotta go. It's lights out now. I didn't get a chance to tell you about the train ride or boat ride or nothing, but I'm at Newport News, Rhode Island.

I'll send you my address tomorrow.

Love always,
Chunky

PS: When you write to me, don't call me Chunky. Call me by my real name, Roy. The Navy just calls me Harrison.

December 17, 1941   (Letter #2)
Dearest Evelyn,

Before I forget or run out of time, I want to give you my address so you can write to me. If I'm doing the same things every day, I might run out of things to say, so I'll need your letters to answer.

Roy Harrison
U.S. Naval Training Station
CO #45
Newport, R.I.

I know I said I would write every day, but I've been kinda busy. I really will write as much as I can. I'm going to tell you about my trip here first. But don't you get mad at me because I didn't do none of those things some of the other guys were doing. There were even girls on the train ride, so you can guess what happened. Use your imagination. But it wasn't me.

It was long and noisy and hot. There was plenty of beer to drink and other stuff. Some of the guys had cigarettes and one of them offered me one. I didn't take it. I did try a beer though. But it was so hot on the train – yeah, even in the winter – and it was rocking and I thought I was going to puke so I didn't drink much. I moved to a seat in the front and started thinking about you.

You'll have to pardon the handwriting because I'm writing fast. Boy if you only knew how much I miss you and everybody. Maybe I'll get used to it, but I reckon it takes a long time.

Well let me tell you some more about when I first got here. After we went through all those lines and got needles and stuff they gave us a duffel bag with everything that we would have while we are here. I think that's three months. It was heavy. It had a mattress wrapped around it and that's what I sleep on.

In the bag was a whole bunch of stuff that's mine now. It's all I got cause they kept my clothes that I wore here. Anyhow, it has clothes and a knife and a toothbrush and washrags and shoes and socks and blankets and a whisk broom and shoe polish and well you see what I mean, it was heavy.

We have these things that look like boots but don't have a bottom. After we put on our uniforms and our shoes, we have to put them on over our pants. Just the new recruits have to wear them. That's why they call us boots.

We don't stay in the same place the other fellas here do but I can see them sometimes. They don't wear those things over their pants legs, so I know they're not new like me. We're in D Barracks. Everybody calls it detention. I guess that's what the D stands for. It's kind of like being in jail. But don't tell nobody I said that.

Well, everybody else is hitting the sack, so I'll write some more tomorrow. I hope you're not mad at me for leaving. I just couldn't stay home after what happened. I hope you understand. We're supposed to be in training for 90 days, then have 10 days leave.

I'll see you then.

Love,
Roy

December 20, 1941 (Letter #3)

My Dear Evelyn,

I'm sorry it's been three days since my last letter. I been real busy. I hope that I get a letter from you real soon. If my writing looks funny, it's because my arm is sore. We got needles again today. Then, we had to carry those big rifles. That was hard.

I'm already doing guard duty. I walk up and down on the waterfront carrying a gun that weighs near about 12 lbs. It's cold here and tough, but the food is good. I never had to wash my own clothes before, but I do now, and I think I do a pretty good job. Do you wash your own clothes? I bet your Ma is teaching you because you're a girl and you're gonna graduate in a few months. I wish my Ma had taught me, but I know how to do it now.

I have to tell you about this one thing that happened. This one guy on guard duty caught this other fella going A.W.O.L. - Absent With Out Leave - and he put a bayonet through him. Boy I hope I never have to do something like that. I'll be glad when this schooling is over. Everything has to be just perfect and they really put the clamps on you. It's just like jail.

I don't want you to think it's so bad, they got to do it to make us tough. But I guess I just have to tell somebody my troubles and I miss you and my Ma and Pap and my friends. I miss home, too.

You know how we talked about going to New York? I heard we might get to go there. Depends on what ship we get assigned to. Maybe you could come see me and we could go to a show just like you said you wanted to do. That is if your Ma will let you come. I know you're still seventeen and all.

I get paid four times while I'm here. I think it'll be about 40 dollars all together. I'll be waiting for your letter. I miss you.

All my love,
Roy Harrison
US Navy Training Station

8

December 25, 1941 (Letter #4)

Dear Evelyn,

This is the first Christmas I ever been away from home, and let me tell you it's not a good feeling at all. Sure they try to make us feel better by feeding us good and playing lots of Christmas songs. They even let us have today off from training, which is pretty good, I guess. But somehow it might be better if I was real busy and didn't have so much time to think.

I sure am glad I bought you a Christmas present before I left home. Did Sally Jane remember to bring it over to your house?

I got some Christmas cards the last few days and they were real fine. I liked the one from you the best, especially the way you signed it with XOXO. Real hugs and kisses would be better, but I guess that will have to do for now.

There's this one guy in my barracks named John that's from New York. He was telling me about a big new battleship that was built in Brooklyn Navy Yard not far from where he lived. He said it was the first battleship been built by America in more than 18 years and it was the biggest, baddest thing you ever saw.

John said that ship hadn't gone to war yet, and he hoped we would get assigned to it. Its name is the Battleship NORTH CAROLINA. He said it would be the best ship to be on. You never know where we will be though.

Merry Christmas,

Roy

1942

JANUARY

January 1, 1942

Dear Evelyn,

Happy New Year! I hope you had a fine celebration with everybody back home. Guess you'll be going back to school any day now. Not much longer before you graduate. What are you planning to do then?

Now that I'm in my new barracks, the work really started. We've been running and practicing with our guns and all kinds of training. I'm learning to talk and send messages with semaphore flags. It's real hard cause some of the things they mean are a lot alike and you can get confused. I'll show you what I'm talking about when I come home.

I like getting your letters. I showed your picture to the guys and they think you look swell. They said they bet you were nice, and I told them you were. They started calling you Peaches because this one guy said that he heard they grow real good peaches in Georgia. I said yeah, I reckon we do.

Most of the guys have nicknames, but they haven't given me one yet. I didn't tell a soul my nickname is Chunky. I might have been fat when I was a little boy and my grandma started calling me that and everybody else did too till it stuck. But I'm getting right skinny now. All that running and not so much eating. But the food is good and they do let you eat all you want. It's just that sometimes I'm too tired to even eat.

We might not be training 90 days after all. They said it might be cut to 60 days. I guess that war is heating up and they need some more sailors on the ships. I'm ready to get my leave time and come see you. I want to see my Ma and Pap and everybody else, too.

All my love,

Roy

PS: I decided putting numbers on all these letters would be crazy so I stopped. That's my New Year's resolution. No numbers. Six years is a long time and a lot of letters.

January 10, 1942

My dearest Evelyn,

If my handwriting looks funny, I can't blame the shots this time. We've been loaded up on a train and headed somewhere. It's bumping and so's my hand so I can't write steady. They don't tell us where we're going. All I know is that they cut our training short, and we're headed to assignment. Keep writing. They said the letters would find us, but I don't know how long that will take.

The bad thing I have to tell you is that we don't get that leave they said. We didn't train 90 days like they said, and we didn't train 60 days like the second thing they said. I guess you can't believe everything the Navy says. Seems like we're slowing down at some train station somewhere so I'll close for now. I'll mail this as soon as I can and write again when I know where I'm going.

All my love,

Roy

January 13, 1942

My dearest Evelyn,

You won't believe where I am. I don't hardly believe it myself. That train took us all the way down to Florida where we spent the night. Then they lined us up and marched us out to the docks carrying our big ole sea bags. Then they put so many of us on this little ship called a destroyer that we bunched in there like cattle gone to market.

They took us out in the ocean where it was rough and we were being tossed all around. It was foggy and you couldn't hardly see nothing. Then all of a sudden rising out of the ocean like a monster or something we saw the biggest darn ship ever. There was the number 55 on the back and that guy John was standing beside me. He said, 'That's it! That's the North Carolina.' And sure enough, it was. That's where I am now. Got here yesterday.

Everybody seemed to have heard about this ship but me. Said there was a lot of stuff on the television and in the newspapers and all. Guess that news didn't get to Simms Hollow or we just didn't pay attention. Must of thought something going on in New York wouldn't ever matter to us.

Anyhow, after we got onboard, we had to gather up in the mess hall and get our assignments. They acted like we had a choice – even asked us what kind of work we wanted to do. But in the end they just put us where they wanted us to be. But I think I got a pretty good deal.

I've been assigned to the 5th Division, which means I get to work on the deck and take care of a bunch of boats and run a crane and everything. I'm not below deck and that's good. The ship has a lot of different Divisions and the one you're assigned to tells you what you gonna be doing and where you'll live and sleep and work.

Then, we have what's called a battle station. Mine is the 5-inch gun mount. I don't know so much about it yet, but I'll tell you when I start training on it. We'll do a lot of training before we go anywhere to fight. I have a lot of catching up to do because some of the fellas have been on here since the ship was commissioned last spring and they already been firing the guns.

Well, that's all for tonight.

All my love,

Roy

USS Battleship NORTH CAROLINA

January 15, 1942

Dear Evelyn,

Your letters haven't caught up to me on the ship yet, but I do have a few left that I can answer. First, let me tell you about being on the ship.

The fellas in my division gave me a nickname. You won't believe what it is. They didn't know nothing about what the fellas at boot camp called you. Now they're calling me Peaches. There's this other guy onboard who's from Georgia, too. They call him Atlanta. I like that better but once you get a nickname it sticks and you can't do one thing about it.

Almost everybody has a nickname – there's Atlanta and Mud (he's from Mississippi) and Broadway (guess where he's from) and Rocky is from Colorado. I think I would like to go to those mountains sometimes. Way he talks, they're mighty fine. He makes out like they're even better than our mountains back home. Then there's other names they get not because of where they're from but because of something they did. Not something good.

There's this one guy they call Sparky because he did something dumb with some wiring and almost started a fire. That would have been real bad. We can't go nowhere but in the water if the ship catches on fire. And it better not be one of us who does that. Probably the Germans. They say the Germans have submarines in the Atlantic and they're going to try to attack the good ole USA. I hear that's why we didn't go fight the Japs yet. We got to take care of the Germans first. I'll protect you, so don't you worry.

Now, back to your letters. I'm sorry that you made a bad grade on that math test. I know you want to do good on all your tests, but sometimes everybody makes a mistake. Just like Sparky – at least your mistake didn't almost burn the school down!!

Anyhow, don't let what Jeb and those guys say get you down. They just probably want to take you out on a date and they don't have enough sense to know they should be nice first. It's ok with me if you don't go with any of them. Can't you just go with a bunch of girls to the soda shop? That would be better than staying home. I bet my brother Billy would still go fishing with you.

Most of the guys on the ship have pin-up girls in their lockers, movie stars and such. I'm glad you sent me that picture so I could put you in my locker. It's little but that's ok cause I don't want everybody looking at it every time I open my locker. I can see it.

Yes, I do know that song, 'This Love of Mine.' The whole gun crew knows it. They sing it all the time. I think they might be making fun of me, but I don't know. Most of them have girlfriends or even wives. One of the fellas has a picture of his new baby boy. I wouldn't want to go away and leave my wife to have a baby without me. I guess he really don't have a choice though. He said he hopes he gets back home before that baby's all grown up.

Your last letter I got was written before Christmas so I guess you didn't have your present. I hope you like it when you get it.

Well that's all for now.

Yours truly,
Roy

Jan 19, 1942

Dearest Evelyn,

Well, we haven't received any mail call in a while now so I don't have much to write about. We've been practicing our guns every day and shooting at targets in the air.

You saw the pictures of the ship I sent you, right? You know those planes on the fantail (that's the back of the ship). You should see them take off. They shoot them out of there with gunpowder. They fly around a while and come back. They can't land on the ship so they land in the water then we hoist them up with the crane and put them back on the ship.

We're still down south but we hadn't gone to war yet. I heard we'll be headed to New York before we go. Wish you could meet me there.

Love,
Roy

Jan 31, 1942
Dear Evelyn,

We just got to New York today. I cannot even begin to tell you what it was like to see the Statue of Liberty standing there with her arm held high. It was foggy so I couldn't see it when we were a ways off. But I stood on deck and watched it come into view. I tell you it made me swell up with pride.

I'm glad we got back safe. We went through a part of the ocean near North Carolina where the Germans been busy sinking ships with their U Boats. I don't know how many ships they sunk but they didn't get us. We didn't get them either so that's not good.

I got a bunch of letters when we had mail call today. To start with I didn't think I was going to get any. We had mail call and they didn't call my name so I went back to my work station. Then after chow we had another mail call and I still didn't get any. Next time they said mail call I didn't even go, but I was working on the crane and somebody brought me a whole bundle of letters.

I got six from you and two from Sally Jane and three from my Ma. I guess I better not make this letter too long so I can write Ma. She sounds real sad. She said my cousin Stuart joined the Marines. I'm not so sure about how he'll like that. We got some Marines on our ship but I don't ever see them much. I hear they can shoot though. Stuart should like that. He always did like to go hunting.

Hey, did I tell you we get to watch movies on the ship sometimes? We just saw this one called 'Swanee River.' Did you see that one? I hope you saw it. I guess you were right when you said I was sentimental. That movie did it to me. This guy got married and he told his wife to wait up in a boat in the moonlight while he wrote a song. But he took a long time – like two or three hours – and when he got back she was mad. She tells him to leave. But he don't say nothing to her. He just starts singing 'Jeanie with the Light Brown Hair.' She wasn't mad anymore.

Well I reckon I better write to my Ma now.

Still loving you,

Roy

PS - Did I tell you we have our own ice cream making machine right here on the ship?

MARCH

March 8, 1942

My dearest Evelyn,

I got your letter yesterday. It was a very happy day for me. It's been so long since I heard from you I thought you were mad at me about something. Not a single letter in February so we missed Valentine's Day. I hope you got my card, but I didn't hear nothing so maybe you didn't. I guess you been busy at school and I been busy here on the ship. I'll try to do better writing letters if you will.

I didn't have time to read it right off because I had to be in crew with Lawson. Lyle Lawson is new in my division but we're good buddies now. Anyhow, I was in crew with Lawson in a motorboat. I did get to see the picture. It was swell. We were riding around in the motorboat and picking up different officers from different ships. I guess you don't know but we're in Casco Bay, Maine now. I had the letter under my life jacket and every minute or so I would feel it to make sure it was still there. I didn't want to lose it. I wish I could explain the thrill I had. I'll try.

It's a great feeling to know you have a job to do and not everybody gets to do that job. And it's a good one. It's not a hard job but it's sure a good one – except sometimes it's cold. But it's a great feeling to be speeding along in the water with the wind in your face. The boat motor doesn't make a lot of noise and the water just speeds by. Lawson and I stand in one place in the stern (that's the back of the boat) and the coxswain is in the cockpit steering the boat. Maybe I'll be a coxswain one day. Anyhow the stern goes down in the water when we go faster and the bow comes up (that's the front of the boat) and the water just ripples along behind us. I hope you can understand the feeling. It was swell.

After we picked up all the officers and took them where they needed to be then took some other ones back to their ships, I got to have a little time to read since I wasn't on watch for another hour. But I didn't have time to write anything til now.

I been missing your letters but I know you are busy with school and your friends and all. I'm glad you like the bracelet I gave you for Christmas. I saw a silver one kind of like it when I was on liberty and I bought it for me. It was a man's watch but it was silver and looked kind of like your bracelet so I bought it and thought about you when I look at the time.

I'm not good with words so I can't always say exactly what I want to say. I know I'm gonna be gone a long time, but I want you to be my girl. You can still go and have fun with a bunch of people. You don't have to just sit at home. Maybe just not go out alone with any of the other boys.

The fellas on the ship all go out on liberty whatever port we're in. Some of them get real drunk and do stupid stuff and there's always girls at the places we go but I don't even look at them.

They're not you.

Thank you for the invitation to the prom, but I don't think I can come home. You don't have to go by yourself though. Why don't you ask my brother Billy? I know he's a year younger than you but he's tall and he won't do nothing stupid. He's a good dancer too so you wouldn't have to sit around watching everybody else dancing.

Susan is crazy asking a serviceman to take her to the prom but not to wear his uniform. First, he probably can't come home and second, even if he could he'd have to wear his uniform. It's against the rules for any serviceman not to wear his uniform in a crowd during wartime.

I can think about the prom and pretend (in my mind) that I'm dancing with you. We have a pretty good record collection. We had 'I Dream of Jeannie with the Light Brown Hair' but somebody broke it. We got 'Friendship' and 'I Don't Want to Walk Without You Baby' and 'How Do I Know it's Real' and 'I'll Pray for You' That one's swell.

Chow time. I guess I'll close for now.

YOUR sailor,

Roy

Mar 26, 1942

Dear Evelyn,

When I wasn't getting any letters from you, I got so tired of hearing that song 'Somebody Else is Taking My Place' because I figured if you weren't writing to me you might be getting you another fella. I didn't like mail call so much when I didn't get a letter from you. I like getting letters from my Ma and Sally Jane and sometimes Billy even writes me but it's not the same. Stuart even sent me a letter the other day. He hadn't left the states yet and he don't know where the Marines are going to send him. Wouldn't it be something if he ended up on my ship? Probably not.

We had a scare today. We're still trying to guard against the Germans attacking the good ole USA and there was an air raid alarm in Portland - Maine not Oregon. That meant we had to go to our battle stations and stay til the all clear was sounded. We stayed a long time but we didn't have anything to shoot at. Must have been friendlies (that's what they call our own planes).

I got that letter from Sally Jane and she said that the school has gotten to work on graduation. You know I'm making $64 a month and I don't have anywhere to spend it so I'm sending you some money to buy your ring. I know you're working at the drug store, so people can think you bought it. But you got to let me do this for you. I want to real bad. That's what the money order in this letter is for. I sent Sally Jane one too so she won't be mad. Since she's your best friend she's the only person you can tell. Ok?

Thanks for the pen and paper set. It's real nice and I'm using it, see? But all I want you to send me is letters and cards. You save your money for what you need. I know it won't be enough for you to go to college, but it will help you get along after school. I got everything I need on this ship. Except you.

Yours truly,

Roy

PS: Your last letter had the stamp upside down. Did you do that on purpose? I know what it means.

APRIL

April 5, 1942

Dearest Evelyn,

I'm glad you like the pictures. I don't think that one of me is too good, but at least you have one with my dress whites now. So you think Lyle is cute. He has a girlfriend. He doesn't know I sent you that picture with him in it.

Today was a bad day for me. It was visitor's day on the ship. A lot of wives and children came aboard and they had an Easter egg hunt on the bridge. Those kids were laughing and having a good time. I was glad, but it made me sad. Visitor's day and I had no visitors cause everybody I love lives too far away. I wasn't the only one though, so some of us single fellas just went to the fantail and played a game of cards.

We did have a bunch of good food. Lots of ham and turkey and yams and stuff like having Thanksgiving at Easter. Then we had ice cream. I told you we have our own ice cream maker on ship right? I made mine a sundae with nuts and stuff. Made me think about when we went down to the drugstore after school. Remember that day when we went for a walk down by the river? I remember it.

When you get your ring, I want you to take a picture. Hold your books up like you're walking down the hall at school. Not like a fella does it down by his side. Hold them up to your chest and have Sally Jane take a closeup. Then the ring will show up and I can see it. Don't forget.

Yours forever,
Roy

April 9, 1942
Dearest Evelyn,

I'm tired tonight but not so much from working as from having some fun for a change. Today our ship the 'USS NORTH CAROLINA' is one year old. Well I guess she's really older than that – at least parts of her are. But today one year ago was the commissioning. Some folks call it an anniversary but we fellas call it her birthday. So we could have a birthday party.

A lot of the fellas were already on the ship when they had the commissioning and they talk like it was a grand celebration - one like you never seen before.

Today seemed like a big deal, too. Some fancy folks came on

the ship. But the best thing was the tug of war. We had two teams with about 75 guys on each team. It was the deck force (me and Lyle) against the engineers. The deck force won! I reckon that's because we spend more time working with our arms and making muscles but the engineers spend more time thinking with their brains. That might not be true but it's a good way to put it.

Of course we had good food. That's one thing I can say about our ship. They feed us real good. Even though I been working super hard every day I been putting on some weight. A lot of it could be muscle. You wouldn't believe my muscles. You would like them.

Talking about weight - you said in your last letter that you weren't eating so much because you didn't want to get fat. That last picture you sent me – the one of you and Sally Jane down by the river. You looked swell to me.

I had a dream about you last night. I think it was because I was reading your letter when I fell asleep and probably because the fellas were talking about when their wives come to a hotel and they have liberty. Everybody in my division is married now. Everybody but me and Lyle. You should hear them fellas talking. Some of them sent for their girls to come to them to get married. As long as we're in Casco Bay, they get to see them when they have liberty. And when we go out to sea now we don't stay too long. We come back to port real often. Chatter around here says we might be leaving soon, but we never know for real.

Back to my dream. I can dream if I try really hard. I sent for you to come to me and you got here real late. We had a room. You were tired so you went to sleep and I went out. When I got back you were still sleeping. I was going to kiss you good night while you were asleep but you weren't really asleep and well - what a night.

I know I sometimes answer your letters in the wrong order but let me tell you why they get all messed up. I'll use states instead of ports so you can understand better. You send me a letter. Say the ship is in Florida then so the Postmaster sends it to Florida, but before it gets to me in Florida we leave and go to New York. Then the letter has to leave Florida and go to New York but then we might be in Kentucky. So you write another letter when I'm in New York and the Postmaster sends it to New York but we left to go to Virginia or Maine and your letters are going where we were instead of where we are and by the time I get the one that went to Florida I already got the one that went to Maine when we really were in Maine. My letters don't have that problem because you're always in Simms Hollow, Georgia.

I'm glad you got your ring. I told the fellas about me buying you a ring and they thought it was a wedding ring. They all been doing it. We talk about it too. Those talks are long.

Write to me and tell me all about the prom – ALL about it is what I mean. Won't be long before graduation and you're not in high school anymore. What are you going to do then?

Your sailor,

Roy

MAY

May 7, 1942

Dearest Evelyn,

I was glad to get your letter today. They been coming in the right order since we've been in Maine so long but word is we're leaving soon. Us fellas all been talking about what would happen if we did run up on one of them German U Boats and had a fight. We would win. But I guess just in case something went wrong, we had to abandon ship today. It was just a drill.

I been telling you about the guys going to liberty and seeing their girls. Well I don't much go on liberty since we been here. It's been real cold and windy and icy – not rain, real ice. I have to be out in it sometimes to take care of my boats and to lower them for liberty, but the ship is a long way out in Casco Bay when we anchor and the liberty landing ain't close. By the time you get to liberty you're all wet and freezing and that don't sound like fun to me. I guess them guys that have a wife to warm them up got a reason to go. Not me. I get done with my duty and just stay on the ship. You might think I should be writing more letters if I got time, but I been studying real hard to make another rank. If I get to be coxswain I can be in the bow of the captain's gig and not at the stern. I would get to navigate. That will take a lot of studying and working to get there.

We have blackouts every night, sunset to sunrise. So when we're on the night watch we can't do nothing – not even smoke a cigarette but I don't smoke. I tried one but that stuffs not for me.

You didn't tell me much about prom. I thought you'd be excited and tell me all about it but you didn't say much. Sally Jane didn't say much in her letter either. Are you going to tell me? Here's something a fella showed me on his letter. I know I don't have to worry about you. Here's what it said – Be good. But if you can't be good. Be careful.

Love,
Roy

May 20, 1942

Dear Evelyn the graduated,

I got your letter today with a bunch of pictures. Why did you say you didn't like the proofs? I thought they were great. I really like the one with you looking over your shoulder. Your eyes are so big and green like the pasture in spring. (That sounded kinda like a poem didn't it?) You know I always liked your red curls and they were hanging down your back and it looks like you don't have any clothes on. I really like that one.

And I like the ones of graduation too. You and Sally Jane and Emma Sue and Judy Ann all looked real nice. So, you're not in high school anymore. Congratulations! You still going to stay at the drug store or are you going to look for a job somewhere else? I heard that women were starting to work in lots of places now that the men are all going to war. But you might have to leave Simms Hollow to get much of a job. Not a lot to do there. I bet your folks wouldn't want you to do that. Sally Jane says she's going to go to work for the phone company. But she's got to go to Atlanta. I don't think my folks are going to let her do that.

I'm glad you finally told me some stuff about prom. Sounds like you all had a good time. Yes, I do know the song 'Wherever You Are.' I'm sorry that one makes you sad because you don't know where I am. But you did know where I was most of the time. I think that is going to change soon. We hadn't been told nothing but it's just a feeling I got that we're going to go to the Pacific Ocean and go to war for real. I'm not going to be able to tell you anything when we leave and go to war.

'Loose lips sink ships.'

Your sailor,
Roy

JUNE

June 8, 1942
Dearest Evelyn,

I haven't had a letter from you in a while so this one may be short. I don't have anything to answer. You should have got a lot of letters from me. I been trying to write almost every day but we been real busy practicing and getting ready. I know why I hadn't got your letters. You know we left Maine and went to Virginia but your letters didn't catch up.

Today we left Virginia. Some of the fellas think we're going to the Pacific but we don't know. When we do go where we go my letters might look a bit funny. We've been warned. All our letters get read by the censor before they get mailed and if we say something we're not supposed to say it might get a big black line through it or it might get cut out so if you get letters with holes that's why.

Last week in the 'Tarheel' - you know the ship's paper - there was this thing called the censor's dream. I thought it was pretty good. Here it is –

Dear _____,

Miss you. Love You.

Write soon.

Love,

———

I'm going to try to write more than that but if it gets messed up you understand.

We got a change of uniform today. Now we're wearing dungarees and shirts that match and we had to dye our Dixie cup hats blue too. I'll send you a picture. I think we look swell.

I been trying to write better like you said. Take my time so you can read it and not write on both sides of the paper since the ink runs through and makes a mess. Can you read them better now?

Yours truly,

Roy

June 24, 1942

San Francisco, California

My dearest Evelyn,

If this letter has holes it's because I said something I wasn't supposed to say. I want to tell you some of the stuff I saw but boy oh boy you probably wouldn't believe it. It's ok that I tell you we're in San Francisco because it's still the United States and people see us here. The reporters are around sometimes taking pictures like they did in New York.

We had to go through the Panama Canal to get here. If you don't know what that is look it up in the encyclopedia. Our ship is so big we almost didn't fit and people could reach out and touch us. They threw things like bananas at us, or maybe to us.

We were in this one place but I won't tell you where and there was this whole line of battleships lined up. They were old ones cause they weren't as big as us and you could just tell they were old. But man what a sight!

I better write something else. I got a letter from your Ma. That was real nice of her. Tell her I will try to be safe so she can thank me when I get home. I thought that was a swell thing to say. I get lots of letters saying things like that but nobody says it the way she did. She has a fine way of saying things. I always liked your Ma.

I told you how proud I was that you can save so much money even though you don't make near as much as me. You don't have to blow me out for lending mine to some of the fellas who need it. It's kind of like saving it. I lent out twenty, kept 40, get paid 32 next payday. I'm saving it cause I got some plans I can't tell you now. I got a hundred dollars saved already. We been hearing that Congress is passing some new bills that will give more money to us service men. One of them will give Seamen twenty more dollars for being married.

Yes, the fellas do talk about being married. If you don't hear it from somewhere else I'll tell you one day all about being married. Some of the fellas that didn't get married when we were in New York were wondering if you could get married through the mail.

We been hearing some good songs. Do you know that one 'There I've Said it Again?' It's a swell one. This one guy Paul told me about a swell song but I forgot the title. It's about a girl throwing a kiss out to sea. I think it's called 'I Threw a Kiss to the Sea.'

When I'm on the night watch I think about that song 'Blues in the Night.' I can't listen to nothing when I'm out there at night but when the sky is clear I can see all the stars and think about a lot of things. I think about you a lot. I hope you think about me. I wonder if the stars I see are the same ones you see.

You didn't tell me what you're going to do. You going to wait until summer's over to look for another job or are you going to stay at the drugstore? Did you figure out who that man in the fancy suit was you said came in the drugstore?

I saw some of the other fella's mail and it had S.W.A.K. on the back. Do you know what that means? All you really have to do is put on your lipstick and kiss the envelope then that would be for real unless you get tired of kissing paper.

I think that's not true about a sailor getting 96 letters at one time. They're going to find us to get us our letters. Sailors love mail call. Some say they'd rather have a letter than eat.

Remember that you are the only one for me. But you can go on out and have a swell time, at least for now. One day you might have to forget about me and that will make it easier.

That's all for now.

Yours truly,
Roy

JULY

Pearl Harbor: July 11, 1942

I been following all the rules since I been on the ship, but I'm breaking one now. Sometimes you just gotta get stuff off your chest or you can't sleep. What good would I be to the US Navy then all tired and worn out? I been seeing other guys writing in a diary at night. Hiding them good before they hit the sack. I don't have no fancy book like they got so this letter paper will have to do. Might be

27

better. Just look like I'm writing a letter.

I been writing a lot of letters, especially to my girlfriend Evelyn, but now who knows how often I'll get to write her or anybody else. Sometimes I write to my Ma and my Pap and my cousin Stuart and my brother Billy and my sister Sally Jane. But I can't tell any of them the truth now.

I can't tell them where I am. I can't tell them about hearing that porthole cover creaking when our skiff stirred up the water around the Arizona. Back and forth. Back and forth. Made the hair on my neck stand up. That ship was sunk all the way up to the captain's level but it still had a flag on the masthead whipping in the wind. The flag was flapping and the porthole was creaking and I just wanted to get as far away from there as I could. What kind of sailor does that make me? A yellow-bellied one. I can't tell them that.

Bobby Messersmith from back home is down in there somewhere. Been seven months. No telling what he looks like now. My Ma sent me the newspaper clipping in a letter before we left New York. It told about him being on the Arizona and getting killed.

A lot of the guys said they had never heard of Pearl Harbor before that day it got bombed. Some of them that were already on the ship had gone on liberty. Some were at a ballgame in New York. They all got called back to the ship real quick.

I remember where I was. I suppose everybody does. I was sitting on my couch holding hands with Evelyn when the announcement came over the radio. We didn't know what it meant exactly. But we figured out how bad it really was the next day on the radio when the President declared war on Japan. My Pap was right.

A bunch of the fellas that were already on the ship then told me they were cheering when the president said that and were all gung ho – yeah, let's go get those Japs. I guess they didn't know what war really meant. None of us did. Not till today.

Most guys say they ain't scared. I think they're lying. Maybe not before today cause we hadn't seen much before now. Just been practicing. But I saw all the bits and pieces of those ships the Japs blew apart floating in that oily water. Hell, I was so close to the water in that skiff that I could reach down and touch it. But I didn't cause I think I saw part of somebody's leg. Least ways that's what it looked like. I can't be sure but I wasn't taking no chances. That was at the end of the day. It really started out pretty good.

Been out on the seas for days and days. Glad to see land. The Navy don't never tell us where we're going, so when we left Bremerton and started down the west coast, we just done what they told us to do. Tore up all the linoleum and threw it overboard. Scraped all the paint off the bulkheads and painted them all over again. Something about fire hazards. We had left a bunch of my boats back there. I called them my boats since I had to take care of them. Course they belonged to the Navy not me. But they were wood and they would burn so we left them. Didn't keep nothing but the captain's gig. We scrubbed and we cleaned and we practiced and we just kept going. Then this morning, I heard somebody yelling – Hey look at that mountain! Come to find out later it was called Diamondhead and we were seeing Hawaii.

Pearl Harbor. That's where we were headed.

We had to dress up in our whites and get to our stations. Lined up next to each other on every level of the ship. When we got real close, there was an escort ship waiting for us like we was something special. Heck, I guess we were if you believed everything the papers back home said. My ma cut out and saved every single thing. Sent some in her letters back then so I could see them. And we could see the papers, too. Back when we were in New York.

Back before.

Anyhow, those guys on that escort ship, they stood and saluted us. That was just the beginning. As we started moving on into the harbor, all the sailors on all the ships stood and saluted us. Some of

29

them even had their bands on deck playing for us. They raised and lowered their flags in salute and we saluted right back.

They all started cheering for us. Made me feel real funny, like I was a fake or something. We kept passing ships that had been sunk and the sailors there were all dirty and trying to clean up stuff and here we were standing up there in our spiffy dress whites looking all grand. At first I thought it was real nice, but then when I seen what really happened there and thought about what those guys went through. Didn't take much of an imagination to see the bombs and hear the screams and feel the fires and smell the smoke. And there they were cheering and saluting me. I hadn't done one thing to deserve all that.

Guess I better write to Evelyn now.

July 11, 1942
My Dearest Evelyn,

Not much going on with me. Everything is just swell. Don't get mad at me if this letter is short. I been trying to think of things that they'll let me say and I just don't have nothing. I don't have any letters from you to answer. I know you probably wrote a bunch of them, but they just hadn't caught up with us yet. I guess all I can say right now is I miss you. Keep writing.

I love you,
Roy

Pearl Harbor: July 14, 1942

The letters home are getting harder to write because I don't know what we can say and what we can't. A man came onboard today with a big camera - somebody said he was what they call a war correspondent. So I reckon I could say where I am but I ain't gonna try.

I went on liberty today for the first time. I bought me a book for this writing. This is a swell and beautiful place if you get away from the harbor and the landing field. In town, there's all kinds of fellas from every branch of the service. We had some more Marines come on our ship. I saw them. I reckon they're going to stay.

There's this one place where all the fellas stand in a long line to get in. I ain't stood in the line yet and hadn't ask nobody what it is. I don't want to sound dumb, but it must be a pretty good place. I might do it next time if we come back here. I hear we're pulling out soon. No telling when we'll be back.

You wouldn't believe all the supplies being loaded on our ship – all the food and all the ammunition and stuff. I reckon we'll be gone a long time. I better try and write Evelyn now so she'll at least get one more letter from me before I'm gone.

July 14, 1942

My dearest Evelyn,

I been sitting here for a half hour trying to think of something to write. Don't be mad if you don't get another letter for a long time. You should get this one but I don't know about any more. That don't mean I won't be writing them but they won't go out except when mail leaves the ship.

Have you seen the movie 'Jukebox Jenny?' That's the last one we watched down in the mess hall. We have a radio down there too. There was this song called 'O Genevieve' in the movie. It talks about never being blue when you got a sweetheart. That ain't the truth though.

I started to write down the words to a bunch of songs that would tell you how I feel but I forgot them now. I'll try to find them so I can have something to write.

Love,

Roy

AUGUST

Guadalcanal: Aug 4, 1942

I wasn't sure at first where we were going in the Pacific but we are at war now. We been shooting at this island called Guadalcanal with our big guns (16s) and the fives (me). It's our job to kill as many Japs as we can and blow up their guns and their landing strips and stuff so the Marines and soldiers that go in on the ground have an easier time of it.

We travel with a bunch of other ships - aircraft carriers, battleships, cruisers, and destroyers. When we're shooting at the island, we get in a line of three battleships and just sit there and shoot. Our other job is to protect the aircraft carriers when we're out in the ocean so we're always looking for enemy planes that might be trying to attack us and the other ships. When the radar picks up signals in the sky we have to go to our battlestations. We call General Quarters GQ for short. We been going to GQ a lot lately. The enemy must be everywhere, but I hadn't seen none yet.

Solomon Islands: August 5, 1942

Tonight our division officer called us together in our sleeping compartment. He said in two days the Marines would invade Guadalcanal. I hope we did our job good so not too many of them get killed. Hadn't wrote any letters to Evelyn lately. They won't go out anyway when we're in the battle zone.

Solomon Islands: August 7, 1942

Up at 0330, ate breakfast and relieved the watch at 0400. Worst time for the enemy to attack is 0530. So our planes took off from the aircraft carriers – about 30 from each. The fighters go in and clear the way for the bombers. They set a bunch of planes in the bay on fire. The Japs took to the woods. Heard we lost five planes when they ran out of fuel.

While the cruisers were shelling the beach it started to rain. Marines were supposed to land at 0800 but because of the rain getting harder they waited til 0830. They got little resistance so I reckon we did our job good enough. But the Japs were just back in the woods a ways so they sent our planes out and machine gunned them and dropped bombs. We ate sandwiches in the mount.

I sure am glad I'm on this ship. I got food every day and a bunk to sleep in. I don't much think I'd like being down there. I hope that don't make me a coward. I told Evelyn a long time ago that if I die in this war, I want to die a hero.

Solomon Islands: August 8, 1942

Ate breakfast at 0400 after midwatch. Got a nap on the deck before GQ. No planes or nothing come in this morning. About eleven we got word that Jap bombers were headed our way. They didn't do much damage cause we were ready for them. There were 25 – we shot down about half. Ate sandwiches in the mount again today. One of our destroyers got hit by a Jap bomb. Ended up on the beach. Makes a good target for anti-aircraft practice.

August 9, 1942

Dearest Evelyn,

I don't know when we'll get mail going out again but I had a minute so I thought I better write. We been real busy. I'm going to answer some of the letters I got earlier.

I'm glad to hear you got a raise. I got one too. Congress is always passing bills for the service men. I make about $80 a month now. My buddy Lyle gets about $100 cause he made third class. I'd go up for third class too but I don't feel like taking all that time to study. I got too many letters to write and we don't have much time. I still got about a dozen to answer.

I like how you started that last letter off saying you couldn't write much. When I say it I mean it but you wrote eight pages. I enjoyed getting it. Don't never say your letters are boring. I like getting yours better than anybody elses.

When you gonna do that picture I want with your class ring? You got it a long time ago.

What do you think about that song 'Don't Sit Under the Apple Tree with Anyone Else But Me?' I think it's swell. I reckon you'd be sitting under peach trees.

I'm going to save you some time and trouble. Don't ask nothing about where I am cause I can't tell you. That's a serious thing during war. You'd get a letter with a great big hole in it. I could get prison or death. Some of the fellas try stuff like that in their letters. It's not worth it in the end. Even if you knew where I was you couldn't do nothing about it so why make you worry. It's a war. You already know that part.

I like the pictures you sent but you gotta quit sending so many. Pretty soon I won't have room in my locker for my clothes. That's why I can't keep your letters either. I'm glad you're keeping all of mine but I just don't have the room.

So you been studying for tests to get a job with the Civil Service. I'm sure you'll do swell on the tests. You always were the smart one. Where would the job be? I bet you can't get a job in Simms Hollow. If you go anywhere else, you better send me your new address real soon so I don't send your letters to the wrong place. It's hard enough to get time to write them. I don't want them to get lost trying to find you. What would you be doing in that job anyhow? I don't want nothing bad to happen to you.

I gotta hit the sack before watch. I love you as big as the ocean and believe me that's pretty big.

Love,

Roy

Solomon Islands: August 24, 1942

Now I know just a little bit how those sailors at Pearl Harbor felt when the Japanese planes started dropping bombs and shooting up the ships. We were attacked today. We lost a sailor – V Division. I don't know his name yet but I want to find out. I know he was on the 20s – that's the antiaircraft guns and they don't have a long range so if a plane gets close enough that the 20s have to start shooting everybody's in trouble.

It started out like most other days. I was on watch all morning and nothing much going on. I was off watch and standing on the boat deck about 1330 hrs when a Jap plane started closing in on our task force. It went down in a cloud of smoke when one of our fighters got him. But we knew he wasn't all by himself so we went to GQ. Then all hell broke loose. I ain't never been a cussing fella but that was hell. Can't say it no different.

About 1700 we got word of a bunch of planes heading our way. They were going after the Enterprise. But then they saw us and started coming after us too. I was in my mount ready to go but I dropped the first round before I could get it in the gun. Then we got into rhythm and everything was fine. There was dive bombers and torpedos and when they was coming in close they would machine gun the ship. We were zigzagging the ship to try to keep from getting hit from them bombs they were dropping. One plane even looked like it was trying to fly into the carrier but we shot him down. The fighter went after him and made him bail out and he still machine gunned him too.

35 planes attacked us. We got 31 of them. Some fell pretty close to the ship but lucky for us they didn't hit it. I reckon I never thought it would really happen. It was almost dark when we could come out of our mounts.

Next thing we did was put that V Division man over the side. That's the only way we could bury him. He was sewed up in a bag.

Somebody said they put the five-inch shells in with him to make him sink. They didn't just chunk him over. We had a funeral of sorts. I climbed up on my mount with a bunch of the other fellas to watch. They had an American flag laying over him before they slid him off in the ocean. The chaplain said some words and the band played too. Sure did hate leaving one of ours back there in that big old ocean but we had to keep going so we wouldn't get hit again. We went up to high speed to get out away from the main action for a bit. We gotta fuel up tomorrow. That's a dangerous job and I have to help do it.

SEPTEMBER

Sept 12, 1942

My dearest Evelyn,

I finally got some letters from you today. They were all dated from July and August. At least I'll have something to answer and maybe I can make this letter longer. You said you like long letters. Well I can try but there ain't a whole lot I can tell you.

I read a swell story today. It was called 'Always Remember.' That's what I do you know – always remember you and how it was back home. The story's about the war and this old woman gave the young officer a talking to. She told him that no matter what happened he had to keep thinking about when he'd see his girl again and if he kept thinking it then it would happen. So, I'm thinking it.

I don't think you're eating enough. That last picture you sent you looked real skinny. You said you were getting fat but that ain't true. I know you got food you can eat. That's the best part about living on a farm. Anyway, I eat every chance I get. We still got some pretty good food in the mess hall. And we got ice cream. That's the best. Makes me think about you and me at the soda shop after school. That was the good old days.

No, I hadn't heard Glenn Miller's song. Least ways I don't think I have. You didn't tell me what the name of it is.

I got an idea. Whenever you don't get letters from me just say I wish you would write me and I'll say write soon. I know you're writing letters and you know I'm writing letters but they're not getting where they're supposed to be going. I guess they might find us after the war is over.

You hadn't said whether or not my letters have black marks or holes in them yet, so I guess I'm doing a pretty good job not making the censors mad.

Sometimes when we fellas get together we talk about our girls back home and what she's like and how ours is the best. We talk about the things we did back home like us liking to go down to the edge of the river for a picnic under that old oak tree with the rope where we could swing out over the river and drop in and go swimming. I told about the time we went swimming in our underwear cause none of these guys will tell anybody we know. Don't be mad for me doing that.

I didn't have the best story cause this one guy they call Shorty came from Florida and him and his girl went swimming in the ocean one night with no clothes – skinny dipping. You probably think I'm lying but I'm not. But they got a real scare when they thought they saw a shark swimming in the water and they had to run out real fast. Lucky for them they didn't see nobody else around before they got their clothes back on.

But the best things are the sea stories that the other guys that's been on different ships before this one tell. Some of them are real whoppers so I don't know if they are true or not. You might not even believe it if you heard it but I think some of the strangest things happen out at sea. When the sea gets rough, it really changes things.

You tell them guys that's been coming in the drug store to leave you alone if they say that stuff anymore. The Navy makes a fella real strong and puts a lot of fight in us. Those civilians better watch out if they mess with our girls.

I could just see you the way you described you were writing those letters. You sitting on the porch. The radio on. The pouring rain on the tin roof. I can just see and hear it. I shoulda been there.

I got real dirty today. I was out working on the crane and my face and my hands and my dungarees were all greasy. You wouldn't have liked it too much. I know you don't mind some good old mud and dirt, but the grease smelled nasty.

So you got a $2 a month raise at the drug store. You're doing the books now and not just the counter. That's real good and you got it because Mr. Wimbly knows you're smart. Maybe he's worried you're going to get a new job and move away and that's why he gave you a raise. Maybe he'll give you some more and you can just stay in Simms Hollow.

Well you got to think this is a pretty good long letter and I didn't write on both sides of the paper. But I got to stop now. I'm out on the deck and it's getting real dark and I can't see no more.

But I'll tell you this. We might have to start using that V-Mail soon and if I do - look out. Those will be real short letters cause they don't have much room to write.

Hugs and Kisses,
Roy

South Pacific Ocean: September 17, 1942

I don't know exactly where we are right now but I do know we're headed to an island called Tongatabu with a great big hole in our side from a torpedo. But the good old NORTH CAROLINA hadn't hardly even slowed down. That same day - it was two days ago - the WASP was sunk and a destroyer too I think. But we got hit and kept right on going. The Japs got lucky that day. Three hits and maybe more torpedoes than that but three ships got hit.

They been asking around for some sailors to volunteer for a bad job. They're not getting many takers, but I believe I might be brave enough to do it. I reckon I better start from the beginning or anybody ever reading this diary won't know what I'm talking about.

It was two days ago. September 15, 1942. Really it was the day before that we got word there was a Japanese task force headed our way – a bunch of carriers and battleships and cruisers and destroyers. The planes went out from our task force but they didn't find nothing to shoot at.

The next day one of our planes shot down one of their planes about 15 miles away. Weren't so long after that our task force was just moving along to the next place we needed to be and all of a sudden somebody yelled they could see smoke. It was the WASP looked like she had been hit and was on fire.

Since there weren't any planes around it had to be a torpedo and before we could get to our battlestations somebody was yelling torpedo wake and then we got hit. We had to do what we been trained to do and if you were in the wrong place when that thing hit that was bad. The fellas down below decks had to batten down the hatches. Had to close them to keep the ocean from coming in through that hole and sinking the ship and all that oil from the compartment that got hit was running in too.

Bad thing was there were men down there that didn't get out. Come to find out, there was one fella got blown overboard and there were four more got killed or trapped down below. Now they been down there for a couple of days in all that oil and water and it being real hot here in the South Pacific. Makes me think about my buddy trapped in the Arizona. They can't be in too good a shape, but we got to get them out.

We're headed to Tongatabu to see how bad the ship's hurt and to get them guys out and bury them.

Tongatabu: September 20, 1942

Well I did it. I reckon in a way I'm glad I did, but that's a sight I won't ever forget. They gave us liquor. Supposed to help us be able to do the job without getting sick I guess but I had never drank nothing stronger than a beer and didn't like that. So, I couldn't do too much of the liquor. Too strong for me.

We had to put on boots to wade in the oily water and they suited us up best they could but the stink was something awful. They had drained a bunch of the water out so it was below the hatches and they could open them without that water and oil coming back into the ship. I forgot to say we're at Tongatabu now and not still out in the ocean.

There were four bodies been in there five days. We had to find em and bring em out for proper burial but there weren't but six of us doing it and it took two for each body so two had to go back in a second time. I'm glad somebody else volunteered to do that. They were hard to find but we found them. You sure couldn't tell who was who by looking at them. Except for their dog tags you couldn't tell. We brought them out and laid them on the deck down in second. The pharmacists mates had to try and clean them up and get them ready to be buried. Those sailors were so swole up that one of them had his dog tags sticking straight out. I'm glad their family ain't got to see them looking that way.

Then after that I had to go get cleaned up and get my dress whites on. I was on duty to take the boat out and ferry anybody over who wanted to go to the burials. Some fellas just wanted to go on liberty and forget all about that torpedo and the dead shipmates. I reckon some people just need to do that. Get drunk. Find a girl. I wanted to go see them get a proper farewell. I reckon I felt kinda like it would help me forget the other things what with the flowers and the prayers and TAPS. It may sound funny but I feel like they're my friends now even though I didn't know them before. It will be hard to leave them buried on that island when we head back to Pearl Harbor, but it's better than the ones we done left back in the ocean.

We're going to be here in Tongatabu for a few days while they do some repairs to that big hole in our side, but they can't fix us good enough here. Word is we'll be headed back to Pearl Harbor so they can fix us up right before we go back out there where the real action is. But we still have to be careful, especially since we been hit once already. The Japs will think we're damaged goods and they can finish us off. But they don't know the good old BB55 too good if they think that.

We'll get them back for what they did. You can't kill nobody from the NORTH CAROLINA and get away with it. They'll see.

September 30, 1942

My dearest Evelyn,

I can't tell you where I am but I can tell you that I got a lot of letters from you today. We had a big mail call and all the fellas were getting a bunch of cards and letters. That makes us feel real good and gives us something to write back home about.

So you already gone to the new job in Washington, D.C. Is it with the State Department? You traveled by train from Atlanta to Washington and you thought it was swell. Was that your first long train ride? I can't believe you been there four weeks already. I guess your letters did take a long time to get to me. Just remember those Washington boys might not know how to treat a southern girl like you. I been around some fellas from the north and some of them don't act the same as us. I saw one fella when I was on liberty back in New York that didn't even open the door for his girl. Let her open it up herself. At least he did let her go in ahead of him.

Where I am I get to do some shopping and I already been scouting out some stuff I want to buy you for your birthday. See I didn't forget that it's on October 29. I better go on and buy it and mail it while I got the chance. I might just do that but then I don't want it to get there too early either. Sally Jane's is Nov 12. I gotta get her something good too so she's not jealous but if she's still back home and you're at your new job then she won't see what I got you and if you don't tell her it will be alright.

Yes, I know you can take care of yourself. I just wish I was there to take care of you some. So, you're working in an office in a big fancy building with a balcony where you can see the White House Rose Garden. That sounds swell. You can tell me some more stuff about your new friend. You say her name is Mary White and she has blonde hair. Is she short or tall? Is she skinny as you? Maybe she'll be a good cook and you can eat more. You really should eat more. That's probably why you fainted that day at work. You gotta be careful cause if you faint they might think you're sick and if you're sick they might think you can't do the job and give it to somebody else and then you would have to go back home.

So Mary's working in the same office as you and you stay in the same boarding house with some other girls. Does Mary have a fella back home? What about the other girls? What does the apartment look like? Do you have pictures of me on the wall? I'll be sending you some new ones so you can hang them on your wall and sit them on your table. That way if any guys come over they won't get the wrong idea. You got a guy and he's in the Navy.

You might know where I am when you get the pictures. It's got palm trees and a lot of flowers. And pineapples too. I went on liberty the other day and we rode a train right through the pineapple fields and went to the pineapple plant. It was swell.

I finally heard that Glenn Miller song, 'A String of Pearls.' It gave me some good ideas. I got liberty today so I'm going ashore. I'll answer some more letters when I get back. I'm just reading them one at a time and in the right order according to the postmark so you may have already told me something I asked in this letter. If you did you don't have to answer it again. I'll mail this letter before I go on liberty.

I almost forgot. You can tell me how much money you make. It won't make me mad.

All my love,
Roy

OCTOBER

October 1, 1942
Dear Evelyn,

I just got your letter about the strikes going on back home. It makes me mad to hear stuff like that. You had a lot to say about it. Do you think they're right? I don't and this is why.

They don't have nothing to complain about. Maybe they don't have enough gas to joy ride around with or maybe they can't get new shoes whenever they want to get dressed up and go out on the town. So what if they're working seven days a week some weeks? They get to go home to their bed at night don't they? Maybe they think they got it rough, but let me tell you they don't know nothing.

Here's what you need to think about. All of you. What about the service man that might get back home on leave and could get to see his family if there's a little bit of gas left over for him to get there. Or the soldier who every muscle in his body is sore and tired and needs those leather shoes so he can do his job to protect you.

I know from experience what's tough. We waited three days and nights for some nut jobs to take a shot at us. Some fellas hadn't been back on American soil since the war started, much less seen anybody that they love like their Ma or Pap or wife or kids. Those defense workers might work long hours and they might be tired, but they get to go home to their families at night. I know a mess of guys who would trade places with a defense worker any day.

I met merchant marines who hadn't seen a movie in months. We're lucky cause we got them on the ship. But where does the soldier go when he gets tired and don't hardly have enough food to eat and can't talk to his family and don't know when or if he'll ever even see them again?

And you say that those guys are striking cause they got it bad? I tell you what they need. They need to see what war is really like. They need to be put in one of those hell holes for a while and see what they got to complain about then. I don't care if they get mad they'll get over it. They don't know what they're talking about. Seems there's folks that don't even know there's a war going on and sure as hell don't know what people are going through when they're fighting in it. I know I got it good as far as the war goes. I could get blown to smithereens any day, but I ain't laying in no fox hole in the cold and the rain day after day. And neither are those people doing the striking.

I don't want to hear no more about that. You need to not listen to that crap and you need to stick up for the guy who's really got it tough out here trying to end this war and get back home before he gets killed.

People like that are the ones that's going to keep this war from being over. I ain't got no patience for it at all and I'm sorry if that makes you mad.

I still love you,
Roy

Pearl Harbor: October 10, 1942

They put us in dry dock today. Looks real funny seeing our ship all the way to the bottom with no water under her. Makes her look even bigger than I thought. I never seen her out of the water before. That torpedo sure did knock a big hole in the side. Big enough you could drive a bunch of trucks through it. But it's getting patched up.

In the meantime, us sailors have got to clean the ship and start painting. We have to go over the side on ropes and hang almost upside down sometimes to scrape the barnacles and stuff off the ship so she can be painted. I just about fell off the scaffolding today and that was not a good feeling. I lost my Dixie Cup hat. Fell right off my head, but it wasn't too big a loss because it was so full of stuff I had scraped off the ship that it probably couldn't of ever come clean enough to wear again. I got another one.

I'm hanging there working but I look over at the other fellas – each division had to do a different part of the ship – and I'm thinking we look like a lot of little spiders hanging down from our webs. Makes me think about the barn back home and the way the morning sunlight would sparkle on the spider webs in the corner of the doorway when they were still wet with dew. I saw them every day when I went out to milk the cows.

Anyways, we're going to be here for a while and that will give me some time to answer all of Evelyn's letters. I got to write her back about that last one where I was so mad. She ain't said nothing about it yet, but then she probably hadn't had time either.

But here's the other thing. I can't tell her how worried I am about that fancy new job of hers in a big city where she's never been before. I'm so far away I can't see her and I can't take care of her. She says she can take care of herself and for me to take care of me so I can get back home. She's probably right. But she's probably mad at me too so I got to write and straighten that out.

I know we're going back out there. I can't tell her I'm scared. Heck, I can't tell nobody that. I know the other fellas have got to feel it too but nobody will ever say it so it makes me wonder if I'm the only one. Maybe if I said it then somebody else would say it too like they were waiting for another fella to say it first. But if I say it and nobody else says it, then that'll be bad for me. Probably a new nickname or maybe they won't trust me to do my job in the mount.

We all gotta trust each other. Our lives depend on it. No, it won't be me to say it first. Or probably ever.

October 11, 1942

My Dearest Evelyn,

I got some more letters from you but you hadn't said nothing about what I said about your letter about the strikes.

I wanted to write sooner about that letter I wrote. It sounded pretty bad. I reckon I just blew my top when you said those things. I wasn't in the mood to hear stuff like that and I reckon nobody out here fighting in the war would be in the mood for that kind of crap.

You know we need your help and we can't do it without the support of everybody back home. I know it's hard on folks back home, too, but it sounds like you're doing alright. I know you miss me, but you got a good job and a great place to live and you're doing exciting things in a big new city. We just got to all stick together or we won't never get the big 'V' and be able to come home. Please just don't write me nothing else about that.

We got to talk about the good stuff so we don't get mad at each other. Some of the fellas talk about how much fun it is to make up with their wives after they had an argument (if you know what I mean). But we're too far away to make up so I don't want to argue.

There isn't much I can write about now. I'm plenty tired and got a couple pair of white sneakers I have to scrub up for my trip in the captain's gig.

I really love you,

Roy

October 19, 1942

Dearest Birthday Girl,

Happy Birthday to the prettiest girl in the world. I hope this package gets to you just in time for your birthday. I sure am glad you sent me your new address there in Washington, D.C. or your present would be going to Georgia. I tried to time it right so it didn't get there too early but it wasn't late. Now open your present before you read the rest of this letter or it might give it away.

I can tell that office job has changed you already. Those jokes you told me – well, I let some of the fellas read it – and they said it was worse than some of the jokes the sailors tell. You better be careful or you'll ruin your reputation.

I mean we all knew about June B. when we were in school. I wasn't surprised when you told me, but I was surprised they got married so fast. I pity the poor guy. I bet he's from a good family too. Maybe he wanted to marry her but I bet he didn't want to marry her that soon. You said he was Army and leaving town soon. I guess they had some fast thinking to do.

I got a letter from Sally Jane and she says she sure does miss you a lot. You were her best friend and you left her back in Simms Hollow. She's worried that you will get a new friend and not write to her anymore. She wants to take a new job but our parents won't let her leave town yet. So she said she's got your job at the drug store now. She helps with the books and works the counter when they get real busy. She sees a lot of the high school kids coming in. She said that Billy got himself a girlfriend. I sure hope he don't mess up and have to get married too. He's too young for that kind of stuff.

You need to write to Sally Jane even if you miss writing one to me because of it. She sounded pretty sad in her last letter. She and our cousin Stuart were always good friends too and he hadn't sent her too many letters since he joined the Marines. She doesn't even know where he is and I don't either. I better write her more letters myself. But she still won't know where I am either.

Now did you already open your present? If you didn't go do it before you read another word because here's the deal. You remember when I said that Glenn Miller song gave me some ideas?

Well, after that I went on liberty and this store had the most beautiful string of pearls you ever saw. I hope you like them and wear them to work or out to dinner and if someone asks where you got them you can say your sailor bought em at a faraway place.

I hope in some of the letters I haven't read yet that you tell me what you want for Christmas. I don't know if I'll be somewhere I can buy you something you want, but I'll try.

Yes, I know that radio show Tokyo Rose. We listen to it but I didn't know you could hear her too. Don't pay no attention when she says they sunk the NORTH CAROLINA. That's what they call propaganda. She's trying to make all you back home think that we're not doing good but we are doing just fine. I'm just fine and so is my ship. So unless you get word that the official Navy officers went to my Ma's house and told her I was dead then you don't worry about me. Yes, I'm sure that Sally Jane would let you know. You did send her your new address didn't you?

I hope you have a swell birthday. If you have a party remember that I would be if I could. It's ok to dance with the other fellas but remember that you are the only one for me. I know you don't want me to talk about <u>that</u> subject but you sort of did when you told me about June B. Please be careful, especially if there are sailors in Washington. I know what they think about.

Yours truly,

Roy

NOVEMBER

November 15, 1942

Dearest Evelyn,

Are you going to take the train home for Thanksgiving? I know your family would like that if you could and so would your old friends. I'm glad you made new friends in Washington. So, you saw the inside of White House. Is it as big as it looks in the pictures? You really got to go inside? Boy, I bet that was swell. Did you see President Roosevelt?

I bought a $100 War Bond and I'm sending it home. I'm sending a $100 money order, too. It's alright if you don't buy me a Christmas present. When you're at war you can't stop for a holiday so all days are the same. Except they do try to give us some real good food.

Yes, I do a lot of scrubbing and sewing and cleaning in the Navy. I learned how to tie knots too. There's this one cartoon I saw – I might try to find it and send it to you – where there was this sailor and his wife. She's in the galley (kitchen) and he's got the baby on his lap. The sailor is saying 'they showed me plenty of knots in the Navy but this one's got me stumped.' Yes, he is trying to tie one of those three corner deals. That might be me one day.

I'm sending two pictures in this letter. How do you like the white uniform? I like the one of me leaning on the palm tree the best.

Sometimes I get the newspaper from back home. Last one I saw where George and Eddie and Fred and Bob had all joined the Navy. Mike was going to the Army and Ben was in the Marines. There won't be any boys left at home if they keep that up. Is your brother still at the university in North Carolina or did he have to join up too?

You remember that boy Henry? The paper says he was supposed to have seen action in the Solomon Islands too. And Larry. He got killed there.

Well, it's almost time for chow and I'm real hungry so I'm going to sign off for now. Remember there's no one for me but you.

Love always,
Roy

Pearl Harbor: November 16, 1942

Today I done something that don't make me very proud but I didn't know what I was doing until it was too late to not go in there. Tomorrow the ship is pulling out to go back to war and some of the fellas said we all needed to go out and have us a good time cause we might never be coming back. I reckon that's the truth.

So a bunch of us guys from 5th Division went ashore on liberty and they asked me had I ever stood in those long lines and went in that house. They said it was a sight to see and something I should experience before I might get killed. They said I needed to have three dollars and I had that much and more.

We got in line with the other sailors and the soldiers and the Marines and it was a long line so we had time to do some talking and some listening to the other fellas talk. They seemed real excited. I knowed that some of them were married cause they were talking about their wife and their kids and some of them were talking about girlfriends back home. But they were kinda joking around most of the time.

One of them looked at me and asked was this my first time and I said yeah. He said he could tell by the look on my face but that it would be swell and I'd have me a mighty fine time. He said all the fellas need to go in that house sometimes and that's why the government set it up. I couldn't let on that I didn't know what he was talking about.

When it came my turn to go in the front door I had to wait some more in a chair against the wall. There was four doors and women kept coming out each door without much on. The fella at the first door was already coming back out before the girl came out the last door and called to me. I couldn't not go in and let the other fellas see I didn't cause by that time some of the ones in my group were already in the waiting chairs too.

So I went in and she said 'three dollars for three minutes, what kind do you want' and she took off her clothes right then and there except for her high heel shoes. Well she was a beautiful sight but I said I got a girlfriend and she said they all do and your time's ticking down. I said I don't want nothing but she put her hands on my shoulders and it did feel mighty good when she pulled me up close and kissed me. But I didn't want to do no more than that. Heck, I didn't know how anyway. I ain't never done it, I just heard the fellas talking. And I want to do it with Evelyn. By that time she had my shirt unbuttoned and was pulling me to the bed and my man parts were telling me I did want to do it. But I said no ma'am. You done enough and gave her the money. I said you're a mighty fine woman and she said you'll be back. It's going to be a long war.

I reckon she might be right but I better write to Evelyn now.

November 16, 1942

My one and only Evelyn,

We're pulling out tomorrow so I won't be having liberty again any time soon and I don't know when I'll get to send out another letter so I'm going to write this one tonight and put it in our post office so it will go out before we leave.

I don't think I ever told you all the things we have on this ship so I'm going to tell you now. We got just about everything we need and then some – like an ice cream maker. We got a post office and a dentist office. We got the sick bay that's just like a hospital. They say that all the ships don't have that and sometimes we might have to take people on from other ships so we can take care of them in our hospital.

We got a laundry and we take turns having to do the clothes. We got a mess hall – that's like a great big dining room and we get assigned duty there too. All of us have to do the mess hall duty sometimes so no one person has to do it all by himself all the time. We got a butcher shop with a real butcher that cuts up all the meat.

And we got the galley (kitchen) where we got some guys that that's their work station and they're in there all the time like I'm on the deck duty as my work station. But then we all got to take a turn in the galley mostly peeling potatoes in the potato peeler. It takes a lot of potatoes to feed all us sailors on this great big ship. But you got to pay attention to what you're doing cause if you start thinking about something else then you might grind those potatoes down to nothing and have to start over. You get in trouble when you waste food. Oh, and we got a brig that's like our jail. You don't want to go there.

Let's see now. We got a chapel that's like our church and they have services on Sunday in all the faiths. Seems a lot of the guys are Catholic and there's a priest on board, but sometimes they try to do a Baptist service too for fellas from the south like me and Methodist and Episcopalian. I've learned a lot about religion talking to the other fellas. I reckon you think a lot about that when you might get killed any day. Makes you think about a lot of things you might miss too and makes you wonder why you didn't already do some of those things.

Down in the mess hall we got a real good radio and that's where I hear the songs I tell you about. The mess hall is like a great big dining room with a whole bunch of tables where we can sit and eat and sometimes watch movies.

We have a band on ship and a boxing team and they're getting together a baseball team too for when we are places that we might be with other ships and play against their teams. There's some places that are pretty safe far away from the Japs that we can rest but most of the time we can't. And their planes came all the way to Pearl Harbor one time so I reckon no place is really safe anymore.

We have a barber shop too and when the Marines are in there they cut your hair really short. That's why my hair is so short in that picture I sent you. You said you're about to forget what I look like. Well, I have changed.

I look forward to getting some more letters from you and hearing all about your new job and your fancy new life in the big city of Washington. So you walk right past the Capitol building to go to your office. I bet that's a sight. Yes, I mean the Capitol Building but I mean a bunch of pretty young girls walking down that sidewalk together in their high heels all dressed up for work and talking and giggling.

I bet there are a lot of military guys in Washington, D.C. Some fancy ones with high up jobs. Just remember that you're the only one for me. I'll get home as soon as I can.

Your one and only,

Roy

PS - I got to listen to the Hit Parade a few days ago and I forgot to tell you. It had some swell songs on it. Some I had already heard but some I hadn't. I don't remember them all but I do remember the top three. I'll count them down backwards for a surprise at the end. 'My Devotion' was in third place. Second place was 'Praise the Lord and Pass the Ammunition.' There's a story behind that song. Do you know it? It's about something that happened at Pearl Harbor and a chaplain said it then somebody wrote a song about it. You know we have hoists that move the ammunition along to the guns but theirs broke and so they formed a line of fellas to pass the ammunition from person to person. That's where that song came from. The number one song was one I hadn't ever heard before. It was called 'White Christmas.'

Figi Islands: Nov 26, 1942

We've been out to sea for nine days but today we moored on one of the Fiji Islands. Every time we get to an island that don't belong to the enemy we get to have liberty. Some places are better than others, but there's usually something to do. Sometimes I don't like to go ashore though because you can get in trouble if you drink too much or you get too close to those island girls without much clothes on. Makes you think things a guy with a girl back home ought not be thinking or doing.

We spent the last nine days practicing shooting and dodging periscope sightings and getting where we're supposed to go. I don't know where that's going to be just yet, but I do know it's bound to be where the action is. We just got to find it before it finds us.

They gave us a map with all the islands in the Pacific on it. Some of them are safe and some of them have Japs on them. Those are the ones we got to shoot at first so the soldiers and Marines can go ashore and take it back. And we still got to always be careful out in the ocean to take care of the enemy submarines down below and airplanes up above. And sink their battleships and cruisers and destroyers before they get ours.

The way I understand it we got to make our way taking back those islands all the way to Japan and then we got to defeat them right there on their home turf. That's when we really get them back for what they did at Pearl Harbor. Maybe when we get that done this war will be over. Except I know they're fighting in other places like Germany too. But we can't rightly do nothing about that so we got to concentrate on what we can do where we are and hope those other fellas are getting along alright where they are. We all just want to go home.

November 30, 1942

My dearest Evelyn,

I hope you had a good Thanksgiving. We were in a place - I can't tell you where - but we were able to have some good old Thanksgiving dinner with turkey and ham and stuff. I ate a bunch and it was good. I bet your folks were glad to see you if you got to go home. I bet you and Sally Jane and a bunch of the girls and guys from home got together. Well that's good. I'll be looking for letters from home to tell me if you behaved while you were there. Did y'all build a big old bonfire down by the river like we used to do?

So you went out on the town for Mary's birthday. I bet Washington's got a lot of places to go out and have fun. But you got sick, huh? Well, I know all about that because I've seen the other fellas. I kid them about it and that makes them feel worse and sicker. I wish you got sicker than you did then maybe you wouldn't try it again. It can get you in trouble.

You can't get mad when it goes a long time and my letters don't get to you. I'm writing them but ships don't stay in one place all the time. We're moving around and even though we got a post office onboard ship our mail can't go nowhere from it when we're not in port. Except sometimes we get mail from another ship out at sea. They pass it over on a line and we pass ours back to them to go out, but they got to get to somewhere to mail it so it takes a long time.

So you haven't told me much about your new job. I sure would like to know about what you do every day and some more about what you do when you're not at work.

What do you mean there's a girl in your apartment skinnier than you. I didn't think you could get much skinnier if you want your clothes to stay on. You got enough to eat in that apartment?

You're making how much money? That's almost more than me. Must be some kind of job and I'm glad you got it. I know your Pap is glad when you send that money home. It's a fine thing you're doing cause I reckon sometimes the farming don't bring in a lot of money and things are getting scarce back home. Least ways that's what my Ma said in her last letter. She said she was glad they had turkeys on the farm and she was going to invite some of the rest of the family over for Thanksgiving dinner. I sure wish I coulda been there. Having Thanksgiving dinner with the fellas was alright, but we were all missing home pretty bad and some of them songs on the radio make it a whole lot worse. 'Blues in the Night' is an old one, but it sure says how I feel sometimes. And they play that 'White Christmas' one all the time. One of the fellas just played a record called 'I Want My Mama.' On the other side it's a song called 'Angel.'

I read in the newspaper (the one Ma sends me from home) that George Linden from over in Beatty's Gorge got killed in the Solomon Islands. He was a Marine. If you read the paper, you heard about those islands. The Marines took it back from the Japs. I was there. It says so in the paper. I reckon if you take the paper from back home, you'll know where I been. You just can't know where I am now or where I'm going.

The other night it was a nice night so I took my bedding topside to sleep under the stars. You remember when we found the Little Dipper that night down beside the waterfall? Well, I didn't have no sound of water running over the rocks or falling down the side of the mountain, but I did get to listen to the waves and pretend. I rolled my bedding up long ways and was wishing I was holding you. I was looking at the Little Dipper and I think I fell asleep that way.

So Billy wrote you a letter and said he wanted to get away from home. Maybe he thought you could get him a job when he gets out of school. I just want to go back. I've about had enough of this war. I sure hope he don't have to go but he's gonna graduate in a few months. My folks don't have no money to send him to college so I reckon he's going to have to join up or get drafted. I been telling him the Navy was a pretty good place to be. I wouldn't want him to be in the Army or the Marines. They're the ones that have to go in on them islands like the Solomons and get right up close to the Japs. It's bad enough where I am. I wouldn't want him to have to do that. He's my little brother.

Signing off for now. I gotta get your package of Christmas presents ready to send off.

Your sailor,
Roy

DECEMBER

Figi Islands: December 6, 1942

Well tomorrow will be a year since the Japs attacked Pearl Harbor and put us in this war. I hear we're leaving Fiji today and getting underway for the island of Noumea, New Caledonia. I'm sure glad I got this map cause it helps me know where we are and where we're going. Sort of anyway. I hear Noumea is a safe place – as safe as we can be I reckon. It's where we'll meet up with other ships and pick up supplies and ammunition and refuel and all the things we need to do to go back out there and fight some Japs.

A whole bunch of us ships are traveling together. We never go anywhere alone. I need to remember to tell Evelyn that – she shouldn't go anywhere alone in the big city of Washington, D.C. either. Being alone can be dangerous. But she don't seem to want me to tell her what to do anymore – not that I ever did tell her what to do – but I want her to be safe and sometimes if you ain't seen the bad you don't really know what's out there.

I been thinking a lot about Bobby Messersmith today and how the Japs sunk the Arizona and he didn't have a chance to get out. He's still there. And I been thinking about those fellas we pulled out of that oily water back at Tongatabu and glad we could give them a decent burial, not leave them in the water for fish bait like Bobby.

And I been thinking how our mountains back in Simms Hollow may have some snow already. We might be in the south but we're so high up we get snow before Christmas sometimes but probably not. Anyhow it gets so hot here that sometimes I think it sure would be nice to get all bundled up and go out to the barn and milk the cows. I reckon I miss the cold. Never thought I would.

I know my Ma's been worried a lot about me. She says so in all her letters so I try to write to her and tell her not to worry. But our neighbors down in the holler got a visit from the Army. Drove up in a big fancy car. Had to pass our house to get there and Ma was out in the yard hanging up laundry. She saw it. She knew without even asking nobody what it was and what it meant. Mas just know things sometimes. So she's been going over to the neighbor's house helping to take care of the little ones. Their Ma's just so heartbroken she ain't been out of bed for two weeks. I don't ever want to break my Ma's heart that way. She just don't deserve it.

And now I got things to worry about with Evelyn. Things I can't rightly tell her in a letter. It might come out all wrong and then she could get mad and break up with me. But she's got this really good paying job in Washington, D.C. of all places and she lives with about five other girls and they go out on the town and to dances and stuff. And there's lots of servicemen around there and politicians and a young girl like her just don't know how guys think. Heck I didn't even really know til I heard all the fellas on the ship talking. When you grow up in the mountains like we did you just don't know all the ways of the world. In the South we're taught to respect our elders and women and stuff. If I ever said some of the things I been hearing fellas say, I'd a had my mouth washed out with soap. But I found out that ain't the case everywhere.

And now I expect we're getting ready to get back into some real action. Least ways it looks that way considering how much supplies we been loading on the ship. And everybody's fueling up. That's a part of my job I really do like but sometimes that scares me too. It's a dangerous job when we're out in the open waters and can't stop. The last time we fueled out at sea, the ships got too far apart and a fuel line busted. We got railed for that.

December 25, 1942

Merry Christmas my dearest Evelyn,

I know you won't read this until sometime way after Christmas but it is Christmas Day and I wanted to write to all my family. You will be my family one day. I wrote to my Ma and Pap first. I don't ever write a letter just to my Pap cause he don't like reading too much so Ma said I could just talk to him in the letters I send to her and she would read them to him. I wrote one to Sally Jane and one to Billy and I even sent one to Stuart since you sent me his address that you got from his Ma. He's in Germany. I don't think that could be a very good place to be right now and I hope he makes it back home. Anyhow, I saved the best for last so I could write longer.

I'm sorry I hadn't been sending a lot of letters, but I been real busy. Besides all the regular stuff I have to do with my battle station and my work station and us practicing and stuff, I been studying. I should be up for third real soon. I'll get a raise when I make third and then I can send more money home. I should have a pretty good bank account by the time I get home. Maybe you'll be ready to come back home by then and we can get married and buy a little piece of land in the mountains. I sure do miss the mountains. Do you?

I hope you got your package before today. I can just see you opening it up and wondering where all those things came from. I been buying you something in every port and putting them in a box to save for Christmas. I put some postcards in there, too. Did you get them or did the censors take them out? I'm going to tell you something that you will think is interesting, but if you see a big hole after this sentence, you'll know I wasn't supposed to say it. I think it will be alright though because we aren't there anymore.

We went to this one island – I won't tell you the name of it. But all the houses there weren't really houses at all. They were little grass shacks. And all the people were very dark skinned but the women had red hair or blonde hair and they didn't wear nothing but a grass skirt. No dear, I didn't stare but it wasn't something I couldn't see unless I stayed on the ship the whole time. The men just wore a little bit of cloth hanging down in the front.

I got my chess and checker set you sent me. It was a mighty fine Christmas present and I will use it a lot once I finish studying and make third class. Sometimes we do have time to sit around on the deck and us fellas like to have some games to play. Cards get boring after a while. I never played chess but I can learn. I'm sure there's somebody here that knows how and can teach me.

The harmonica is really swell. Now I got to learn to play it so I don't get ragged by the fellas. The Hit Parade I was listening to was the same one you hear but maybe mine was recorded. That would make me hear a different top three than you that week.

I hope you got to go home for Christmas so you can tell me how my folks really are. I get letters from my Ma and I know she's worried about me. My Pap too although he don't really say it. I don't never complain to her when I write cause there's no reason to worry anybody else with my troubles. You know that song 'Pack Up Your Troubles in Your Old Suit Bag' or something like that. Well, it's got this one line that says something like there's no use of worrying it never was worthwhile. I reckon that's the way I'm trying to look at life. I got a few more years in the Navy and if I complained all the time those years would sure seem a lot longer.

They fed us good today and we sang some Christmas songs down in the mess hall. Now everybody that's not on watch is writing home and playing card games and stuff like that. Some of the fellas went on liberty, but there's really not much I want to do on the island so I just stayed onboard.

I think I'm going to read the Christmas story in my Bible and think about that play we did every year back in church when we was growing up. That last year, I got to be Joseph and you were Mary. That's a long way from where we started out as a sheep and a donkey when we were little.

Well that's about all for now. Merry Christmas my love.

Thinking of you always,
Roy

December 31, 1942

Dearest Evelyn,

It's New Year's Eve and I can't help but wonder what you and all your friends are doing tonight in Washington, D.C. Do they have a big celebration there near the White House or anything? We're in the same place that we've been since before Christmas. I'm sorry I can't tell you where that is, but I did receive a bundle of letters from you dated back early December.

Sounds like you had a swell time with all your new friends at Thanksgiving. You really cooked a turkey? I didn't know you could do that. Did you do the dressing and everything? I'm sorry you didn't get to go home. I'm sure both our folks missed seeing you.

So there was a military ball and you all got to go. Did you each have a date? What was his name? I sure hope he treated you right and didn't try nothing. You don't ever tell me those parts. But you said that one girl Helen stayed out all night and still had her evening gown on when she got home at lunch the next day but no shoes. She had to take a taxi? That don't sound like she was with no gentleman. Must not have been a sailor, probably Army or Marine. Although they got plenty of good guys and I reckon the Navy probably has some bad ones too. Anyhow, you be careful when all you girls go out. I hear them fellas still talking about being back home and going out on the town in New York.

I been running the crane a lot lately. That's one part of my job I really like. I can make it do just about anything I want it to do now and so I'm loading stuff on the ship all the time. And I use it to lower the captain's gig into the water before I take the Captain where he needs to go or take the fellas on liberty.

I only heard that song 'White Christmas' one more time since we don't get to hear the Hit Parade very often. Sure does make a fella think about back home in the mountains, though. Did we have a White Christmas? I know we don't much but sometimes we get lucky. I remember that one time it snowed so hard on

Christmas Eve that we didn't even get to go to my grandma's house. We had to stay at home but it was right much fun anyhow. Me and Sally Jane and Billy got out and built us a great big snowman and rode our sleds Pap built down the side of the mountain over by the creek. Billy ended up in the creek and he was a mite too cold to stay outside so we went in and Ma had fixed us hot chocolate with the milk I had went out to the barn and got that very morning. Those were the days.

I reckon I can tell you it's hot where we are. Ain't seemed like Christmas a bit and it sure don't seem like New Year's. If there was a hole or black line there it's because I said something I shouldn't have but I didn't tell no secrets so I think it will be ok. It's hot a lot of places in the world right now.

Yes, I do get a little homesick. Do you? I wondered if getting a chance to go home would make it better or make you more homesick when you left again. You can tell me now that you went home for Christmas. You did go, didn't you? I ain't never been far from home but this one time and I don't know when I'll get to go back again. Don't seem like this war is anywhere close to being done.

Well I better hit the sack. We been told we'll be real busy on the crane tomorrow loading a lot of provisions so I bet we're getting ready to head out somewhere. I probably won't be getting no letters from you for a while and I won't be able to send none either, so please don't keep starting all your letters saying you hadn't got none from me. I explained why that happens and it will probably get worse. So don't be sore if you don't get letters. I'm writing them and I think about you everyday no matter what I got to do.

Have a Happy New Year,
Roy

1943

JANUARY

Jan 3, 1943

My dearest Evelyn,

Well, I remembered to write the new year date this time but I bet I'll forget in some of my letters but you'll know it's 1943 and not '42 so please forgive me. I was wrong when I thought we were getting ready to head out on New Year's Day. We had a ballgame instead. You remember how I told you that all the ships have bands and boxing teams and baseball teams, too? Well, we had a baseball game and I got to go. I ain't playing. These fellas are pretty good – one even said he was supposed to play pro ball. Had signed a contract and everything but then Uncle Sam got him and he's in the Navy now.

Anyhow, we were playing the team from the other battleship. I reckon I can't tell you which one. But you ever heard of that baseball player named Bob Fellar? Well he's here and he was coaching that other team. They did pretty good. They won 6 to 2.

I hadn't got any letters from you since the last time I wrote. But that's only been three days. They usually come in a big bunch so I'll probably get the ones about Christmas real soon.

Ma sends me letters and she says she's doing just fine, but Sally Jane says she cries a lot. I want you to tell me how she looks for real. I'm not wanting to worry her none, but I can't help it that I had to join the Navy. I bet she's real worried about Billy. He'll turn eighteen on Valentine's Day and graduate in May. If the war ain't over by then he'll be leaving home too. I know it and my Ma does too so I'm sure she's worried. But she don't tell me that. She just tells me about the farm and my favorite cow Millie and how the horses run around in the mornings when there's frost on the ground. She don't know that just makes me more homesick.

We had one of my favorites at chow tonight – meatloaf and mashed potatoes – so I'm all full up and getting sleepy. Got the early watch so I'm going to hit the sack now.

Yours truly,
Roy

February 25, 1943
My dearest Evelyn,

I got a letter today from you dated December 18, 1942. It was wet so the ink had run, the stamp fell off and the envelope was torn. The papers were all stuck together but from what I could read it was a pretty good letter. Except that it was all old news since it got lost.

We been doing a lot of practicing lately getting ready for whatever comes next. It don't take no thinking at all to load and fire the guns when you do it so many times every day. That will come in handy when we take on the Japs again. That will probably happen sooner than later.

I did get some other letters from you but you didn't say a whole lot I could answer and I ain't really got too much to tell you except that we had that actor fella Joe E. Brown who came on the ship and entertained us right there on the fantail. I been told that I don't have too much of a sense of humor but he made me laugh. That sure did lift our spirits.

I'm glad you got the roses. I wanted to send you something special and I heard one of the other fellas sent flowers home. I hadn't thought about that. So I sent you some in Washington and I sent Sally Jane and my Ma some too.

I did get your letter that said my Ma looked too skinny when you went home at Christmas. I reckon she's worrying herself about sick. I don't know how to do nothing about it except write her more letters, so I might have to skip some days writing you til she's better.

That don't mean I don't think about you every day. I know you're getting skinnier and skinnier too but that's because you girls are having a contest to see who has the smallest waist. I think it's dumb but at least it ain't from worry. What do you mean that Helen's waist is getting bigger?

You hadn't told me much of nothing about that fancy new job of yours except that you're making a lot of money. No, I don't think it's wrong that men usually make more money than women cause they have families to support. Most people would agree with me about that. Most of the fellas here have wives or girls back home that aren't making so much money or none at all. But if you get any more raises, you're going to be making a lot more money than me. I reckon I better start studying for a new rank so I can keep up.

Well that's about all for now. Except I did send a birthday card home to Billy. I hope he got it in time for his birthday. I hadn't heard back from him.

Love to you always,

Roy

PS - Yes, you are right. My birthday will be in March. Do you remember which day? Do you remember how old I'll be? One year more than you.

MARCH

Mar 1, 1943

Dearest Evelyn,

We been in the same place doing the same things for a while now. Some of the fellas are getting restless and want to go ahead and get this war over with. I want to do the same thing.

That was a swell picture of you and your new friend Mary. My buddy Lyle likes blondes and he don't have a girlfriend back home no more. He was wondering if maybe Mary would write him a letter or he could write her if you send the address. He's a good fella from over in South Carolina – a real beach bum. Ha! The truth is he's a real good guy and he don't get enough letters so if she could write him that would be swell. I'm sending a picture of him and me together on the island so she can see what he looks like. She can use the same address as me.

We found out we're going to have to pay income tax – probably. In 1942 I made nine hundred and twenty dollars and forty-two cents. I only got a hundred and thirty on the books right now so I hope that's enough to pay the taxes. I been sending home some war bonds and money orders and buying some stuff.

I hadn't heard nothing about third class yet. We're supposed to find out soon whose name is going up this month. I had time to study but having a hard time settling down to do it. If my name goes up, I'm going to have to buckle down and get to studying. Probably go on a battle and not have any time, then I'll wish I hadn't waited so long.

So your roommate Helen is going to have a baby and she don't know how to find the Pap cause she don't know his last name. That was from that party when she didn't come home at night. You never told me he did nothing to her and now you said she didn't want him doing it. She shoulda called the law.

Where's her folks live? She probably just needs to go on home and let them help her out. Unless her folks are like this one fella George's girlfriends' folks. He can't write her letters no more cause her Pap don't want her having no sailor for a boyfriend. He had to mail them to a different address but she put them in a box in her closet and her Pap found them and he was mad and she paid the price for that. He punched her around for it. George said he was going to take care of that old man when he got home from the war. But right now he can't do nothing but stop writing letters. She still writes him though.

The reason you fainted again is probably because you hadn't been eating. I reckon if you think you got to stay that skinny that's fine by me but you better watch out. That fancy paying job of yours probably won't last long if you don't eat enough to stay awake and work. Are any of the other girls fainting too? Maybe you got something in your apartment making you sick. You better get that checked.

Love you always,

Roy

Noumea: March 18, 1943

We been back and forth around Dumbea Bay, Noumea ever since before Christmas. We been here with a lot of other ships and been fueling out at sea and practicing firing the guns and stuff but I'm ready to get on with it. We need to take care of them Japs and get it over with so we can go home. Now I hear we're going back to Pearl Harbor. Got to get something fixed on the ship probably. And maybe pick up more supplies and ammunition. Usually when we go there we get new troops too or somebody from our ship gets transferred to another one. I think I'm staying right here. At least I hope so. I like my ship pretty good and the fellas on it too. Supposed to take us about nine days to get to Pearl. I reckon we'll be doing some more practicing and fueling and stuff along the way. They got a lot of places to visit on Pearl when we get liberty. Evelyn's been going to parties and stuff back home. Maybe I'll try out one of them USO dances while I'm there. I will not be getting back in that line on Hotel Street. The war ain't been that long yet.

Mar 31, 1943

Dearest Evelyn,

I don't think I'm supposed to tell you where I am but you might can tell by the postcards. I thought they were mighty fine pictures of here and one day we might come here for a honeymoon or something after the war is over. It's a swell place.

Lyle got that letter from Mary with a picture in it. He was grinning all the day he got it. He's talking about her now, about how maybe we can double date if we ever make it back to the states. I think that's a swell idea.

Yes, I did hear that song 'All I Need is You' and 'He's My Guy' but I didn't hear it on the radio. One of the fellas bought some records and we get to play them sometimes. I sure do miss you and listening to music makes it worse. But I don't want to stop listening so I reckon I'll just have to keep missing.

Are you missing me too or are you having too much fun in Washington? Sounds like you and the gals are having a good time – museums and restaurants and dances and stuff.

Wait a minute. I got to kill a fly that keeps bothering me. Ok I got him. Pretended he was a Jap.

I did not understand something you said in your letter dated March 10. I thought Helen was going to have a baby, but now you say she decided not to. How do you decide not to have a baby?

Yeah I reckon it is a good thing you live where you can just walk places or take the train or the bus since the gas rationing is going on. I wish you could walk across the ocean cause I sure do miss you. I don't know when I'll get to come back home but it can't be soon enough for me.

I know we hadn't really talked about getting married, but in all your letters you say you love me and you know I love you too. Maybe we better talk about that one day.

All my love,
Roy

APRIL

April 9, 1943
Dear Evelyn,

Today is the second birthday for the good ole Battleship NC. She's the best in the fleet and I'm glad to be aboard. Looks like we'll have many more years together. I expect that we'll have some birthday cake later on and maybe some ice cream, too. We can celebrate since we're not out at sea. She's still being patched up a bit to make sure everything is ship-shape, then we'll be going back to the war zone. Take care of things so we can get back home.

That was interesting what you said in your last letter – that you don't know or can't tell me anything about your new job but that all you been told is that you're helping end the war. Not sure how you're doing that back there at home but it's fine with me. The sooner the war is over, the sooner I can get home, and we can start our life together. There's this song I heard the other day called 'Flying Home.' That's what I want to do.

I got the watch now for the next four hours, so I gotta go. But you know that old Lena Horne song 'Stormy Weather?' That's what we're getting ready to have. Will make the watch interesting and wet. At least it's warm here.

Love always,
Roy

April 25, 1943

My dear Evelyn,

Are you alright? I just got your letter dated March 15. I don't know why it got lost unless it was because it was so fat and didn't have enough stamps on it. I bet you think I'm a no good son of a gun. Please don't be mad at me. I been writing you letters and never saying nothing about your friend.

But I got other letters from you dated since that one and you never mentioned a word about Helen. I reckon it's because you might be just so sad and you want to forget all about it. I can't hardly believe all the things that you told me in that letter. But you were a good friend to her to go along and help her like that even though you didn't rightly know where you were going or what was going to happen. Now you just stop feeling guilty about it.

I know that it had to be hard for Helen not knowing who the Pap was or anything. She musta been all mixed up and real sad to try and kill her baby with drinking turpentine. You knew when she did that? It made her sick and she threw it all up. I bet you took good care of her.

You said that lady you took her to was a nurse and that other girls had gone to see her with their problems. That it was a house on the edge of town and there was other girls there then. Nurses are supposed to help people feel better so that makes sense. I bet you didn't know she was going to do nothing bad.

I can't rightly understand what she did when she went to see that nurse if she did it on purpose. I'm sorry, I know your friend is dead and I shouldn't be saying no bad things about her but I just can't understand it. Tell me you won't ever do nothing like that.

You were a good friend to take her to the hospital after she went to see that other person and did what she did to her baby. I bet you tried to take good care of her when you got back home, too. But you came home from work that day and she was burning up with fever so you did what you needed to do even though she begged you not to do it. You tried to save her by getting her to the hospital. I reckon that infection was just too bad by the time you took her and the doctors couldn't fix it. But you got to remember you tried. You and Mary tried. Where were the other girls that live in your boarding house? Did any of them help her at all?

I'm sorry you couldn't go down to Alabama for the funeral. It musta been real hard for you to just see her carried away like that by her Ma and Pap. Her Ma sounds like a real sweet woman, but that Pap of hers sounds like a piece of work. I reckon that's why she couldn't go home like she was.

I'm real sorry about your friend. Truly I am. If this war would get over soon, I could come home and make your feel better.

Love always,
Roy

MAY

Pearl Harbor: May 6, 1943

We been in Pearl Harbor for over a month now and the big girl's all patched up and ready to go. I'm glad. Hawaii is a mighty fine place to be but it ain't getting the war over by us being here. Evelyn told me in her last letter that ain't ain't a word and I reckon I know that but it's the way we talk so I was writing that way too. I don't want to be no haughty taughty kind of person. But I reckon I better try a little harder in my letters – write neat, don't say ain't, don't write on both sides of the page. She's up there in Washington with all those smart people in high places. I don't want her to forget about me and the fact that we are country folks, or used to be. I sure hope she still wants to live in the mountains when I get home. I don't think I can be no city boy.

May 7, 1943

My dearest Evelyn,

We've been in port for a while now. It sure has been nice getting your letters faster. I been trying to write more to my Ma and my sister and other people at home, so I'm sorry if you didn't get as many letters as you would like. I been thinking about you every day. I even bought you a present while I was here, but I've decided to wait a little while before I send it.

You really saw President Roosevelt and he waved at you? That must be some view from the balcony at your office. Being able to watch the President walk around in the Rose Garden. All you girls out there taking a break in the spring sunshine must be quite a sight to see. I try to think what it might look like. What kind of clothes do you wear to work? Do a bunch of working girls giggle as much as you did in high school? I reckon you're too sophisticated for that now.

I'm glad you send me letters and not cards. When it's mail call, we ask the other fellas did you get a letter today and if it's just a card they say no just some old card. It means a lot more when somebody takes the time to write a letter. I like it when you send me a postcard in the letter though cause I get to see some of the sights where you live now. I never been to Washington.

I got my work logged for me for the next week. The Navy found out that the paint on the bulkhead (that's a wall to you) would burn if we get bombed. So we got to scrape it all off so it'll be easier to put out the fires. I'm in charge of ten men to make sure they do the job right and all the paint comes off.

No, I won't get mad if you end your letter 'write soon' or 'I hope I get a letter from you soon' but you got to remember what I told you about the letters. Sometimes they don't go out for a long time and then they go all over the place before they go to you and sometimes they might get lost or wet or something. It's a big ocean and it's a long way from home.

Lyle has been getting more and more letters from Mary. Since we been in port, he got them regular like me – except for that one important one for me that got lost. I'm still sorry about that. He really likes her and it sounds like she likes him, too.

We had some interesting things to do tonight, like listen to the Hit Parade, watch the movie 'My Heart Belongs to Daddy' which don't sound too bad. Or, I can listen to Artie Shaw. He's playing on the fantail of the ship. Yep, that's the tail because it's at the back of the ship.

No, we do not run around in our whites all the time. I can blame the movies for making you think that. Whites make you too easy to see, so we just wear them when we go ashore. On the ship we wear dungarees and even our hats are dyed blue so we blend into the color of the ship and the ocean. You know how we camouflage our clothes back home when we go hunting. Well, it's kind of the same thing except we don't wear green and brown cause there ain't no trees out where we are.

Well it's time to go down to the mess hall and have some chow then decide what I want to do, so I'll close for now.

Love you only,
Roy

May 25, 1943
Dear Evelyn,

We got nine bags of morale aboard ship today and when it was all handed out, I had five letters from you. I usually read them from the oldest to the newest, but today I wanted to read the last one first. I don't know why but I reckon it's a good thing I did. Lyle got one from Mary and it's probably the one you didn't want me to know about until you told me what you did.

I could tell you that it don't make me mad, but it would be a lie so I won't. But that guy Joe sounds like a pretty smart fella and had some good lines that messed you up. I reckon I can't blame you too much cause you didn't know the score.

I bet his uniform started it off – Junior Officer at that. He tells you he just finished some training and is going to be shipped off to some hell hole. Then he tells you all the things he's probably gonna go through. He tells you how lonely he is because all his buddies are gone and he's away from home and don't know when he'll get back.

Then he thinks that's about the right time to ask you out and you're feeling sorry for him so you said yes.

I don't want to know what you did in those three hours. I'm not interested. You can say I'm a jealous kind of guy and maybe I am. Why shouldn't I be? Thinking about him I could tear up half of what I could get my hands on.

Bright eyes will probably come back and when he does you tell him he better watch out if we ever meet up cause one wrong word will set me off. But I reckon you spoiled his plan cause he told you your boyfriend was a lucky guy. Did you really tell him you were the lucky one?

I thought I could write more clear about this but it sounds all mixed up. If you talk about it on what some people did, we don't have any ties like you said. I wanted to do that plenty. But you were still in school when I left. If I had known how long I was going to be gone even that wouldn't have stopped me.

You're damn right, you would get mad if I went out with some other girl and when we're in port I could do that. Plenty of fellas do, even the married ones. But I don't never plan to give you that chance to get mad.

I sure pray everything's alright with us cause there ain't much I can do about it way out here. I hope I never get another letter like that from you again. I can't ever stop loving you.

Only yours,

Roy

JUNE

New Caledonia: June 5, 1943

We spent a little over a week making our way back here to New Caledonia. For about a month now, we been going out in the ocean to practice firing at targets then coming back to port. Lots of liberty time when we get our two cans of hot beer and get to go on the island. I ain't never liked cold beer and sure don't like it hot. I usually give mine away to some of the other fellas.

There's a lot of other ships here with us going and coming. We have to fuel the other ships when we're out in the ocean and that can be a dangerous job, but me and the other fellas been ready to get going to some action and finish off this war. I want to go home. There's a lot I need to take care of there.

I know troops are fighting somewhere, but right now we just ain't doing a whole lot to get it over. But I found out today that we don't have to be fighting the Japs to get killed. We got these planes on the ship called Kingfishers. They mostly do spotting jobs like checking out where we're going before we go there or flying over the land to help us gunners know where to aim. When we're just practicing they pull targets for us to shoot at. But they got machine guns on them in case they get shot at and have to shoot back. The way I heard it, the timing on the machine gun is set up with the propeller so it fires in between the blades when it's turning. I don't know how they do that.

Well, today I was on the deck holystoning and I heard that machine gun fire. It weren't supposed to fire when it was on the ship. I looked up and saw this guy falling over with blood spurting out everywhere. I yelled for help but the medics were already running over there and I wasn't allowed to leave my post.

I learned later that the fella's name was Neilsons. He was a young guy from California. Hadn't been on the ship long. It was his job to clean the propellers and check the catapults and the plane to

75

make sure everything was ready before it took off. Nothing supposed to be in those machine guns after the plane lands. But I heard he was turning the propeller to check it out and that gun just fired right at him. Hit him between the eyes and killed him on the spot.

They buried him on the island. Woulda been nice if they could send him home, but I don't think they can do that. I didn't hear nothing more about it. Seems it means more if you die when we're in a battle, but the fella was just as dead as the others. Don't know why it wasn't just as important. Sure would be to his family back home cause he ain't coming home neither.

June 6, 1943
My dearest Evelyn,

What do you mean you got an offer to go to a job in Australia? Who is your boss and why does he want you to go to Australia? What does that have to do with anything? I sure hope you told him no but you said you won't have a job there in Washington when he leaves. Are the other girls going to Australia? I don't know why you don't want to go back home to the mountains. Georgia is not a bad place to be. I know there aren't a lot of good jobs in Simms Hollow, but what if you went to Atlanta? I'm sure there are some places that need a good secretary and you could stay there until I come back home.

I know I shouldn't yell at you and tell you what to do, but I'm already on the other side of the world and if you go that far from home I don't know if I'll ever see you again. I couldn't bear that. I don't know what I would do.

In this one letter before you talked about going to Australia you said you wondered what would it be like when I came home. Well, this is what I think. You would meet me at the train station and I would see you before I even got off the train. You would be standing there in your flowered dress – the one with the little white collar and the pink belt. And you would be waving to me even though you couldn't see me. There would be a lot of people there and we might get jostled around a bit but when I came down those steps you would start running to me if you could get through and I would drop my duffle bag and take you in my arms and kiss you like I never kissed you before. We're both older now and that will make a difference.

We would have to go see my Ma to make sure she was alright and spend some time with Billy and Sally Jane and my Pap, but then we could go down to the river where we like to sit and listen to the water run over the rocks and well you can just imagine the rest. Especially if it's the summertime. But that can't happen if I come home to Simms Hollow and you're in Washington, and it sure can't happen if I come home and you're all the way to Australia. What are we going to do?

All my love,
Roy

JULY

July 4, 1943

My dearest Evelyn,

Well, it's Independence Day and I guess you're getting ready to celebrate with your friends. I'm sure glad you decided not to move to Australia but I was really surprised when I got that letter saying you had already moved to New York. It's hard when the letters are so far behind. You already got the job offer in New York when I was worried about you deciding to go to Australia. You move too fast for me.

Seems like you really like New York City, but you must be making a lot of money to be able to get an apartment that close to Central Park. I'm glad that Mary went with you. It's good to have a friend around when you're in a new place. I'm glad I got Lyle. He hadn't got his letter from Mary about New York yet. I shouldn't have told him about it but I thought he knew. I hope he gets his letter from her soon.

Maybe our ship will come back to New York and we can all go out on that double date. Wouldn't that be something. But I bet there will be a lot of other ships come in before we do.

You and Mary have got to watch out for those sailors when they go on liberty. You remember we were there for a time before we went to war, and I know what sailors do when they get off the ship, especially when they been away from home for a long time. I know what they're thinking.

You really went to see a Broadway show? You got to tell me more about it in your next letter. No, I hadn't heard that song, 'Oh What a Beautiful Morning.' You say it's from the show 'Oklahoma!' Well, I hadn't heard much of nothing about that, and I don't know that song either. It's a love story you say. Well, that's good. Is it as good a love story as we got?

I know what you mean about all the noise and people in New York City. I don't think I liked it good as you do. I reckon girls like all the stores where they can go shopping. Since you got another big raise when you moved, you can afford to buy a lot of stuff. I like that knife you sent me. I'll use it every day.

Just don't forget to keep saving some money. When we get married and have kids, you might want to spend it on them when we move back to Georgia. I know you don't want to keep working after that, do you?

Well, we can't have no fireworks or nothing like that where we are, but I suppose we'll have some ice cream or something. I'm betting the band will play us some music and the baseball team may be playing again against one of the other ship's teams. I might go ashore and watch if they do that. We got some good players, and it's a good way to pass the time.

Since you moved away and don't keep up with my family so much anymore, I guess you hadn't heard that Billy got drafted in the Army after he finished high school.

He wrote me a letter – which he don't do often – and told me he was going to boot camp in August. I sure wish he had just joined up with the Navy before he finished high school, but he didn't and the Army got him.

In case you don't write to her anymore either, you might want to know that Sally Jane left the drug store but she didn't have to leave home. She's working for the bank right there in Simms Hollow.

I asked her about Ma and she said that she was eating a little better but that she was still real thin and she was tired all the time. Now that Billy is going away, I don't know what she'll do. I sure wish you were closer home so you could check up on her now and then like you used to do.

Well, this is about the longest letter I wrote in a long time, maybe ever. And I didn't write on the back of the page. I took my time, too, so my words are easy to read. But I got to write some other letters home, so I'll close for now.

I hope you hadn't moved again by the time I get your next letter. I bet mine are real slow getting to you since I sent it to the old address instead of the new one.

All my love,
Roy

July 12, 1943

My dearest Evelyn,

I wanted to find a different way to start this letter but I tried a lot of different words like sweetest and honey and rarest, but when I say dearest that's what I mean so I'm going to keep saying it. It comes from the heart.

Another ship came alongside today and we got mail. It's a

destroyer. We had to fuel it a few days ago and today it came back with mail – the old morale bag. I got several letters from guess who? You, of course.

I also got one from my Ma, but it was short. When you're at mail call and waiting to hear your name, I can always tell when the next letter is for me because of all the wonderful Xs and Os you put on the envelope. Even the fellas know. They say – hey Peaches, there's another one for you.

I already read them all so now I'll answer some. I was glad to hear about Joe. Sounds like you been put to the test and came out with flying colors.

I couldn't be no prouder of you. Don't think I didn't believe in you and us before, but you did get me a little worried when you went out on a date with that officer. But I could just about see his face when you told him what you said this time. I just want you to know I love you and I'm proud of you. There won't never be another girl for me.

I know some guys get leave and that's why they're back at home for a while. When I enlisted way back in '41 they told us we would get 30 days leave a year. But we just can't go home right now. I know one guy whose Grandma's real sick and he won't get to see her before she dies.

And there's other fellas on the ship and everywhere else in this damn war whose wife's gonna have a baby while they're gone and they have to wait and see a picture and if we're somewhere we can't get mail that picture might be real old by the time they get it. By the time they get home that baby will probably be walking and talking. It just don't seem fair.

You ask me about getting gun captain. I think I answered that a long time ago, but I don't mind saying it again. The test was bad but yes I made gun captain. I had to know how the gun was wired up – that's kind of electrician stuff. I had to know angles and positions of targets and firecontrol and everything about how the gun fires and actually firing it. And about what the gunners mates do. You know I don't really mind studying and going up for rates if I know I'm going to make it.

That pretty much answers the first letter. In the next one you asked me about the captain's gig. I reckon you want to be in the know about my job even if you won't tell me much about yours.

The captain's gig is a little boat that the captain uses to go places. I don't know how it got the name gig. But when we're in port with a lot of other ships and the captain needs to go to another ship to talk to another captain or whatever he does or if he needs to go ashore, then we take him there in the captain's gig.

But we don't drop him off and leave. We have to wait right there until he's ready to go to another place or back to our ship. So I usually take a book to read or stuff to study. One day we took him to every ship in the harbor. One after another.

Now the admiral's boat is called a barge. I don't know as much about that one and don't want to bore you with anymore details about boats.

I sure have some troubles not being about to see you. You don't know how many days go by that I'm troubled. But every day that goes by is one day closer to being home. That's the way I gotta look at it but it sure enough is not an easy thing to do.

Missing you,
Roy

AUGUST

August 12, 1943
My dearest darling Evelyn,

I hadn't gotten a letter from you in a few days so there's not a lot to write about but I had some time and writing makes me feel closer to you. I reckon there's some stuff in the old letters I can answer.

You been talking a lot about Frank Sinatra. Well, I haven't heard any of his songs. We got one here that keeps getting played all the time. I don't exactly know who sings it. It's called 'Always in my Heart' and it gets played over and over again. I still like it even though it's about all you hear around here. I reckon it's the truth of it that makes people want to play it. One of the guys has the words all wrote down. He said it was Glenn Miller. It says that even though he doesn't know when he'll meet her again, she's always in his heart. Yeah, that's about right.

I used to worry all the time that I wasn't in charge of the boat. I'm a gun captain in charge of the gun so I'd feel pretty good if I could be in charge of the boat too. Remember when I wrote you about waking up in the morning with a bunch of nerves worrying about it? Well, I'm over that now. There's some things I got to learn that ain't all that interesting.

But here's what I do that makes me feel better. Makes me feel smarter and bigger. I like to make drawings of the bay or the harbor where we are with all the ships where they are and chart a course. Makes me feel like an old sailing skipper charting his course home. You reckon I been watching too many movies? Anyhow, the good part is when I run a course in the daytime, then I have to do it again at night in the dark and I get it right. Perfect. That's harder than you might think and then I know my efforts weren't wasted.

I don't have much to write about except my duties and I reckon that can get kind of boring for you. About me making snaps to secure the life ring and stuff like that. I wished I could write more interesting stuff but I can't think of nothing.

I got a Simms Hollow newspaper from my Ma last time she wrote. She sent the whole thing. It had some news in it about folks we know. Old man Pickett got arrested for the moonshine he's been making for twenty years. I reckon they finally caught up with him. Norton's got to go off to war with the Army so him and Sue got married before he left. Makes me think of what we shoulda done but I reckon we couldn't seeing as how you were so young and all. Lenny was in the news. He's been to Africa and made it back home safe. It said something about Mary Lou and Sarah – you remember them, the Husten sisters? Well, it says they had a party before going off to some new job in the same town together but it didn't say where they were going.

Remember how I told you those swell pictures of you in your new bathing suit were bent a little when I got them? Did I tell you how good you look in that bathing suit? Well you do and the fellas here all want to look at them pictures and I needed to hide them. Besides they were bent so I put them under my pillow to see if I couldn't straighten them out. Anyhow, that night I had a long dream about you. I woke up and didn't want to be awake and not be so close to you and so I went back to sleep and the dream just kept right on going. We were at that beach where you been going with your friends but it was nighttime and we weren't with nobody else. You had on that new bathing suit and I had on my bathing suit that we wear on the islands and you know it ain't too big. That's the most skin I ever touched and it was so soft and felt real good. I just wanted to keep on dreaming and coulda just about killed the guy who woke me up then. But we had the watch and I was about to be late so I reckon I should thank him instead.

No, this sailor life don't bother me too much. We doing what we got to do and I know I'm a lot luckier than those soldiers over in Germany and France and places like that all over the world. I got a bed to sleep in at night and I got food to eat and I am not in a foxhole somewhere in the mud wondering when some guy's gonna walk up and shoot me or throw some grenade or something. I ain't saying what we're doing is not just as dangerous. I done seen a lot of men die or be hurt real bad. It's just that I think we got the better end of the deal.

The only thing I really worry about is home and when I'll get there. It can't be too long now. At least I hope not.

All my love,

Roy

SEPTEMBER

September 5, 1943

My one and only Evelyn,

Did you like that beginning better? It's what I hope is true. You are the only one for me and I hope I'm the only one for you. What do you know. That sounded kind of like a poem. I hadn't been able to write any good ones lately.

You been telling me sometimes about the blackouts in New York and I reckon they can seem pretty dark to you. But I bet they'd seem like daylight to me. Let me tell you about our blackouts. We have them all the time. Anything above second deck is out and anything around the hatches on second deck is dark too so nobody can see anything when you open the hatches. When you got the night watch, say 8-12 or 12- 4, you got to go up in the dark. They are some narrow ladders and when you get to the top your eyes aren't adjusted from being in the light below and you can't see nothing even to know if the man you're relieving is there or not. Sometimes they like to play tricks on you so you can't find em. You got to keep calling to them but not too loud.

Sometimes they'll say ok so you know where they are but if they want to play a joke on you they won't say nothing or they'll start tapping and you won't know where it's coming from. Then sometimes they ask you can you see yet. This one time I ask a guy could he see and he said yeah but I set a bucket in front of him and he walked right into it. I proved he couldn't see. When you been out there in the dark your eyes are adjusted so you can see the fellas coming up but they can't see you.

I figured out one reason the lifelines around the ship are so important and why they're called lifelines. One night this fella was coming up and he couldn't see and he walked right straight over to the side and into the lifelines. If they hadn't been there, he would have been a goner. Right in the ocean. Enough about blackouts.

No, the boat isn't really mine. It belongs to the Navy, but I'm in charge of it, so I call it my boat until they give it to somebody else. It's my job so I take good care of it. It was hoisted aboard and it sits in skids. I'm the coxswain of it. I probably should explain all about the boat but I don't have time. Maybe I'll do it in another letter if you want to know and it don't bore you.

Yes, I do want children. Maybe a whole passel of them. We can name the first boy Roy, Jr., and he's going to be the best. Best in school, best in sports – probably football – and best in everything he does. He's not going to be like me. He's going to be smart and get ahead.

I been up since the 4-8 watch and it's been a busy day. I started this letter later than I wanted and now I'm just too tired to make it any longer. I can't keep up with your twenty page letters. I reckon you'll always win on that account.

I think I'll put your picture under my pillow and see if I can dream again.

Loving you always,
Roy

September 6, 1943
Dearest Evelyn,

I'm in a swell mood today even though I hadn't had any new letters lately. I got some old ones that still need answering. You made me feel better when you said that you just had a good feeling about me and the boat. I been having some nights when I couldn't sleep. I would wake up all nervous and sweating and worried because of my first command of a boat.

I have to worry about the crew and making sure the boat is ship-shape and being in a strange harbor I had to worry about the course and making sure I got where I was supposed to be going. And I could get called on a second's notice and have to get into my whites cause I'd be taking the captain somewhere.

If you want to know some more about it I can write a whole letter sometime. It's a pretty interesting job to do and I like it. I like the crane, too. I'm getting better at that all the time. So, my jobs are pretty good on the ship.

When you going to tell me more about your job? Do you like New York? I reckon you're working in a fancy office typing and filing and stuff. But what does your boss do? Is he a lawyer or a banker or what?

Yes, the seaman gets the dirty jobs and gets orders at just any ole time, sometimes bad times like when you're reading a book or doing an important job of your own. PO is a Petty officer. PO for short.

No I didn't take a test to be a 2/c PO. I took three tests – one for seaman, one for coxswain, and one for gun captain. I passed all three on the first try. I hadn't started on my second class course yet because I want to learn all about being a good coxswain first. I got to learn how to make a monkey's fist (that's a knot). I need to learn about all the gear, too. I got time. Don't look like I'll be going anywhere anytime soon. And that means I just got to miss you all the more.

Yes, the fellas do a lot of talking about their girls and comparing. But I don't get in on all that. I got the best and that's all there is to it.

No, I don't go messing around. I know the guys are supposed to be wild and there's some wild girls too. It's suppose to be worse for a girl to be messing around at a young age. I reckon people expect it from the fellas. But I don't do it and this is why. I want a good bright future with you. I know this one guy he was messing around and he's gonna be suffering now. He got some germs in his blood and he's breaking out on his body and his leg done swelled up. It's a sorry story for him. He was one of the ruff ones from New York.

Alright so I got it mixed up. House coat, negligee, they're all the same to me. So yours is thin. It looks heavy in the picture. The one I saw in the store window you could read a newspaper through it. That was thin. Don't – no do – get some ideas. But I got a lot to learn about women's clothes.

You don't have to stop wearing earrings just cause I don't like them. I reckon they're ok on you. I like what you said about them getting in the way when you're with me. Sounds like you're cleaning ship for action. That's what we do aboard ship getting rid of all the junk you don't need before you go into battle. But I'm not going to be battling you. No ma'am, no way.

You sent me some swell pictures. My album is filling up. You remember that movie 'White Cargo' with the native girl who was driving all the men crazy. Well, you sorta look like her in that last bunch of pictures and you sure do drive me crazy.

That was a good saying you found in the 'Reader's Digest' about loving something more when you might lose it. Don't worry about me. I'm going to be coming home. I just can't say when.

Some more about clothes. That picture of you in the bathing suit is really something. It's just swell, best I've seen. In them advertisements they say that the clothes can make you look good, but it's the other way around. You're the one that makes the clothes look good. Don't matter what you got on to me – might be nice with nothing at all.

Well that's about all the news except I got my teeth cleaned aboard ship. They're shiny and white now. First time I seen a dentist since I came on the ship and I didn't have nothing that needed drilling.

I hope this letter makes you as happy as your letters make me.

Loving you always,

Roy

Somewhere out in the ocean: September 15, 1943

Things here don't seem like they're changing very fast, but they sure are back home. Evelyn got that job that sent her to Washington, then before I knew what happened, she was in New York City. I hadn't had a letter from her in almost two weeks now, so I'm not sure if she's still there or if that job has moved her somewhere else again. Or if she met somebody else more exciting in New York. She sure was taken by that place last time I heard from her.

We been back and forth participating in some action in what they called the New Georgia Group Operations. We were at New Guinea and Efate and New Hebrides. We fight a while and capture the small islands and make them safe as a gathering place before we move on to the next group of islands. I reckon we're headed straight to Japan but we got a lot of work to do before we get there.

Well I found out now that even if you're a ship, you don't have to be in the war zone to get hit. I done wrote about how we travel with other ships in this big circle and how we go out and practice our shooting. We got this new destroyer in our task force called the Kidd.

A few days ago, we were out practicing a fake torpedo attack at dawn and the NC was lighting up the Kidd with what we call star-shells from the five-inch. That's my guns, but we have more than one mount on each side. Well something went wrong from one of the mounts and one of the shells hit the Kidd just above the waterline. It weren't supposed to hit her at all. I hear tell that nobody got hurt aboard her, but it was a bad thing that messed up the ship a bit.

Today, the Kidd had to come alongside us to refuel. She probably weren't too happy about being that close to us. Well, while we were going along, the North Carolina's band came on deck and started playing some music to entertain the crew of the Kidd. Down in the bakery they had been real busy trying to do something to make up for what we done.

They brought up a huge cake in a box. On it was the words 'USS Kidd' and a great big Purple Heart made out of icing. We passed that cake over on the heaving lines before we started fueling. We passed over a bunch of fresh made ice cream, too. The captain sent us back a message thanking us for our special kind of damage control. It was the best we could do at the time.

September 16, 1943
My dearest Evelyn,

I haven't heard from you in quite some time. I hope that next mail call I will get a whole bunch of letters that just got lost somewhere along the way. When we get mail call, we call it morale call, and my morale hadn't been too good lately.

I'm sending this letter to New York and hope that you are still there. The way your boss likes to move you around, I just can't be sure. I wish you could tell me more about what kind of job you have other than you're a secretary. What kind of stuff are you writing and filing and all?

Sally Jane is leaving home. She has a new job somewhere in Tennessee but she can't say too much about her job either. I don't know what all the fuss is about. We can't tell you where we are because it's a military secret and if it fell in the wrong hands could get a lot of people killed. But you and my sister are in the good old USA. What could be so secret about a job you have?

My Ma wrote me a letter. She sounded real sad in between all the lines of telling me about the farm. She said that the cows miss me and aren't giving as much milk since I been gone. She said the sunflowers weren't growing as tall and the cucumbers didn't put out much this year. She had a good harvest of tomatoes and canned right many. I reckon the rest of the vegetables did alright.

But what with me out here in the ocean somewhere she doesn't know, and Billy in boot camp in North Carolina, and now Sally Jane moving to somewhere she don't know about in Tennessee, I'm real worried about her. My Pap don't write cause he never learned how so now with nobody left at home but the two of them, I'm real worried about my Ma. You reckon you could write your Ma and ask her to check up on my Ma and let you know how she's doing so you can tell me? I'd be much obliged if you could.

In one of your last letters, you were a little bit confused about the ranks so I'll try and explain them to you. You are right about me being a little thinner but my tailor made uniform makes me look that way, too. I'm eating, how about you?

Anyway, the expert rifleman mark I got sewed on my shirt isn't a pointers rate. That one has a cross in the middle of a circle with a star above it. The watch mark is the white stripe on my blue uniform and the blue stripe on my whites. I don't think you understand about the coxswain and boatswain mate either. I already explained that in a different letter, so I'll make sure you get that one before I explain it again.

You did say something in the last letter I got that made me happy. You said I wrote swell letters and that you are proud of me for making a new rate. I'm glad you're glad. I wouldn't trade you for anybody else either. Somebody would have to beat the life out of me and even then I wouldn't change my mind. I hope that tells you how much I love you.

I have a present to send to you, but I want to make sure I have the right address before I send it. Hope to hear from you soon.

Love always,
Roy

Pearl Harbor: September 17, 1943

We're back in Pearl Harbor. The ship is getting some work done on her shafts, and I heard she's got to get a new paint job. I reckon it's hard to camouflage something this big, but you got to do what you can.

I suppose we're going back to the heavy action when we leave here. That's the scuttlebutt anyhow.

Last time we were here, I went in the jewelry store and looked at rings. I was going to buy one and asked Evelyn to marry me, but I chickened out and bought a bracelet instead. I mailed that to her in Washington, but by then she had moved to New York.

I hope she got it.

This might be my last chance for a while so I'm going to do it this time. I'm going to count my cash I got hid before I go, then I'll come back and get it when I find out how much I need.

When I get another letter from Evelyn and make sure I have her right address I'm going to send the ring and ask her to marry me. I wish I had someone I could send it to that could make it special and do it for me, but that ain't the case since she moved away and my brother joined the Army and my sister moved away. I'll just have to do the best I can and hope she still loves me.

I'm going now. I'm really gonna do it. I am.

Well, I did it. It's a beautiful ring set with a single big diamond in the middle and one smaller one on each side. The wedding band has little diamonds all the way around it. I'm going to keep it with me for now. I hope I don't lose it or the ship don't sink, but I wanted to get them matching and I probably couldn't find a band to match when I get home.

Now I just got to wait until I hear from her. Maybe while we're here in Pearl Harbor, the mail will catch up to us. It usually does.

OCTOBER

October 1, 1943

Dearest Evelyn,

I finally received a whole bundle of your letters today, so I will read them one at a time starting with the oldest date to the newest and answer them as I go. They took a long time getting here.

I can't believe you left New York for your job without even knowing where you were going. You must really trust your boss or love your job or something. I don't understand, but I'll keep reading.

Ok. So your boss told you the office was relocating and he couldn't tell you where but he wanted you to go. And he wouldn't tell you what you would be doing or how far you were going or how you would get there or how long you would have to stay wherever you were going. And you said yes without knowing anything at all? Now I'm worried.

Sorry, I just can't do this one letter at a time. I have to read ahead so I know what's going on. This first ones got me all worried and confused.

Ok, I'm back. I read them all and I can tell you I am relieved that none of them said you found a new fella in New York. I can't lie. I was worried that some fancy sailor had come into port and swept you off your feet or that you were going to fall in love with your boss and marry him. I see you did go to some dances at the USO and you had a good time. I'm glad you enjoyed being in New York, going to the Broadway shows and shopping and going to dances and parties. I'm just glad you're still my girl.

And now you are in Tennessee. I gotta tell you that sounds weird to go from Washington to New York to Tennessee for the same job. Are you doing the same thing? Did you get my letter about Sally Jane? She moved to Tennessee for a job, too, and the only thing that they told her was that her new job could help end the war. They told you that, too. Are you in the same place? I hope so. Maybe you can find her. That shouldn't be too hard, should it?

You asked me if I ever went on liberty in any interesting places. Well, I'll tell you about this one time I went on liberty and I got a black eye. We were at this island and the fifth division went on a little beer party. We had to go in a boat that they launch from the ship because it's too big to get close to shore. The skiff took us up to the dock with our beer. We each get two cans of hot beer but some of the guys managed to get more than their share. And we went through this path in the woods and ended up on the beach. A little H___ was raised.

Well this storm came up and we went hurrying back down the path to the dock to get back to the skiff and I was one of the first ones in. Everybody was piling in and there was these two big guys. The first six foot guy went sailing into the boat, dove right in without touching and knocked me over. Then before I could get up the next guy who had to weigh at least two hundred pounds just stumbled in and made a one point landing on my eye. It was a beaut and the whole division admired it – dark blue and reddish blue, then it turned yellow when it was healing. I gotta tell you I swore off those liberties after that. I just rather stay by myself.

So you can tie a clove hitch. I reckon that's good. No, a lover's knot is not when two people get married. It's two regular knots tied at the same time and one fits right behind the other and they can slide. Look at it this way. You know how when two birds make love they rub heads. I know you've seen it. Well that's kinda what it reminds me of. You pull one side and it moves apart but you pull the other side and it goes closer together.

I'm glad you feel better about Helen. You hadn't talked about her in any of your letters for a long time. Yes, you were a good friend to her and tried to help her. That's all you could do. Yes, I expect that you will miss her for a very long time. So Mary went with you to Tennessee but not any of the other girls. That one that was so skinny, even skinnier than you, went to the hospital after she passed out too many times. They didn't want her to go with you because she was too sickly. Did they tell you that or did you just figure it out? I hope you're eating more now.

The rest of the girls wouldn't go or did they even get asked? They might have just asked the best ones you know – you and Mary. Lyle got some letters from Mary today too. I'll have to see if she told him she moved. I won't ask direct, I'll just hint around and see what he tells me. He's pretty hung up on her. Got her pictures all over his locker. I'm glad she likes him too.

Thanks for all the pictures you sent in your letters. They're perfect. Now I know what it looked like in Washington and how you could see the White House from your work. And I really like the postcards from the Statue of Liberty in New York. But I like the pictures that have you in them the best. You are so beautiful. You have really changed since I left. A beautiful woman instead of a teenage girl.

Yeah, well it's hard for me to explain what lubberly means except it would go kinda like this. If you came on the ship, you might call it a boat. That would be real bad. And you would say wall instead of bulkhead and floor for deck and pail instead of bucket and mop for swab and stuff like that. We have words we use for a lot of things that you wouldn't know if you weren't in the Navy. But you won't need to know them in Tennessee. Won't be any ships there.

I like that you're in Tennessee if you're not in Georgia. It's closer to home than Washington or New York.

I'm glad that you're proud about my rate. Now that I'm third, my old job will go to a seaman. I wanted to be a pointer so I could see where we're shooting and get to pull the trigger sometime. But I'm a gun captain so my job is to make sure everything goes right and no one gets hurt. I reckon that's a pretty important job.

I would write until my fingers break but I got some work to do yet. I got to fold my laundry and put it away and get my dungarees dry and folded and a few other things.

I'll write you again soon and I got a package to send now that I have your new address. You gonna stay in Tennessee for a while I hope so this package can get to you. I wouldn't want it to get lost.

All my love,
Roy

October 2, 1943

My beloved Evelyn,

Do you trust me? Well, if you do, please wait and open everything in the order I tell you to open it. That's very important.

First I want you to open the small envelope. It has some pictures in it that I took at night where we are now. If you opened it and looked, you can read on.

I had liberty that was two days long so I was free at night. I took the one of the sunset and then got up early in the morning to take the sunrise. During the day, I put on my dress whites and had Lyle take the picture of me standing next to the beach with a package in my hand. That's the little package in the box. But don't open it yet.

Now open the picture in the bigger envelope. Did you open it? Now read on. I wanted to send you real flowers but I knew they wouldn't get there at the same time as my letter, so I took a picture of the prettiest flowers I could find on the beach and am giving them to you.

Now open the bigger box. Did you do it? That's called a lei. I'm sure the flowers aren't very pretty anymore but I want you to put it around your neck anyway and think of how pretty they were when they were fresh.

Now, I want you to look at the picture of me standing by the ocean. It's quiet and there's a nice cool breeze. In the sunshine, it's nice for swimming, but at night it gets very cool and is nice for snuggling. The breeze makes the palm trees rustle and make a little noise. It would be a wonderful place for a honeymoon.

Make believe with me. I hope you've heard Ella Fitzgerald sing that song 'I'm Making Believe' so you can hear it in your head when you read the words.

<blockquote>
I'm making believe that you're in my arms
Though I know you're so far away
Making believe I'm talking to you
Wish you could hear what I say
</blockquote>

Now, open the little box. There's a picture on the top. I'm on one knee at the beach offering you a diamond ring and this is what I'm saying. Evelyn, I love you with all my heart. There will never be anyone else for me. I don't know when I'll be home, but will you wait for me? When I get there, will you marry me?

Anxious for your answer,
Roy

Oct 5, 1943

Dearest Evelyn,

I'm writing this letter from the #1 mess hall and the fella that plays the organ is making me homesick. He keeps playing all the good ole tunes like 'I Dream of Jeanie' and 'Danny Boy.' I reckon I could go out on the deck and write but it's easier to do it where you have a table.

Since you said that my letters usually take about six days and sometimes a lot longer, I know you hadn't got my package yet so I'm not going to ask you about it, but boy do I want to know when you get it. Now he's playing 'For Me and My Gal' and you're my gal so that one does make me think of you.

I saw 'Journey for Margaret' last time we did a movie in the mess hall. It made ole Lyle cry a bit, but he's a tender-hearted fella. Mary is lucky that he likes her. I hope we'll get to go home soon so they can actually meet each other. She does a good job writing letters, though, cause Lyle feels like he knows her just fine.

He knows she grew up in New Jersey. But he don't care that she's a Yankee. He's from a little island off the coast of South Carolina. There's not a finer fella I know on ship. A real Southern gentleman. Sounds like you think Mary's a pretty fine person, too. Lyle says that Mary has two brothers and three sisters and her Pap is a doctor. Did you know that?

Truth be told, that movie made me cry too but I tried to hide it. I can't know how it would feel to lose a baby before it was even born, but I think it would be pretty awful for the woman especially and the man too cause he would be excited to be having a baby. And all those little kids in that orphanage – that was sad. I won't tell you no more in case you hadn't seen it yet, but if you get the chance to see that movie, you might like it. But it might make you think about what Helen did, so maybe you don't need to see it.

He's playing 'I'll Never Smile Again' now and that one means something to me. I really like the second verse the best. Do you know it?

Now that first line is the truth. I won't never love nobody else but you. In one of your letters you asked me about that song 'It Can't be Wrong.' Well I never heard it before so I tried to find out about it and one of the fellas had the record. So I listened to it. You're right, it's a good one. I don't think it would be wrong for us to stand in the moonlight and kiss because of the way I feel about you and you feel about me. So if it's not wrong, it must be right. But I just hope you don't stand in the moonlight in Tennessee and kiss some other fella you meet at your new job. Cause that would be wrong just like I don't plan to kiss no other girls even the ones with grass skirts.

When we're where we are now, there are a lot of normal people. Some places we go, there's not much in the way of folk but the ones who don't wear much clothes. I told you about that – the women in grass skirts and nothing else at all. The men with just some cloth hanging between their legs in front. But here is normal.

There's restaurants and hotels and a hospital and normal people dressed in regular clothes. There's lots of different kinds of military here, too, so it's not unusual to see the sailors and marines and soldiers all in the same place.

So you had blackout warnings when you were in New York. What was it like? What kind of whistle did they have and what did you have to do? We have blackouts all the time when we're out in the ocean. Even when we're in port out there at some of those islands in the Pacific we have to do blackouts. Can't even light a cigarette if you're on deck. Not that I would do that anyhow. I don't smoke, but a lot of the guys do.

The fella on the organ is still going at it. Now he's playing 'Blueberry Hill.' He's a pretty good singer, too. I like the part that says they're still part of each other even when they're not together. That's about me and you.

Well now, I'm in a heck of a mood. I don't care much about what goes on around here. All I want to do is get this war over and get home to you. But the mail sure helps in the meantime, so please write soon.

All my love,
Roy

October 10, 1943

My dearest Evelyn,

I received two letters from you today, but they don't mention what I really want to know so you must not have gotten the package before you wrote these letters. I'm going to try and answer some of what you said.

I'm glad you're getting settled in at your new job. You say it's a new place that doesn't have much sidewalks. You ruined your new shoes in the mud. I bet that made you mad. After being in Washington and then in big ole New York City, you probably don't like being back in a hick town and this one sounds like a hick town. What is the name of the town? Is there a town in Tennessee that it's close to that I might know?

I heard somebody say, or maybe it was in a song, that war turns the whole world to sex. Maybe that's why you're talking about that. Yeah, my Ma lied to me too. She said that babies were kept in little baskets in the hospital. They had boys in one room and girls in another and you'd just go in there and pick one out. But I got to wondering how they did twins and things like that cause I had a friend who had a twin sister. He was boy and she was a girl. They would have been in different rooms.

It really took you til you were sixteen? I wanted to find out sooner than that so a bunch of us fellas started digging around and asking questions. I never had the nerve to ask my Pap. I got a lot from books and advanced guys. It weren't like we didn't know some things. We did live on a farm. And I never saw no baskets when we went to visit my Grandma in the hospital. She died there when I was about 13. We didn't have no hospital that close to our house anyhow. But I never knew where they got Billy or Sally Jane. I was pretty little and they just up and sent me to stay with my Grandma for a few days and when I got back, there was a baby.

I'd like for us to have some babies. Maybe at least a couple of each. One of the fellas that just came aboard, his wife had a baby right before he left home. Cute little thing in the picture he got. He seems awful sad a bunch of the time having to leave them like that. I wouldn't want to have to leave you again and I sure as heck wouldn't want to leave if we had a youngun.

I gotta close even though I would like to keep writing. I need to write to my Ma and I got to be in bed by nine. All good boys are in bed by nine. But you have to stay up all night if you're on watch.

I hope I get the letter from you that I'm hoping for soon.

Good night my love,
Roy

Pearl Harbor: October 22, 1943

Well they finished all the repairs to the ship and moved her out of dry dock. That means we'll be going back to the war soon. Not soon enough for me. We can't get it over with if we don't just go ahead and do it. All this waiting around is killing me. But not as much as waiting around for Evelyn's answer. I know she should have got that package by now, but none of her letters has said one thing about it. I hope that don't mean she won't say yes. What if she got it and she wants to say no and she just don't want to tell me while I'm out fighting in a war. I hate waiting.

NOVEMBER

November 2, 1943

My dearest Evelyn,

It's been exactly one month today since I sent you a package. Hadn't you got it yet? I got some more letters from you today, but you hadn't said one word about a package. Is that place you're living in got a post office? You don't tell me nothing about the place or about your job or nothing. I'm just wondering where you really are and if you're even getting my letters or my package or anything cause your letters don't really answer my letters like I try to do when I write you.

Ok, so yeah, I'm in a foul mood. I just get that way sometimes. You would too if you were all this far from home and don't know what's going on and can't do nothing about it. I got a letter from my brother Billy and he's being sent overseas. Probably gone by now. He finished up his boot camp and he's got to go. He's been lucky to be back in the states so long but he's been getting some kind of special rifle training or something. He got to go home one time, but he don't get to go back home and see the folks before they ship him out. He thinks he might be going to Germany. From what

I hear that's a bad place to go.

Sally Jane hadn't written me one letter since she moved to Tennessee for that job. Have you found her yet? You hadn't mentioned that neither. Sometimes I get so frustrated not knowing what's going on back home and not being able to do one thing about it.

I think I better stop now and go do something else and see if I can get my mood better. I got some liberty. Maybe I'll walk on the beach or something. Look at pretty girls.

Alright, I'm back and I'm in a better mood. I'll get back to answering your last letter, but first I want to tell you that there weren't no girls on that beach prettier than you.

So you've got a new friend named Mildred James Malpass. She just got married, huh? Well, I guess if you're real good friends, she can answer some of the questions you been having about things. Seems she's already started your education if she told you about French kissing. Oh, so you had me trained the way you wanted me. Well, that's good to hear. I tried to do it right. If you say I was, then I musta been. She's married to a sailor and you want a sailor, too. I sure hope you mean me. I'm real sorry her sailor shipped out right after they got married, but at least they had a chance to get married.

Ma said nobody's heard from cousin Stuart in about a month now. Nobody's come told Aunt Sue nothing either. They don't know what's going on with him or where he is or if he's alright. Sure does make everybody back home sad not knowing. And my Ma tries to sound cheery in her letters to make me feel better I reckon, but with all her younguns gone from home, I can tell she's real sad. I sure wish Sally Jane had at least stayed home. She didn't have to move off for no new job but I'm not surprised. She never did like the farm. I sure do miss everything about it.

Well, that's the end of your letter so I don't have nothing else to write about. I hope you get my package soon and answer the letter inside it. I sure wish there was some other way for us to talk straight out because these letters take way too long.

Your sailor,

Roy

PS - I like all those Xs and Os you've been putting on my letters, but I like the lipstick kisses on the envelopes the best. When I get home, we'll catch up on all of those.

Still in Pearl Harbor: November 6, 1943

We been going out for firing practice now that the ship's shipshape again. I reckon we're just testing everything and getting our aim before we take on the Japs again. Today we thought they might be coming for us like they did back in '41. Had an air raid warning and we had to go to General Quarters. Turned out it weren't nothing to worry about, but it sure does set you on edge. I still remember that first day we came into Pearl Harbor and saw everything the Japs did. I won't never forget it.

I still ain't got no response to my question from Evelyn. I been getting letters but she don't say a word about it. I don't know if she didn't get it yet or she got it and just don't know what she wants to answer so she's pretending she ain't never got it. Or she wants to say no but don't want to do it while I'm out here. I know back home they get this stuff all the time about keeping up the morale of the troops. We do need it.

But every one of her letters talks about how much she loves me, and now that she's got that new friend that married a sailor, she talks about that, too, so I gotta keep my hopes up. I just hope I get some kinda answer before we set sail again. I believe that's going to be real soon and there's no telling when I'll get mail then.

Scuttlebutt has it that the war's picked up something fierce in the Pacific. We're winning, especially after Guadalcanal and all. But I reckon that just made them Japs madder than heck and they been getting ready to retaliate. We got to get out there and help take back some more islands so we can get to the Japs. We're ready to do it. Go all the way to Japan and get them where they live if we have to.

November 10, 1943

My dearest darling Evelyn,

I never been so happy as I was today. The ship was pulling out to go back to war and at the last minute we saw some mail bags being brought on board. We couldn't get mail call right then cause we had work to do while getting underway, but after chow we got mail call.

I got six letters from you today and one package with an earlier date on it than all the letters, even earlier than some letters I already answered. I had to open the package first thing. I hope you don't mind. The box is a little beat up but that's the way things usually are when they get to us. At least I don't think it got wet.

So you copied me and I didn't mind that but it sure was hard opening one thing at a time. I was going to try and answer while I opened it, but that was too hard so I did it all first, then started this letter. Here's how it went down.

The first envelope had a picture of you wearing your lei and a note. Yes, I know the flowers are a little wilted but they sure look pretty on you in that blue dress with your red curls hanging all down. It's a swell picture. I know you're just standing next to a swimming pool because there's no ocean where you are but that water is blue as the ocean. Where did you find those plastic palm trees? They look almost real. But the best part of the picture is you.

Ok, next in the big box was a little box with a number 1 on it. I had to get out my knife you gave me because you put so much tape on it. The fellas gathered all around me. I reckon I looked sort of excited and they wanted to know what was going on.

Where did you get those wooden baby blocks? There was two

in that box. I had to keep turning them around like your note said until I made a word that made sense. Figured that first word was probably 'MY.' I saw some more little boxes and they all had a lot of tape on them. They had numbers too so I would open them in the right order. It was hard but I did it. Well, almost.

Box number 2 had six blocks in it. It took me a few minutes but figured it out. Every block had six different letters on it and there was six blocks. It took a while.

I made a lot of words that didn't make sense but then I made one that did. I told the fellas the rest would be easier because I figured out what you were doing. Pretty creative aren't you? That second word was 'ANSWER.'

I really wanted to skip to the last box but Lyle said I had to do it the way you said. I bet if he got a package like this from Mary after he'd asked her an important question he'd cheat and go right to the last box.

Ok, so you got me. I did open box number 4 next and it didn't have no blocks in it. Just a note that said 'Don't cheat!' So I took my medicine and went back to box number 3. Why did you have to use so much tape? It took a long time.

Box number three had two blocks in it. That one was easy. The word is 'IS' so then I had a sentence with no ending. It said MY ANSWER IS. But I didn't see no more boxes so I still didn't know the answer. And it didn't look like there was anything else in the box. I started to think you were playing a real bad joke on me.

I turned the box every which a way and looked on the bottom and the top and the sides and couldn't find nothing. Lyle said let him try. I told him there weren't nothing there but he said let him try and I did. He started messing with it and figured out you put a extra bottom in it. Now I don't know why I couldn't figure it out but I'm mighty obliged to Lyle because I don't know how long I coulda gone without seeing the answer. He thought I was going crazy so being a good friend he helped me out.

Under that tricky bottom you put in there was an envelope that felt like it had another picture in it. I was praying it was my answer that I wanted.

I never been so happy and excited! The picture on top was a close up of your hand with the ring on it. It sure looks swell on that pretty hand of yours with your fingernails painted pink like the lipstick you kiss on my letters.

The second picture was one of you with a big sign in your hand that says YES! YES! YES! That's the prettiest smile I ever seen on the prettiest girl I ever knew.

I'm a happy sailor right now. Got the biggest grin on my face. The fellas in my division they're all patting me on the back and saying congratulations Peaches and just a whooping and hollering. I reckon we're going to have us a party later on with some ice cream. Lyle just said he was going to go down to the butcher shop and see if he could roust us up a big hunk of boloney all our own cause he knows the guys in there and he's going to find some cheese and mustard and stuff and have us a party.

Did you have a party with your friends? I'm hoping your letters tell me all about it. I reckon it's a good thing I opened the package first in case the letters give it all away.

Well, I got the watch now for the next four hours so I better put away all my stuff and get ready. I'll be looking at the stars and thinking about that song 'Me and My Girl.' Cause I got me a girl for sure now and I can't wait til I can come home and we can get married. I just don't know when that might be but I'll let you know as soon as I get an idea of when.

Your gonna be husband,

Roy

PS - I never loved nobody in my whole life as much as I love you and I can't wait to show you how much and try some of them things we both been learning about by listening to other folks talk.

Somewhere in the Pacific Ocean: November 11, 1943

It's funny in a strange way not a Ha Ha funny way how you can be so excited one day and then the next day things happen that make it hard to stay happy. I got my answer from Evelyn yesterday and she said she would marry me. All during my watch last night I thought about how great it would be to get home and marry her and have us a few younguns and raise a family right there in Simms Hollow. Or maybe even up on the side of the mountain that looks down in the holler. There's a fine place up there with some flat land where we could grow a garden and have some horses and maybe a few cows. And the rhododendron bloom in June all over the side of that mountain. It would sure be a fine thing. I need to ask ole man Scruggs if he'll sell me a few acres. About 50 ought to be enough. I don't plan to be just a farmer and I'd still be living close enough to do the farming on my daddy's land if he wanted it that way. I been learning some skills here on the ship that could get me a good job, maybe running a crane for somebody.

But we found out today where we're headed and why. We're going to the Gilbert Islands to Tarawa and Makin and some others. Seems the first landing by the Marines weren't so successful. Our task force wasn't there yet but some other ships bombarded Tarawa for a few hours. It weren't enough. The Second Marine Division went in, but there was some coral reef that got their landing craft stuck and they had to wade in and the first wave of them nearly all got killed. Almost every one of them.

If I'm remembering right the last letter I got from my Ma said my cousin Stuart had been heard from finally and he'd been transferred into another Marine Division. I believe it was the Second. I reckon I got to wait and hear from my Ma again before I know for sure. I can't write nothing home about it to ask. It would just get cut out of my letters for sure. So I reckon I just gotta wait. Her last letter said that Billy had wrote home and told her he was in

Germany. She hadn't heard from him for over two weeks then but I told her that letters just take a long time even more for them than us sometimes. I didn't want her to worry but I really don't know much about what's going on in Germany or France or nowhere else for that matter. We hear about what the folks back home hear about that. What they tell us here is what we got to know to do our job.

Tokyo Rose done claimed that the Japanese sunk the North Carolina two or three times already. I have to keep telling everybody in my letters that we ain't been sunk. That radio station gets heard back home and gets them all riled up. I told my Ma she just needs to never listen to it. It don't tell the truth and it don't do no good to worry about something that might not be real.

What we're fixing to do is real enough though. We been told the Japanese are all riled up about us taking back those other islands and they ain't ready to give up. We got to expect anything and be ready for things we don't expect.

I don't rightly know when I'll be writing any more letters home. I hope Evelyn won't think I forgot her cause that's the last thing in the world I could ever do.

November 14, 1943

My dearest future wife Evelyn,

I want you to know that you might not get many letters from me for a while. I'll do my best to write whenever I can but they might not get mailed and I don't want you to worry. You just start planning a wedding even though you don't know when it will be. I hope that don't make it hard.

I read all the rest of your letters and there wasn't a whole lot I could answer. I see you didn't tell me anything about you saying yes. I reckon you didn't want to give away the surprise and you're waiting to get a letter from me saying I got your package before you tell me anything else about it. I do hope you had a fine party with your friends.

Have you told your Ma and Pap yet? I sure hope they'll be happy that you said yes. I didn't tell you but I did send a letter to your Ma to read to your Pap asking if I could have your hand in marriage. I had to wait to get a letter back from her saying it was alright before I sent your package. That sure took a long time but they gave me their blessing. I was sure glad cause I know some fellas who said their girlfriends' folks didn't fancy the idea of her marrying a sailor. I reckon since your folks know my folks and they been knowing me since I was little that it made a difference.

So your new friend Mildred's been getting sick at work in the mornings. You really think that might mean she's going to have a baby? I don't rightly know much about those things but I know you said that's what happened to Helen at the beginning before she knew. You say Mildred's husband is on a Destroyer. Do you know which one? We got some Destroyers that travel with us. I think I told you unless the censors cut it out that we travel in groups with a bunch of different kinds of ships – some battleships like us and some aircraft carriers and some cruisers and destroyers. Then there's supply ships that bring us supplies and tankers with fuel. We get our fuel from the tankers and then because we're so big the other ships pull alongside us and we fuel them. That's part of my job and it's a hard one but I won't bore you with how it's done.

We do have to throw some lines between the ships. That's why I had to learn to make that monkey's fist knot that I was telling you about. Anyhow when we're out in the ocean we can't stop so the ships have to go along beside each other. But the ships are hooked together that way and we pass stuff over the lines that aren't the fueling lines. Sometimes it's mail or stuff we need but sometimes it could be a person. Today was one of those days. You know how I told you we have a real operating room on our ship. Well today there was a fella from another ship that had the appendicitis and they transferred him across that line to our ship so he could go down to sick bay and get operated on. I hope none of this stuff gets cut out cause it's the most interesting thing I can tell you.

So Mary talks in her sleep sometimes. Does she say anything interesting about Lyle that I need to tell him or some other fella that I really need to tell Lyle about? He's right smitten with her. He said he reckons he needs to meet her before he proposes so he might do that at our wedding, but don't you tell her I told you so. You just tell me if she's smitten too cause I don't want my buddy to get his heart broke and be thinking something that ain't true about the two of them.

I hate to have anybody sleeping near me that talks in their sleep but it's worse if they snore. And there's this one fella who was sleeping in the bunk above me before he got moved. I was sure glad when they moved him cause he was gritting his teeth so loud it would keep me awake sometimes.

Here's the sounds on the ship when I'm sleeping. There's the motors for the vents blowing and the engines running. I know the waters washing up on the side of the ship but you can't rightly hear it where my bunk is. But those motors and engines can put you to sleep with a steady hum.

I never heard that one from Bob Hope but we did get to see the movie 'In Which We Serve.' It's about a British destroyer if you haven't seen it, it's a good one. It makes you think real hard about why we're in this war and how we want to win it and get on back home. That was a British movie but I know they think the same things we do. I wonder sometimes if the Japs are thinking the same thing too. I know they bound to have wives and children back home. But I might get in trouble for thinking that so I just remember that they're the enemy and I can't think twice about what we got to do to win the war and get home. That's all for now.

All my love,
Roy

November 16, 1943

Dearest Evelyn,

We're still headed to the next place we're going so I have a little bit of time to write. I think it might get mailed but if not at least I wrote it and can put it in the mail sometime later.

I've got some new nicknames now so they don't call me Peaches all the time. One is 'Boats' because that's what they call the boatswain mate. They call me Cox for coxswain too. They ain't called me Crane yet cause I run the crane but somebody did call me 'Mouse.' You might wonder about that one. It's not because I'm quiet. We have these phones we have to take turns wearing when we're out at sea and on watch. Each one wears them an hour a piece. I had my head out the hatch on the top of the gun mount and I would duck back in to look at the ship through the periscope. Then I would stick my head back out and back in again and they started calling me mouse cause of the way I was ducking in and out kinda like in a mouse hole.

When we were back at a place where I could do it – I forgot to tell you I did it – I took out another allotment to the Treasure Department for a bond every month. I been wanting to do a $50 allotment but had to wait until I got some money on the books, about $100. That payday I had $100 even on the books so I did the bond. The guy trying to sell it to me told me it would be good for my future and to think about the people back home and maybe having a family and such. That sold me so I did it. I got a $57 allotment now with it added to the other.

So I got $40 going home every month, about $2 insurance, $18.75 bonds adding up to about $61. That leaves me $32 a month. That's $8 a week for me to spend which ain't too bad. I think that's about right. I make mistakes when I start adding it all up. I never liked math. That's why my wife will have to take care of all that stuff in our family.

I know you're still not getting as many letters as you want but I do the best I can. Whenever we're in port or getting ready to leave I always get a letter off because I know it will get mailed. But when we're out at sea it's impossible to mail a letter even though we got a post office on the ship. That's why you have to wait sometimes and I'm real sorry but it can't be helped.

They told us to tell our loved ones back home why our mail didn't get there very much so that our sisters and Mas and girlfriends wouldn't write to Washington and say that Johnny hadn't written in a long time and where was he and why hadn't they heard from him. My only reason is I'm out at sea. If there were some carrier pigeons I would send a letter that way but I hadn't seen none.

Did you ever hear that song 'Here Comes the Navy' sung by the Andrews Sisters to the same tune as the Beer Barrel Polka? It's a pretty good one and maybe it will be true one day when our ship comes in. You can sing it.

You said in that last letter I read that you bet you know where we are. Well, I bet you would be surprised if you really knew all the places I been since we left home. There's places we're going that I hadn't ever heard of. I'm glad I got this map they gave us so I can kinda tell which way we're headed next. You can tell me where you think I am but I can't tell you if you're right. Military secrets.

Since I know I might not get to write again for a long time, I'm trying to make this letter real long. I got to try to beat those 20 page letters you been writing. I got one that was 24 pages. How do you write so much and how do you find the time?

I got a book with all the ships in the Navy and I been checking off the kind every time I see one. I've seen a lot of the battleships but I'm sure there's a bunch I haven't seen. The book has all the different kinds of planes in it too and I been checking them off when I see them.

So the weather in Tennessee is cold right now. I wouldn't mind having some cold weather like in the mountains. Here we get the heat rash. You can't get cooled off. Even when you take a shower and get back out and dry off you're just as wet as when you got in cause of the sweating. It's worse for the fellas down in the engine room. At least I'm out on the deck a lot of the time. But then we got the sunburn and get a whole layer of skin peeling off your nose.

So you heard that word 'Asiatic.' I'm not that yet and I hope I ain't never gonna be. But sometimes if my letters don't make sense you can just blame it on being Asiatic. That means you're going crazy from being out in the ocean all the time and not seeing land. What makes me Asiatic is being out here all this time and not being able to see you. There's not a thing wrong with me that a little visit with you wouldn't fix up. I hope and pray it's soon, even before that. Sometimes I just want to jump ship and stop doing all this war stuff. But then I know I got to keep going so we can win this war and I can get back home to you.

I heard that the fellas that go back home are supposed to wear a yellow band on their arm. I hadn't seen any, have you? They said the President's wife wanted them to wear them so that people would know they might be Asiatic and not responsible for their actions.

I don't think I'm going to be able to make this letter that long after all. I'm writing in the library and they have confessions in here and the chaplain just came in so I have to move. I gotta go on watch soon anyhow.

Loving you forever and always,
Roy

November 17, 1943
My dearest Evelyn,

I'm trying to write a letter every day as long as I can. I don't know when I will get to mail them but at least if I get them done and pass the censors and put a stamp on them and they get to our post office, then if the mail goes out you will get some.

I hadn't told you too much about this one fella on my boat crew. He's a real good kid and he can keep the boat cleaner than anybody else on my crew. His name is Smitty and he's from Kentucky. Well, that's not exactly right. His name is John Smitherton, but the fellas all call him Smitty. Everybody thinks he's a swell kid. He just came onboard at the last port and he's not handling the sea very well. He gets sick. I just let him go puke over the side of the ship, then he comes back and works hard as he can. I hope he gets his sea legs soon. I feel responsible for seeing he's alright.

You said you been having a little bit of trouble sleeping in your new apartment at your new job. Well, I hope you can get some sleep cause I know that can make you tired when you don't. I hope you're eating good, too, instead of trying to be too skinny. Have you fainted anymore? You said in your last letter that Mildred fainted but that's because she might be having a baby. Well that can't be the reason you fainted so it must be because you didn't eat enough.

Even when I get a chance to sleep all night I usually can't sleep from taps to reveille. I'm used to standing watches and that means you can be sleeping but have to get up to do the midnight to four watch or the four to eight. It's different every night but we all have to do them. You might have the 8-12 one night and then do the 8-12 the next morning, or you might do the 4-8 in the morning and then have to do the 12-4 in the afternoon. We do them all day and all night. So you get tired. How would you like to be so tired that when General Quarters sounds you're halfway to your battle station before you know what's going on. It's happened to me already and I expect it's going to get worse.

You telling me about making those dresses didn't bore me at all. I think a person should be proud of what they do and I'm always interested in what you're doing. I'd be interested to know more about your job, too. And you can tell me about your friends and the other folks you've met and what the town is like. I'd be interested to know it if you would just tell me.

You might not be thinking about Christmas yet but you probably are because it's already almost Thanksgiving. A while back when we weren't thinking about Christmas the ship and the Navy already was. They got this program where they arrange with some store to send a present home to the children of the sailors on the ship if they got them listed on the books. I think it's swell but it doesn't apply to me because I'm not a husband or a Pap. Not yet.

Well we got the news about the Waves and that they might be put to sea if the bill passes in the house. I could really write a long letter if I was to tell you all the things that was said among ourselves when we heard it. I'm not the only one that thinks outpost duty would be fine for them, but not on the ships. It would be like an American Yacht Club or something if they let them around here. They don't need to be on sea duty and I didn't just say that myself.

Yeah, Lyle and me talk about a lot of things cause we spend so much time together, especially late at night when it's just the two of us on watch. Probably about like you and Mary talking about things you don't tell nobody else. Or like you used to be with Sally Jane. I got a letter from her and she said that she hadn't seen you. She don't believe you work in the same place as her. She told me the name of the town. She said it was a new town called Oak Valley or Oak Hill or something like that. I believe the oak part is right anyhow. You hadn't never even told me the name of it. Is that the same one where you're at? Sally Jane said she got her shoes muddy cause they didn't have no sidewalks so I thought maybe it was the same place.

What do you mean you wouldn't tell Mildred some of the things we done? I wouldn't be ashamed of none of it. Oh, I get it. You think since she's done a whole lot more then she might not think much of it but to you it means everything. You treasure it but she might laugh at it. I bet she wouldn't if she's a real friend. Even married people had to start somewhere just like us.

I'm that way too, but I told Lyle. He understands that there's more we'll get to do one day. What about Mary? Has she done those things yet? If so, Lyle hadn't told me none of it but she might not have told him yet either. I don't read all her letters, just the parts he wants me to read. She's got some fancy words that sound real pretty on the page.

Some of the fellas have some Navy slang they use when they talk about what they're going to do when they get home. They say they're going to be 'training in and securing.' Best I can tell that just means they're going to be getting away somewhere alone with their girl. I'm ready to do that, too.

You asked me a question one time that I don't think I ever answered about navigating the boat when there's other boats around. It was a good question so I'll try to answer it so you understand. All boats have what they call running lights. They're red on the port side and green on the starboard and white on the bow. You know which way the boat or the ship is going just by seeing one of the lights. So, you know if you see the red light, that boat's going from your right to your left. I hope that sort of explains it. There's a lot more to it but I don't want to bore you with the details.

It's about time for chow so I'm going to close now and send this one to the censor. Don't know how many more I'll get to write before we get where we're going, but I'll try.

Loving you forever,

Roy

November 18, 1943

My darling Evelyn,

I was thinking today about the way you started one of your letters a while back that I really liked. You said, 'Hey hon, I sure do love you.' That's the way to lift a fella's spirits. I hadn't got any more letters from you because we hadn't had mail call and it may be a while before we do again. And since I wrote one almost every day now, I'm about out of stuff to say.

But I learned a secret for how to write long letters from some of the other fellas. There's this one guy who says that he just reads a book, then rewrites it in his letter and that makes it a long letter. I don't think that really counts, do you?

I don't think you should write all that stuff about what you read unless it has some meaning behind it. Like a magazine article or something.

There was this one thing I read that's got real meaning. It's about this fella who had been writing this girl back home for over a year while he was in the South Pacific. But she hadn't sent him a picture. But they had feelings for each other from the letters just like Lyle and Mary.

Anyhow, the sailor was going on leave in New York City and she was going to meet him. She was going to wear a red flower on her coat so he would know who she was since she hadn't ever sent him a picture. She told him exactly what kind of red flower. Well, when he got there he was looking for a girl with a red flower on her coat. He saw one and stared at her and started walking toward her but it was the wrong kind of red flower.

So he waited and waited. Then this real pretty girl walked by him and said, 'Going my way sailor boy?' He wanted to follow her but right behind her he saw this old lady wearing the red flower. It was the right kind. So he looked at the young pretty girl that had walked by him but he went to the old lady wearing the red flower. If she was the one keeping his spirits up while he was at war, he wanted to do right by her. So he asked her out to dinner.

She just smiled at him with almost a toothless grin and told him that young girl who just walked by him begged her to wear the flower. She said that the young girl told the old lady that if the sailor asked her to dinner to tell him that she (the young pretty girl) would wait for him at the corner diner. It was a real test and he passed with flying colors. Now that kind of story has a real meaning to it, so it's a good one to write about.

There's something I been wondering about for a while and wanted to ask you. How is the price of jewelry back home? Everywhere I been able to see it is plenty high. Like the navy rings you used to could buy for two or three dollars are almost ten dollars. You can't find a wrist watch for less than $25. It's not like I'm looking for something made cheap, but those are really high prices. I was wondering if they were like that back home or if they just make them that high in places where they think the sailors and soldiers and Marines are going to be wanting to buy something.

You never told me if your Ma checked on my Ma to see how she's doing. I hadn't heard anymore either about Stuart to know if he's ok or not. Sometimes I wish you were still back home in Simms Hollow – you and Sally Jane. With both of you gone I don't seem to really know what's going on back home anymore. Pap can't write and I can tell Ma's not really telling me the truth when she writes. She tries to sound all cheery. I might not be the sharpest tack in the can, but I can read between the lines. It's like when she would talk real fast at home when she was worried about something and didn't want to let on. She'd just ramble on and on about nothing really. That's how her letters are now so I know it ain't right.

I hope she's heard from Billy by now. Not knowing's gotta be the hardest thing in the world. Ma and Pap never talked about it much but they had five other young'uns before me and none of em made it past their 3rd birthday, some not even past the first day. I reckon if you lost that many kids you're always worrying more about the ones you got left.

I'm going to write her another letter now, but I don't know when it will get mailed so she'll probably be worrying more about me too. There just ain't a thing I can do about it and that makes me worry about her.

Well write and tell me about your new job and new friends and all the new things in your life so I'll have something to answer next time I get a letter.

I only have eyes for you,

Roy

Somewhere in the Pacific Ocean: November 19, 1943

We're back in action now and I hope we get it done and over with fast. Today we got called to General Quarters at 0430 hours. The Enterprise was launching planes so the task force had to turn into the wind. Now it don't matter how big your ship is when you turn into the wind fast with those great big waves they wash over the bow and nearly knock the gunners over. I got to my station and climbed in the mount but I saw the waves coming over before I did.

Then we had to wait. Sometimes I envy the fellas on the 20s because they can see what's going on. Whether there's a torpedo wake or a bunch of planes coming in. I just have to stand in the mount with my headphones on waiting for the sign to give a signal to my men in the mount to start shooting. They stand there and stare at me waiting for me to say something but there weren't nothing to say. After a while they started trying to find a place to sit or lay down cause we had to stay there but weren't nothing happening. The bogie contact was lost but we couldn't take a chance to secure from GQ when something might be out there fast.

So it's hot in the mount and there's a dozen fellas in there along with all the guns and stuff. The time passes real slow. It's dark in there too even when its daylight outside but especially when it's still dark like the wee hours of the morning. The only light is a red one that reflects on my face so the fellas can see me a little. I can kind of see them too, staring at me waiting for me to tell them what to do.

And they sure do stare. Waiting to do the job they been trained to do but not able to do it until I give the command.

We were at GQ for almost four hours. I heard tell that it may get so bad that we stay in GQ for days. I reckon four hours weren't so bad. Then we got to go to the head and then the mess hall and have some chow. We even got a few hours sleep if we weren't on watch.

November 20, 1943
My dearest Evelyn,

I don't know why I'm even writing this letter except that it makes me feel closer to you. I haven't had any letters from you and I can't tell you where I am or what's going on. I don't know even when this letter will go out. I just wanted to say that I love you and always will.

I hope you are busy making wedding plans. I'll tell you as soon as I know when I'm coming home. I hope that job of yours really does help end the war soon. I don't know how, but I still hope it.

All my love,
Roy

Near the Makin Islands: November 23, 1943

For the last few days we been in and out of GQ over and over again. Sometimes we didn't stay long but sometimes we were there for hours. Sometimes we're in there so long that they send up sandwiches in a bucket from the mess hall so we have something to eat. It's like I tell Evelyn, you got to eat to keep up your strength. Otherwise, you can't be much good at your job. When the radar picks up some activity we have to go to GQ to get ready. Sometimes it's a false alarm or the bogeys turn back. But we're just waiting and expecting the big attack. We've been told the Japs aren't happy that we're taking back so many islands and they are going to fight back hard. We have to be ready for anything.

The ships needed refueling today so we made our way back out in the ocean a bit to meet up – away from danger as much as we could be. Fueling is a dangerous job but running out of fuel would be even worse what with the enemy bearing down on you.

This is the first real time I've had to use the skills I learned to be gun captain. We been practicing a lot and I know what I'm supposed to do, but when it's real it just seems a lot different. I hope when the time comes for me to give the signal, I do a good job. It will be a matter of life and death – my buddies, my ship and me.

DECEMBER

Underway in the South Pacific: December 1, 1943

We finished up our work at the Makin Islands and now we're on our way again. I reckon we did alright. The captain even said the five-inch battery did a fine job. That includes my gun mount and that makes me feel proud. We didn't let no enemy planes get too close. We either shot them down or scared them away. I can't think about the pilots in those planes. They're enemy planes and it's them or us.

I was a bit worried about how I'd do at gun captain when it was the real thing, but I got a great group of gunners and they all know their jobs real good. All I had to do was say, 'Stand by' and they'd be ready in an instant. Then when I'd say 'commence firing' they worked together so good that nothing went wrong. A fine group of fellas indeed. I'm real proud of them.

Word is we're headed to Nauru so I marked it on my map. Even though the island's been bombarded some already, the Japs are still flying planes out of there. Our job is to fire on the island until those landing strips can't be used at all. Our task force looks bigger this time. There's two other battleships plus us, some carriers and about half a dozen destroyers. That Nauru ain't going to know what hit it when we get done.

Dec 5, 1943

My dearest Evelyn,

They told us mail would be going out today so all us fellas are trying to get a letter written. I was in the library but it got so full I came out here on deck. I did find this swell card in the library though so I'm putting my letter in the envelope with the card. Lyle done asked me how many stamps I had. He wants to write to Mary too but he don't have no stamps and no money to get any right now. I got a couple to share. That way both of you girls will be happy.

There ain't a whole lot I can tell you cause I hadn't had any letters from you. Mail call would sure be good.

I been asking the fellas about that double ring ceremony you talked about. Seems like it's a good idea but don't many of the fellas here have wedding bands. They ain't supposed to wear them cause they could get caught on something and tear their fingers off. So if we have a double ring ceremony I might not be able to wear my ring. But maybe the war will be over and I won't have to come back. But I still got almost four years to go, so no telling what will happen. Sometimes I think I should have listened when my Pap said, 'Six years is a long time, son.' Maybe I wouldn't have signed up voluntarily like I did but I think I'm better off than the fellas who didn't do it. Like Billy who got drafted and had to go to Germany. I sure hope my Ma's heard from him by now.

I hope you had a fine Thanksgiving and can write me and tell me all about it. Maybe you already did and I just hadn't got it yet. Folks back home hadn't got any letters through either so I hope they had a swell one too. The ship always feeds us good when they can but that ain't always the case anymore.

Well, they're about to call for the mail and it's still got to go through the censors so I better hurry up. I'll be glad when I can show you how much I miss you and not just tell you. Then you'll know.

Loving you always,

Roy

Efate, New Hebrides: Dec 12, 1943

Well we did a fine job bombing Nauru. No way the Japs are ever going to fly planes out of there again. Might not even be any Japs left there either. That last part's probably just wishful thinking but it makes me feel good to think it.

It was a pretty impressive sight to see all the US ships lined up one right behind the other all of us aiming at that island. I was proud to be part of it and my gun crew did a fine job. It weren't as tense a time as when we're waiting for the planes to fly in at us and not knowing when they're coming. That island just sat there and our Kingfisher planes were up in the air letting us know when we were aiming right and we just kept on firing til they told us to stop.

December 13, 1943

My dearest Evelyn,

I got a bunch of mail at mail call today and it felt swell to know so many people back home are thinking about me. I got one from my Ma and she said she heard from Billy. The letter was dated November 12 but when he sent it he was doing swell. He didn't tell her too much about what was going on in the war but he did tell her about going into some town in Germany and that he had a pretty good time. There was lots of Army and Marines there and they had already taken over that town so it weren't too dangerous. Then he had to go back somewhere else but he wasn't excited about it. He told Ma he was alright and not to worry. I know she does anyhow. I been trying to send her letters when I can.

Sally Jane sent me one too. She said she finally saw you on a bus when you were going into town to do some shopping. I'm glad to know you are in the same place. I hope you can be friends again even though you have a new best friend with Mary. Sally Jane said she would never get to see you at work because y'all don't work in the same exact place. You're in an office in one part of town and she's in a factory in another part of town but maybe at Christmas you could see each other again.

She said maybe they would have a big party or something and you could all be at the same place. Seems she's found her a fella but she probably told you that already. I hope he's a good one and not like that one she left back home that only wanted what fellas want and didn't do right by her. I reckon that's why she left town like she did.

I know that Mary will be in our wedding but it would be a mighty fine thing if you could ask Sally Jane to be in it too next time you see her. Lyle's going to stand up for me as my best man. Depending on when it is and if the war's already over, maybe Billy can be there, too. I know it's hard to plan a wedding when you don't know if it will be winter or summer but it can't be helped. I reckon you just have to choose stuff that will work either way.

Are you thinking we can go back home to Simm's Hollow to get married or do we have to do it in Tennessee? It's gonna be mighty hard for my folks and your folks to travel anywhere, what with the gas rationing and having to tend to the farm and all. Maybe you could think about that. It might be easier for you and Mary and Sally Jane to get off work and travel back home.

That little white church down in the valley would be a mighty fine place to get married winter or summer. They got the wood heaters to keep it warm and the windows open with fans for the summertime. Maybe it will be spring or fall and not be too hot or too cold. That would be swell. But I reckon we should probably get married in the church where we grew up in Simms Hollow. That would make both our Mas real happy. What do you think?

I reckon maybe you are thinking about getting married at home since you mentioned Freddie Green. I didn't know he was a preacher, but he's probably a pretty good one. Wouldn't that be something. Getting married by the boy who used to sit behind me in sixth grade. He threw spitballs at my head and one time the teacher caught him. What she did must of set him on the right path. I never did like her paddle and tried to keep from getting it myself.

Well I been worried about Smitty. He's been sick an awful lot lately and it don't seem to be getting better. Every time he has to go down to sick bay it takes longer for him to come back. Three days last time. He's a good kid. I hope he can get his sea legs soon. I didn't never have no problems like that so sometimes it's hard to understand. I still go see him down in sick bay when I can.

I'm going to be able to send you a Christmas present after all. We got to a port yesterday but I can't tell you where. It ain't Hawaii. But it's got some stores and I can buy you something you probably couldn't get back home. I don't rightly know what it will be but I'll try and make it special and get it mailed so you can have it before Christmas.

Scuttlebutt has it we'll be here til after Christmas if nothing happens so I may get some mail and Christmas presents before we head out again. That would be swell.

We might have some real good food too if we ain't out in the ocean fighting. Talking about food makes me hungry and it's about time for chow, so I'll close now. I will answer some more letters soon.

All my love,
Roy

December 16, 1943

My dearest Evelyn,

I just read your letter dated Nov 23 that said about Frankie not making it back home. Ma had sent me the newspaper clipping. She's been keeping count and that makes five from our school that didn't make it. And the war ain't over yet. It don't seem fair. Simms Hollow High School is just a little old place and there's already so many that ain't gonna make it back.

There was one girl, too. You remember that girl Lela that was a year ahead of me. Maybe you don't but anyhow she was a nurse in the Army and she was doing good stuff taking care of the soldiers over in France I think but they bombed her hospital tent and she died. Ma sent me that clipping too. Seems she sees all those things and that makes her worry even more. I wish she'd quit sending them things to me but I hadn't got the heart to tell her.

When you write don't talk about the fellas never coming home. I know that it's the truth but I just rather not hear about it.

That was a swell group of pictures you sent me in that frame. There's a fella in my division that has a frame just like it except his has one big picture and two little ones. I like mine better cause it's got a medium size picture and four little ones. That means I get to see more pictures of you.

I can't have too many more frames though cause my locker will be all filled up and there won't be no room for me to fold my uniform and get the creases right. I can't keep all your letters cause there's so many but I got an envelope with the best ones and the cards. I put that locket of hair you sent in another envelope. That's a mighty pretty red curl. I like your hair short in that last picture. Well it ain't so short that it don't still touch your shoulders but it ain't way down your back no more like it used to be. Makes you look like a real woman but it will be alright by me if you let it grow back out.

I been able to play my harmonica you gave me more since we

been in port. Makes the time go faster at watch and calms me down when things get to bothering me too much.

The ice follies sound like a swell thing to go see. I wish I coulda been there to go see it with you. So you been ice skating now instead of roller skating. I like both ways, but I think I like the roller skating better. I just like the sound of it with the wheels rolling across the wood floor. I bet if it weren't a war going on some folks could have a swell time roller skating on the teak deck. But that's a foolish thought. I reckon I'm just getting a bit tired. Stood two watches in the last day and we been cleaning the boat better than usual. I miss Smitty. He's real good at that.

I had to take the captain's gig out a bunch of times since we got to port and had to wait while the captain did whatever it is he does from ship to ship. It ain't my right to know what he does just to make sure he gets where he needs to go and back safe. I made a pretty good map of the harbor and all the compass courses so I know where I'm going even when it's dark. I think I got to go out again tonight. That's better than going out in the day right now cause my arms and nose are pretty burned up and peeling.

So what if it looks funny with no paint on the walls. You said walls but they're really called bulkheads. Anyhow, it will help save the ship so who cares how it looks. Why did you say that now? I told you about that a long time ago. I reckon maybe you been reading my old letters all over again cause you didn't have no new ones. I do that too sometimes.

I'm sorry that you're blue. I feel blue too but I reckon I stay too busy to think about it as much as you. Every time you ask me if I can tell you when I'll be home so we can get married but I just can't. I'm real sorry about that. It's the best I can do to tell you I'll be home as soon as I can and I'll tell you as soon as I know when it will be. I won't even know where we'll come to. It could be Bremerton or New York or Boston or San Diego or Norfolk. Who knows. Not me.

Till next time, I'll be loving you and thinking about you all the time.

All my love,
Roy

December 20, 1943
My dearest Evelyn,

We had mail call today and I got 25 letters so I will have a lot to write about for a while. I just don't know when I'll have time to write. I been real busy taking the boat out all day from morning til night and then at night too. Some important things must be happening is all I can think and the captains have to talk to each other about it a lot.

All the letters weren't from you. I got 15 from you and 5 from my Ma and 2 from Sally Jane and I even got one from Billy in Germany. So he's still alright as far as I can tell. That leaves two. One was from your Ma saying she saw my Ma and they had a good talk in the five and dime down in town. So she invited her over to lunch one day and she went so they got to talk a while. She said she knows that my Ma is real worried about Billy and me and even Sally Jane, but she told her to try not to worry. She said my Ma had a good cry while she was there and then she drank some fresh coffee and ate some of your Ma's special cinnamon apple cake and she thought maybe she felt a little bit better when she went home but that she'd be sure and check on her again for me. She said she'd be glad when I was her new son. Then she'd have two. She said your brother was about to graduate from Carolina and that he was going to be an officer in the Air Force. That was a mighty swell thing for your Ma to say about me. She's a fine lady.

And the last one that makes 25 came from Mary. She said she told you she was writing me so you wouldn't be mad but she's worried a bit about Lyle. I reckon she told you that. She hadn't had too many letters from him but I need to tell her he's been real busy too and he talks about her all the time. I think they really have got to meet each other when we get back home. Maybe at our wedding would be a good time or before if we have a party or something first. Depends on how long we get to be home. I don't want to waste too much time before the wedding that'll take away from the time I get to spend with you after we get married and you are my wife. I like the sound of that.

Yes, I do think we need to take a honeymoon and get away from everybody else even though they'll want to see me since I been gone so long. It don't matter. I want to spend all that time with you and don't want no interruptions from other people. So I reckon we better not tell anybody where we'll be going. From the things I been hearing, we got a lot to learn and I'm ready to get started. We need to buy a strong bed. I'll tell you more about that later.

I wish I could use all those fancy words Mary uses in her letters to make it sound all nice and tell you how much I really love you and miss you. But I'm just a simple farm boy and I hadn't never heard some of those words. So I'll just do the best I can to let you know how much I love you. And that's as big as the ocean. You wouldn't never know how big that is unless you seen it like me.

Loving and missing you every day,

Roy

December 24, 1943

My darling Evelyn,

It's Christmas Eve and I been thinking about you every day. I been pretty busy with the boat and other stuff. Word has it we'll be heading out tomorrow on Christmas Day. I hadn't got the present you sent yet, so I hope we have mail call before we leave. I hope you get your present, but I hadn't had a letter that said so.

I want to answer some of your other letters. I'm glad you like the last pictures I sent. I had been swimming near the hotel. Don't be mad about the lei. I had a little cash and thought I'd spend it. They make them fast right on the street. Yes, the picture of me in my bell-bottoms does make me look a bit bow-legged and knock-kneed but I'm glad you like it anyway. Don't worry about how much I weigh. I'm up to about 180 lbs and that's good for my height. Now you tell me how much you weigh. I bet you don't weigh a hundred pounds and you're too tall for that.

There's two flies in the library that are driving me crazy. I may have to quit writing and smack them both if they don't leave me alone.

No, I don't have a gun on my boat. I got a pistol when I'm out there and that's all. Yeah we do fire the sixteens. They ain't there just to look at. Those big guns are something. When it goes off, it just about takes your clothes off. You might as well forget about wearing a hat cause that thing will blow right off for sure. I was standing outside next to my mount one day when they fired to starboard. You see the fire and the noise and hear it whistling through the air and then you don't see nothing but a big explosion over on the beach and you know it's a hit. It's something alright. I told you about the 19 gun salvo they did back before I got on ship. The fellas talk like it made the whole ship jump sideways away from the direction they was firing. My guns were part of that too, but I wasn't onboard then. Don't get me started. I'm like a gunners mate when it comes to talking about the guns. Enough about gunnery.

That ends that letter. The next one was a card with the mountains on it. They might be Tennessee mountains and not Georgia mountains but they can sure make a fella homesick. Especially at Christmas.

No, I don't think much of hunting myself. I'd rather just go in the woods and sit down by where a stream runs down the mountainside and listen to it all – the water, the birds, the squirrels chattering. I learned real young that if I was still enough not to make no noise or motion the deer would come out of hiding. Especially if I put out some of the sweet potatoes from the field. I know, I know, we wouldn't have had food on the table sometimes neither if Pap hadn't shot a deer or a squirrel but he didn't never make me shoot one and I was glad of that. Billy liked hunting just fine, but I never did.

I got a little time off today so I want to make this letter long enough to answer all the ones you sent me. I'm glad you found the kind of hope chest you wanted and had the money to buy it for yourself. That's a fine job you got. You said you wanted to keep working even after we got married and I reckon that will be fine for a while cause I'll still be in the Navy and you'll need something to do unless we have a kid right away. But I think you should probably stop working when the war's over or at least by 1947.

Well, it's time for chow and it should be a good one, so I'll close for now. I hope they ain't playing Christmas songs down in the mess hall. I heard 'White Christmas' and 'I'll be Home for Christmas' about as many times as I can stand cause ain't neither one of them true for us.

Merry Christmas darling,
Roy

December 26, 1943
My dear Evelyn,

I didn't expect to write again so soon but I had a wonderful surprise after I finished your letter yesterday. We had another mail call and I got a package. Yes, my Christmas present from you came and I was very happy to get it. You had a great idea about the photo album. That won't take up as much space in my locker as the frames do and I can keep more pictures. Yes dear, I will use it to put some of the letters in too. The watch was a fine gift too and I liked the inscription on the back that said 'Roy and Evelyn Forever' cause that is true for sure. And it was smart of you to put the date.

That way when we're old we'll know when I got it. The book was fine too. I like westerns and I do have time to read every now and then. You said I could read it when I'm waiting for the captain to come back to the boat and that is true if it's daytime. I can read it in the sack at night. And the joke books got some good stuff in it. I read a few already. But the song book is the best. It has a lot of songs in it about sailors and the other military.

I was blue all Christmas day cause I couldn't be with you. I thought about how it would be back home in the mountains with maybe some snow if they're lucky and the families together by the fireplace with the tree and presents and turkey with dressing and sweet potato pies. And you have to wear your coat and gloves to go out and milk the cows first thing before everybody starts visiting around. I hope you got to go home and see everybody.

We had good food – turkey and ham and all the good stuff – but it just ain't the same. You're not supposed to get sunburned and sweating and heat rash on Christmas Day. Anyhow they try to make it as good for us as they can and we had some movies. That night they had a news reel made just for us. Remember how I told you about the Navy making sure the kids of the sailors on the NC had Christmas gifts. Well, they made a news reel of them kids getting those gifts and opening em up and getting all excited.

Once in a while the news reel would have a picture of our ship getting underway but I wasn't sure where it was taken. At the end, the kids were all singing 'Merry Christmas sailor, Merry Christmas to you.' Well it made my eyes water all up and weren't none of em my kid.

You said you wouldn't like to see 'Lady of Burlesque' and you probably wouldn't but it was alright. I saw 'Hello Frisco Hello' and it was pretty good, but nothing I seen is better than that movie with those kids in it. I can't stop thinking about it.

You don't need to be worried. We'll make it just fine. Everything will be swell if we just both go at the goal together.

I think any color is fine for the cake. I'm partial to chocolate but it can be yellow and alright with me. Yes, I believe white on the icing would be good but you could add some colors if you wanted to like yellow or blue. You like purple, I don't have a problem with it. I probably will be too excited and ready to leave that I won't even eat cake. No ma'am don't get mad at me for that. I'll just be thinking about the honeymoon.

Here's a joke for you from the book. Have you heard the one about the guy with the big nose? When God was handing out noses, this fella thought he said roses and he asked for a big red one. Ha! Makes me think about this one guy down in the butcher shop. He's got the biggest nose I ever saw and when he gets mad it turns red.

I don't know when I'll get to write again or when this letter will go out. We're underway and heading back to try and finish off this job so we can come home. Whatever you and Sally Jane are doing at your job to end the war, I hope you hurry too.

In case I don't get to write for a while, I hope you have a very Happy New Year.

All my love,
Roy

1944

JANUARY

January 8, 1944

Dearest Evelyn,

I had a hard time writing 1944. I wrote 1943 two times and had to start over. I'm glad it was at the beginning of the letter and not after I wrote a lot. I don't have time to keep starting over. We been out where the fighting is and I can't tell you where but if you hear Tokyo Rose saying they sunk us it ain't so. We're fine.

I been busy but I had time to look through my song book and here's what I got I think you will like. It's like a song story.

'You'll Never Know' the 'Things That Mean so Much to Me.' 'I'm Thinking Tonight of Your Blue Eyes' 'If You Please.' 'It's Always You' 'All or Nothing at All' 'Sunday, Monday and Always.'

Pretty good, huh. I need to change the titles to green eyes like yours, but then that wouldn't be right. And all these songs were on one page. There's a lot more. But I can't spend a lot of time on that now. I been studying my second class books. I had the old one but now I got a new one that I hope will help me see things a bit more clearer. I handed in one test and should take my progress test in February. I want to be second class by the time I get to come home.

I got to secure now since it's only an hour before somebody relieves me from watch. Then I can go to chow. I believe I'll have some ice cream tonight. I hadn't had none in a while.

I hope I get a letter from you soon cause I don't have nothing to tell you that they'll let me write about.

I love you and always will,

Roy

January 10, 1944

Dearest Evelyn,

I got the package from you with the chocolate candy. You know I love chocolate and I thank you for the thought, but don't waste your money on it no more. By the time it gets to me it's all smashed and melted and just a big ole mess. I tried eating it anyway but mostly I couldn't. I think it might have got wet too. That's too much money to spend. Save it and we'll eat chocolate together on our honeymoon.

No that don't mean I know when I'm coming home yet but I'll be sure to tell you as soon as I know. I'm saving up money so I can send a telegram. See, I'm thinking ahead.

I'm glad you got your Christmas present early and could open it and wear it to Christmas dinner at my family's house. I got gold so it matches your ring.

I'm glad you like the tablecloth. I found it in a shop on one of the islands where I was and thought it would be real good to go in your hope chest. It has a bunch of colors embroidered on it so it should match anything you decide to do in our house. I will be glad when we have one. I'm sending you a drawing I made of the kind of house I want us to have. Tell me what you think about it.

You won't believe who I got a letter from today. It was my cousin Stuart. So now we know he didn't get killed with the 2nd

Marine Division. I was mighty worried about that and nobody hearing nothing. I reckon his Ma mighta got a letter and just forgot to tell my Ma or my Ma forgot to tell me she told her. Anyhow, I'm real glad. He's in France now.

That last picture you sent me was swell. All the fellas from my division were standing around and man did they say some compliments. If we had to pay for them we'd be broke because they were worth a whole bunch. Like – 'she looks like a movie star' or 'you're a real lucky fella' or 'wish I had somebody back home like that waiting for me.' Then there was this one – 'You could make chief if you pinned her up in your boat and the old man got a look at her.' Old man's what we call the captain but not to his face.

I'm glad you got to go back to Georgia for Christmas and see your family. Thanks for spending some time at my house. I know my Ma was real happy to see you. I'm glad you said she didn't look too bad. Her hair is grayer than it used to be and she is thinner but you don't think she looks real sick. Just worried. I been real worried about her but I can't do nothing about it way out here and Billy sure can't do nothing from Germany or wherever he is now.

I got to keep studying for my second testing in a few weeks. We been busy practicing the guns and getting better at all the jobs we do. There's this saying that there are only two kinds of people who fight in a war zone - the quick and the dead. I want to be quick.

So you like to flash your ring around and hold your hand so people can see it. I'm glad you like it and will expect to be properly thanked. I'll let you know when to get ready.

All my love,
Roy

January 20, 1943
My dearest Evelyn,

There's some things I want to tell you that I might not can say, so if this letter's full of holes that's why. I'm not going to tell you where we are because I know I can't do that but I want to tell you about how bad the weather was. You would think with these ships as big as they are that a little old wind and rain storm wouldn't do no damage, but that ain't so. I think you know we got a bunch of ships that travel together and not by ourselves so we can protect each other.

Well the weather was so bad today that we got word that some sailors got washed overboard on one of the other battleships and one of the destroyers. That's how big the waves were. We had one man get hurt bad but he caught hisself and didn't wash overboard and die like the others did. So sometimes it don't take bullets to kill a fella. It just takes a storm.

Or it might take some kind of sickness. I'm feeling pretty low today cause Smitty's real sick and it ain't just the bad weather or being seasick or not getting his sea legs. He's down in the sick bay and he's got some kind of infection. He might not make it. We had another fella just keel right over and die one day. It was his heart they said.

Now this next part I think is something they'll probably have on the news reels so I don't reckon it will get cut out. But I could be wrong. This whole letter might be a bunch of shreds. I'll be interested to know when you get it. You probably heard that the groups of ships is called a Task Force. You been watching the news cause you said you did. Well we are a new task force now with a new Admiral. We're Task Force 58 and the Admiral is Halsey. So if you hear anything on the news, that's us. I heard real good things about him. I wanted to tell you cause I just have a good feeling that we're gonna get this war over with now and I can come home. I want to come home something awful to see you and get married. I believe my blues would go right away if I could.

I heard a fella say something the other day that I think he meant in a bad way but I reckon what he said is true. 'You can take the boy outta the farm but you can't take the farm outta the boy.' I ain't the only farm boy on this ship and if he gives me any more trouble we might all have to show him what hard working on a farm can do for your muscles. But I might get throwed in the brig and I don't want nothing like that.

Yes dear, I told Lyle he better do more writing to Mary or some other fella from that place where y'all work might catch her eye. I think he's been writing more and longer and talking about things they can do when he gets home. Did she get those letters? Don't tell Mary but I think he really might bring a ring with him when we come. He asked me if I minded if he proposed during our wedding celebration cause that's when he would get to see her. I told him it would be alright but not where anybody else would know cause that would take away the specialness of the day for you. Don't give nothing away now or he'll be fighting mad at me.

No, I don't think you and me will do much arguing. I'm not the type. But I did hear some of the guys talking about how much fun the making up is after the arguing so maybe we should do some friendly arguing and find out.

I had my boat for seven months now and out of that seven months I only had about ten days off. That's why my face is a mess all the time cause when I'm in the boat I get sunburned but I got some white salve I can put on it to make it feel better. No, I don't think it will look bad for the wedding because it will take me so long to get home it will get all healed up before then. Yes, I will wear my uniform for the wedding. The white one or the blue one?

So I wouldn't make a pin-up boy. Who cares. So all the girls you work with like Frank Sinatra, ok, but we got Betty Grable. There's so many guys with Betty Grable in their locker you see her everywhere you look and it's a pretty good sight. But my eyes are only for you dear.

I reckon I about got used to you not telling me nothing about your work but have you seen Sally Jane anymore? Can you get in touch with her so you can see her on purpose and not by accident?

That accident might not ever happen again and I think it would be swell if you two could be friends again. I know my Ma would sure like for Sally Jane to have some good friends where she's at since she's so far from home.

I didn't know this was leap year. I wouldn't want any girl to propose to me. But we're already engaged so we don't have to worry about that. I will warn the other fellas though so they know to look out.

I'm glad you like the outdoor life too. It can make you feel a whole lot better just to sit by the creek and listen to it going over the rocks. I reckon you don't get to do that too much where you are now but maybe we can do it together when we get back to Simms Hollow and build our house.

But sometimes I might have to go off in the woods by myself cause I like to explore and it can get thick and cut you up. There was this one beach we went to on an island. I been there more than once. There's places you have to get to by swimming and some paths you have to cut or knock the vines and briers and stuff out of your way. Talk about thick jungle. You could get lost pretty easy but I never did.

Let me tell you about this one fella that got in trouble with the Petty Officer. Wasting water is real serious. You got to get in the shower, turn the water on and get wet, turn the water off and soap up, then turn the water back on to wash off the soap. Well, this one guy was just standing there letting the water run. I just came in from a late boat trip and was waiting to get a shower. The PO told him to quit letting the water run but he didn't listen, even got mouthy, and the PO had to put in a report. So it goes from the chief in charge of making sweet water to the chief master at arms who told the executive officer who gave the fella a captain's mast. That's like a court and if you lose you go to the brig or get extra duty. He got extra duty.

I don't have to worry about my watch getting tarnished and

turning black anymore. I found out what will clean it – toothpaste – and it works just swell.

I guess this is the longest letter I ever wrote so I beat some of your long letters. But I got to be honest. I didn't do it in one day like a normal letter. I knew the mail wasn't going nowhere so I just been writing on the same letter.

I reckon I'll close this letter now. We're getting underway tomorrow and that means it might go out before we do if I can get it to the censor in time. You tell me if it's cut to shreds when you get it, alright?

Always yours,
Roy

Roi & Namur Islands: January 30, 1944

We been real busy since we left Efate a couple weeks ago. Maybe it hadn't even been that long but when you're in battle the days all blend together and you don't know for sure. The next big prize is the Marshall Islands and we been working on the little ones first to get them back. We shot down some Bettys. That's one of the names we call the Jap planes. The islands have names like Tarawa and Roi and Namur and Kwajalein.

I hadn't wrote home to Evelyn in a while now. It wouldn't go out anyhow and I think that last letter might have said things the censors won't like. Thought I needed to lay low for a while.

I shouldn't have said stuff about people dying either. I told her not to talk about fellas not coming home then I did it myself. That's why I decided not to tell her anymore about Smitty. He never did come out of the sick bay. He died from septicemia. I wrote it down when the Pharmacist Mate told me so I could remember. He was a fine young fella. It's bad enough when you die from enemy fire in the middle of war, but he just got sick and died. Somehow that don't seem right.

And we had to bury him at sea – no time or place to do anything else. I couldn't help it but the whole time I watched and listened to the preacher then saw his body dropped off over the side and sink in the waves I couldn't help think about my cousin that time we went swimming in Mount Sever River. It dropped out over a little ole waterfall that wasn't big as nothing but had a deep hole at the bottom. We was taking turns. But my cousin Luther just never came back up. He went under the water just like Smitty and we never saw him again.

We're going to be bombarding the islands again before the landings. The better job we do the fewer fellas get killed when they get there. That's a mighty heavy burden to carry. We just got to do the best we can.

FEBRUARY

Feb 6, 1944

Dearest Evelyn,

I'm sorry I haven't written. There just hasn't been time. I think this letter will probably be like the last one where I write on it when I got time. It may take days to finish but I'll try to get it out when we got the chance. I couldn't get a Valentine card. I tried but there just wasn't one to get. That's why I drew the hearts on this letter. I hope that you know I love you and you are the only Valentine for me.

I think I told you I took my test. I didn't do great but alright. I got two more to take and the practical part. I was told I'd be going up the last of the month. So keep your fingers crossed I make second. It's going to be tough.

This is another day and I got some letters from you. I'll try to answer as much as I can. So you got up with Sally Jane and she went to the movies with you and Mary. I'm real glad about that.

How did you find her? Nevermind, I reckon you probably can't tell me. Military secret.

I'm glad your Ma got the handkerchief I sent her for Christmas and that she liked it. Yes, it was mighty fine looking but I didn't think it would make her cry.

Glad you liked the songbook story. Maybe I can do another one if I ever have the chance. Jim in my division got a letter from his wife and the whole thing was made up of song titles. I didn't know anybody else ever thought to do that and I didn't copy nobody neither. That letter was swell though and you would like to see it.

Yes, I think pink is a fine color if that's what you want your bridesmaids to wear. I don't much have to worry about it. The fellas standing up for me will have to wear their uniforms. We can't go out in public without having our uniforms on. I sure hope Billy is back home to so he can be there. I reckon I might should wear my blue so I look different from the other fellas and they can wear white. Or do you want it the other way around? I could wear white and they can wear their different colors for the branch they'e in. I got to find out the regulations. I need to read up on it.

No, I don't think it's too early for you to have a bridal shower if you got a place to put the presents. I still don't know how long it will be before I get to go home so you might have to store them up for a while. Some of it might fit in your hope chest.

Sounds like you girls see a lot of movies. You need to tell me the titles of them. I'm going to have time to see more movies and more time to write, too. I saw that one movie about Mae West.

See, I won't be on the boat no more but back on the deck. After eight months – that's a long time to do one job – I'm about tired of it. It held me back plenty when the other fellas had time to do stuff. You'd be in the middle of something and have to stop to do the boat, or you'd get woke up in the middle of the night to take the boat out. I got plenty to do on the deck and I got to get back into that. It'll give me more time to study for second too.

But there's one thing about being in the boat. Us fellas in the two boat crews got around more than anybody else on the ship. I got to see a lot of places and go to some ports that the other fellas didn't. I didn't really want to leave the boat, but it'll probably be a good thing. I can study more.

No, I don't have a weak stomach so don't worry about it. If you say you can cook, I'll take your word for it. I can't cook so I don't reckon we have a choice if we want to eat.

Since I'm not in the boat I got to stand gun watches. I got the 12 – 4 watch tonight. Supposed to be a full moon so that will be good. I'll be able to see lots of stuff. Last night some of the fellas was running around in the bay about 10 o'clock the moon was so bright they could do it.

You been having some strange weather – 60 degrees in January. Must be making it hard on the ice skating. Bet it made it that much worse that you complain about it all the time too.

Well, I been writing this letter three days and I'm going to send it out so it makes it before we ship out again.

One more thing though from your last letter. You tell whoever said the Navy ain't doing its part that they're wrong. The Navy is right out there with the Army and the Marines and we're working just as hard to get this war over with. I'm glad I'm in the Navy but it's just as dangerous as the rest. The thing I can count on is better food on a pretty regular schedule and a bunk to sleep in if we're not in General Quarters waiting to be shot at.

Let's don't talk no more about the war. It puts me in a bad mood. I hear enough about it anyway.

All my love,

Roy

PS - I didn't get the letter out yesterday but I'm going to do it now because we are getting underway again and I don't know when I'll get mail or send mail. I wanted to say you don't have to be scared about me saying 'Watch Out Evelyn' on the first time I see you. But it's going on three years since I kissed a girl and that girl was you.

MARCH

Majuro Atoll: March 20, 1944

We been real busy the last few weeks. I wrote to Evelyn every now and then but not as much as she wants I know. There just ain't nothing I can tell her about what's going on and she can't tell me nothing about her job and not much else either, so the letters don't say much. Just a lot of love words and I'm about running out of them. If I don't get to kiss her and do other stuff soon, I might bust. I keep thinking about what that woman at the cat house said about me being back there because the war's a long time. I just hope it ain't much longer.

We been giving Truk a hard time but hadn't done a direct attack yet. It's gonna be a hard one, so we're just shooting at it every time we go by to let em know we'll be back. We been shooting down enemy planes and launched strikes against Guam and Tinian and Saipan. We done real good there shooting down all kinds of planes and sinking some ships. I'm real glad I got this map so I can sort of keep up with where we are and where we probably going next.

What we do when we take back the islands is make a safe place to go back to not far from the next place we got to be. The safe place for us to be now is Majuro Atoll so we been back here over a week now. We been replenishing supplies and refueling and practicing and stuff. But we get some down time too that we need to be sharp when the shooting starts. There's this real great place to swim here.

Yesterday started out real good but it didn't end up that way. We were getting off the ship in recreation parties and everybody had their two cans of beer. The stuff is hot and I don't care none for it even when it's cold so I gave mine to whoever wanted it. Lyle did the same thing. We just don't need or want the stuff.

All the islands are in a little circle that make a swell lagoon to swim. They took us over to the little island called Peggy Island where we could do some swimming but they told us to stay there on that island and in the lagoon right there cause the current was too strong to try to get to any of the other islands on our own. The coloreds and whites don't usually do nothing together but we were on that island together and we was all having a good time albeit we weren't that close together.

But there was this Japanese gun left over on one of the other islands that one of the colored fellas decided he wanted to get for a souvenir. So he started to try to swim over and get it and he just disappeared under the water and didn't come back up.

It took a while but they found his body later in the day. There weren't nothing nobody could do for him then. Today we had his funeral on the island. I reckon it's better than being tossed over at sea but I feel bad for his family what with him being buried so far from home. They built a coffin for him down in the carpentry shop on ship and his steward mate buddies were his pall bearers. I just felt like I should go to that funeral even if he was colored since I was right there and saw him drown. I don't rightly know nothing about him except he ain't gonna make it home and I bet he has a family back home waiting. It wasn't a Jap bullet or torpedo that killed him. He was just having some fun. That just ain't right.

We head out tomorrow or the next day. Looks like the next places on the map are Palau, Yap and Woleai. Those islands are just south of Guam and we did a good job there. But every time we do a good job, it makes the Japs that much madder and we gotta really watch out the next time. Used to be attacks only came in the early hours of the day right at dawn and then again right before dark. That ain't the way they do it anymore. They like the night time now.

I better try to write to Evelyn now. Don't know when I'll get another chance.

March 20, 1944

Dearest Evelyn,

I got some letters from you today that I can answer. I know 'No Letter Today' is a song but you say it a lot and I do too. It's just the way it is. There's lots of days when we won't have letters.

You know that fella that was saying things about not taking the farm out of the boy. Well, he's about to get on my bad side. He's calling us country boys 'plow jockeys' now and that don't set right with a bunch of us. He's from New York City and he don't know near as much as he thinks he does. Maybe we're all just getting a little Asiatic.

I don't remember if I told you, but I made second so your good lucks and wishes worked. Now I got to learn all the duties of second and start studying for first. I don't know if I'll make it that far but I plan on trying.

Yes dear, I know I went a long time without writing. I didn't have much to say. I'm glad you let me know about that letter that was cut all to shreds. Now I know that I can't say some of the things I thought I might could say. Was there anything in that one left for you to read?

I told you I was going to copy that letter the other fella got from the girl who used all the song titles to write a whole letter so here it is. She did a swell job.

'Dearly Beloved'

'Never a Day Goes By' that I don't 'Miss You' even 'From Taps to Reveille.' 'You are Always in My Heart' 'As Time Goes By.' 'I Realize it's Always You' so I'm not 'Taking a Chance on Love' as long as I know you love me.

'I'm Thinking Tonight of Your Blue Eyes' as I do 'Every Night About This Time' 'In the Blue of the Evening' just before 'I Hit the Road to Dreamland.' 'You'll Never Know' how 'My Heart and I' feel.

'By the Light of the Silvery Moon' I go into my 'Moonlight Mood.' You know that 'You're the Only Star in My Blue Heaven.' 'Memories' prove that 'There are Such Things'.

'It Started All Over Again' when you won my heart 'At Last.' I know that this is 'The Right Kind of Love.' 'It Can't be Wrong' because 'You Made Me Love You.' 'I Don't Want to Set the World on Fire' but 'I'll Never Smile Again' if I lose you.

'Time Was' when 'Anchor's Away' meant 'Goodbye Now' but when I hear you sing 'Here Comes the Navy' I'll say 'I've Heard That Song Before.'

'Honey' 'I'm Getting Tired So I Can Sleep.' 'I Just Kissed Your Picture Goodnight' but it wasn't 'As Though You Were Here' so I'll say 'Goodnight Sweetheart.'

'I Love a Military Man' (that's an old one)
PS – 'Please Think of Me' 'Sunday, Monday and Always'

That was a pretty good letter wasn't it? Sorry I didn't think of all that first. Til next time I'll be thinking of you and loving you always.

I sure do love you,
Roy

March 21, 1944
Dearest Evelyn,

I found I had a little bit of free time today so I'm going to try to get one more letter off to you before we get underway again. I hadn't got any more new letters but I still got some old ones I can answer and some news.

I'm feeling swell on my birthday. I turned 21 years old. I got a good tan now cause I can work on the deck without my shirt sometimes. When I was with the boat I had to wear my full uniform all the time. I get to go to movies now too without worrying about getting called out in the middle of it.

I didn't get a birthday card or packages but I know you sent them because you said you were. And Ma did too. They'll come sometime. We just never know when.

I saw some good ones like 'Gung Ho' about the first raid on Makin Island in the Gilberts (I reckon it's ok now to tell you I been there) and then there was 'Destination Tokyo' with Cary Grant. That one's about a submarine. All the movies I see are aboard ship. The very best one anybody saw was called 'Lost Angel' and that one will give you a feeling you hadn't never had before.

I broke my tooth and had to go to the dentist. I reckon it's a pretty swell thing that we have our own dentist right here on the ship.

I stood boatswain mate watch the other day. It was the first time in almost a year since I was on the boat so long. About six o'clock in the evening a boat came alongside our gangway. The officer came aboard and I was talking to the fella in the boat. He said there was a sailor from Georgia on his ship. He believed it was a town with Hollow at the end but he couldn't remember the first part.

I didn't like that clipping you sent about the girl who had been true for two long years and the fella was running around with some Chinese cutie.

You are right about something. Some guys say 'Keep the Home Fires Burning' but then they do things with a French girl or island princess or some other girls where they are in Germany or Italy or places like that. But that ain't me.

I hadn't seen a girl in over four months and that one was when I was in the boat and she was on the beach a thousand yards off. And she was a native.

But don't think I'm true cause I don't have a chance not to be. I'm true because I love you. Your letter said you hope I am and you don't like to think about it. Get this thing out of your head and don't worry about it no more. I gave you my heart and my word and I'm gonna live up to it no matter how long this war lasts.

I'm sorry to tell you that the knife you gave me got broken. We were at an island where we took a swim over to a place with a lot of coconut trees. I climbed up one and got the coconut and was using my knife to cut it open. It worked swell.

But I loaned it out and got it back broken. I got paid back with a brand new one cause he was sorry, but it ain't the same as having one from you.

We got the list up today for how much we made in 1943. Mine was $1,092.42. If I was married it would be more. It's going to be more in 1944 anyhow cause I got a new rate. I hope it goes up cause we get a chance to get married too. I'm making $122 a month now. That ain't bad but it's not as much as you make at that fancy new job of yours.

My nose is better cause I'm not sitting in the boat all the time in the sunshine without being able to get in the shade for even a minute. But it's been over a month and a half and it's just stopped peeling.

I'm not going to talk about how much I miss you cause it makes me feel bad and makes you feel bad too. I'll just talk about how much I love you and that is bigger than the sky and the ocean put together.

All my love forever,

Roy

PS - I better wish you Happy Easter in this letter because I don't know how long it will take it to get there or when I will get to write again.

APRIL

Majuro Atoll: April 9, 1944
We been anchored back at Majuro Atoll for a couple days. The

last few days before that were so crazy that we hadn't had time to write or sleep or hardly even eat. It was the worst yet as far as how long we had to fight. Since we been back in port, we been so busy I hadn't had no time to do anything. When I got time to stop, all I wanted to do was sleep.

We didn't take no direct hit and neither did the other ships, but there's got to be some repairs on some of them before we go back out again. That won't be long. The Japs are trying new things to beat us but we're still winning. The NC is three years old today and I hadn't even had time to remember that til now.

I need to try to write Evelyn while we're here but I first wanted to put down the things that happened. We went to Palau and Yap and Woleai. We weren't the only Task Force there so we had a whole bunch of battleships and aircraft carriers and cruisers and destroyers. The Japs would have had a good day if they could've got some of our ships. They got some planes but no ships. But we sure got a passel of theirs.

Even in all the time of fighting we still had to fuel other ships. That's the dangerous job and when you're so tired from being at General Quarters day and night without no break it makes it a harder job. But we didn't get nobody hurt and that's a real good feeling.

The Japs played a lot of underhanded tricks on us to make us think they were getting ready to strike. Then they wouldn't but we couldn't leave the mount cause then they might be there again. They liked attacking at night time this time thinking we couldn't handle it but they were wrong. We did just fine. We just didn't get no sleep but we still got the Japs.

The captain gave us a report on how good we did. We lost 25 planes from the whole task group (that's all the task forces put together) and that's a crying shame. But all of us together shot down 150 enemy planes and damaged a bunch more. We sank 29 of their ships and hurt about half as many more. We sank some little boats they had too. There was some more planes, almost 30 that we think we got but they don't know for sure. He said we did a mighty fine job to be proud of.

April 10, 1944

My dearest Evelyn,

I'm sorry there's been no time to write but the mail wouldn't have gone out anyway. It couldn't come where we were either. We got 20 bags of mail aboard today, so I got some letters from you and everybody else. I'll try to answer what I can. I'm fine so don't worry about me right now.

How have you been? I know it's pretty back home in Georgia right now with the trees starting to bud out and the flowers trying to bloom and the pastures turning green. I always loved how many different colors of green they're are in the mountains. Is it like that in your part of Tennessee too?

We get the same color about all the time – blue skies, blue ocean, blue mood. I reckon that might make a pretty good song. 'All I See or Feel is Blue.' Maybe I'll try to write it sometime.

I finally got some good sleep last night for the first time in a long time. We got back to a place that's safer so we don't have to worry about being attacked any minute but we been working day and night ever since we got here so I still hadn't had no sleep.

But last night it was raining and that kind of cools it down a bit. When you gone so long without sleep like we done the last little while, you don't just fall asleep - you pass out. That's what I did.

I don't know when or where we'll get to meet but don't you worry about what anybody says or thinks when we do cause after going on three years already, we got a right to be excited to meet each other and I'm gonna hold you so tight you won't never think I'm going to let you go and kiss you like we hadn't ever kissed before. That's a promise and I don't care how many people are around or who they are.

Think about it. You were just a senior in high school when I left and I just graduated that summer. But I been gone a long time. That means we're not kids anymore but a man and a woman in love.

That harmonica you gave me was made in Germany. That's why you can't find another one. But they can take all their harmonicas and go to heck. I'll learn to play something else if this one breaks.

Yes, there really is a life belt called a Mae West. It's not very big but it fits around your hips and that makes them stand out. Use your imagination for the name.

Looks like you're running out of stuff to write in your letters too. This last one is telling me what I wrote about in '42 and '43. I already know that stuff. I need something new.

I saw Alfred from back home the other day. I couldn't hardly believe it. We got the word in our division to stand by to fuel a destroyer. We've got extra fuel tanks to carry more fuel than we need but the tincans (that's what we call destroyers) are so little they can't carry very much so we have to fuel them. But we have to do it while we're underway. I told you all about that one time before a long time ago. Anyhow I was standing by the lifeline all ready to do the job and I saw the number on the can was '512' so I started looking for him. Ma had told me his Ma told her that number like our number is BB55 his is DD512. So I started looking for him and I saw him and he saw me but we couldn't do much about it til we got all squared away with the fueling. We still couldn't talk because of all the noise and the mail going between the ships but it sure was swell seeing somebody from back home. I hope to see him for real if they go to the same port as us sometime. I hadn't seen that tincan since we been here this time.

Well I got to do some chores and have chow. Then I'm going to go to the movie tonight. We hadn't had one in a while and it should be a good one I hope. It's called 'Honeymoon in Bali.' Maybe I can learn something.

I'm glad to hear you got your wedding dress. I will let you know as soon as I know when we'll be headed home. I just don't know nothing yet.

Waiting to hold you,

Roy

PS - Yesterday the ship was three years old. We had birthday cake and ice cream. It was swell.

April 11, 1944

Dearest Evelyn,

I'm still answering the letters that came aboard in that 20 bags the other day. I got a feeling I may get some more before it's all said and done.

So they're sending you papers about your income. You must of made plenty. Now you have to pay taxes on it. Charlie's girl had to pay $200 income tax.

So how do you know about stars? You want to know how many we earned. Well, I can't tell you that. Anything the ship does is military secret so if I wrote it the letter wouldn't pass and would end up like that other one all in shreds. I tried to be careful since then so you get letters in one piece. So just skip it.

Why do you keep saying you'll be afraid of me? It's been a long time I know since we seen each other but that don't change things between us except to make them stronger. I would never do nothing to hurt you and you know that. We can just take our time and do what we do when we want to do it. You been talking to too many people that don't know what they're talking about or reading too many magazines or movies or something. It's gonna be just swell. You wait and see.

So how is your friend Mildred doing that's going to have the baby? You hadn't mentioned her in a long time. That's not what's got you scared is it? Did you find out which destroyer her husband is on? What's his name? Maybe I met him when we were in port.

So you have tennis courts in your town where you work and you're learning to play. I never played tennis but I reckon I can learn if you want me to when I get home. Now that it's getting on toward spring you should be able to be outside and enjoy that.

I just got some more mail call. It was a package with an Easter card and some books and some hard candy and some gum. I just finished off my last stick of gum and now I got a new supply. The cookies are swell too. The best part was the picture of you and Mary all dressed up in your Easter dresses and hats. Lyle got one too. You know just what a fella needs. Thanks a whole lot.

I'm worried about having to go up for first. We got two firsts in the division now. One is going up for chief and the other heard he's gonna get transferred to the old country. One of the seconds will get first which ain't too hard when you been in long enough because first is supposed to lead its division. There's five of us seconds and everybody keeps saying its gonna be me but I don't really want it. I been studying up on what the firsts have to do and I just want to finish out my Navy life as a second. It's the best rate in the Navy.

If you're a second, you ain't in charge of the division. When the fellas are gone, you don't have to worry. You can go ashore on liberty and forget about the Navy. If you're a first, you got to take care of everybody and there's things you got to schedule and take care of. I know I couldn't go nowhere without worrying that I did what I was supposed to do and had everything scheduled right and all my men were safe as they could be. If one of my men got hurt - or worse killed - I would feel like it was my fault even if it weren't.

Nah, I'll just stay second. I know I told you one time I'd try to be an Admiral. I hope you don't mind that I don't want to be one anymore. I just want to do what I got to do and get home to you

153

and raise a family on a farm where there's seasons like winter and spring and summer and fall not just water all around and hot weather all the time.

Its chow time so I'll close for now. Don't you worry about nothing. Just plan our wedding and think about when we'll be together. I'll be home as soon as the Navy lets me come.

Loving you always,

Roy

April 12, 1944

My future wife Evelyn,

We got one more day before we're underway again and won't be able to send or get mail so I wanted to write one more letter before we go. I still have some of yours to answer.

So, you know how to hang wallpaper. You're a girl of many talents. You and Mary did it in the baby's room for Mildred. That was a fine thing for friends to do. Did you really have all the tools you needed like scissors and glue and ruler and a ladder and razors. I didn't know you ever hung wallpaper before. I hope you did a good job so it stays on the walls and Mildred don't end up looking like a mummy all wrapped up in paper when she goes in to check on the baby. She hadn't had it yet has she?

No more joking. I believe you can do anything you set your mind to do.

Last night I had to load stores and help get everything onboard so we can get underway. We take turns doing working parties and I had to get up at four in the morning for my turn so I'm sure tired.

You got some pillow cases from Mary. That was swell of her to think of you (us) when she went shopping. I bet that hope chest is getting full already. No, I don't usually sleep on a pillow cause it's too hot. I fold up my blanket and put it under my mattress too. I don't need it. But when I get home it won't be like it is here. I can sleep on just about anything so no embroidery on a pillow case is going to keep me awake.

I got a letter from Sally Jane today. She said she moved to another place in the same town and got a different job with a promotion and a raise. She said her boyfriend is real smart and real nice. He took her on a picnic and being a country girl she really liked it and thought he was a good person to think of something like that to surprise her. I hope you can get to meet him sometime. Sally Jane told me that they're getting ready when the weather gets just a little bit warmer to start having dances every Friday night on those tennis courts you told me about cause they got lights and they're big enough for all the people to get together and dance. Did you know that? Maybe you will see her then.

Why have you been putting 10 cent stamps on your letters? They're not that long. We only have to put six cents on them unless its airmail and I hadn't done much of those. If you write on both sides of the paper then your letters aren't so heavy. This paper works better than the last cause it's thicker and the ink doesn't go through to the other side.

If my writing looks funny its cause I hurt my hands playing tug-of-war. We have to do stuff sometimes to have fun when we're in port and not on a work party or on watch at the time or it gets boring. All the teams on the starboard side won tug-of-war no matter what sailors they had. I think they must have had a truck hid or something. Sometimes we play acey-duecy or checkers or just read. I told you about our baseball team and then we got a boxing team. They set the ring up right on the fantail and the fellas box each other from our ship and from other ships. We got the winner on our ship.

I got the watch again in a few hours and I still got some laundry to do and other stuff so I will close for now. We're getting underway again tomorrow so I don't know when I'll get to write again.

Keep working hard at your job if it's going to end the war

sooner and I'll keep working hard at mine. Maybe that will get me home so we can get married.

All my love,
Roy

MAY

May 9, 1944

My dearest Evelyn,

Sorry for the delay in writing. I got some letters from you and now I got a bit of time to start answering them. It will probably take me a year to catch up. Maybe I'll be home by then and we can just talk about it so I don't have to write my answers.

So you got a new bathing suit. When are you going to send me a picture of you in it? It ought to be warm enough to put it on about now. Yes, I would like to see your tan but I might want to see your tan lines better. I did say that. What you think about it?

What do you mean that you could have twins? Your grandma had twins and your aunt had twins so you think you could have twins. That would be alright with me. If we have one at a time or two at a time I don't care. I want a boy and a girl, but if they're born at the same time maybe they should be the same. That talk about quadruplets scares me silly. Ain't that four babies at one time? Has anybody really ever done that? Enough of that. I hadn't never passed out not even when I was getting the needle and that big fella passed out, but that many babies at one time I might. Triplets might be ok but that's plenty.

So you want to know my boatswain mate duties. It's swell most of the time but sometimes it can be trouble. You have to find the people for the work parties. See the deck division is in charge of rigging for church or for the movies when we do them on the fantail. When we're in port we do the movies topside where it's cooler. Well at Easter, we needed to get rigged for church but I was having a hard time finding enough for the work party. I found seven and they worked a while then I had to find more and then more again to get all the work done cause they had to keep relieving the other party when they worked their time.

Yes, 'No Time for Love' was a good one. I did see it and it's got a good ending. That 'Lost Angel' was a great movie and you need to see if it you hadn't already done it. The fellas still talk about it all the time. If they show it here again I'll watch it another time.

No, I don't want to get married just cause I'll get more money. You know why I want to get married or least ways you should know. Maybe I won't be attached to a ship when I get to come home and I can stay longer. But if I got a ship and it's pulling out then I don't know how long it will be. No, I don't know yet when I'll be home but you'll be the first to know.

Yes, the ships do have their own bands and ours is real good. There's this one guy that can play anything. Sometimes he plays the drums and then he'll play the trumpet and then something else. He's a little guy but good looking. He's real good on the piano and at night he'll play it but some of the songs he plays makes you think about home and gets you sad. When it's peace time the band will play in parades and stuff but when it's war time they're in charge of damage control. They gotta go down below deck and repair any damage from battle. At night in port they can play for us.

It's time for chow so I'll close now but I'll try to write some more answers sooner than later.

All my love,
Roy

May 20, 1944
Dearest Evelyn,

I still got plenty of letters to answer from you. Yes ma'am I did get my birthday card and my package. It was a swell card. I like the hearts you drew all over it too.

Thank you for the new knife. I didn't expect to get a new one from you. No, I won't let nobody borrow this one to work on coconuts.

I know there will be plenty of people around when I first get home but we can get rid of em after a few days. That's why we probably ought to wait about a week to get married. By then I been around my Ma and Pap enough that they won't be so worried when I leave with you and spend all my time with just you. We got to take a honeymoon away somewhere though so none of em can find us.

Lyle said there's a little cottage on the island in South Carolina where he lives that his Grandpa owns and they don't stay there all the time but we might can use it for a week or so if we have that much time. It'll just take us a while to drive there and we got to have gas so be saving up on your ration cards. My Ma and Pap don't get off the farm much and she told me she's been saving hers so I can have em when I get home.

I hope you got a car that we can use cause my ole truck hadn't been drove in a while and I don't know if it would make it that far. I reckon we could take the train if it were a city but it ain't and the bus don't go out on that island either so we got to drive if we go there.

But I been in the ocean so long I miss the mountains. If you hadn't got a real hankering to go to the beach, then we could just stay closer to home as long as nobody knows where we're at. I reckon you'd want to be close to a town too so we could go to the movies or skating or something. You think about it and let me know where you want to go. It wouldn't take as much time or money if we stay closer.

The abandon ship drill weren't bad. All we did was put on a life jacket, climb down a ways, jump off and swim back aft then climb back up. We got these ladders that we use to get to the boats when we go on liberty so that's what we use for the abandon ship drill. We got life boats too but we don't put them down for the drill. We gotta save them for the real thing.

I hope that don't never happen cause when a ship gets damaged there could be fire and there's lots of oil that gets in the water and it burns your eyes.

You saw that one picture I sent in my dungarees. That's what we wear most of the time aboard ship. We just wear our uniforms when we go ashore or when we're coming into port.

I'm sending back the V-Mail like you asked so you could see what it looked like. It was short.

I do like that Frank Sinatra song 'This Love of Mine' just like you. It's my favorite too cause you're my love. It will go on and on like he said and you're always on my mind. Don't let it make you sad. We'll be together one day soon I promise.

You say Frankie keeps up the girls morale. Why do you call him that? I say he sings pretty good but he's got a big adam's apple.

I still got to take a shower yet tonight and this is a good time that the lines not too long so I'll close for now. We're leaving soon so I got to get it mailed.

But I just thought of something I gotta tell you about some movies I saw. One was 'Miracle of Morgan's Creek' about this woman with a lot of kids. I think it was six. It was Betty Hutton. The one they're going to show tonight is that dog movie 'Lassie Come Home.' I reckon that one will be alright if you like dogs and I do. I'll close for now.

Til next time Love of Mine,
Roy

May 31, 1944
My dearest Evelyn,

We got mail call again today and I got some letters from you. Some are dated older than ones I already got and answered. I still don't know what happens to our mail but at least it got to where I am.

This first letter was dated way back April 10. So you gave Mildred a baby shower. I bet she really liked that. Was the wallpaper already done then? I got confused about when you did what since the mail got so mixed up. You say she got pink stuff and blue stuff. I reckon she don't know what the baby will be but she'll have enough things for it. Why don't people just buy yellow blankets. Then it don't matter what the baby is. Seems that would make more sense.

So seeing all that baby clothes and blankets and diapers and bottles makes you want one. Well, I'll see what I can do about that when I get home. But you can't do nothing about it before then.

What's all this talk about red PJs? No I don't wear PJs and I don't have no red ones. I rather sleep without nothing on but I got to wear my skivvies here cause you never know when you got to get up and go to GQ real fast. Hadn't got time to put everything back on. Oh, so they're just for the foot of the bed in case of fire. I see. So you think I'm going to get tired on our honeymoon. What you got in store for me? I tell you what. I'll bring a bottle of vitamin pills just to keep up my strength.

I got a pretty good supply of gum so you don't have to worry about sending me none seeing as how you say it's hard to get. I got plenty. About the candy. I'm sorry it was all messed up when I got it and I couldn't eat it but it has to come a long way to find me and could go from one ship to another before it ever gets to me. The packages sometimes get squashed and get wet. It's mighty hot out here where we are to so it gets all melted.

I do love fudge like that Ma used to make and pour up in the platter then it would get hard and so good. Did you know there's a new kind of chocolate made by Hershey? It's called the 'Tropical Bar' and it ain't too bad when you been wanting chocolate something awful and hadn't had any in a while. It's made special for the tropics so it don't melt like the other kind. I'll send you a wrapper some time so you can see.

I like the magazines and papers in the packages that you been sending. We share them around the ship when we already read ours and another fellas got a different one. I like the 'Reader's Digest' you send and the newspapers from back home that my Ma sends the best. I liked the 'New York Times' you used to send when you lived there too. Had some good stuff about the war. But I don't have a lot of time to read em so don't send so many, ok?

I coulda seen 'The Fighting Sullivans' tonight but I rather write to you. I think that movie would put me in a bad mood anyhow. I heard it was about five brothers and they all died when their ship sank. What they were all doing on the same ship I don't know. I reckon it could be a pretty good story but I'd feel awful for their Ma and Pap.

I'm in charge of the boat deck now and the starboard crane and the gear locker and other stuff plus 35 men every day. I don't mind. It keeps me busy.

I'll close for now. Keep thinking about our wedding and the honeymoon and the PJs on the foot of the bed.

Loving you forever and always,
Roy

JUNE

Underway from Majuro Harbor: June 1, 1944

Well it's been a long time since I wrote anything other than letters home. Evelyn keeps sending me so many I can't answer them fast enough. I ain't complaining cause they're what keeps me going. When the battles are over and we get some down time, I just think about getting home to her and starting a new life that don't have nothing to do with war.

I get letters from other people back home and my sister. I just wish I would get one from Billy but I hadn't in a long time. I hadn't wrote him like I should either. I write Evelyn even when I don't write nobody else and between writing her letters and doing all the other stuff I got to do that don't leave much time. Billy's busy too.

We been going back and forth in some real heavy fighting the past few weeks. Been in General Quarters more than out of it when we're out to sea. Japs ain't liking us none and they been trying their best to take us out, but it ain't gonna happen.

When we finished taking care of all the little islands we went back to Truk. Worked on it hard but it still ain't secure. We shot down planes from the air and sunk ships and demolished planes on the ground. Not just the NC but all the ships in the task force and there were plenty of us out there.

Back the last day of April we had a pilot from the NC made a rescue people been talking about ever since. The Kingfisher planes on our ship do a lot of different jobs and one of their jobs is to rescue pilots that's been shot down before the enemy gets to em. They been doing a lot of that all that time we were fighting at Truk. But this one was special I hear.

They ain't supposed to be able to rescue more than one or two at a time and take them back to the sub that's waiting to carry them back to their ship. Those Kingfishers ain't very big but they got pontoons so they can land on water. To take off, they got to be shot out of a catapult on the fantail of the ship. It rotates out toward the water so the planes can get shot off without hitting the ship.

The way I heard it this fella Burns (that's the pilot) had already rescued three pilots at one time and that surprised everybody but he went back out and rescued ten pilots at one time. They was sitting on the wings and the pontoons and everywhere just riding along on the outside of that plane going to meet the sub. I heard the pontoon was taking on water and so the plane was listing over to the side and they were about to run out of gas and everything going wrong, but Burns got them all to the sub.

That's why he got a medal and a transfer anywhere he wanted to go when we went back to Pearl. Yeah, we been back to Pearl Harbor to get one of the rudders repaired and then we were back at it again. Been in Majuro Harbor some. Takes five days to go from Majuro to Pearl Harbor and five days back.

There's always the danger of torpedos when we're going out there almost alone. Got some tincans along to protect us but it ain't like being with the whole task force. But we made the trip safe there and back and got patched up so we're ready to go again. Still no word when we'll get to go home or much about how the war is going other than what we know from what we're doing out here. And that's winning a little bit at the time.

Scuttlebutt already has it that when we get to the big island of Japan that ain't gonna go easy. I reckon we'll do what we got to do when we get there. I'm glad I'm on the ship and not a soldier or Marine that's got to put their boots on the ground.

But we got to take it one day at a time and right now we're getting ready to head out for some big ones in the Marianas Islands – Saipan, Tinian, and Guam. But the problem they tell us is that Truk still ain't secure and the Japs can still fly out of there and we have to go right past it again to get where we're going. I'll be glad when we just take care of that one and don't have to worry about it no more. But I reckon the Admiral knows what he's doing and we got to follow orders.

June 4, 1944
My dearest Evelyn,

I got mail call today and wished I hadn't never even looked at the letters. I was happy to get yours, but I got one from my folk's neighbor Alice and it was a bad one. They don't know where Billy ris. The big black car that nobody likes to see drove down our road at the farm and it stopped right at our front door. Miss Alice said Ma ain't been right since. She put her to bed and been coming over everyday to help out. She found the last letter I wrote home and figured she better let me know. That's how she got my address. That was a month or more ago that Ma and Pap found out. I wondered why I hadn't had no mail from home but sometimes it gets lost or Ma just don't have time to write, especially with spring planting then the early vegetables coming in and the cows calving.

He was in Germany and the last time somebody saw him it was a big battle at night. There was injured soldiers and he went back in to get one of his buddies. Nobody saw him no more nor his buddy neither. They didn't find him with the dead ones so they thinking he got taken and the Germans have him locked up somewhere. They don't know that for a fact so they're calling him a MIA and not a POW. Least ways, they don't think he's dead. Not yet anyway. Sometimes I think dead might be a better way to be than the other but I can't say I want my baby brother dead.

I'm wishing you were back home so you could check on my Ma. I'm hoping Sally Jane can go home for a little while and help out with our Pap. Surely that job ain't something she can't leave for a family emergency. I sure hope somebody let her know. I'll write her a letter now but can you try to find her and be sure she knows?

Could you write your Ma and get her to go check on my Ma for me please? I need to know how she's getting along and I don't reckon Miss Alice will be sending me no more letters.

I just wished I could get home and do it right now. I'm sorry I don't have it in me to write no more tonight. I just can't think about movies, and songs, and weddings and having fun when I don't know what in hell is happening to my brother.

But I still love you and always will.

Yours,

Roy

June 6, 1944

Dearest Evelyn,

I wanted to try to answer some of your letters. I'm still worried as I can be about Billy but there's not one thing I can do to help so I got to concentrate on other things. I hope to hear some news from you soon about Sally Jane. I got some letters from her that don't say nothing about Billy so I don't know if she got the letter I wrote.

So you been crying about a lot of things lately huh. One of the girls you work with got married and that made you cry. I reckon it would make you blue since you don't know when you're going to get to wear your wedding dress. But I hope you're happy when we have our wedding.

Then you been crying when you saw Mildred have her baby. A little girl. Well that's real good. I bet she's a pretty little thing if she looks like her Ma did in that picture you sent of you and her and Mary. You been helping her out some after work. That's a swell thing since her husband is out at sea.

Yes, I think if the baby is crying and it don't need a new diaper and ain't hungry but just not sleeping then you gotta walk it. I remember Ma doing that with Billy. I wasn't very old but he cried at night and she walked him and sang to him. Try it. It might work. What did she name the baby?

Thanks for sending me Mildred's husband's name and ship. Johnny Malpass on the destroyer Hull DD350. I might run into him when we're in port if he's part of one of our task groups.

Did I tell you that the Spence DD512 is in one of our groups and when we were all in port not long ago I got to see Alfred when we went ashore? It was sure swell to meet somebody from back home and talk about the old days. Remember he was on the football team. He recalls your brother Sam.

I'm glad you like the picture of my division. It shows you some of the ship too. That was on the fantail and those are the 16s behind us. You want to know what that is behind the guns you're right it's leather. We call it elephant hide. They're called 'bloomers' and they keep water, gas, and flash out of the turret.

That is not a whistle around my neck. It is called a bos'n pipe. You got to get your terms right using the Navy way. Yes, walls are bulkheads and doors are hatches and the floor is the deck.

Yes, you are right. To rig church means to put out everything you need. We rig an altar and use the benches in the mess hall for sitting.

I heard about the movie 'The Fighting Seabees' but I hadn't seen it yet. That's the one with John Wayne and Susan Hayward. I think that ones pretty new and we just get to see them later when they're older. I'm glad you get to go the movies where you live. Sounds like a pretty good place with all the things you need. Having a hospital right there where Mildred could have her baby was good too.

I'm glad you're telling me a little bit more about where you live. I reckon I'll get to see it when I come home. You still don't tell me nothing about your job though. I wish you would. I try to tell you as much as I can about mine.

I got the night watch so I got to sign off now.

Loving you forever and always,

Roy

June 10, 1944

Dear Evelyn,

This may be the last time I get to write for a while so I'll try to answer as many of your letters that I have left as I can.

So you think fall would be the best time for me to be back home and us get married. Yes, a fall honeymoon in the mountains would be nice. But what if I get to come home in August? Now don't get your hopes up I don't have no information. I was just asking.

So your morale is better now that it's summer and you get to go swimming. You have tan lines now. I would like to see them for myself. If you go to the Friday night dances on the tennis courts try to find Sally Jane if you hadn't already talked to her. Maybe she's done gone home. I still hadn't heard anymore but it's only been a few days since the other letter.

You asked me how is my morale. I know you wrote it before I told you about Billy but here you go #1 - I'm a sailor. #2 – I hadn't been home in going on three years. #3 – I'm in love with the perfect girl and need to prove it to her. #4 – My brother is MIA and my Ma is taken to the bed with worry.

I could go on but I reckon you get the picture. The only thing that keeps me going is getting back home to you. I still haven't any news about that. But it could happen on short notice so you need to be ready.

You don't have to send me no more pictures right now. I take a beating about how many pictures I get. I can take it, but the fellas want to know how you get so much film. Most folks are having trouble with finding it. They say you must have some link to the black market or something. They just kidding but I'm really running out of room.

You wondering why some sailors get to come home on a leave and I don't. Well, it could happen cause they're getting a transfer to another ship. They might could get some leave if that happens or they got to have some special training back home or something else like that. I hadn't got a transfer (and don't want one I'm on a fine ship) and all the training I need I get right here so the only way I get to come home is if the war ends or the whole ship comes back home. I don't know what would make that happen cause if we need to get fixed up we go to Pearl Harbor. That's when I can send you the swell cards with Aloha on em. That would be a fine place for a honeymoon but I don't reckon we have much time for that and I been there enough lately anyhow. Maybe we could do it for our anniversary about ten years or 20 years. It sure will be swell to spend my whole life with you.

When I'm on watch and it ain't too busy or dangerous where we are right then I do a lot of dreaming about all the things we can do and places we can go. Even if we got a farm, I plan to have some hands to help us so we're not tied down like my Ma and Pap and yours been all these years. What do you think about raising horses? There's a fella in my division that's from Kentucky. His folks raise horses and they have a fine place to live and lots of land. I said I hadn't got no money to buy that kinda land and he said they started out with just a little bit but they worked hard and did a fine job with the horses and made enough to keep growing and growing til they got what they got now. It sounds like a fine place to raise some kids.

Well I got the watch soon so I reckon I better sign off for tonight. Keep your spirits high and I'll try to work on my morale to have good reports next time.

Loving you more every day,
Roy

Somewhere near the Marianas Islands: June 21, 1944

I haven't wrote to Evelyn in nearly two weeks now, but we just hadn't had time. What with all the going back and forth we been doing out here at sea and not going back to a port nowhere, the fueling duties been keeping us real busy. And we been even busier fighting the Japs.

We been to Guam and Rota and Chichi Jima and Iwo Jima. We been close to Saipan. But we mostly been doing the fighting out at sea, the aircraft carriers launching planes to fight in the air and us trying to protect em and shoot down as many Jap planes as we can. Try to sink their ships too if we get the chance. We hadn't sat and shot at no islands lately. That'll be coming for sure if we're going to get them ready for the Marines to invade and take over.

We been at General Quarters so much sometimes we don't get to get out to eat or nothing. That's when they send sandwiches up in a pail from the galley. There's an old saying back home when you don't have much money that you're so poor you don't have a pot to pee in. Well we got a pot and that pot makes us feel mighty lucky when you in there so long. The mount ain't a big place. I stepped it off about 14 feet across and the guns take up an awful lot of room. There's about a dozen fellas each with a job they got to do and if you don't do it just right at the right time then you don't get the job done. You only got seconds to do it. We got to fire fast to keep the Japs from hitting us before we shoot them down. There ain't no way to see out except for the spotter. I listen on my headphones and just tell when to shoot. We got a computer below deck that helps the guns know when to turn and where to fire. It's a mighty sophisticated thing when you think about it.

We been in the Phillippine Sea and the Mariannas Islands. We got word yesterday that the pilots done such a fine job of shooting down planes they said it was like a turkey shoot. I reckon there was so many of them coming at em they just kept firing and fighting. We lost a few planes mostly cause they didn't get a chance to come back in and refuel. I hear they been searching for pilots in the water.

They hadn't told us if we're going anywhere else so I reckon we'll be out here near the Marianas Islands for a while till we get the job done. A good night's sleep in my bunk would sure be a welcome thing. But when I start to think about it, I gotta tell myself it ain't so bad where I am. I worry about my brother Billy all the time. Nobody knows where he is. If the Germans got him that ain't gonna be a good thing. I can't hardly stand to think about it. But I been doing a lot more praying lately. Hoping that God's still gonna listen since I hadn't been speaking to him right regular like my Ma taught me to.

June 30, 1944

My dearest Evelyn,

We hadn't been where we could send or get mail lately and I hadn't had much time to write. I'm sorry if you got worried. I know Lyle hadn't been doing much writing to Mary neither, but we been just fine. Doing the work we got to do to get back home. Still no word on when that will be. I wish every day I could tell you to set a date and be ready but all I can do is tell you it's gonna be one day and you can do as much as you can to make it happen when I get there. Sounds like you been pretty busy and got some good plans. I'm glad you want a church wedding. I do too. I been talking to God more lately like I shoulda been doing all along. I can't wait to say them I dos to you in front of him.

I still got a couple more of your letters to answer so I'll get right to it. Don't know how much time I got. They could say we got a couple hours but something could happen any time to change that.

You say you'll be a different person when you go back to work after the wedding and I reckon that will be the truth and not just because your last name will be Harrison. That's a fine sound – Evelyn Harrison – almost like a song. I hadn't heard any new good ones lately. No time. And we hadn't seen any movies either. I'm betting I'll be a changed fella too and it ain't got nothing to do with my name. I'm gonna have the biggest ole smile on my face and be ready to take all the ragging from the fellas. But that'll be fine with me. I'll know a whole lot more about stuff than I do now.

There's this one fella in the division that hadn't been here but about six months. He got a picture from his wife of his new baby boy. 9 lbs and 12 oz. Gonna probably make a football player or a good farm hand when he gets bigger. Cute little old rascal. They named him Joseph Alexander Wright, Jr. His Pap is called Joe so they gonna call him Joe Jr.

I don't rightly think we ought to hang the name Junior on a baby even if he does have his Pap's whole name. He'll have a middle name and you could call him that. There's this one fella in the division that's got a boy and a girl back home. His name's Big Bart cause he's so big, but they call the boy L'il Bart. Don't know what'll happen when he gets to be six foot three like his Pap. That could happen.

I been thinking about names for our boy when we have one. I don't want to call him Roy Jr. or Little Roy but we could name him Roy Lawrence Harrison, Jr. and call him Larry for the Lawrence part. There's another fella that ain't in my division but I talked to him when we were at liberty on the island. His name is David Winston DeBose and his son's a Jr. but they call him by the middle name Winston. I reckon if they ever go in the military they gonna get called by their first name or their last name and not the middle one even if that's what they go by, but if we do what we got to get done out here maybe there won't be no more war to take the sons away from home.

Now about our little girl. I hadn't thought past the first one but I think she ought to be named after her Ma. I hope she's gonna have red curls just like you. We could name her Evelyn Marie just like you but instead of calling her Marie we could call her Ellie. I just think that's a fine name for a little blue-eyed girl with red ringlet curls. What about you?

I know I might be getting ahead with all those thoughts about babies and what we gonna call em but it sure makes the days and nights go faster and makes my morale better than thinking about what we're doing out here. Ain't nothing good about the war.

I hadn't told you or nobody else this but I just gotta say it. Sometimes I think about those pilots in the enemy planes and the sailors on those ships we sink. I wonder what they're really like - if they're just like us doing a job cause their country needs them to. Even if they're in the wrong. What if they got families back home waiting just like us? I don't tell nobody else that cause we ain't supposed to think that way. They're the enemy and we got to kill em. At least I don't have to look em in the eye when I do it. That's another reason I'm glad to be on the ship and not on the ground. They ain't as real when you don't have to look em in the eye.

I bet it's feeling real good back home about now and looking right pretty with the rhododendrons bloomed out and all the leaves full. Won't be long before the blueberries and the brierberries on the side of the mountain'll be sweet enough to eat. And the peaches. I could sure use a juicy one about now. You ever get to go back home and see your folks?

Thanks for reminding me a while back about Father's Day. I did send my Pap something I picked up on the island. It was a knife carved out of stone with a wood handle that was made out of wood from a coconut tree. I reckon he'll like it pretty good.

I bet y'all might have some kind of celebration at your town for the 4th of July. See if you can find Sally Jane. She sure needs to go home. I hadn't heard from her in some time and I don't never hear from my Ma anymore. More likely than not, she's still laid up about Billy.

Don't know exactly where we'll be when Independence Day gets here, but you can bet we'll be making our own kind of fireworks.

Til next time, I'll be loving you more and more every day.

Waiting to hold you tight,

Roy

JULY

July 2, 1944

My dearest Evelyn,

I have some letters to answer and I have some news. I think I will answer the letters first and make you wait for the news. I am a bad fella.

First, I want to tell you I got a letter from Sally Jane. She did go home but just for a visit because she said she would lose her job if she stayed away too long and she needed to make the money to send home to help Pap. They got a lady coming in every other day to do some cooking and cleaning while my Ma gets better. She said they still hadn't heard nothing else about Billy but Ma is getting up some ever so often and sits on the porch in the rocking chair. Pap's about lost his patience a time or two with my Ma Sally Jane said. He told her he tried to make her better but he stays in a foul mood. I reckon it's no surprise but she found some shine hid in the barn when she went out to milk the cows. After supper, Pap goes out and stays in the barn and only comes in to go to bed.

The two stars in the window at our house are still blue, but that's not the case at Aunt Rose's house. Sally Jane said she hadn't heard a word and I hadn't neither cause nobody's been writing from home. So she went over there when she saw the gold star. Stuart ain't never coming home. They sent him over to Africa and he got killed.

I can only write to you every third day cause this is my routine – I got the watch one day and I have to stay on the deck the whole time even after. On the second day I got the duty and I have to get all the work done and make sure my crew does what they're supposed to do and then wait for the Chief Bos'n Mate to do the final check. The third day, I got some of the night to myself so I can write like I'm doing now but I better get to the news before something happens and I have to stop.

If everything goes right – but don't get your hopes up too high in case something goes wrong—but if it don't go wrong I should be home the very end of this month or the start of the next but at least by the end of the year. No, we hadn't won the war yet, so I'm probably going to have to leave again but we get to be home for a while. Long enough that we can get married and maybe even have a honeymoon if we don't go too far and take up too much time in the travel. Can you get some days off without losing your job?

Get ready cause I think I'm coming home and when I do I'm gonna be holding you tight.

Loving you always,
Roy

PS - I hope my Ma will be better enough to come to the wedding. Maybe we better have it close to home if that's alright with you. I'll be writing her today too, and maybe that will make her happier to have one son home at least.

July 20, 1944
My dearest Evelyn,

I'm sorry I hadn't written sooner. We just been real busy and there hadn't been no time. But it's official now. I'M COMING HOME! It looks right now like it will probably be in August but even when the ship gets back that don't mean I get to take leave right off. We're on our way to Pearl Harbor now and I can tell you more after we get there. You just keep sending my letters to the same address and they find the ship wherever we are. Since we're on our way to Pearl Harbor now, they will probably just go there.

I won't have much time to be off. About 15 or 28 days and it will take part of them to get home and to get back to the ship. Looks like we'll be going somewhere near Seattle, Washington. Even if the ship is getting worked on in dry dock at Bremerton we still got to have a crew aboard, so we take our leave half at a time. I won't know til later if I get the first leave or the second one. Scuttlebutt has it that they try to let the married ones go first and the ones getting married so they have more time to spend with their wives and kids. But if that's more than half, we got to draw for it. Here's how it's supposed to work.

If I get the first leave and we get married, I can bring you back to the West Coast with me if you can get off work that long. It would be thirty days plus time for the trip back to Tennessee. Paul

174

is going to bring his wife to stay in the houses they got there for the sailors families. When I have to leave you got to go back home by yourself but you can travel with her part of the way cause she lives in Virginia.

That's all I got time to write now but I'll let you know when I have more to say. I don't think I'll answer any more of your letters because it will be a whole lot better just to talk about it than writing it down. I been wanting to do that for a long time.

Your soon to be husband,
Roy

July 24, 1944
My dearest Evelyn,

We got to Pearl Harbor yesterday and will be heading home tomorrow so it really is going to happen. I still don't know if I get the first leave but I think I probably will. I heard I can take the train or the plane but the plane is faster. I reckon it will only take me to Atlanta then I got to take the train to Simms Hollow.

It takes about a week to get from here to where we're going. I'll send you a telegram when I get there and know which leave I get. I hope it's the first one and you can take the time off so we can be together longer.

We got to get blood tests. I know you have to wait three days after you get it before you can get married but I don't know how many days early you can get it. We need to know that cause I might can get it in Hawaii. But I really need to spend some time with my folks before we get married so we can leave after and that would give me time to get the blood test done. I know I hadn't got to worry about it like some of the other fellas might cause I hadn't been with no women. I wanted to wait for you.

I can wear whites or blues for the big day. That's up to you. I was thinking it might look striking in our wedding pictures to wear the blues with a little bit of white on them standing next to you in your white wedding gown. But if I wear the blues then my best man (Lyle) needs to wear whites or we could do it the other way around and me wear dress whites. I got them both so you decide. I got one more surprise that my uniform will tell when you see it.

Did you decide on pink for your maid of honor or did you change your mind to the blue? You talked about it but never said for sure. Can Mary still come if we get married in Georgia? I hope she can be there because Lyle sure is hankering to meet her. You gonna have any other bridesmaids? I reckon if you do I gotta have some more fellas. I hadn't rightly thought much about it but maybe my Pap could stand up with me too. I don't know if he would or not. Depends on how my Ma is doing and if she can come and he needs to sit with her instead of standing up with me. I don't know much about any of my buddies from back home where they are so I don't think I can ask any of them. And with Billy and Stuart gone, I just don't know. But what about your brother Sam. Is he still in the states?

I'll let you know soon as I can what's going on and when to expect me. That way you can set a date and get everything pulled together. You got preacher Freddie Green on the stand by? I still can't help but laugh about getting hitched by the boy who sat behind me in sixth grade. I think its swell.

I been waiting a long time to say this – <u>I'll see you soon.</u>

Loving you forever and always,
Roy

July 30, 1944
My dearest Evelyn,

We hadn't made it to Bremerton yet but we're almost there and we did the draw. I got the first leave for sure and its 25 days. If I take the plane and the train and not the train the whole way I should be able to get home in three days instead of five.

I hadn't got my blood test yet so I'll do that when I get home. I reckon I should spend about five days with my folks. We can get the blood tests at the same time together unless you want to get yours before you leave Tennessee. We got to get the marriage license anyhow at the Polk County Courthouse if we're getting married in the Simms Hollow Baptist Church.

I sure hope you get to take some time off and go back to Bremerton with me. I know you hadn't had time to tell me yet. I thought we'd just take the train all the way back to Washington. If we're together it don't really matter how long it takes. They got some sleeping compartments and maybe I can get us one of them. We can see the countryside that way too. Be one of our first trips out of all the things we're gonna see and do for the rest of our lives together. I hope that's at least 80 years or more.

They told us to send a telegram home when we get there so you'll be able to start planning. I hadn't ever been so excited.

Loving you forever and always,
Roy

WESTERN UNION
WU5 3 TOUR = SEATTLE WASH JULY 31 1944 316P
MISS EVELYN MARIE MOSELEY=
PO BOX 921 KNOXVILLE TENN=

LEAVING WASHINGTON WILL ARRIVE IN ATLANTA
WEDNESDAY LOVE = ROY

AUGUST

WESTERN UNION
WU6 7 TOUR = ATLANTA GEOR AUG 2 1944 1016P
MISS EVELYN MARIE MOSELEY=
PO BOX 921 KNOXVILLE TENN=

ARRIVING SIMMS HOLLOW THURSDAY NOON LOVE =
ROY

Blue Ridge Mountains: August 16, 1944

I did not bring this diary home with me thinking I'd have time to write or even want to. But I couldn't leave it aboard ship since I'm not supposed to be doing it and could get me in trouble if it was found. I can't let Evelyn see it cause it says stuff she can't know. But right now I'm mighty glad I got it. It helped me some times aboard ship to write down my thoughts when I couldn't sleep.

I thought when I got home to Evelyn that nothing else would matter. I wouldn't think about war nor what I did in the name of the Navy. But even with her laying next to me and breathing soft with all those red curls spread across her pillow and mine, I been having trouble sleeping. I doze off after we make love the last time for the day but not for long. Late at night here in these mountains with the windows open and the cool breeze blowing in I wake up in a cold sweat when I hear the coyote howl or the owl screech or even the woodpecker looking for food. Sounds I used to love. Now they make me think of screaming planes and bullets and bombs. I sneak out most nights but try to get back to bed before dawn so Evelyn don't know.

Yesterday when Evelyn came out on the porch with a cool glass of lemonade, the screen door slammed shut and I bout jumped off the steps where I was sitting. She didn't mean to sneak up behind me like that but I almost yelled at her for it. I wouldn't never forgive myself if I did that.

I always loved it down by a mountain stream with the water rushing over the rocks. In the early morning light the cobwebs glisten in the leaves and grass. They're as pretty as Evelyn's diamond ring. But now I see it making white water and I think about it rushing between the ships when we're fueling and how if I do one little thing wrong somebody could die when we transfer crew from ship to ship over the lines cause they got an appendicitis and need our doctors and sick bay. It ain't just the fighting that kills fellas out at sea.

At the wedding somebody planned a big fireworks celebration. It was not the right thing to do with so many military men there that been in battle way too long. I made it through but some of em didn't. I heard the noise and could see our guns blazing, shooting down planes, blowing up islands.

One night since we been here, Evelyn thought it would be fun to roast marshmallows down by the river and have a little bonfire like we used to do in high school. I told her it was alright but I didn't do so good that night trying to sleep. Those blazes took me back to the WASP sinking after it had been torpedoed and all the flames and crew trying to push burning planes off the deck to save the ship. Far away as we were, we could hear them screaming.

When we went fly fishing and caught the trout, Evelyn wanted to cook them in a pan on the stone fire pit outside so it didn't stink up the little cabin, but I made an excuse. I told her I could fry them better in the house.

We didn't get married for more than a week after I got home so I could spend some time with my folks and Evelyn could too. She hadn't been home since last Christmas. We had to get the blood tests and the marriage license and make arrangements for the picnic after. My ma was a sad sight. She tried to smile when I walked in but it didn't sparkle in her eyes the way her smile always did before. And Pap just weren't himself either. I could smell the shine on him when he came in from the barn at night.

But then I believe it was Tuesday that week when a car we didn't recognize drove up in the yard. I walked out on the porch and Pap came out of the barn cause I reckon we all expected some bad news. But it was a fine surprise. When Billy got out of that car we couldn't believe it.

We don't know if he was a POW or just lost somewhere. He was banged up pretty bad with cuts and bruises on his face and head. He was limping something fierce and his arm was in a cast but he didn't give us details and I don't know when he will. It don't matter. He stood up for me at the wedding but he didn't never smile not one time. That look in his eyes was so empty and cold and scared.

I hope he don't never have to go back. I hadn't talked to him about nothing he saw but maybe one day years away he can tell me. Or maybe what we seen and done in war best be forgot for both of us.

SEPTEMBER

September 24, 1944
My darling wife,

I don't know when I was so sad as I was to see you waving from the train as it started down the tracks. I stood there watching with the other husbands til it went so far we couldn't see it no more. When I walked away I couldn't stop the tears from running down my face. When I got on the ferry I saw I wasn't the only one. The other husbands were just as blue as me. A bunch of crying sailors heading back to their ship. But it didn't matter right then what anybody else thought about us.

I was blue from the time you started packing, but I tried not to show it too much cause I didn't want you to start worrying about me and make it all worse - if it coulda been any worse. I never thought it could hurt worse to be away from you than the last three years, but there's just no comparison to before and now. I'm so glad you could get time off and come back to Port Orchard with me or we never would have had that time to see what it was really like being husband and wife, me going off to work and you being a housewife. You're a good cook and the best wife any man could ever want.

Lyle talks to me about Mary every day. He said he wished he had got her to go ahead and marry him while he was home instead of just getting engaged. But she talked so much about how she loved our wedding and wanted one just like it that he didn't have the heart to disappoint her. Seeing as how she couldn't come back to Port Orchard with him since they weren't married he wrote to her every day. She don't tell him nothing about her job just the way you don't tell me, but she went back to work when he had to come back to the ship. It was good she had that week off and could go to South Carolina with him right after our wedding. His family really liked her and she liked them too. But I reckon she'll tell you all about it when you make it back to your apartment. He got the plane back here from Charleston and she took the train to Tennessee.

I'm back on the ship since the house in Port Orchard is just for couples, and I'm not a couple with you gone. I still get liberty every other day til the ship pulls out for good. We can stay at the 'Y' at night just to give us something different than being on the ship. I'm gonna stick close to Lyle when we go on liberty or maybe with Paul if Lyle doesn't get liberty the same as me. I like Paul. I hadn't known him very good until we got to live next to him and his wife Sue at Port Orchard. I'm glad you had her to be your friend when I was at the ship during that time.

I know if I'm with Lyle or with Paul I won't get into trouble and we can keep each other from getting ragged by some of the fellas that think they got to get drunk every time they get off the ship. We don't none of the three of us drink or smoke and I aim to keep it that way.

I know you hadn't had a chance to send me a letter yet but I'll be glad when I get one. I hope you have a good safe trip back to Tennessee.

Your loving husband,
Roy

September 28, 1944
My darling wife,

I hope by now you are back home and settling in just fine. Tell Mary that Lyle speaks of her every day. Maybe we can get this war over with and you can help her plan her wedding just like she helped you. Lyle already asked me to stand up as his best man. He said we could stay in his grandpa's cottage on the beach when we went for the wedding and could stay there long as we wanted for a visit.

We had some meatloaf at a restaurant last night but it wasn't nearly as good as that you made. They don't do much fried chicken in this area so I hadn't had none since the night you made the fried chicken and mashed potatoes and green beans. Nothing better than some good old home style cooking. I didn't know you could make such good biscuits, but they sure were delicious and I wish I had some more.

But I would rather just have you. I can never tell you enough how much I love you and there ain't no words to describe how bad I miss you. I been listening for a song that might explain it but I hadn't even heard one of them good enough to say it right.

I figured I'd tell you about how my days go when I'm on the

ship. We're getting ready to go back as soon as all the repairs are finished. That won't be long now so we been loading ammunition and supplies. That keeps me busy on the crane all day and into the night. We have to stand the night watch just to keep folks off the ship that aren't supposed to come on, but it's not like standing watch out at sea.

I love the new writing paper you gave me and that's why I'm using it. The cartoons with the song titles are swell. I'm going to be saving every bit of money I can while I'm out at sea cause when I get back home I want us to have our own house to live in and raise a family.

I talked to my Pap about a piece of land and he said if we were wanting to be farmers he had some he could spare and that old man Johnson on the next land over will probably be wanting to sell out in a few years. He don't have no kids left around that want to farm even though the land's been in the family since his granddaddy's daddy.

I'm glad you liked the horses when we went riding on our honeymoon. That was a fine horse farm. We could raise some horses and maybe some cattle, too. Have a few chickens for fresh eggs and some goats. They make fine milk, better than cows. And cheese.

You hadn't never said for sure that you will be willing to leave Tennessee and come back home to Georgia, but I figured if that job of yours is just to end the war then when I get home the war will be over and your job will be done. It would be good if you could stay at home and raise the family. But if we're farming, we can both be at home and taking care of everything together. I can't think of a finer way to do things. With all your secretary and bookkeeping smarts, you can be the brains and I'll be the brawn of the Harrison Horse Farm.

Maybe you can come up with a better name for it. Be thinking about it and the creeks and hollers and ridges and stuff around there. Maybe we could name it after one of them or one of the trees or something.

I won't have a lot of time or a lot of new stuff to say for a while but I'll do my best to write every night if it ain't nothing but just to tell you again and again how much I love you.

You were the most beautiful bride I ever saw – even better than in the magazines you had. You are the best wife I could ever dream to have.

Your loving husband,
Roy

September 30, 1944
My beautiful wife Evelyn,

I hope you hadn't been tired of getting a letter from me everyday that said the same thing over and over again about how much I love and miss you. There ain't nothing more important going on.

I'm glad to hear you're back home and settled into your apartment with Mary. So Mildred has gone back to work and there's another mother there in your neighborhood helping take care of her baby during the day so she can work. I hope she's a good mother and can take care of her own and somebody else's too. I hope you don't never have to do that after we have children. Don't forget to let me know about the monthly thing. I hope that turns out for the best.

So you say you're spending a lot of time over at Mildred's at night because you like her and you like to be around the baby girl. What did you say her name was? It's a good thing her apartment is close to yours so you don't have far to go back at night. I would worry about you more. Is the wallpaper still hanging? I'm just kidding. I'm sure if you put it up it's just fine cause you do everything the best it can be done.

So you think that when we have a family you want it to be a girl

184

first and then a boy. I was thinking the other way around. But why don't we just have one of each at the same time. You said you might could have twins. That would be good but I hope it don't happen until I get home to help you out.

It must be hard for Mildred with her husband away at sea and her having to do a job all day and come home to take care of the baby by herself. I hadn't had a chance to meet him yet, but if his destroyer is in the same task group as us when we get back to sea, I'll be sure and ask for him in port.

I'm glad you and Sally Jane got to talk when she was home for the wedding. I know you said that nary one of you could talk about your job, not to outsiders and not even to each other, but at least you know she's in the same town and you know how to contact each other now. Maybe you can do some shopping together when you go into Knoxville. It won't be that long before Christmas.

We finished loading today and are going to head out tomorrow, but we'll be taking our time down the west coast. We got to make sure the ship is fixed up right and do a lot of gunnery practice to get the crew back into shape since we been gone for a while now.

I'll write as much as I can but I don't know how much it will be. I will look forward to getting your letters and hearing how things are different now that you're a married woman.

I know for me the biggest thing is that I'm the happiest a man could ever be. The only thing that would make me happier is to be able to stay with you and not go back to war. But I'm hoping it won't take us long to get it over and done with so we can come back home for good.

So til next time, my love, sleep tight and sweet dreams (of us).

Your loving husband,
Roy

OCTOBER

October 8, 1944

My beautiful loving wife,

I can't wait til the end of each day to have time to write to you. Until we get back to the war I should have time to write a little every night. We stay busy during the day and really get tired but never too tired to talk to my loving wife.

I was in my bunk writing tonight because the library was full and they're having a movie in the mess hall. I'd rather write to you than watch a movie. Jim was in his rack writing to his wife too and we got to talking about Port Orchard and the time we got to be with our wives. It was a swell time how we got together once in a while and had a neighborhood picnic with the other couples. I hope you can stay in touch with some of the wives while we're gone. Jim has a fine looking wife but not nearly as beautiful as mine.

He told me when his wife got on the train to leave he got on with her. Theirs was a little bit later than yours. He said it was filled with Navy wives and they were all crying and carrying on. His wife too. He said he couldn't take it and he couldn't let all them wives see him crying so he had to get off the train as fast as he could. It weren't no easier for him to see her go than it was for me to let you go and they been married five years. I hope that was our last time we've got to leave each other in our whole lives. I don't want to go through it ever again.

It hadn't hardly been much more than a week now and it seems like months since I saw you and touched and kissed you and held you tight. It's been hard sleeping at night without hearing you breathing and feeling your copper curls tickling my nose when I snuggle up to your back. I hope me talking about it doesn't make you too blue. I like to close my eyes and pretend that you're here but that's not easy around a bunch of sailors snoring and all the other noise on the ship.

We got a lot of work to do tomorrow - painting and other stuff for a big inspection so I reckon I better hit the sack now and try to get some sleep. I put a picture of you under my pillow hoping to dream of you. It's the one in your two piece bathing suit. You remember how we went swimming that day and when we got back to the house I was glad we didn't have nothing on but bathing suits cause it didn't take much to get them off. That was a good afternoon. They all were.

Sleep tight and sweet dreams,
Roy

October 18, 1944
My dearest Evelyn,

I know the letters I been writing everyday don't have a lot of news in them but when I write every day I run out of things to say. The most important thing is that I love you more every day. I hope you don't get tired of hearing it.

Ever since I got back on the ship I been hungry between meals. That hadn't never happened before. I miss how we used to raid the ice box after making love and sit in the bed and eat. I been getting more ice cream down in the gedunk than I used to do but it don't taste near as good as the ice cream I ate with you. That was a swell day we walked down to the waterfront and had ice cream cones sitting under the big tree next to the water. Every day with you was swell.

Jim just came in and said I should tell you what we ate today. We had chili at chow and fried spuds and some broke up lettuce. Later we was able to get some crackers and bread and peanut butter. It tasted good. Don't know why I'm so hungry all the time now.

I thought it would get easier being away from you but it hadn't yet. I don't think I'll ever get used to being apart from you. I hope it won't be much longer we can go back to the Pacific and finish the job so we can come home.

You know that ole saying – you don't know what you got til it's gone – well that's how I feel now that we really been together. We had such a good time and the wedding was swell. So much good things to remember and think about. Blue as it makes me feel to miss it all I don't wish it hadn't ever happened. I guess what I'm trying to say is I'm lonely but I'm happy.

I finally got the allotment all worked out with the paperwork. They said you should get it the end of the month. It will be at least 100 maybe 150 .

How did you like the postcard from Long Beach, California? We were there a few days but probably gone by the time you got the card. It would be a swell place if you were here with me. I'll send a few I picked up like the one from San Diego. I like the one of the ships in the bay best. We were there but not on that postcard.

I told you about how we do the fueling. Today we tried a new way and I got stuck with the deck winch. When thing's got to going wrong, everybody cleared out and I had to figure out how to slack out the wire with the winch. I couldn't never trust it to work just right. Then the next day (yesterday) I told them somebody else could do that job today. But when the time came again I heard them saying where's Harrison. I knew what was coming. But I did it better this time because I had practice and knew how to make it work.

It would be swell if you send me that record you said and other ones too but if you can't find it that's ok. It would probably just get broke anyhow and we can't play them much. Save your money and buy something for the hope chest. I hope we can get us our own house soon as I get home.

If you want to buy the records, that's ok but keep them there.

That way when I get home we can dance in the kitchen like we did at Port Orchard. Or leave the windows open so the music pours out of the house and we can dance under the stars. When I have watch at night, I try counting the stars just to pass the time. I think of you and when we were in the mountains how the stars just felt close enough to touch. Then there was the shooting star and we made wishes. You know what mine would be.

Time for chow and we're eating fish tonight. They're pretty good most times. I'll close for now but write again tomorrow.

Your loving husband,
Roy

October 23, 1944
My Dearest Wife,

I hope you been liking the postcards from Hawaii. I thought the one with the hula girl was swell. When we go on liberty, a whole bunch of the fellas get together and the hula girls give lessons. I tried to do it but my hips don't work that way so I made a fool of myself. I probably won't try no more. Won't have the time either with us getting underway tomorrow. That means the mail won't go out or get to us like it has since we been home.

I like this piece of writing paper with the sailor and the girl making a toast. 'To you a Greeting, to the Axis a Beating.' Not soon enough for me.

I got the duty again today and was waiting for the bos'n to check the deck before I could go to chow. Then I got a couple hours before I got the watch so I thought I would try to answer some more of your letters.

I know it's foolish of me to tell you not to cry. I do it myself – that day I saw your train leave and other times when I was just thinking about how bad I miss you and wish I was home. I'm not the only one. You can see a fella just sitting off to himself all quiet and you know not to bother him cause he's thinking of home. They got water in their eyes too.

It's foolish for you to ask me if I miss our little house in Port Orchard. I miss everything about it, but I miss being with you most. I miss everything we did even if it was just sitting on the steps holding hands while the sun went down. There's some things we did I miss even more. Use your imagination.

So you almost passed out again. That don't sound good. You eating enough? You ate swell when we were together, and I don't think you ever felt like passing out one time. Or did you fool me?

I used to pray every day after we left home and got into the war. Then it got bad and busy and to where I didn't pray much. But then I did start praying to the Lord again that I could get home to you and all my dreams come true. I got to go home and we got married and I got to spend some time with you.

I been praying every night now not just to ask for things but to say thank you for all those days with you. I am asking for some things though. I want this war to be over so all us fellas can go back home safe. I ask to get back home to you and not have to leave no more. And I ask the good Lord to watch out for you and keep you safe since I can't be there to do it myself.

I know you miss me and I want to get back to you as much as you want me to come home.

Yes, I did enjoy 'Snow White' when we saw it in Seattle. It's not a movie they would show here on the ship so I was glad we got to see the new version. Remember when we first saw it? A whole bunch of us went together on Saturday morning. I was barely in high school so it musta been around '37. It was the first color movie I ever saw. Even though there was a bunch of us together you ended up sitting right by me. What were you 13 maybe? I think I fell in love with you right then and there watching you smile and cry and laugh all in one movie. I think I missed some of the movie cause I was watching you. You probably didn't know that did you?

We were in a restaurant the last night before we left California to get some dinner and there was a whole bunch of sailors in there. The waitress didn't know from nothing and she got the orders all fouled up. Then some of the fellas at our table were about finished with theirs before the other ones got theirs. And some of em been drinking and you know what happens then. Fighting. I got lucky cause I was there but I didn't get in the middle of nothing and none of the swings hit me. I didn't get to eat my food though so I was hungry. I was on liberty and didn't go back to the ship. I stayed at the 'Y' and they had some peanut butter and crackers.

I know that anniversary cards are supposed to be for years not months, but the way I figure it I saw this card and it's been two months since we got married so it was an anniversary of sorts. I like it said 'being married to you is perfectly ideal' cause it is. The only way it could be better is if I was home.

We got to eat some apples today and it made me think about the apples we got when we went horseback riding at the ranch in Washington. They were good apples. I like that horse farm even better than the one where we rode on our honeymoon. I'm glad you're thinking a horse farm might be a good thing.

That's all for now. I just about answered all your letters and won't get none for a while so I better save some to answer tomorrow. Til then I'll be loving you now and forever more.

Your loving husband,
Roy

October 31, 1944

My darling wife Evelyn,

I have time to write today. The reason is I'm in sick bay. Went down for more typhoid shots and the doctor said I had a fever. I got a bad throat. I'm trying for medical discharge, but it's not working. I was just kidding but I reckon that's not a good thing to kid about. This is not a bad place to be. I got time to write, a radio, and air conditioning.

I like this sheet of writing paper. The couple sitting on a bench holding hands and he's kissing her on the cheek. It says that song 'Don't Sit Under the Apple Tree With Anyone Else But Me.' All the songs we listened to make me blue when I hear them now and that's about every song playing.

I'm not sure if it's true but Charlie (he's another guy in my division not married so you never met him) said that he read in 'Our Navy' that once you had eighteen months out of the states you could get shore duty. I wish something like that would happen but we wouldn't have no fellas left on our ship if it did. Most of the fellas I know have all been out of the states for years before we got home this time.

I got a letter from Ma and she sure does sound better. I can hear her smiling in her words. She said Billy's been helping Pap out and things around the farm never looked better. I sure hope she stays good when he leaves again. I got a letter from Billy, too. He hadn't told Ma yet that he's got to go away again. But he hadn't got to go overseas. He hadn't said what happened when he was MIA but it was something that makes him not have to go. He'll be doing desk duty at Fort Bragg til his years are up. That's in North Carolina.

I was thinking about how many different military we had standing up at our wedding. Me and Lyle was Navy – me in my dress whites and him in his dress blues. Billy was Army. Your brother Sam was Air Force. We didn't have a Marine standing up for us, but your friend from work had a beau who was Marine so they were there, too. That about covers it all. I wish my cousin Stuart could have been there.

I was glad this was the end of the typhoid shots. They make your arm sore even when you're just writing. When I get out of here I'll be busy with fueling again and that's hard even when your arm's not sore.

There's this one fella in my division, he's been real quiet and not talking much. But we're getting to be friends now. I knew he had a daughter. I thought his wife was dead cause he never talked about her. Come to find out, he got a divorce. He's a big ole Texan but not as tough on the inside as he looks on the outside. When the war first broke out he was still stateside and working nights. Somebody gave him the word that his wife was having a visitor. One night he got a reason to go home and didn't tell her. He caught the fella right there. It was his best friend and he didn't never get over that. I feel bad for him. He's a nice fella. His Ma sends him pictures of his little girl. She's a pretty little thing with blond curls and big brown eyes.

Yes, I do believe that we can be happy forever. There's no reason we can't be.

Well, it's lights out now. Most of the fellas here in sick bay are worse off than me but I got to follow the rules anyhow.

Never forget how much I love you. I'll be home as soon as I can.

Your loving husband,
Roy

NOVEMBER

November 4, 1944
My darling wife,

I got out of sick bay yesterday after I wrote you. It's night now. I'm writing down in the mess hall next to the radio and I'm getting blue. They're playing the song 'You Are My Sunshine' and it makes me want to be with you even more. Sometimes when you get so lonely it's like you're walking around without a soul.

This place is full. All the fellas are waiting to hear Tokyo Rose, the Jap Victory girl. She speaks good English but she don't tell the truth. That's why the folks back home thought we had been sunk when we weren't. They're crazy when they lose islands and ships. She don't tell the truth about it but makes it sound like the Japanese Empire is winning when they're not.

I had fueling duty again today. Don't worry, it's the old way again. That new way was some dumb head's idea. Me and Lyle make a good team doing it the old way and got the job done.

I can't hardly hear myself think in here it's so loud. I think I'll go see if there's room in the library or maybe topside and find a better place to write. It's a nice night.

I found a good place and now I'm ready to answer some of your letters. I sure did like those pictures you sent of us in Port Orchard. I know you bound to have a lot more but I may have to wait and see some of them when I get home. They make me blue but happy too.

Some of the fellas weren't so lucky as me when they went home. There was this one fella that got married right when he got home but he had the second leave so he didn't get to bring her back to Port Orchard like us. Turns out that things weren't so peachy as he thought before he went home and married her. He got back to the ship and he had the venereal disease called the clap cause she had been with other fellas and they had it so she got it and gave it to him.

He's paying for it now. That's a painful thing. The treatment sounds real awful and painful too. Then you got to keep taking some pills if you ever want to get rid of it. The clap gives you a funny color in your skin and makes you lose weight. He hadn't been doing too good but is getting better now. I bet he will be getting a divorce too when he gets back home.

You said in your letter that you're starving for love. Me too. We can't do nothing foolish though. I can wait and I know you can too.

No, we hadn't got to worry about getting syphilis. You hadn't got it and I hadn't got it and we hadn't been with nobody else to give it to us. And we never will be so we'll be fine.

Til next time and I'll try to make that soon.

Faithfully yours,

Roy

Nov 8, 1944

My loving and faithful wife,

Last night me and Lyle had the watch together. It was the 8-12 so it was dark. The wind was blowing something fierce, worse I ever seen out here. Could be 60 knots or better. We were doing pretty good til we got hit with a big ole salty wave that wet me up to my hips and almost knocked me down. We got probably 30–40 foot seas. It started getting real bad yesterday and they think it stays this way another day at least. We're going through a typhoon.

Today we just been watching the waves and the wind. Not much more we can do but try to keep the fueling gear hooked up where it supposed to be. We might lose that battle but can't let it take us over the side if we do.

We got the election results. It was pretty close. All we want is for Roosevelt to bring us through the war safe and get us home. He needs to do it fast.

I got the wedding pictures that we had made at the photographer in town. They are swell. I got the big one hanging up in my locker so I can look at it every day.

So Mary and you been making plans for her wedding. Lyle is a lucky fella. I think Mary is a swell girl and she's pretty too - but not as pretty as my wife. I like red hair better than blonde and green eyes better than blue, but that's because it's you.

Lyle's been talking about it too. He asked me about being married and I been telling him it's the best thing I ever knew. Better even than I expected. He was glad that Mary was just as pretty and sweet in real life as she was in her pictures and letters. I was glad too. I know you said she was a real sweet person but I didn't know if they would still get along in real life. You never know. But it all turned out for the best and when we get back home you and me get to be in another wedding but this time standing up for our best friends.

Yes, I believe you would like California. On the days that the sun is shining it's nice and warm. Sometimes they have fog and rain. But the nights are nice and cool. I would like to be stationed there if you could come live there with me. Yes, I heard Florida is good too like California. I went through it so fast, I really don't know too much. I believe we would like California better if we weren't living at home.

I'll try to see 'Til We Meet Again' but it will probably be a long time before we have more movies. We're not in port anywhere anymore. It must of been a sad movie if it made you cry. Somebody leaving somebody I reckon. That sure enough will make the man and the woman cry. Jim still tells me how many weeks it's been since we left. Don't matter he's been married all them years. He wants to get back to his wife as much as I want to get back to you. We gonna be like Jim and his wife - always in love.

I saw this funny cartoon in the Saturday Evening Post. It was this girl sitting on the soldier's lap real close and she said, 'Ooh, your good conduct bar is sticking out.' Use your imagination.

You hadn't said nothing at all about your job in a long time. You still like it? You're making a lot of money and I'm doing alright, too, so we can save a lot and get us some land to build a house and a barn soon as I get home.

I've got to go take a shower now. Sorry you can't scrub my back. That would be swell. I got a three-day beard to shave off too. I never would let it get that way if I was with you because I wouldn't want to scratch your soft skin and ruin that pretty face.

That's all for now. I'm loving you now and forever.

Your faithful husband,
Roy

Nov 23, '44

My loving wife,

How is the weather in Tennessee? I bet it's cool there now and back home too. It's so hot here we can't sleep so we (me and Lyle) took our mattresses topside. Lots of fellas do it. I dreamed about you. We were laying on the beach at Port Orchard in the night air under the stars. My arm was around you and I was touching skin right out there in the open cause you had on that two piece. I was sorry to wake up.

You asked about how the mail comes to us. It's in different ways and however it can catch up to us. Sometimes it comes to a port where we go. The fellas used to go up on the beach and get it and bring it back to the ship. It can come out at sea too from a ship where we get fuel or a ship joining the force might bring it. It gets transferred in bags from one ship (mostly destroyers or cruisers deliver the mail) to the other over the lines we toss when we got to fuel. Sometimes we do crew that way too. I hadn't never missed a mail call thanks to you and all the letters and cards and packages that you send. I get something every time. We just don't have mail call as much as I want and go long times between letters then get a whole passel at one time.

I forgot to tell you last time we were in port the Hull was there too and I asked for James Malpass. It took a bit of time because I was asking after the wrong name, but a fella said he knows a Johnny Malpass and I said that's the one. I found him and told him who I was and that you're his wife's friend and neighbor. He had a swell picture of his wife holding his baby girl in his pocket. He says they go with him everywhere all the time. I believe I'll do that too with that little copy of you in your wedding gown you sent.

Today is Thanksgiving. I know you said you couldn't go home because you had to work yesterday and tomorrow so no time to travel but I hope you and Mary and Mildred and your other friends have a swell day. I hope you get to see Sally Jane too. Can you do that? Kiss that baby of Mildred's for her Pap. He sure does want to get home bad as me because he's got two of the best girls waiting for him. He's a fine fella.

We had a good chow – turkey and dressing, spuds, cranberries, beans, buns, pie and ice cream. Woulda been better if it was you and me doing the cooking and the eating in our own house. I hope we have a table big enough we can invite my family and yours and they can all come to our house on the horse farm for Thanksgiving. That would give our Mas a break. I bet I could help you cook. And you already said I'm good at drying the dishes. Heck I didn't even mind that part when we were in Port Orchard cause we were in that little house and it was like it was ours. Dish time was a mighty fine time to talk about our dreams – not the night ones but the daytime ones when they're really wishes.

No I hadn't got the cookies yet. It's been five or six weeks since you sent them. Maybe some other fella got them and ate them all.

I saw Jim today and he said it's the 23rd you know what that means. He don't ever let it pass by weeks and specially not months. It's been exactly two months today since we put our wives on a train and hadn't seen them no more. Shows me he thinks about her all the time just like I think about you.

You said Mildred's husband told her about getting a certificate for crossing the equator. I woulda told you but I thought it would get cut out by the censors and I know you don't like getting letters with holes in it. Sometimes there's a party too depending on where you are and what's going on. It's not just any kind of party but a special one. You get a certificate for crossing the international date line too. That makes you have two days with the same date. If you go back and forth in that one spot you get your dates all messed up and don't know what's what.

I've got a lot to be Thankful for and the best one is you.

All my love forever,

Roy

Nov 28, '44

My dearest wife,

I hadn't ever got a letter like the one I got today. You sure know how to surprise a guy. You started out making a Thanksgiving list and it was all the things I would think about being thankful for -

#1 - being married to you

Then you said all those other ones like a good job and food to eat and friends and a warm place to live and all that, but when you got to #10 I bout lost my socks with shock.

#10 – I am thankful to be having a baby

I never been so surprised and happy and scared all at the same time. We got to get this war over with so I can get home to you and be there when he's born. Or I reckon it could be a her. I don't want you to do it alone.

How are you feeling? Do you get the morning sickness? You been fainting anymore? Don't being in the family way make you faint sometimes and you already been doing that so does it make it worse?

So the doctor said the baby will probably be born in June. You really think we made a baby that last night when we stayed awake all night before you got on the train? That was a swell night. I can remember every minute of holding you and loving you. And eating ice cream in bed. That was a perfect night and this is going to be a perfect baby.

I'll do my best to get home as soon as I can. I can't think of nothing else to write right now. Heck, I can't even think straight at all. Maybe I can think again tomorrow.

I gotta tell the fellas now. You just made me the happiest man in the world.

With all my love forever,

Roy

Out in the Ocean somewhere: November 30, 1944

Well November has been a month like I never had before and for most never want to see it again. The good thing is I'm going to be a Pap but I'm real worried I won't get home in time or won't get home at all. I don't tell Evelyn that because I don't want to worry her but things are getting worse out here. If it ain't the Japs it's the weather. I never saw nothing like the typhoon with waves so big they wash over the bow. Other ships are pure hidden when they go down into the spots between waves 40 and 60 feet high.

We didn't lose anybody yet but the other ships did. Fellas got washed right over the side the waves were so big when they hit the ship. But it ain't just the weather.

We've been taking back islands and making safe places for the force to go back and refuel and get provisions – food and oil and ammunition – and we hadn't never had any problems cause we took the islands back from the enemy before we ever stopped there. Ulithi was the last one where we were. But one night a submarine snuck in the port and shot a torpedo right into a tanker. It sank and 50 of its crew died right there in our safe spot. Ain't nowhere safe now.

We've been fighting at Leyte trying to stop the Japanese from being able to ship supplies. Then at Luzon they started something we hadn't ever seen before. Those Japanese pilots weren't just flying by and shooting at us. They would shoot til they ran out of ammunition and then they would just use their plane like a torpedo from the sky and fly right straight into the ships, blowing up and starting fires and killing people. We didn't get hit and we shot a bunch of em down before they could hit the ships but a lot of sailors died on other ships. I heard tell there was 50 here and 30 there and more somewhere else. Probably 100 in all or maybe more, I don't know for sure.

We been refueling ourselves then fueling other ships all the while the flags flying at half-mast to honor the dead. They might not have been on our ship but they're still in our group. Way I see it that makes them family. We are responsible for keeping them safe. It hurts when any of em don't make it. And it's scary too cause it could just as well been our ship, our crew, me and my buddies.

I used to worry about getting killed and not making it back home to Evelyn. Now I worry I might not ever see my kid either. I hoped we wouldn't have babies til after I got home from the war but Evelyn said that she wanted to have a baby. That way if something happened to me and I didn't make it home she would always have a part of me with her. I don't want Evelyn to have to be a Ma all by herself. I just gotta get home soon.

DECEMBER

December 1, 1944
My darling wife,

Well this is the month of Christmas and it looks like it will be another one away from home. My 4th one. Don't forget to put my name next to yours on the Christmas cards you send out.

How you feeling? Do you get sick or tired during the day? Some of the other fellas been telling me about when their wife was expecting and how all she wanted to do at first was sleep and puke. I hope you don't feel that way especially since you have to go to work. You don't have to, you know. I been making good money. I can make my allotment bigger. I don't really need money here because they give me everything I need. Except you. You could go back home and live with your Ma and Pap or my folks and sleep in my old bed. You wouldn't have to do the job every day. Then when I get home we can have our own place.

I got eight letters from you yesterday and one had the end burnt. They told us some mail got on fire at a post office and some were burnt completely up. I hope none of them were yours.

We get free haircuts now. We had been having to pay for them all this time so that's just a little bit more money I can save for our horse farm. I figure depending on how long we're out here, my not having to pay for haircuts could save enough to buy a horse. Or I can just send it home to you so you can rest and take care of having a baby.

There's something I forgot to tell you about crossing the equator. If you ever see a fella at the beach and he's barefooted look at the top of his feet. If he got a chicken tattoo or a pig then he crossed the equator or the international date line. One's for one thing and the other for another but I can't remember which. You hadn't got to do it and I won't so don't worry. I watched a fella get a chicken. That top part of the foot is mighty tender and he was sweating and making faces the whole time he got it.

I'll try to write as much as I can tonight cause tomorrow I have the boatswain mate watch and won't have time for much of anything else.

You got five letters from me. There might be more out there that hadn't got to you yet. I been trying to write every day when I get the chance. Some are short but I been making some of them plenty long too.

What do you mean you wish they wouldn't have so many cartoons before the movies? Sometimes that's the best part. I like the rabbit best. He's always saying 'What's cooking doc?' After we had a movie the other night – it was a western, 'Roy Rogers' – it had the rabbit cartoon and we went to chow a bunch of us fellas were in the line saying it over and over again. Some fellas didn't think it was too funny though.

The needles ain't too bad just make your arm sore and when you got to get one in both arms that makes it hard to work. It's best to use your arm and work your fingers in a fist to help keep it from getting so sore. Some fellas get fevers but I didn't except when I had the bad throat. If they keep away all the stuff they're for, like typhoid fever, then I say shoot away.

That's all for now. Hope to get more letters soon. Take good care of both my babies – the grown up one (you) and the little one. I love both of you very much.

Proud to be your husband,
Roy

December 7, 1944

My darling wife,

Today is the day that started all this madness. Pearl Harbor. I wished today was the day we could end this war and start going back home. That would be fitting.

Some fellas don't wear their wedding ring because they say it bothers them when they're working but mine don't bother me none at all. I want to wear it because you gave it to me and it means I am yours. Even if I took it off it would look like I got it on. My hands are tanned from being out in the sun all the time. When I slide the ring a little bit one way or the other you can see a white skin ring in its place.

We got mail today but let me tell you how messed up it is. We got about 80 bags aboard of mail and cards and packages and I didn't get one package so you're going to be mad that it hadn't got here yet. We'll be leaving soon so I don't know when I'll get it. Might be after Christmas but that'll be alright I reckon. I did get letters and I'm always glad to get them so that's something.

When you get all my letters there will be one date missing. That night I didn't write to you. I should have taken the time but I was doing V-Mail Christmas cards for Ma and Pap, and Sally Jane, and Billy, and my aunt and uncle that was Stuart's Ma and Pap. You met them at the wedding. There weren't nobody else I needed to send one too since you're putting me on all the ones you're sending and you're doing so many even to people I don't know but that's alright cause we're a team. Maybe I will get to meet some of your friends one day since they couldn't leave work in Tennessee to come to the wedding.

I saw a movie last night. The short one was 'Donald Duck' and it was a good one. The long one was 'What a Night' and I didn't care much for it. It was about a bunch of diamond crooks. I like the flag waving movies the best.

So you got the 'Give My Regards to Broadway' record and it's got some good songs on it. What kind of song is 'Don't Fence Me In?' I reckon I would like to be fenced in somewhere with you for a long time where nobody could get in and we'd be all by ourselves doing just what we wanted.

I won't get to send you much present for Christmas. We hadn't been where I could get something good but I'll put a little something in the mail before we go out again. Don't you worry about sending me nothing. Just save your money. Me and Lyle and Jim ate all the fruit cake. It was good and it survived the trip better than some of the other things like cookies and candy and even the gum was melted last time.

So you been thinking about names for a girl. I like all the ones on your list but 'Ellie' isn't there. I like that one, don't you? You hadn't said names for a boy. It could be one but we don't want to call him Roy, Jr. We both got good middle names. Maybe we could use that.

That Tokyo Rose is a nut. I told you not to listen or believe anything she says. She's telling about ships they sunk and planes that got shot down and stuff that ain't happening to the Americans. So if you ever hear it don't believe it and worry yourself over nothing. I think she said we been sunk four or five times already. She dares us to put down our guns and go home. She's crazy.

The music's playing now and its 'The Way You Look Tonight.' That brings water in my eyes thinking about you. I'm in the mess hall with a bunch more fellas so I got to be careful.

That's just the way it was for me when I got the wedding pictures too. I'm glad they made it back to you safe even if it did make you cry to see them again. Don't be too sad. We're both working to make this war end and then I'll be home and we can make up for all the time we lost with me not there.

Well, I better close for now. I still got to do my laundry and I got the watch later on.

Always loving you,
Roy

Dec 14, '44
My darling wife,

I had to start this letter three times before I just had to overhaul my pen. I been using it so much it's not working too good. But I got it back together and doing better now. I had to wash it out real good with hot water. I switched back to the blue ink too. Works better than the black.

We got mail yesterday. Nothing like getting mail at sea. Remember I told you that happens sometimes when we're fueling other ships. Sure does make a fella's day better when he gets a letter from home.

You notice the dates on my envelopes? I had a hard time keeping your letters straight and I like to read them in the right order. So I took to writing dates on the back of the envelope that's the same as the date on the letter. Cause sometimes the letters all go out in one bunch with the same postmark and you don't know which one I wrote first. I get them from you that way too so if you write a date on the outside of the envelope I can figure out which one to read first when I get a whole bunch like I did today.

They're playing Christmas songs on the radio now. Not but a few days away. I hope you have a good one and get to go home and see both families. They're gonna be real surprised since you hadn't told them about the baby yet. I hadn't told nobody back home because you said you wanted to make a big deal about the surprise and that's a good idea. I sure wish I could be there and us do it together.

That picture you sent me standing sideways and holding your dress close to your middle was swell. Yes I think I could see that little bit of bump you're talking about but I don't believe it's enough anybody will notice unless you tell them. That's your Christmas surprise? How do you plan to do it?

I just had to stop writing to listen to 'Together.' That's a swell song and it's what I want us to be real soon.

I got the watch so I'll close for now. Loving you and our baby more and more everyday. I'll do my best to be home before the baby comes. I hadn't never seen a baby person born outright but I seen a calf and a colt and I know it's got to hurt the mama. I don't want you to go through no hurt, but that's a swell thing between a Ma and her baby right off when it ain't but a few seconds old. You're going to be a good Ma even if I'm not there. But I want to be. I will try.

All my love,
Roy

Pacific Ocean: December 20, 1944

It's been a bad few days and I hadn't wrote home at all. I reckon I better do that later but right now I got to get all these things out of my head and down on the paper so my letters home don't have no sign of what we been through the last few days. It's been a storm like I never seen before and hope to God that I never see again in my life. It was worse than some of the fighting we been doing and that's about as bad as it gets.

At night the stars are out now and the seas pretty calm but I swear we still think we hear sailors screaming for help. There's been a lot of sharks swimming all around the ships. I reckon they figure they can get a free meal without working too hard for it. I hope we got all the live ones out before the sharks started their Christmas dinner.

I better start from the beginning or nobody ever reading this will know what I'm talking about.

Back about a month ago we run into a storm. Lyle said back home on the coast they call them hurricanes. Out here they call them typhoons. When you're out in the ocean the wind whips the waves up so bad they come washing over the bow of the ship big as it is. The waters rough and got big swells so the ship rises up on the swell then drops down in the trough and the water washes over the bow. Thought that other one was bad enough but it was nothing.

It was about four days ago the weather started to get real bad and they told us to prepare for fueling everybody but especially the tin cans. The big ships like us can do pretty good cause we got a lot of fuel to last us plenty of days. And that goes for the other big ones too like the carriers and even the cruisers are not bad. But the destroyers - that's the tin cans - they don't carry much fuel because they are little and have to travel fast. Bad thing is we gotta fuel them every few days. Well, the last few days before the weather started, we'd been fighting at Luzon and it's probably been four days since we fueled them. So they were about empty.

About three days ago, the force started pulling away from the fighting so we could do some fueling. The storm was getting bad and if the tin cans run out of fuel they got no way to stay upright in the water. So there's this big line of ships waiting to fuel. We mostly just do one side at the time cause you got to keep going and the ships have to stay the same distance apart so they don't run into each other by getting too close or break the fuel lines by getting too far away. It's hard enough when the seas aren't bad and we're just doing one side.

Here's the way it works. We got to take all the fueling hoses down from where they're stored. Then we take the lifelines down from the stanchions on the side of the ship. Nothing between us and falling in the ocean. You lose your balance and you're shark bait, especially if you hit your head up against the ship on the way down. Then we have to shoot a line across to the boat we're gonna fuel and they secure it over there. Then we run the fuel hoses over that line. All this time we keep on going cause we can't stop in the ocean. If we did, there wouldn't be any way to keep the ships the right distance apart and we'd be too good a target for torpedos.

We'd been fueling for more than two hours when the SPENCE pulled alongside on our side of the ship. My buddy Alfred from back home was on the SPENCE and he helped with the fueling detail just like me. We've been seeing each other some when we were in port and that's good catching up about back home. Well he was working on his side and I was on mine. We couldn't let go of nothing to wave cause the wind and the rain and the waves were so bad. We just nodded to each other and kept doing the job. Next thing I know this great big wave washes over the side of the SPENCE and takes him right away. When the water disappeared he wasn't standing there no more. He was just gone. Weren't nothing me nor anybody else could do to help him but pray he drowns before the sharks got him.

About that time they called off all the fueling because the weather's too bad to risk it. I looked at that line of tin cans still waiting to fuel and I got right sick to my stomach thinking what's probably going to happen. The next in line was the HULL where Evelyn's friend Mildred's husband was aboard. I just hoped and prayed they weren't that low on fuel that they couldn't make it through ok. We had to send them away.

We couldn't just leave all the fuel hoses laying around on deck so we had to start storing them and securing them down best we could. Lyle and me were doing our best to get one of the hoses in the place where it was supposed to be. It's pouring down rain and the winds whipping us every which a way. Then this big wave came washing over the side of the ship. It had to be six foot higher than the deck because it was over Lyle's head and he's a big guy. Knocked him down and I saw him washing away. Next thing I know I'm going down the fantail too.

I thought for sure I was a goner. I just prayed to God to save me so Evelyn wouldn't have to go with no husband and that baby with no Pap. I grabbed out for anything I could get and caught hold of the splinter screen around one of the 20s. Looked up and saw Lyle with both legs and arms round one of the stanchions. We had to both hold on while another wave came over the side and washed down the deck then we scrambled fast as we could and went below deck before we got washed all the way over.

Down in the mess hall all my crew was accounted for and we didn't get word of anybody from the NC getting washed overboard, but the ship started rolling. This a big ship to roll but stuff was sliding across the mess hall deck and off the tables. Had to put everything away and wait it out. Weren't nothing more we could do. You could feel it roll one way and you would wonder how far it was going to go and would it ever straighten back up again. Then it would but she would roll again and even more over to the side the next time and you're just waiting for it to keep going over. But it didn't.

My left hand was banged up pretty bad from where I grabbed hold of that metal screen. It was bleeding a bit too so I got sent down to sick bay when they were checking on everybody that had been topside when it got so bad. Down in sick bay they had to cut my ring off my finger because it swelled up so bad. They didn't throw it away so I got to put it in my locker. Gonna see if I can get it sautered back together or something. I got blasted for wearing it.

Lyle had to go to sick bay too but he was just mostly bruised and scratched up on his legs and arms. Had a gash on his face too where it hit the stanchion when he caught hold. He said his man parts was hurting something fierce but leastways he didn't go over the side. He made a joke about it saying he sure hoped it would work right when he got to go home and marry Mary. He worried about having kids too. You don't never know about those things.

There were other fellas banged up a lot worse – cut faces and broken bones – so the sick bay was real busy and we got to leave pretty fast. Weren't nothing to do while we were waiting it out but go somewhere safe and stay til we got word to do something else. I should of wrote to Evelyn while I wasn't doing nothing else but I just couldn't get my mind off Alfred long enough to make my words sound right. I might just write a bunch for those days later and put the dates on them so she thinks I wrote every day. Didn't think I'd ever do something like that – kinda dishonest - but drastic times call for drastic measures.

Well the next day we got word that the HULL and the SPENCE and the MONAGHAN all sunk. They ran out of fuel and couldn't make it in the storm. That makes me feel mighty bad that we didn't do what we needed to do to help save them. I couldn't have done any more for Alfred once I saw him wash over the side. But all the rest of his buddies might of been saved if we finished fueling them.

And we never even got to the HULL. It was right there waiting and we started taking in the fuel lines before they could pull alongside showing them we weren't going to do nothing for them. How will I ever look at Mildred's face when we get home and I get to meet her? She was one of my wife's best friends and she's got a baby girl that might not have a Pap no more. I didn't do nothing to save him.

Yesterday when the storm got better we refueled everybody then turned around and started back trying to find anybody who might still be alive. Instead of being the circled up groups like we usually are, the ships all made a big line and it backed out like a bow. It was like a net made of our ships trying to catch anybody still there. There was bodies floating everywhere and you could see the sharks circling in. All in all about 30 off the HULL were rescued. I don't know if any of them was Johnny Malpass, but I sure hope it was. I can't ask Evelyn right out but maybe I can find out somehow. If he's safe it sure ain't because of nothing I did to save him.

Dec 17, '44

My dearest Evelyn,

I already answered all your letters and I hadn't got anymore today so I'm trying to find something to write about. Not much going on here. We got some bad weather like we had back last month. The winds pretty bad so I'm writing down in the library.

I know my letter of December 12 said Happy Anniversary, but I'm feeling bad cause I didn't get to send you a card. There just wasn't a way to get one. We been married four months now. In about six more months we're gonna be a Ma and a Pap. I sure hope I make it home in time.

I know you're planning on telling everybody when you go back home for Christmas. I'll be glad when you do cause then I can brag about it in my letters. It's been real hard not letting the cat out of the bag.

What color do you think would be good for a baby's room? I know we hadn't got a house yet but I hope to have one soon after I get home. I reckon it will make a difference if it's a boy or girl cause you can't use pink for a boy's room.

There's some colors like green or yellow that you could use for both I reckon but maybe we better wait and do that after I get home. I don't want you climbing on no ladders hanging wallpaper or painting right now.

Have you been to see Mildred and her baby lately? How are they getting along? I believe you said she was from Tennessee. Does she have folks close by to where you're living and working? I bet she gets letters from Johnny about as often as you get letters from me. But they come in bunches with lots of time between them sometimes. That don't mean somethings wrong so you and her don't need to worry when you don't hear for a while.

It's about time for chow so I gotta close for now.

I will always love you,

Roy

Dec. 18, '44

My darling wife,

Still no new mail so I haven't much to write about. Everything here is swell. I hadn't done much today but try to stand up. The sea's still pretty rough from the storm.

It won't be long before Christmas now so I reckon you'll be headed back home pretty soon. You got to let me know how that goes and what everybody does and says when they hear about the baby we're gonna have. I bet they will want you to come on home and take good care of yourself and the baby. That's probably not a bad idea.

I had a little accident and hurt my finger so I had to take my ring off til the swelling goes down. We're not really supposed to be wearing them just for that reason so I might just put it in my special box in my locker for awhile. That's the box with your red curl in it from where you cut your hair a bit and sent it to me in a Valentine Card. I got my lucky penny we found at Port Orchard in there and it's about the same color as your curl.

Well, there's not much going on so I haven't much to write. Tell Mary I said hello and give her my best regards. And Mildred too.

Don't ever forget how much I love you. Sorry for the shortness of the letter, but I got some chores to do before chow.

Your loving and faithful husband,

Roy

December 19, 1944

Dearest Evelyn,

Still no mail from you. Not much news to share. You asked me one time if I ever saw any sea creatures and I don't think I ever answered you about that. Sometimes we see fish jumping out of the water.

When we're in port and get to go on the beach we see crabs and things like that. Sea birds flying close to shore and sometimes so far out in the ocean that it makes you surprised. I hope that answers your question. Today we saw some shark fins but most of the time we're too busy to look in the water for anything.

I been looking through some old letters trying to find something I hadn't checked off as being answered. That about the sea creatures was one of them.

There's not much else I hadn't already answered. I know you're wondering when I'm going to get your package and I don't know when we'll get a chance to get mail call. It won't be today for sure, but maybe if we get back to some port before Christmas we might get some mail then. And maybe I'll get a chance to get you something to mail even though it won't get there before Christmas. Maybe it gets there before New Year's Day.

So our baby's birthday will be sometime in 1945, probably June. Well, mine's in March and yours is in October so that puts the baby right in the middle.

When did you say Mildred's baby has a birthday? Just wondering if they'll be close enough together to be friends and play.

I wished I had got to meet her since she's your friend. I think your friend Mary's a fine person. Lyle sure does, too.

I got some work to do, so I'll sign off for now.

Loving you always,

Roy

December 20, 1944

My dear wife,

Well it's not long before Christmas now. I hope you have your shopping all done and didn't spend too much money. We gotta keep saving up to get our farm and house. I was thinking that big old tree down near the river would make a fine place to hang an ole tire for the baby to swing on when it got a bit bigger. I might could make something different for a swing when he's still too little for the tire. Maybe a basket swing or something like that.

I remembered something you said I hadn't never answered. You said you're taking an interest in the war and been reading the papers and the magazines every chance you get. You read one about the B29s bombing Tokyo. I'm glad they're doing that. I'm sure it won't be the last time.

Tell me about anything you read in the papers about the war and send me some clippings sometime. Since Billy went missing and then came home and had to leave again, my Ma don't read the paper too much and don't send me things like that. I know I said one time I didn't want any papers but I'm hoping it might have some good news soon. This war's just got to be about over.

There's a fella playing a record by Frankie called 'Come Out.' I'm sure you like that one because you and your friends like anything your 'Frankie' sings. I still don't know what's so hot about Frank Sinatra and why all the girls think he's the best thing since fresh molasses on hot biscuits.

There's Christmas songs playing now and a couple of the guys singing along over our PA system (that stands for Public Announcement) and that means everybody can hear them. I guess it really is just about Christmas. I wonder if it will be my last one away from home. Four is enough.

That's about it for now.

Loving you always and Forever,

Roy

Christmas Day, 1944

My dearest wife,

Merry Christmas Darling. I am so sorry that you have to spend your first Christmas as a married woman without your husband. That goes for me too. I would want to spend every Christmas with my wife and never be away from you. I will be sore if we don't end this war and I miss the first Christmas with our baby.

We got the best present ever today – a whole bunch of mail bags. I reckon Santa Claus didn't forget about us sailors out here after all. I got to help deliver the bags since I had the boat today. I told you I got it back right? I expect I'll have to go out and take the captain somewhere too. There's a lot of ships here and that usually means he has to go see the other captains. But maybe tomorrow.

I didn't get any packages from you yet, but I did get nine letters and three cards. The cards were swell. I hadn't had time to read the letters yet but I'm going to the noon meal now and can read while I eat. Or maybe after. It won't be much for lunch because we're having the big meal tonight.

Ok, I'm back. It didn't take long. Just some sandwiches and fruit. Your first letter starts out telling me how many days we've been apart before and after we got married. That letter was dated Nov 15 so it's got a lot more days on the married number now. There ain't much I can say about it except it makes me just as sad and lonely as it makes you.

We got a menu when we went to lunch so we know what's for supper tonight. I told you they feed us good.

We're having mixed olives, mixed sweet pickles, cream of pea soup, croutons, roast young turkey, applesauce bread dressing, whipped potatoes, giblet gravy, cranberry sauce, English peas, buttered asparagus, fresh carrot & pineapple salad, Parker House rolls, butter, nut pound cake, hard mixed candy, shelled mixed nuts, ice cream, coffee, cigars and cigarettes.

The menu was made like a card and on the front it says Merry

Christmas, Seasons Greetings, and Happy New Year. It's got a cross on it and a picture of the U.S.S. North Carolina and the date. I'll send it to you in another letter. I want to keep it a little while longer to make me remember how lucky we are instead of like the Army and Marines that no telling where they are or what they're eating for Christmas dinner.

Let me know when you get my letters and what kind of letters Mildred is getting from her husband Johnny. I reckon you girls share how many letters you get every time – not what's in them but just that you got them. I know mine and Lyle's probably come to you and Mary about the same time but I wondered about Johnny's if they come about the same time too.

Well that's about all for now so I'll close with a great big MERRY CHRISTMAS and HAPPY NEW YEAR!!! I love you and our baby more than you will ever know so don't ever forget it. Let me know how the surprise went today.

Your loving husband,

Roy

December 31, 1944

My dearest wife Evelyn,

So I'm hoping to get a letter from you soon that tells me all about the surprise you had for our folks at Christmas. I hadn't got a letter about it from anybody else yet either but I hope it won't be long now. This is the last day of the year and I hadn't told nobody at home that I'm going to be a Pap. I'm ready to talk about it to everybody all the time.

So you've been expecting three whole months now. Are you feeling any better or are you still puking your brains out every morning like you said? I hope you hadn't fainted no more since those two times. That falling around could be dangerous for you and the baby. I hope you're feeling all better now in every way.

I got to listen to the Hit Parade today but I don't know how old it was. They weren't talking about it being time for a new year so it might be real old. I was sitting on the hatch watching a couple of seamen making up the fueling gear and making sure they did it all just right. I heard the fella say 'your number three song is' so I started listening real good.

The number 3 song was 'Time Waits for No One.' The second one was 'Swinging on a Star' for number 2 song. And the last one he did was the number one song and it was 'I'll Walk Alone' that is something I don't want to do. How old was that Hit Parade?

I finally got the package from you and it was all great stuff. I especially liked the baseball bat and the cookies. Thanks for everything. You're a wonderful wife.

Today I've got to do work duty cleaning up the stations but I got some good fellas helping me out so it probably won't take that long. You said in one of your last letters that you wanted me to tell you some jokes. Well I hadn't got any good ones that ain't bad (dirty). But you asked for it so here goes.

There was this Honeymoon Hotel where everybody staying there was newlywed couples (like us). Two men were sitting down in the bar next to the lobby. One of them said, 'Where is your wife?' and the other one answered, 'She's upstairs smoking.' The other one said back, 'That musta been something. Mine's hot, too, but she ain't smoking.'

I told you it was dirty. Here's the other one.

There was these three old maids who lived in the same house. One day they came home to find out they been robbed. So they decided to try to find the crook and each started looking in her own room. The first one said, 'He's not in here.' Then the second one said, 'He's not in here either.' Then the third one said, 'Goodnight girls.'

I reckon it's time to sign off for the year. It hadn't been too bad a year but I hope the next one is the one when I get to come home to stay for good.

Beautiful wife – Wonderful life.

Happy New Year!
Roy

Leaving Ulithi: December 31, 1944

We've been in port at Ulithi ever since the day before Christmas. It wasn't too bad a Christmas except for all that happened right before and us not being able to go home.

But we're making the best of it. I'm glad I got the boat again. I been having to take it out a lot and I never saw so many ships in one place. I heard tell that on our way back here since we were traveling in a straight line and not in groups that the whole bunch of us stretched for five miles long. Now we're in port and there's ships everywhere you can look.

We had Christmas music all over the radio and the PA. The 'Washington' spelled out Merry Christmas on her foremast with the signal flags. Of course we had a good Christmas dinner. We got some shore liberties with plenty of beer and baseball games. Evelyn sent me a baseball bat as part of my present. I ain't on the baseball team and don't want to be but it is fun for some of us fellas just to get out and hit and catch a few balls. I don't like the hot beer too much but I had a few anyhow to celebrate getting through all we got through this year.

Now if I could just find something that would help keep away the nightmares I might be alright.

We been doing a lot of loading up ammunition and stores of food and stuff so I know it won't be long before we're back at it again. We got a special message from Admiral Halsey today. He said, 'This is the Aztec himself. I wish you all a happy and prosperous New Year. All I can say is - Give the bastards hell.'

I reckon if we can do that, we might just get it finished and get home for good in the year 1945. That would sure be swell.

1945

JANUARY

January 1, 1945
My darling wife,

You know how in church the preacher would always say that we should claim victory and believe and God would grant it to us? Well, like I told you before I been praying a lot more and better than I did for a while. I got so much to be thankful for with you and the baby and so much to ask God for to keep you both safe and get me back home to you and our baby.

Well, I decided that I'm going to claim that 1945 is the year of victory and I will be coming home. You can claim it too. It won't hurt to have more than one person doing it. Maybe I'll write home and tell everybody else to claim it too. I don't know why I didn't think of that sooner.

I got your letter about you telling the folks and the family about our baby. I knew they would be surprised. I didn't know my Ma would cry. They were happy tears though and I reckon she hadn't had many of them since that day Billy got out of the car nobody recognized and surprised everybody by being alive.

I wrote a bunch of letters since you told me I could tell about the baby to folks back home. I know you already told Sally Jane but I sent her a letter in Tennessee and called her 'Aunt Sally.' Told her she better get her diaper changing skills ready cause you might need some help right at first. We might even want to go out to a movie by ourselves when the baby gets a bit bigger. But that won't be til later for sure. Once I get home I don't want to be no further away from either one of you than I have to for any length of time. I sent one to Billy in North Carolina too. I was glad to hear that he got to take a leave for Christmas. I was the only one of the whole family not there.

I'll be waiting to see pictures that you took at Christmas. I had a lot I wanted to write about but now it's gone out of my head. I'm in the library and it's so loud in here I can't think. The radio is on. There's guys talking about women. There's this one fella across the table from me trying to draw a nude woman. One fella is writing a letter and he don't know how to spell nothing so he keeps asking everybody how do you spell this and how do you spell that. Then there's two other fellas playing the loudest game of checkers I ever heard.

I got the watch soon anyhow so I'll close for now.

Happy New Year my love!

Roy

January 5, 1945

My darling wife,

Had fueling duty today and one of the tin cans brought us some bags of mail. We brought the mail over the line then sent them back a big ole can of ice cream to thank them for the mail. I got a package from you and it was a great big hit. All the fellas wanted to see what was in it and I decided to share some of the candy you sent. The hard candy wasn't too big a hit but the lollipops were and so were the caramels. They hold up better than chocolate in the heat. I'm glad you sent me some more pictures.

This letter I got today you wrote after you left my Ma and Pap's at Christmas. You hadn't told me in the first letter that my Ma said you were too fat to be having a baby next summer. I know that hurt your feelings especially because you always tried to stay skinnier than anybody else. She shouldn't have said it. Maybe we're just going to have a big ole baby boy. You hadn't got to listen to what she says when she hurts your feelings.

So you been looking at pictures of Mildred when she was about three months expecting and you think you're bigger too. What did Mildred say? I like the picture you sent me and I don't think you look fat at all. I'm sorry your clothes don't fit anymore.

I got pay today and I'll buy a money order and send some extra home so you can go shopping. I'm glad Mildred's going to let you borrow some of her clothes she had before her baby came but you need to buy you some of your own too that are just like you want them.

You said you been staying over at Mildred's a lot since you got back from Christmas. She hadn't got no letters from Johnny lately. I bet it's just because they didn't go out when he needed to send them or they could've got lost on a ship taking them somewhere. That happens sometimes and when you don't get mail it don't have to mean something's wrong. Til somebody comes knocking on your door don't ever think there's something wrong.

I'm glad getting mail from me makes you happy. That's the way I feel too. It's the best we can do since we can't see each other. I like it when you tell me what you been doing during the day and what you're wearing when you go to bed. You like gowns better than pajamas. I like gowns too but you don't have to wear them when I come home unless you just want to. I like the PJs and gowns that stay on the foot of the bed the best.

This last letter makes me very happy. You hadn't said yes or no about wanting a horse farm and I been doing all the talking about it but you sent me the best picture of one that you think ours ought to look like.

So you like the Appaloosa and the black and white horse the best. That one that's almost all black looks like it might be a Tennessee Walker. They're supposed to be good horses for ladies to ride because they don't bump you so bad when they run. We might have to choose one kind of horse to raise though so we're making the best stock around.

That makes me happy you said every little girl needs a pony. We're going to have a happy family and I can't wait to get home.

You hadn't said nothing more about your job. Is everything going alright with it? Sally Jane don't tell me anything about it in her letters either except that she's making real good money and the job ain't too hard. She says they're working to end the war and that's all they can say about anything.

So you never seen a fella with a pig or a chicken on his foot. Well you might sometime in the summer so now you know why. Most times they get them in Pearl. I didn't ever get one and don't plan to so you don't have to look at my feet when I get home.

I love you always and forever.

> Your faithful husband,
> Roy

South China Sea: January 12, 1945

Last I heard from Evelyn nobody told Mildred her husband got killed. She's still waiting for letters from him that probably won't ever come. She probably knows by now but Evelyn hadn't had time to send me the news. I can't tell her but best I know from everything I heard nobody survived on the Hull. The fellas rescued were all on the Spence. I know Evelyn's gonna want to be there to help Mildred through it but I hope she don't wear herself out.

I worry about her already – working all day on her own without nobody to help take care of her. At least I got Lyle to write to Mary and see how she's really doing. Mary's her friend so she might not be telling us what Evelyn don't want me to know, but she said she's feeling better now and not puking all the time.

Mary told Lyle she was trying to do more around the apartment than Evelyn so she can get some rest. They're both exhausted when they get home from work in the evenings. She doesn't tell him anything about her job either except they're real busy all the time and it's important work they can't talk about. I just can't imagine what it is that they're doing that could be such a big secret.

We got important work to do too. We've been making strikes on Formosa and Okinawa. Then more strikes on Luzon. We been fighting the weather almost every day too, but nothing like it was before Christmas. I hope I never see that again.

A few days ago we got a message from Admiral Halsey. It came over the TBS radio then the fella down in the print shop made us all a copy in case we didn't remember what he said. Here's what Halsey said to us all. We didn't know how bad it was at Luzon til we heard this.

'Luzon is now a bloody battleground. The enemy is now fighting to the death to stop our expeditionary forces and troops. Many of our ships have been hit hard in the past two days. Every undestroyed enemy plane is potential death to many of our comrades. This is the time for great effort. Give the best and God Bless you.'

Today we got this message from Admiral Nimitz over the TBS. 'God seems to have given us good weather and a chance of a big bag of the season. Give them the kitchen sink.'

I sure hope he's right about the weather. All I know is we're gonna need all the blessings, good weather, and luck we can get.

January 17, 1945

My darling wife,

I saw in our press news where the Navy released information about the Spence sinking. The ship was lost in a Typhoon but 40 got rescued. That's the ship that Alfred was on. If you hear news from home about Alfred let me know. Did you hear news about any other ships?

How are you and our baby getting along? I hope you're taking good care of yourself and not working too hard when you get home from work. I bet Mary wouldn't mind helping you out. She is a real nice girl.

I had to take my ring off again today. The reason was bad weather and I got knocked down by a big wave. Had to reach out and catch something to stop sliding. That's dangerous with the ring on so I'm going to put it back in the box for a while. It doesn't make any difference about me being married. Ring or no ring, I'm yours forever.

I'm sorry all my letters have been short this year. This one's going to be short too. No letters from you. Some got lost in the typhoon.

> Yours forever and always,
> Roy

South China Sea: January 18, 1945

I sure hope those blessings Halsey asked for last longer than Nimitz's good weather. We had one decent day and then it's been bad ever since. So bad we couldn't fuel. So bad they canceled the strikes on Hainan and Hong Kong. Then we got to strike the next two days but today we needed to fuel all of us and the weathers so bad we can't. It's hard enough fighting the enemy without fighting the weather too. And it's bearing down on everybody's nerves.

Jan 20, '44

My darling wife,

This is going to be another short letter as there's nothing to write about but the weather. I still have no letters from you to answer. I know you are sending them so maybe I'll get them some day. I hope you and the baby are doing fine. I would like to have more pictures that show how he's growing.

All my love,

Roy

Formosa: January 21, 1945

It was a bad day. A Jap plane crashed right into the Ticonderoga on purpose and set her on fire. Then another one dropped a bomb on the Langley before it slammed into the Ticonderoga too. I don't understand pilots willing to kill themselves to hit their target. Or a government expecting them to do it.

A bunch of US sailors had to be rescued out of the water. A lot of them didn't make it that far. We transferred one fella over to the North Carolina cause he was so banged up and burned that he needed our hospital. I helped bring him over the lines but once he got onboard wasn't much could be done for him. I know good and well our doctors did everything they could. But the fella didn't make it and we had to have a burial at sea. We weren't even his own shipmates seeing him off.

Funny thing is this was the first day we had decent weather.

January 22, 1945

Dearest Evelyn,

The good thing I can tell you is the weather. We had so much bad weather for so long I didn't think it would ever get good again, but it did. The last couple of days hadn't been bad but today is perfect. The sun is shining and no clouds in the sky. The wind ain't bad and the temperature is just a little bit cool so we're not burning up.

Well, there has still been no mail so I have no letters to answer. I expect when we ever do get mail, I will have a big bundle and won't be able to catch up for a long time.

I hadn't been sick with my throat anymore so things with me are swell. I hope they are with you and the baby too.

Loving you always,

Roy

January 27, 1945

Dear beautiful wife,

I'm so glad we finally got mail and I have letters from you to answer. I been doing pretty good answering them the last few days, haven't I? At least my letters got longer.

At the end of the last letter I didn't finish answering, you asked me a question about what it would take to slow me down. You use some big words – voracious appetite. I didn't see you wanting to slow down either. But if I hadn't had to leave I think we woulda had to slow down sometime. Or maybe not. But with you going to have a baby we would. I heard say after the first year you don't do it as much. But we got to start our year over when I get home. That first month doesn't count and we got a lot of lost time to make up for.

I got a letter from Sally Jane and lately all she can talk about is that fella she's dating. She sounds real smitten with him. I think if he was all that taken with her he should have come home at Christmas with her and met the family. But you said you didn't see him there. I worry about her. She hadn't always had good sense when it comes to fellas. Since he works at that same place as you do and you work in an office with paperwork, can you check up on him for me? Don't do nothing that might make you lose your job, but I just thought maybe you might could do it. But I don't really know what you do there so maybe you can't.

His name is Ronald Lewis. But I reckon you already know that if you been talking to Sally Jane at all. I hope you two have a chance to see each other sometimes.

So you went and saw a doctor. He says that's going to be a big baby because you still got almost six months to go and you're getting a big belly already. I reckon that's whittled down to about five months to go now. I hope one of these letters I hadn't got around to yet has some good pictures of you in it. I'd like to see another one of you holding your dress in so I can see how big the baby's getting. Don't worry about being skinny now. You can be skinny again later if you want to. Please eat lots of good food for you and the baby.

It's the next night now. I had to stop writing last night and today's been so busy I hadn't had time. It's late but the movie is on so lights won't go out for a while. That gives me time to write. We're in port so I had a lot of work to do today securing the deck, unsecuring it, getting the gangway out, hoisting the boats in the water and bringing them back in. There was this missing part I couldn't find and somebody was supposed to find it and stow it a month ago. It wasn't where it was supposed to be so I been running all over the place looking for it.

We got mail aboard today but so far I hadn't got any letters. The fellas that got them said they were dated January 15 and this is just the end of January so that's pretty good. There's probably some older mail in there somewhere too so when I start getting mine I might wait til I get them all and line them up by date unless I feel one that's got a picture and I open that one first. I should get some mail. We got 300 bags onboard. Maybe I'll get that package you talked about with the flashlight in it. That would be swell.

Well, I just got one letter. It was dated January 3 right after you got back home. You talking about everything happened at

Christmas at my house. Sally Jane put my picture under the Christmas tree because I was not there in the flesh.

I wished it hadn't made my Pap cry. He don't usually cry but I reckon he's missing me bad. Probably he's mostly worried. He was in the 'Great War' in the Army so I bet he's thinking he knows what's happening to me. But it ain't like what he did. I wished I could do something to make him not cry any more. My Ma hadn't told me about it. I reckon he told her not to.

I didn't tell her but when I came home for the wedding he hugged me and kissed my cheek and cried. He held on real tight. Getting old might make him be that way. I couldn't help it. I got water in my eyes.

I just got handed a few more letters. One of them feels like it's got a picture. It's dated Jan 14 but I've got to open it before the others.

Yep, it's got a picture alright of the prettiest redhead I ever saw. I wished I was there to hold you and touch our baby. I can see where it is so good now. I believe he might be a big baby boy. What you think?

I'm going to wait and read this letter in the order of the others but I just had to get the picture out first. There's some other ones in here from Christmas too. Thank you for them. It helps me feel a little bit what was happening at home even if I wasn't there. I been away four Christmases but this one was the worst.

That was a pretty tree this year. My Pap always goes in the woods and cuts them down. We went with him when we was growing up. That was a fun thing to do. Maybe Pap'll be around long enough our baby gets to do that when he gets a little bigger. When Pap ain't doing it no more, then we can start doing it ourselves.

Well I got 10 letters so far now so I'm going to close and start reading them. They dated from middle of December to middle of January so I already got some you wrote after some I'm getting now. And I answered them not knowing what you wrote in the letters I hadn't got yet so it might not have made sense sometimes. This mails gonna drive us all crazy one day but it sure is nice to get it.

All my love forever,

Roy

PS - I see where you said the Navy's been cutting holes in my letters. I try real hard not to write nothing I'm not supposed to but I reckon I made some mistakes.

FEBRUARY

February 9, 1945

My darling Evelyn,

I'm glad I answered most of your letters. We're heading out again tomorrow and I been busy today getting ready. Have more work to do tonight but I just got more mail with one letter I gotta answer now.

I had to tell you how sorry I am about Mildred's husband's ship being sunk with no survivors. He was on the Hull and the Navy said it was the typhoon not the enemy that sank them. I feel real bad about that.

Now don't let that make you worry more about me. Them destroyers are little and our ship's real big. She's a good one too and she's going to protect us so I can get home to you and the baby. You just worry about taking care of yourself and our little football player. I hear tell you can feel em kick even before they're born.

I know you're going to miss Mildred and helping with the baby since she moved back home to be with her folks now that Johnny's dead. But she lives right there in Tennessee. Maybe you can take the train to see her when you get some days off. I know she would like to see you and she can tell you things you need to know about being a Ma. Maybe that might help her too talking about babies instead of other things.

I wish I could write more and I really wished I could just come home and hold you but I gotta go now. It may be a few days before I get to write again and before the letters go out. But just keep believing in me and knowing I'll get home soon as I can. We're gonna have a good family and a long time to love each other.

All my love,

Roy

Underway from Ulithi: February 10, 1945

After all those bad days of weather and pilots committing suicide just to hit our ships we stayed out there making strikes on Okinawa til they figured we all needed to round up the wagons and get a fresh start. So the rest of us headed to Ulithi where the banged up ships had already gone. We all stayed there since near the end of January getting fixed up and loaded up and ready to go. I had time to write to Evelyn every day but it just don't come close to being good as going home.

She's going to have a baby and now she finds out about Mildred's husband not coming home and her having to raise that baby all by herself. Johnny Malpass died on the Hull because I didn't get them fueled. We should have done something faster and not left them without fuel. Evelyn's in a bad way thinking about her friend not having a husband and that baby not having a Pap and about me not making it home either and there ain't nothing I can do to make it better. I never felt so bad and helpless.

But I got to concentrate on my job or I might not make it back home. One thing we know for sure is we got to all work together or somebody's gonna get killed. Next target is Japan for real. We're going after Tokyo. But we got to go between Iwo Jima and Okinawa to get there. I expect we're fixing to do something about those islands now.

February 14, 1945
Happy Valentines Day Darling,

Our first Valentines Day being husband and wife and we're still apart. That makes the first Thanksgiving, the first Christmas, the first Valentines Day and will be the first Easter. I wished I could be home for our first baby being born but I just don't know. That only gives us a few months to get the war over and get home. I'm scared that might not happen. Maybe I'll be home for our first year anniversary. All this missing special days makes me very blue and I know it does you too. We're in love and lonely.

I got my Valentine card and I really liked it. I especially liked what it said. That was a cute mouse couple in the little buggy and it says 'A Valentine for My Better Half.' I'm not sure about that part but I agree with the rest.

We have such fun in all we do
We're happy as can be
We love each other so darned much
That's pretty plain to see
We always get along so swell
And (almost) never fuss
Gee, but I'm sure happy, dear,
Because we married us!

That was swell. I'm glad we married us too. We're gonna have a good long happy life together if we can just get through this one bad time.

I hope you get your Valentine on time too. It's got a little something in it but not much cause I hadn't been where I could get you anything good. I got my package with the cookies and the taffy

231

and the books. Everything was in tip-top shape this time.

They been playing the radio where we're writing and that Bing Crosby song just played 'I Love You Truly' and that's the way I feel about you. Makes me get water in my eyes thinking about it.

They already played 'I'll Never Smile Again' and 'The Nightingale Sang in Barkley Square.' I reckon they just gonna play love songs all day. I'm probably gonna have to go where I can't hear them.

I have to start writing earlier in the day anyhow. Cause now after officers chow all the division boatswain mates like me meet with the bos'n to check everything and make sure it's secure. Then we get orders for the next day. At least if I write at the noon hour maybe the radio won't be playing them love songs.

Well its getting late cause I had to start writing late so everybody's turning in. I'll try to write again tomorrow.

> I Love You Truly and always will,
>
> Roy

February 16, 1945

My darling wife,

I still got a couple of letters to answer. I been doing pretty good writing every day but I might not be able to do it in a few days. I can't tell you why or there will be a big hole in my letter.

I think you got confused when you picture me writing. The ship didn't look nothing like I expected either. But I got a new bunk and it's got a bench beside it where I can write now if I want to. But it don't have a table so the mess hall or library's still easier. I got a new chair too. It's like the ones those directors use with their name on the back. Mine's got the division # and boatswain mate written on it. My division is 5 and we call ourselves the Fighting Fifth. All the divisions got the chairs. I can sit in mine anytime I want to long as I got time.

So you're going to the doctor every month now and you don't

even have to leave your little town because they got a hospital and nurses and doctors. That's swell. I'm glad he says the baby's doing good just already big. He heard the heartbeat good and strong. Did he let you listen too? So the baby kicks you at night and it feels like it's got more than two legs. That's funny. I wished I could feel it but I'm too far away.

I'm glad you got to go into town on the train with Sally Jane. That gave you time to talk. She was buying a new dress for the Valentine's dance. Why didn't you buy yourself a new one? I don't believe what you said that nothing looks good on you anymore. You are more beautiful than ever before.

She's real smitten with her boyfriend and you think there might be a wedding. He hadn't gave her a ring yet has he? It's alright you couldn't find out nothing about him in the paperwork cause you didn't even look. No, I don't want you to get fired. I'm sorry I even asked it.

Everybody you talk to that knows him thinks he's a real good fella. But you didn't know too many people who know him because different parts of the job don't mingle. That's like it is here on the ship. Divisions stick together. We don't see fellas in the other divisions much.

We sometimes see them on liberty and you sometimes see them at dances but you can't have them outside now cause its cold. But you did have a New Year one inside and you're gonna have a Valentine one. You said you are not going but it's alright if you did. You could have listened to the music even if you didn't feel like dancing. It's already over now though. I hope you and Mary both went. Me and Lyle would understand. He's smitten too.

That's all for today. I'll love you 'Only Forever' and I'm your 'Prisoner of Love' cause 'You Are the One' (the song's really called 'Night and Day' but those are the first words).

All my love,
Roy

Chi Chi Jima: February 18, 1945

Took us six days to get where we were going but yesterday morning we started hitting air bases and industries in Honshu. Near about to Tokyo. We been so hot all this time we been at war and complained about it too but here the temperature dropped to 45 degrees and the fellas topside had to put on their heavy weather gear. Still fighting the weather – cold and wind and waves - so couldn't do much in the afternoons. The planes from our Task Force attacked the Yokosuka Naval Base yesterday and got 400 of their planes. Today they got at least a hundred more. The Japs know we are here for sure. No telling what they'll try to do now.

Feb 20, '45

My dear wife,

I wanted to write to you yesterday but I just didn't have the time. I'll tell you why in about 30 days. They told us that thirty days after an operation, we can tell what we saw like if it was an enemy plane falling. But I don't see much from where I am because I'm inside the gun mount. So I don't see much that's going on and probably won't have much to tell except for where we been.

They said that now we could tell what happened up till January. Well we been to Luzon and the Manila area for raids about four times. In that neck of the woods it got real fouled up weather. There's bad crosswinds and the seas always rough. That's probably because it's the deepest out there, about seven miles down. Most all the bad storms start around there.

When we're fueling out in those seas we got the life jackets strapped to our backs and the salt gets all over our faces. Takes me some time to wash it all off at the end of the day if I get lucky enough to have time for a shower.

In one of your letters you were talking about listening to the jukebox. We got one a fella fixed up and when I was walking through the compartment I stopped and listened to the song playing. I can't even remember what one it was right now but it made me think about home and the good times we had with the jukebox at the soda fountain after school. But better times in Port Orchard when we went dancing and the jukebox was playing.

I been having dreams about home the last few nights. The dreaming and the listening make you feel good and bad at the same time. Does it do you that way too?

I haven't much to write about so I'll close for now.

Loving you always and forever,

Roy

Iwo Jima: February 23, 1945

I knew we were going to have to do something about Iwo Jima and that's just what we been doing the last few days. We left Tokyo four days ago for an all out assault on Iwo Jima. We been shooting the sixteens and the fives at the islands and the planes been bombing the islands and the Marines invaded. I heard tell a lot of them got killed cause the Japs were hiding everywhere in tunnels and stuff with their guns.

That first morning they fed us real good – steak and eggs and just about anything we wanted. Then we set to bombarding that island hard as we could. It was a long day and being gun captain I couldn't see for nothing what was going on being in the mount all day long. They brought us up some sandwiches in a bucket and some hot coffee that sure was welcome.

Even when we got done bombarding at the end of each day and thought we were going back to the bunk for a little rest it didn't happen. The Japs came after all of us in their planes and we went to General Quarters over and over again til we just stayed there.

Today they say a bunch of fellas drove a Jeep up Mount Surabachi and put an American flag up there. Us and the

Washington got told to head to Tokyo even though most everybody else is staying here because the job ain't finished yet. We fueled one ship today then got fuel ourselves. Tomorrow we got fueling duty again and the weather's supposed to kick up again too.

February 24, 1945
My darling Evelyn,

I'm sorry I don't get to write everyday anymore but we been pretty busy. I'll be able to tell you about it later I reckon.

I hadn't had no letters lately that I can answer so there's not much to write. I was reading back over some old letters and found something I hadn't answered. You were talking about all the gifts we been getting. The towels with the letter 'H' on them sound swell. And the butter dish with the matching sugar bowl and creamer thing sounds good too for our breakfast. I could sure use some good hot grits full of butter and a cup of good coffee with sugar and fresh cream. What we got here ain't bad but not like back home. You putting all those things in the hope chest is a good idea. It's gonna be so full you can't close it. We're gonna have a fine time putting it all out in our own house when I get home. No, I don't mind a bit helping you do that.

Well, since I can tell all the way up to January, I might as well go into detail about what we done and where we been. We left Seattle on Oct 4, stayed in San Diego a week or so firing and practicing. Left there Oct 14, stayed in Pearl Harbor two days on the 20-22, got to Eniewetok, Marshall Islands the 27th, went to another place we go in and out of once in a while. That's about it.

There's some gossip about the ship being in an article in 'Life Magazine' in May. The ship'll be four years old in April so I reckon that's what it's about. You'll probably be seeing a picture or two. If you see the side of the ship with the crane on it that's my side. That's my station right there. The cranes easy to see cause it sticks up like a sore thumb. It'd be mighty fine if you could find that magazine and save it for me.

That's about all for now. Don't know when I'll get to write again but I'll try soon.

Loving you forever and always,
Roy

Headed to Ulithi: February 28, 1945

Februarys been a hard month but I feel like we might really be making progress now. We're so close to getting the Japs right where they live. But they're not giving up easy. I just don't understand what they're calling Kamikazes.

We do everything we can to protect our pilots. That's what the battleships job is to protect the aircraft carriers and bombarding the islands. If one of them goes down the destroyers do their best to rescue them.

But the Japanese has their pilots just killing themselves on purpose. If we don't get the planes when they're heading toward us there ain't no chance they're gonna miss with a bomb cause they use their plane and just crash right on top our ships. That causes a lot of fires cause of all that extra fuel in the planes themselves. The last few days we been bombarding Tokyo proper but the weather sure is making it harder. We got snow squalls and sleet and it makes it harder to do your job, both the fighting and the fueling.

One day, I can't even remember which one now, the first tanker come to fuel us didn't have enough to fill us up. We dropped down on fuel level lower than we're supposed to and had to do the fueling all over again with another tanker before we were filled up. That was real hard with the weather bad as it is. We done used up so much of our ammunition we're headed back to Ulithi now to get some more.

Feb 28, '45

Darling Evelyn,

We got mail today but I was one of the unlucky ones. Nothing for me. I know you're writing but they're just not getting here yet. So I don't have letters to answer and not much of anything to tell you. But I can think of a few things maybe enough for a short letter.

We were used to being hot where we been before but this place here's so cold we have to wear fur-lined jackets. Mines got a 5-1 on the back. That stands for the 5th division and me being the number one man in the division. Ain't just salt all over my face when we're fueling now. I got ice too.

I heard some of the fellas talking about how their wife been stepping out on them and how next time they get married they're going to choose better. I can't hardly think about that ever happening to us. I know you wouldn't do a thing like that and I wouldn't neither. We're going to be married and happy for a long, long time. Won't never be a next time for me or you.

There's this one fella named Charlie in our division and he bought this ring and sent it home to his girl like I sent the one home to you. He told her in his letter that he wanted to marry her but he didn't know when it could be. He told her he might be home in two months or it could be two years. You remember that's kinda what I had to tell you too and it was a heck of a lot longer than two months. Anyhow, he had a package at mail call today and it was the ring. He told me what the letter said. She told him that if he thought she was gonna wait two years he was crazy. He said to me she could do whatever she wanted and he didn't care no more but I could tell that wasn't so. He was hurting real bad that she didn't love him enough to wait whatever time it took him to get back home.

I'm a lucky man. You didn't care how long it took me to get home for us to get married and now you're waiting patiently for me to get back so we can start our long life together. You, me and the baby and however many more we have. I hope you're feeling good and taking care of yourself.

I don't have a whole lot more I can write about.

Forever yours,

Roy

MARCH

Mar 4, '45

My darling wife,

We got mail call today and I got lucky. I'm going to have plenty of stuff to write about for a while now - I got 21 letters from you today. I reckon that they just all been stuck together somewhere trying to get here. I hadn't had time to read any of them yet so I'll have to do that before I start answering.

I got a little stuff I can tell you now about what we been doing, then I'll read the letters and answer some tonight.

We been to Luzon a couple more times. We raided Formosa, went to the China Sea, hit Hong Kong and back to Formosa again. You might want to get you a map of the Pacific so you can tell where I been since I get to let you know.

You know I got the fueling detail and one day when we were off of Formosa we were fueling a can – that's what we call the destroyer a tin can because its so little. Anyhow, we were fueling and all of a sudden we heard this loud noise and it was a bomb blowed up when it hit the water. We got the fuel lines loose and let the can get away in case we had to go to our battlestations. We looked up and there was three Jap planes heading our way but they didn't get to us and didn't get back to where they came from neither. The good guys took care of them.

That's all for right now. I got to go check on my boys. They're cleaning the weather decks. I'll read some letters tonight and try and start answering tonight or tomorrow.

Well, I'm back and I got about a half hour before I got to go to chow. I put all the letters in order by date and there's a couple dates missing. I reckon you been busy too. This first letter I open sure does smell good. What you dipping the paper in? It makes me want to snuggle up and nuzzle your neck like we did in front of the fire at Port Orchard. That mighta been a little house without much in it but it sure made a nice home for two people and I miss being there. I miss everything we did those days we were there.

In your first letter you said that you been to see Mildred at her folks house in Tennessee. Her baby's name is Sally. That's a pretty name like my sister. They're doing alright but Mildred's sad all the time and don't know what she's going to tell Sally about her daddy.

I reckon she got some pictures of him in his uniform. Maybe she can tell her he was a hero. But I don't reckon that makes it feel any better to be all alone. I know she got her folks but sometimes you can be around other people and still be alone in your heart and your mind.

I'm glad you got to see Sally Jane and went shopping. She's going to be a good aunt to our baby. So she's already buying little things. How does she know what color to buy? You're putting it in the hope chest with the wedding presents. How big is that hope chest anyhow? Sounds to me like it must be plenty full by now.

I'm glad you're feeling better and not fainting and throwing up anymore. You're eating good and got you some clothes that fit. I hope they'll be some pictures in some of these letters. There's not any in this letter.

Well, that's all I got time for tonight. I hope to read some more letters after chow and watch.

Your loving husband,
Roy

March 5, 1945

My darling wife,

Before I get to answering your letters, I wanted to tell you what I'm doing. I know you want me to go up for first, so I got the book and been studying. Some openings are coming when some other fellas move up so I may try and see if I can do it. It means a lot more money that we can save for our horse ranch and our house.

You say you got a raise. That's real good. You been making good money already so you should be able to put some away too. What with that and the allotments I'm sending home, we should be able to get right to starting our ranch and building our house right when I get home. I just can't wait to be with you in our own place.

You wonder would I like a feather bed. I think it would be swell, but I don't care what kind of bed we got long as you're in it with me. I don't care what color we paint the bedroom either or what color curtains or bedspread or anything. I'll like whatever you pick out. I know it's fun to think about things like that. You're right, I hope it won't be long before I come home and we can do it for real.

So Mary got her a hope chest too. You and her been going into Knoxville and looking at wedding dresses. You have to do it on a Saturday cause you have to take the train and you want to have plenty of time. Even if she buys the prettiest dress yall can fine she won't never be as pretty a bride as you. She's a pretty girl but you are the best ever. I tell Lyle that too but he disagrees. I reckon love can do that to you.

I hope when Lyle and Mary get married we can be neighbors too. That's a great idea. It would be swell to have our friends close by and can do things together and have kids playing together and all. When you talk about that it paints such a pretty picture of what life's going to be like when I get home. I'm ready to be there right now.

I hadn't been on a beach since I was back in sunny California, but I get to put my toes in the sand tomorrow. Five of us'll be getting a beach party as a reward. I don't know what this island looks like but I bet it's got coconut trees like the other ones. But we got to swim to shore to get there.

I'm glad you got the money order I sent. I sent it in the China Sea so I was worried if it would get there. It went off on another ship and the story was that the Japs had us all bottled up there. I reckon that was not the truth. Anyhow, I'm glad you got it.

I still got a lot of letters to read, but I'm answering them as I go. I'll try to write tomorrow when I get back from the beach party if I got time before I go on duty.

Lovingly yours,
Roy

March 8, 1945
My darling Evelyn,

The beach party was swell. We didn't do much of nothing but swim and we had some stuff to eat and we laid out on the beach in the sunshine and listened to the birds. It was swell relaxing and not worrying about fueling or fighting or cleaning or nothing. A few hours away helped.

I been reading your letters and I came across the one where your grandpa died. That's a terrible thing for he was a good man. I always did like him. He was the kind of fella that you just like to be around and never felt worried that he wouldn't want you there. I know you are going to miss seeing him when you get to go back home now and again.

You say you saw my folks when you went to the funeral and they were mighty happy to see you. I am not one bit surprised my Ma had to feel your belly. I'm glad it didn't bother you. You say the baby kicked her right in the hand and made her laugh and cry at the same time. Sounds like she's feeling a lot better these days. And my Pap's doing alright too? Planting season is coming so he'll be busy. I know he likes to keep busy. Makes you not think about the things you rather forget.

So you been thinking what it will be like the day I get home. I don't know. I might have on my dress blues and a flat hat or maybe my peacoat. I reckon it depends on what time of the year it is. So you're not going to hardly give me time to get off the train before you're holding me tight and kissing me right there in public. No I don't care what nobody sees or thinks either. That's a nice thing to think about too.

Yes, I would get another raise if I make first. I believe it's about 20 or 22 extra and that would make us putting away about 200 a month. That's pretty good.

I like it when you say my letters make you happy cause you laugh at this or that thing I said. I want you to be happy and I hope that I can help make that come true.

We're in port right now. I can't tell you where but it's not where the fighting is. It's our safe place to go when we need to pick up more supplies and food and ammunition. We get to have movies on the fantail out under the stars instead of down in the mess hall. It's pretty swell to watch them out there. I believe tonight we're watching 'Since You Went Away.' I heard tell it's a damn good, I mean darn good movie but that it might make even a tough sailor cry thinking about home.

I'll write again soon I promise.

Loving you forever and always,
Roy

Ulithi: March 12, 1945

I reckon it's true that there's no safe place when you're at war. I hope that ain't really true because it better be safe back home for my family – both the old family and my new one.

But here in port in Ulithi is where we been coming to stock up

243

and get repaired and rest up and get ready to go back to the war zone. It's not supposed to be dangerous here. We didn't even have to have blackouts here like we do everywhere else.

But all that changed now. Can't even light a cigarette topside at night. I don't smoke so it don't bother me none but that's not what I'm trying to say. What I am trying to explain is that it's dangerous no matter where we are. Makes me wonder will I ever get home.

Last night we were having a movie up on the fantail like we been doing most nights we been here. It's a whole lot better doing it there than below deck. But we won't be doing it no more.

One of those Kamikazes came right in there where we were and nosedived right into the Randolph. That's one of our aircraft carriers. Some of her crew got killed and a lot more got hurt.

We'll be leaving real soon and going back to the fighting. I bet it's going to be even worse now that we're getting close to Japan for real. I heard the next place we got to go is Okinawa. None of us know whether the next day will be our last one.

That's why we better get everything straight with God and the people we love. I reckon I got to do that. I believe everything is fine with my family, but I hadn't been talking to God like I been taught to do.

Not enough anyways.

March 13, 1945

My dearest wife,

I told you we could tell 30 days after a thing happened but there's something I hadn't told you. I reckon I don't have to tell and I thought I wasn't telling because I wanted to protect you from the hurt. There's a lot of things happening out here that I won't never tell you. Won't tell another living soul. It's better left unsaid after it's done. I don't need to be sending home no details about a lot of this stuff going on. You don't deserve the telling.

But there's one thing I hadn't told you that I think I been not telling you because it will make you think less of me. Maybe not even love me anymore. But I ain't being honest and that's not the way I want our marriage to be. I keep telling myself it's for the best that I not tell you, but it's eating at me all the time that I hadn't told you. Especially when you're telling me about Mildred and her baby girl and how they're not doing so good now that Johnny got killed when the typhoon sunk the Hull. She don't understand how it could happen. I do.

I know what happened and it was my fault.

I told you how it's my job to fuel the other ships. Well, that's what we were doing that day fast as we could. But I dropped the fuel line one time and that lost us a few seconds. And then my crew was working hard as they could but maybe I wasn't leading them best I could. Maybe we coulda done something faster. The wind was whipping the ships all around, even our big one, and we was fueling destroyers on both sides. We have to do that when we get in a hurry like a storm or in the war zone itself. We fueled one right after the other and there's a lot of all kinds of ships in each task group and each group got a bunch of them making up a force. The destroyers are small and don't hold much fuel so they have to get fuel a lot. We got to know some of the fellas on the fueling detail just because we saw them every time. Didn't always know their name, just the face.

Alfred was on the fueling detail on the Spence. That was the last destroyer we fueled that day the weather got so bad. The waves were washing up over the side of our ship. Knocked me and Lyle down a couple times. We didn't go overboard but it slowed us down the having to get back up and set things right again. Lost valuable time. But it doing that to a big ship like us you can just imagine what it's doing to the little ones like the Spence where Alfred was and the Hull where Mildred's husband was.

I asked you to tell me if you found out if Alfred was one of the ones got rescued on the Spence. That was a lie, too. I know he didn't. I saw him get washed off the Spence right between our ships when we was fueling. We kept right on fueling. Couldn't start no rescue mission right then so he didn't have a chance. You have to keep on going in a war even when you see your buddies get killed.

The Spence was the last one we fueled. The Hull was right there behind it waiting. I couldn't see Johnny Malpass but I know he was on there somewhere. We didn't even finish fueling the Spence before they made us stop. It just got too dangerous to do anymore. I reckon they was right in telling us that but I just kept thinking about them fellas on the Hull right there watching us stop. And them being sent away so they didn't wash into our ship. And the ones in line behind it that couldn't see what we were doing and were still thinking we were going to do something that'd help save them from that storm. But they get turned away too. I don't reckon nothing I done or didn't do could've give us enough time to fuel them all, but maybe if I had been a little faster or hadn't got knocked down by the waves, we coulda at least finished the Spence and give a little bit of fuel to the Hull to keep them from being empty and lightweight enough to bob around like a fishing cork, then get pulled under by the currents and swallowed up by the waves.

So we didn't fuel the Hull and it didn't have much of a chance in the storm. Our big old ship was rocked so much by the waves that it almost went over too. But she's strong and big and turned herself back up between waves. We all had to go below deck. Weren't safe out there for nobody. The ones didn't get in fast enough or try to finish their jobs before they went below ended up beat up with gashes on their face and broken bones. Me and Lyle got washed down again trying to get the fuel lines put away. He caught himself on the stanchion that holds the lifelines. If he hadn't caught hold of it, he would have gone overboard. I caught myself on the wall around the guns on the fantail. Just about tore my finger off when it caught on my ring. That's another lie I told you. Well I didn't say an outright lie but I told you I hurt my finger a bit and put my ring in the locker. Truth is my finger swole up so much the doc had to cut my ring off. It is in my locker but it ain't in no shape to wear anymore. I'll get it fixed when I get back home and never take it off again.

But I know that nobody got saved on the Hull that day nor the next day when we went back to try and rescue what could be found. The few they saved was off the Spence and that's probably cause we did get to give her a bit of fuel so she probably stayed afloat longer til she ran out. The ones we didn't get to fuel didn't have much of a chance. So that's why Johnny Malpass died and your best friend don't have a husband and that baby girl ain't got no daddy.

It's up to you whether you want to tell Mildred the truth or not. I don't know that it will make her feel any better except she wouldn't be wondering anymore how it happened. But I just couldn't keep pretending I didn't know the truth cause that was like lying to you and I couldn't do it no more. I hope you can find it in your heart to forgive me and not stop loving me for my failures.

I will always love you and I swear I'll do everything in my power to always protect you and our baby we got coming and all the other babies we have in the future as long as I live. Don't think just because I failed in saving those ships that I won't be able to save you from whatever harm tries to come. If you can still love me, we'll have a good long happy life together.

Well I'm going to go straight and mail this letter before I change my mind about telling this truth that's going to hurt so bad to hear it. But it hurt us both more for me not to tell. I will love you forever. I hope you keep loving me too.

Faithfully forever yours,
Roy

Okinawa: March 20, 1945

It's sure been hell the last few days. Not another way to say it. The worst of it started a couple days ago and it hadn't stopped yet. We been called to general quarters so many times I done pulled my mattress topside so it's right beside the mount. Best way I could think to catch a wink or two if I ever get the chance to lay down again.

We're working on Okinawa now and the kamikazes are everywhere. It seems that's the only thing the Japs got left to do so they're sending all their planes in to crash right into our ships. I don't know how they got any left but they just keep coming.

Couple days ago they dropped a bomb on the Enterprise. She's an aircraft carrier. It hurt her some but she kept on going. I hear she lost some crew and had some injuries too. That's not surprising with a bomb that size. They bout got the Intrepid too but the kamikaze attack got stopped before it could do the damage it intended on doing. But they just keep sending them kamikazes in at us in waves. One bunch ain't but just gone when another bunch comes in.

Yesterday they got two direct hits on the Franklin. It was bombs not the kamikaze. The Franklin was on fire and the crew was jumping off into the ocean to keep from burning up. Some already dead, some hurt. Our ship had to turn sharp to keep from running over the ones in the water. Some of the fellas were throwing life vests over the side to the ones down in the water hoping to help them survive till they got picked up and hoping they made it to rescue before the sharks started in on them. You get that many people down in the water bleeding and the sharks come calling. Couldn't none of our ships stop. We had to keep going but somebody was going back to try and rescue whatever they could.

March 25, 1945

My dearest wife,

I'm sorry I hadn't wrote in some time. I been real busy and

when I can tell you about it, I'll tell you some so you understand. We got mail today and I got some from you all dated before you would have got my letter about the typhoon. I'm afraid you'll be so ashamed you won't love me anymore. I sure do love you.

The mail's been held up so I just got my package for my birthday. The cookies held together real good and tasted good too. And I always like getting the gum. But the best part is the pictures of you. I can see the baby getting bigger. I sure wished I was home to help take care of you both. I like the new writing paper and the new ink pen. Mine was getting pretty bad. I reckon you could tell by the looks of some of my letters. You couldn't hardly see the words sometimes cause the ink looked like it be running out and then a big glob when I put some fresh in it. My letters ought to look a lot better but I hope we won't be gone too much longer to need to do the writing.

I got your Easter card too. It was swell. I sure hope this is the last Easter we spend apart. All these holidays make a fella want to be home even worse than just the regular days and that's bad. I heard that song 'Easter Parade' and made me think of you and how pretty you'd be in your new clothes with being able to see the baby so good now.

Your letter says you haven't had any for a time now. I reckon you understand about mail by now. Sometimes it just sits and waits til we get to port or a ship comes that can take it. So even if I write every day you might not get any for weeks then get it all in a bunch. And I been so busy I hadn't wrote every day so the waiting may be longer.

So the baby's been kicking you a lot lately. What does that feel like? I sure hope you both doing swell. I'm glad Mary likes to cook and that helps you come home and rest but still get some vegetables to eat. That's important for making the baby strong.

I been studying up for 1/c. Some fellas done took the test and fell out of the running so I hope I do good when I take mine. It will be some time today so I don't know how much time I got to write.

I got your package with the ball cap. I needed a new one so I'm much obliged. The fellas asked me about it and I said it was my Easter Bonnet you sent to me. They laughed but I don't care cause I like wearing something you touched not so long ago. That's why I like the letters too. I like the words and all but the paper smells good like your perfume. I can just picture you sitting down at the table writing to me. I have to picture you in Simms Hollow in my mind cause I don't have no pictures of you in your apartment in that town where you work. That sure is a secret place. I hope you really are doing ok and not just making it sound good so as not to worry me. I just got word my test is in 15 minutes so I got to go.

Ok. I'm back. It wasn't bad but I only took half. Today was about petty officer first. Tomorrow will be about boatswain mate so that part'll be easier for me. I'll let you know if I pass or not when I find out. This test I had to know about a bunch of flags, how to write a letter for transfer, what the duties are of different people, how to log a guy with a broken leg, and what the duties are of a lot of different people. Stuff like that. Tomorrow will be easier for me because it's about the boat. Stuff like anchoring a ship, compasses, weather, how to hoist things aboard, target repair, towing and stuff like that. I should do fine on that one. If I got through today then I'll be good.

Yes I do know swear words and I have to use them here but I won't use them when I get home especially around the baby. I hear when they start talking they say everything they hear you say. I hate to hear some young'uns of some of these guys. But when I'm trying to get the fellas to do something right and they don't listen I have to swear. No telling what words they use on me behind my back when I had the coxswain and a second class doing something over again. They secure seventy fathoms (six feet to a fathom) of fuel line but they didn't do it the way it needed to be done so I made them take it off and do it again. They call me swear words for sure but I have to let it roll off my back. Ain't worth fighting over. We got enough fighting to do with the Japs instead of amongst ourselves.

Well I got inspection so I gotta sign off for now.

Loving you more every day,

Roy

March 31, 1945

My dearest Evelyn,

Well another month has gone by and I still don't know when we'll be coming home. We still got some powerful important work to do but I believe the end is getting closer. I will tell you about what I can tell you.

It's been more than 30 days now so I reckon I can tell you we were at Iwo Jima. I know that probably was in the news back home because it was important to getting this war over. Our job was to bombard the island before the invasion forces went it. We watched them go in. We also shoot at planes trying to hit the aircraft carriers. That's about it, except before Iwo Jima we went to Tokyo and it was real cold there. That's when I was telling you about having to wear my fur jacket and getting ice on us when we doing the fueling. That was Tokyo.

When we were firing on Iwo Jima it looked like the fourth of July. I'm glad it's over though. Then we went back to Tokyo and let them have some more.

Yes, the bonds do take 10 years for you to get the full value so we need to leave them where they are for that long. I'm glad you agree about that. If something happens and we really need them we can get them early but it's best if we don't.

I heard today I made first but it wasn't official yet so I'll believe it when I see it. I'll let you know.

I saw 'Tall in the Saddle' and it was better than a lot of cowboy movies we got to see. Sure made me miss back home and all the riding. Had some good horses on it and made me get to thinking again about our horse ranch. Have you been thinking much about what kind of horses you like best? I think we need to make sure we got a good calm pony or two for all the younguns.

We hadn't had a chance to do too many movies lately. I still want to see 'Thirty Seconds Over Tokyo.' I try not to even watch them when they're the ones that's going to make you miss home even more. But I did see 'The Very Thought of You.' I reckon more than one sailor had some water in his eyes on that one. We all been thinking about home and the folks we left behind. It's been such a long time since we got to see the people we love the most in the world and we don't know when we'll see them again.

In a few days our ship will have a birthday. She'll be four years old. I expect if there's time depending on where we are and what we're doing there probably will be some birthday cake and ice cream for us to celebrate.

I got some things I got to take care of so I'll close for now. Sorry the letter's short. Running out of stuff to say.

Lovingly yours forever,
Roy

APRIL

Near Okinawa: April 1, 1945

Today's been a pretty good day. The Marines and Army invaded Okinawa. Scuttlebutt has it there was over sixty thousand of them and they didn't have much trouble because we did a good job bombarding the island before they went in. Seems the government learned a lesson when we lost all those fellas on Iwo Jima. They gave us more time to do our job this time before sending in the troops on the ground. The weather's still bad and the bogies still coming in -

sending us to our battle stations for GQ more than it don't, but we're getting closer to the end. I can feel it and the other fellas can too.

April 1, 1945
My dearest wife,

I won't have time to write much but I wanted to try. It being April Fool's Day there's been a lot of jokes played on each other. I hadn't been hit by one yet but the days not done.

I got news that isn't April Fools. It's official - I did make first. So there will be more money coming home now and I hope you are saving it up for buying our own place when I get there. I sure am ready for us to start our long happy life together.

I still got a couple of letters to answer that's dated the first part of March. I just read the one that's got the poem in it and that 'Last Night I Dreamed' is a swell poem. I especially liked the last line 'Only the heart that's strong to love is strong to wait.'

After that letter I sent about the typhoon I sure hope your hearts strong to keep loving me. I sometimes wonder should I sent it or should I just kept that to myself. In one way I feel better since I told the truth but in another way I feel worse for sending you the burden. The knowing might make you feel worse and if you stop loving me for it, I'll feel worse than I ever did.

I got a lot of learning now to do my new duties right so I'm going to close for today. I hadn't the time to do more writing but maybe later if I get a chance.

Forever yours,
Roy

April 4, 1945
Evelyn my love,

Yesterday we got mail but I hadn't had a chance to write til now. I'm sorry the things on the news is making you worry. And now you been having bad headaches. I hope you go to see the doctor about the headaches even if it's not time to see him about the baby. If they're bad enough you're going back to bed and missing work, that's a bad thing. I know how much you don't ever miss work. Hadn't since you were in high school working at the soda fountain.

I know you hadn't even got the letter yet, but I wished now I hadn't told you about Tokyo and Iwo Jima neither cause it makes you worry more. There really wasn't nothing to it so don't you be worrying about me. You take good care of yourself and the baby and I'll be just fine. I won't be telling you anymore of the stuff till I can say that I'm headed on the way back home. That'll be the good stuff we talk about.

Today's been a pretty good day. We did some fueling. Now I got my laundry all put away and had a shower and got some time to write. It feels pretty cool in here and that's good. It's about eight now.

I know it's hard not knowing when I'll be home. It's hard for me too. But we know we got six months out of the way that's closer to me being home.

That ends your first letter. Now I'm going to read the second one and that's all I got. This letter is dated March 15 so it got here pretty fast. I'll read it tonight and answer tomorrow but stay in this same letter to save paper and time.

I'm back. So you did see the doctor and he's worried about how big you're getting already seeing as how you are not quite six months along. Maybe you're more along than they think. We did get married August 12. That could be seven months if I'm counting right, but I reckon not since you had your woman time in Port Orchard. I need some new pictures. You didn't look too big to me in the last one. You looked beautiful.

So he suggested you might want to stop working and being on your feet or sitting at a desk all day cause of the headaches and tiredness and being the baby's getting so big and you're so little a person. He wants you to be able to be in bed more and rest. The money is not that important. If he thinks you should stop working til after the baby is born that's fine with me. I got the raise now that I made first and I can send more money home if you need it. I don't need the money. I got everything I need right here except you.

So you're worried because if you stop work you can't live where you are and have to go back home to Simms Hollow cause you got no other place to live. Then you won't have your friends like Mary around and not have the same doctor for the baby. You'll have to find another one and you don't want to do that. Can't you go see ole doc Taylor? He's been taking care of all of us all our lives. I know he does babies too. That don't make no sense to me about you having to leave town. Why won't they let you stay a little while longer in your apartment if we're paying the rent? What kind of town is that?

If you don't want to live with your folks I'm sure my Ma and Pap be happy to have you there. They got the extra bedrooms nobody's using since we all left home. Mine's upstairs with a window that looks out over the pasture where the horses are. You might like that one and I like the idea of you sleeping in my bed.

Why don't you want to go to your home? Oh, I get it. It'll be like all the getting free and grownup will be down the drain if you end up back at your house. And you still have to share a bedroom with your little sisters cause they're both just seniors in high school. Your ma is still saving your brother's room until he gets out of the Air Force in case he wants to come home. I bet he won't. I can't think how it would be to live back home now either. I like to be close but not the same house.

You don't know how to tell that to your Ma. Yeah I know she didn't never want you to leave in the first place. But whichever place you decide, they're close enough together to visit the other.

You can tell your Ma I want you at my house and I'm your husband now so you're gonna do what I ask. That might work because that's the way our folks was brought up. The man making all the decisions. But things changed now, at least with us. You're a smart woman with a fancy job and been making good decisions all on your own.

It takes a lot of time for our letters to get back and forth and answered, but if you need me to write my Ma and Pap and ask them I will but only if you want me to do it. You may have to do that first though because it'll be so long coming from me. Talk about it to Sally Jane if you want. I'm sure she'll help you ask if you're worried. She always wanted a sister and now she's got you.

I'll close for now and try to write again tomorrow in a different letter. I sure hope you feel better soon. I'm sorry I can't be there to make things easier for you now that you're having our baby.

Loving you forever and always,
Roy

Near Okinawa: April 8, 1945

I haven't written a letter to Evelyn in two days now and I better do it tonight. But I gotta get all this stuff out of my head or I won't be able to write a thing without worrying her and she don't need that. She worries when she doesn't get a letter, but she'd worry worse if she knew what's been going on here. I won't ever tell her about the last two days. Not something she ever needs to hear. She's not doing the best in the world right now. The baby is getting too big too fast and she gets tired and has headaches and worried about me all the time. I hope I get home soon. Hell, after the last two days, I hope I get home at all.

Us taking over Okinawa must of really put a bee in the bonnet of the Japs more than anything else we did. I reckon it's because there's nothing left between us and the main island now. Anyhow, the attacks from their planes got worse and worse. I don't know how they could have so many of them left as many as we been shooting down - not just the NC but all the ships in the task force and all our planes from carriers. I reckon you can send more when you sending them out from land and not off a ship like we have to do, but they just got to run out some time. At least I thought that, but I thought it before and I was wrong.

I already wrote a little about how we travel together but to make this make sense I better explain it a little more. We got task groups that make up task forces and all these groups travel together. If you took a bird's eye view each of us groups might look like a bullseye. The Japs sure think we do.

Anyhow, the aircraft carriers is in the middle of each group cause she's the one with the planes and the best we got to fight the Japs with when they're coming at us through the air. Then around the carrier we got battleships like us. Then in the next ring out, they got the cruisers. Then on the circle farthest out on the very outside we got the destroyers, the tin cans we call them cause they're little and lightweight. They can go fast.

So you start in the middle with one carrier, then you go out to the next circle then the next you get more ships in each circle because the ships are smaller but the circles bigger. We got more than one of these groups in a task force and we're all going in the same direction but zigzagging to help keep away from torpedos down below. Up top from the planes we probably look like a bunch of bulls eyes squirming like a little boy in church.

So you get the picture. When we're shooting up at the planes we're fine. If somebody forgets and shoots when one gets too close trying to crash into a ship it's not going to be a good thing for the ship on the other side of that plane diving in if the shot misses the plane.

The planes have been coming in pretty regular for the last few days but a couple days ago it got worse. It was April 6. A day we won't forget no time soon. We're launching planes from our carriers for strikes on Okinawa. We got fellas in there now and we got to help them out best we can. But the Japs fighting back worse than ever. They send their planes out in what we call waves. A whole bunch at a time, then nothing, then a whole bunch more. We're on high alert waiting then shooting then waiting then shooting.

There were so many of them today that we weren't doing much waiting. All the ships in each group and the whole task force sped up fast as we could go and was zigzagging even more than normal trying to steer clear. Now I can't see nothing from inside my mount but I heard the fellas talking about it more than once before so I can just imagine how it must have been today. They say those planes do a bit of what you call hedgehopping where they come in low and go back up and come in low and go back up like they're playing with you making you guess which ship they're gonna dive into. We gotta shoot at them. Can't let them keep playing us like that. Sometimes they get a good hit on a ship. Even sunk one here and there. But mostly we get them first.

I can't see nothing inside the mount but we can hear. I never heard so much firing going on and we could hear when we hit the planes before they get us. Exploding in the air and hitting the water. The sounds are awful and loud and don't seem to stop for a long time. We just keep doing our job without knowing much about what's going on outside. Following orders to shoot when we're told and doing a damn good job of getting the Japs. It's all so loud for so long. Then there was a bigger noise louder than any the others. We couldn't stop doing what we were doing even though I swear I could hear the screaming.

It wasn't until later when the worst of the danger passed that we got out of the mounts and found out what was going on. It was bad. Real bad. We took a direct hit up in the director. They said it was a five-inch shell like the ones we shoot in my mount. They say it was an American shell – Friendly Fire – but it wasn't so friendly for the fellas right there. Three of them from F Division got killed and upwards of forty more got hurt. Some real bad. I hear tell sick bay is full.

The fellas who were close by say there was blood running everywhere. Fellas laying around with their arms and legs and insides blown apart. Screaming from the ones hurt and the ones trying to help. And if that weren't bad enough, something went wrong when they was hoisting the kingfisher back aboard late today after all the fighting was over for a spell. I don't know exactly what happened but I heard tell the plane didn't hit the sled like it was supposed to before it gets hoisted aboard and the plane dropped back down in the water and flipped over. We can't stop for anything when we're out there so the ship kept going leaving them behind for a rescue ship to go back and get. Our job as a battleship is to protect the carrier so we got to keep up with the group. There's destroyers on rescue mission all the time. They had to go back and get them. The pilot was okay but his radioman was never found.

That's four dead in one day. Don't sound like much when you think about whole ships going down and what happened when the troops invaded Iwo Jima but when it's four of your own, even if they were in a different division and you didn't really know them, it hurts all the more.

I went to the burial. Hell, I think every man on the ship that wasn't hurt and in sick bay must have. I was sitting atop my mount and everywhere you looked there was fellas atop of all the mounts and on the deck and on the other levels too looking down. We had burials at sea before and I usually try to go just to show my respect, but this one was different. There was three American flags covering up three bodies of fellas that won't never get to go home. I don't know nothing about them yet, but you know they got somebody back home waiting for a letter that won't never come. Waiting for a son or a husband they won't never see again. There might be babies back home that won't have a daddy no more.

I couldn't help thinking about that while I sat there and watched them body bags slide out from under the flags and heard the bugler playing TAPS. I prayed for their families back home hoping God will help them get through it. But I was selfish in my prayers too. I begged God not to let me die before I got home to Evelyn and our baby.

All the while we were at the funeral we kept looking up too. I was glad the Japs left us alone for just long enough to bury the dead. It wasn't long before they were coming in again. I wonder what we got to do to ever get it to stop.

April 8, 1945

My darling wife,

I'm sorry I hadn't written in a couple days. We been pretty busy. I know it don't help for me to say don't worry when you miss getting mail, but there's no reason to worry. Everything is fine.

I hadn't had any new letters in a while but we may be getting some before too long. I expect we'll be going out to fuel some other ships and sometimes they bring the mail. I hope so cause that way my letters will be coming home to you and maybe you won't worry so much. I wish there was a way for me to talk to you every day so you know I'm alright but there just isn't a way.

I hope you're feeling better and doing what the doctor says. Let me know what you decide about where you're going to live when you leave Tennessee. I know that will be hard for you since you been away from home working on your own for a while now. But I know you would do whatever you got to do to take care of our baby even before it's born. I just know you're gonna be the best Ma ever was.

I been thinking about something and wondered if you would

mind if I ask my Ma. There's this rocking chair out in the barn that belonged to my Grandma. It's up in the hay loft. I heard the stories about how she rocked my Ma and her brothers in it by the fire and sung songs to them and read books by the light from the fire and from the oil lantern. I was thinking it would be a mighty fine thing to fix up that rocking chair when I get home so you can rock our babies in it too. Would you like that? There's a cradle up in the attic I bet my Pap would bring down and fix up just in case the baby gets there before I do. I know you're going to want some new things for the baby like a dresser and a crib, but I thought the family things might be nice too. But it's whatever you want. We can buy all new stuff if that's what makes you happy. I know it's about time to start thinking about those things. I wished I was home to help you do it all, but I don't know when I'll get there and you can't wait til the last minute for things like that. That baby ain't gonna wait coming just because his Pap hasn't come home yet.

Well I got some work to do so I got to sign off for now. But just remember that everything is fine and I'll be home soon as I can.

All my love,
Roy

April 9, 1945
Darling,

Do you know what today is? Yep, the ship is four years old today. I reckon we might get some ice cream to celebrate. And maybe a cake. Hadn't had none in a while now.

We got a full day of fueling coming up and I'm hoping that one of the ships we fuel brings us some mail. Or maybe the ship bringing us supplies will bring the mail too. That way the letters I already wrote can go out. I'm gonna save this one and try to answer some letters later if I get any.

I'm back. We got mail call late in the day. We hoisted the bags over the line after we finished refueling the ship that brought it. It sure took them a long time to get it to us but I reckon they had to sort it and get ready for mail call. I already had my shower and shaved before they got it to us.

So you decided to go stay at my Ma and Pap's house. You're going to stay at work until the end of March. So I reckon you already moved seeing as how this is already the 9th day of April. I hope you're doing alright there. I'll be dreaming about you sleeping in my bed. I wished I was sleeping there with you. But we won't stay there long when I get home. We'll get our own place straight away.

Hold this letter! Somebody just dropped a whole other stack of mail on my bed and there's one got big letters 'OPEN FIRST' on it. You know I usually line them up by the date you put on the outside like we always been doing. This ones dated March 15 and there's a whole lot more before it. Mostly takes a month for them to get here. This one got here fast and I reckon I better read it before I do anything else since you told me to. I'll be right back to answering after I do.

It's been more than a few minutes since I read that 'Open First' letter. Lyle said I turned all white and he thought I was going to pass out but then I start whooping and hollering and everybody thought I was going crazy. Twins! We really going to have two babies and not just one?

So you didn't wait until the end of March to move because your doctor in Tennessee said your blood pressure was too high and you needed to stop working. I'm glad it worked out you could go to my Ma and Pap's. I know my Ma is fussing over you and trying to help. If she does too much just tell her in a nice way that you need to rest.

Back to the baby, I mean babies. You saw Doc Taylor soon as you got back to Georgia and you say he knew right away you weren't just too big with one baby. And he listened careful and could hear the heartbeat. Not just one but two of them. He let you listen too. Could you really hear them beating? I just can't imagine what that must be like. First you feel them kicking you all day and all night so you know they're in there alive and well, but then you hear their little ole hearts beating. I can't imagine what that feels like. You say they're beating real fast. The doctor said that's normal though.

What did he say about you? You're not telling me anything about that. Maybe you're just too excited talking about the baby, I mean babies, to think about anything else. I reckon I won't be thinking about a lot of other stuff either except how to do my job the best I can and get home to you fast. You're really gonna need me now!

I got to hit the sack now. I'm so excited I don't know how I'm ever going to sleep but maybe dreaming of you in my bed will help me to do it. I'll read some more of your letters tomorrow if I get time, but I sure am glad you wrote 'Open First' on that one or I would of missed it for days!

I love you more than words can say,

Roy

April 14, 1945

My darling wife Evelyn,

I hope you don't mind that my letters of the last few days haven't been about much but the babies. I still can't hardly believe we are going to have two. I know you got to be believing it because you're walking around with them inside you. The picture you sent in the last letter was swell. No, you don't look fat and ugly. You're the most beautiful woman I ever seen. But I want you to rest like the doctor said to do and let my Ma take care of you a bit. It will be best for the both of you.

I figure you heard the news before it made it to the ship that President Roosevelt died on April 12. What is the news saying about it back home? I wonder what difference it will make in the war.

I got a letter from Sally Jane and she said that she misses seeing you but that she went to visit Mary because they are both missing you being there even though you just left the day before the letter she wrote. I think Sally Jane's beau might be alright. Maybe they'll get married and move back to Tennessee too. If that job really is about making the war end and when it ends they should be able to leave and go home just like we will. I can't wait for that day to come. I want to be home with you now more than ever. I got three people to love and take care of now and I can't wait to get home and starting doing it more than just sending home money.

I got a joke to tell you. We hadn't done that in a while now. Do you know the difference between a fairy tale and a sea story? (what us sailors tell). A fairy tale starts 'once upon a time' and a sea story starts 'now this is no bullshit.' I heard that one the other day and thought you'd like it. When you were going to the dances and parties and stuff where there were sailors around you probably heard a lot of sea stories (lies) from them fellas trying to make you like them.

In your last letter you were talking about the view from the bedroom window. It's a pretty sight with the horses grazing. Even when the pasture is brown it looks swell but I bet the grass is turning green now and that's got to be one of the most beautiful sights ever. I like it especially early in the morning when it's just getting daylight and the sun coming up over the mountain. The sky turns all pink and red and sometimes it looks like its glistening on the horse's backs. If you open up the window, it's still a little chilly but you can hear the early morning sounds. There's usually some Robins that build a nest in that tree right outside the window and you can hear them when the rooster ain't crowing too loud. Another sound I love is at night when you can hear the crickets singing and if it rained recently you can hear the frogs thanking God for it. The whippoorwill call is probably my favorite because it promises summer.

It's going to be a fine life we build together when I get home. Just think about all the years we're going to be happy together after the wars over. Us and the babies and the other young'uns we have later. I know you're saying right now you don't think you ever want to be in the family way again. Some days you love it but most days you so tired and the babies kicking you and moving around a lot make you even tireder. Can you really look at your belly and see them move? I can't hardly stand that I'm missing all those miracles. But we'll have plenty of time to enjoy it all together when I get home and these last few years and however many more months will just be a memory that fades away with all the love and joy we're going to share.

So you did get to go see Mildred before you left Tennessee and she's not doing so good. I reckon it's going to take a long time to get over losing somebody you love more than anything in the world. I can't even think about what I'd do if I lost you. No, don't you worry about nothing. I'm going to make it home to you, I promise.

Your faithful and loving husband,

Roy

April 20, 1945

Evelyn my love,

I been reading some more of your letters and answering them when I can. It's taking about a month for them to get here. We been pretty busy out here trying to do what we got to do to get back home to you. All the fellas feeling it bad just like me. We all been gone from home for several years now and some of us like me with just the one trip back. But that was the best time I ever had when we went back and you and me got married. Those were the best days of my life so far, but I know we're going to have plenty more of them soon. Even better.

I don't want you worrying so about having to leave work and not doing anything more to help end the war. You still don't know what that place where you were working was all about or how it was helping but they kept telling you that it was. So you not being there to do the work anymore makes you feel like you're not doing your part.

That's ok because you're doing the most important work that could ever be by taking care of you and our babies. You are the most important thing I'm coming home to. Yeah I love my Ma and Pap and all of them – but it ain't nothing like the love I got for you.

The fellas here that already have kids say there ain't a feeling in the world like you get when you first see that little face and fingers and toes. Then those little fingers wrap around just one of yours and grabs your heart so tight you can't hardly breathe.

So you don't worry about nothing but taking care of yourself and the babies. I'm glad my Ma is being helpful without being a pest. I know she's a good cook and does the best by you that she knows how until I get home. She probably needed being needed to help her along since all her own young'uns are gone. I thank you for deciding to move there.

I've got some work to do then I've got to stand watch so I better sign off for now. Tell my babies I love them. You think they can hear you yet? Well, tell them anyway that their Pap loves them more than life itself and can't wait to meet them.

Your loving husband,
Roy

April 29, '45

My darling Evelyn,

I'm in the mess hall writing. Feels funny to be having a table to write on. I been doing so much writing in the mount and had to use my leg for a table. Maybe this letter looks better than the rest.

I got a couple more letters to answer then I hope I get some more. I been saving em up and answering them in order when I got the chance. That way I don't go a long time with nothing to read and nothing to answer. I'm sure glad you marked that one about the twins with a 'Read First' or I still wouldn't have read it and wouldn't know.

Yes, I am moody sometimes but I been trying not to let it show in my writing. I'm not mad about nothing at all. I just worry sometimes about you and the babies and about my Ma and Pap and everybody back home. I can't see or really know how they're doing. I know you didn't want to leave your job and Tennessee but I'm glad right now you all can be together. It makes me worry a little less. I think about Sally Jane back in Tennessee doing a different job than you were doing. She was not in an office like you. Do you know anything about what she's doing there? She writes me once in a while but she don't ever tell me nothing. I hope it's not a dangerous job. Now that Billy's back home in the states and doing a desk job for the Army I don't worry about him so much. I'm not mad about nothing and especially not about you so if my letter sounds mad sometime don't take it that way. I'll be more careful how I'm saying stuff if that's worrying you.

You don't need to worry a bit about me getting to sleep. If you got to worry, worry about the soldiers down in them fox holes listening for the enemy all around them or the boxcars rattling down a track over their heads. Better yet, include them in your prayers instead of worrying about something you can't do nothing about. When I get time to sleep I got a good bunk to climb in and I got food to eat and even a place to take a shower and wash my clothes. I don't want you worrying at all, especially about that.

So 'Life' magazine is rationed. What else is going to happen back home? This war better end soon before you don't have a thing to eat or drive or read or nothing.

I been thinking about that train ride back to Bremerton and how pretty you looked when you sleep. I'd tuck the coat around your neck a bit and then around your legs just to make sure you didn't get cold and wake up. I could look at you sleeping all day. You're so beautiful.

Ok. So I got another joke for you. One woman asked another one who just got married, 'Does your husband snore when he sleeps?' The other woman said, 'I don't know. We've only been married three days.' Get it?

I think a lot about the day I get home too and how it will be so hard standing behind other fellas trying to get off the train and get to you. I'm going to hold you so tight and kiss you so long you might not get a chance to come up for air. But if the babies hadn't come yet, I'll be more careful than that but it will be hard not to just hold you and not let you go no matter how many people around us trying to get by.

I don't have anything else to say until I read some more letters to answer so I will close for now. I love you more every day.

Forever yours,

Roy

Ulithi: April 30, 1945

We came back to Ulithi to rest and get supplies and have somebody take a close look at the damage done to our director. Scuttlebutt has it the damage is too much to be fixed here. Last time the damage was too bad to fix here we ended up back home at Bremerton and got some leave time. I sure hope that happens this time too. I could see my wife and spend some time getting ready for the baby, I mean babies, before I ship out again. If she'll have me.

I still hadn't heard her say nothing about that letter where I told her about killing Mildred's husband. It eats at me all the time. Letters are taking a long time to go back and forth now – about a month one way and a month back so if I told her round the middle of March she might not have got it until the middle of April and then her letter back to me about it, if she even bothered to write one, wouldn't be to me until the middle of May.

I reckon I better enjoy all the letters I'm getting when I do in case they stop. If we get to go back home I won't stop until I find her and make it up to her for what I done to her best friend's husband and for marrying her and getting her in the family way and leaving her all alone to deal with it by herself. And now she had to leave work and I don't believe she's telling me everything that Doc Taylor is saying. Not that I'm accusing her of lying to me but maybe not telling me the whole truth like I don't tell her the whole truth about what's going on out here because I don't want her to worry more about something she can't do nothing about. What if she's doing the same thing to me? I'm not sorry she's where my Ma can help take care of her and the babies, but it should be me. I should be there taking care of them in our own house.

We just got word we're headed to Pearl Harbor tomorrow to get patched up. That's back home in America, but it ain't back home far enough to suit me.

MAY

May 1, 1945
My darling wife,

If this letter gets a hole in it I shouldn't say what I'm getting ready to say but I think it might be alright. We're heading back to Pearl Harbor to get patched up a bit. Nothing for you to worry about though. I'm alright. I'll send you a postcard when we get there. It's the good old USA but not close enough to Georgia to do us any good.

Today we had to get dressed and go to quarters. The photographer fella from 'Life Magazine' was taking pictures from a plane flying close by us. Make sure Pap buys one when he goes into town. I think they have them at the drugstore most times but if they're rationed he needs to go quick.

When we get where we're going I'm going to get a chance to do a little bit of shopping. I'm thinking on buying you a Mother's Day present even though the babies hadn't been born yet. You're a mother already as far as I'm concerned. It might be late getting to you but know that it's coming. I reckon I better send my Ma something too so she don't get jealous. Just joking. I know she's got to be the happiest she's been in a long time helping take care of you and the babies.

You asked me to tell you which fleet I'm in but I can't do it. It's a military secret. But to tell the truth of it sometimes I'm not sure which one because we'll be in one and then between missions we'll get switched to another one and they all have numbers with the first two numbers the same but the number after the decimal is different so it gets confusing.

I don't have to know the number to do my job good so I don't let it worry me too much. We're all about the same place mostly doing the same thing anyhow. Except now we're not. Maybe something will happen to end the war before we have to go back out there and then we can just come straight home after we get fixed up. Wouldn't that be something!

I'll close for now.

> With all my love forever,
> Roy

May 7, 1945

My sweet Evelyn,

I hadn't got time to write much now but I just heard the news and it makes me one happy fella. I know they're probably dancing in the streets in the cities and even the cows are probably happy back home in the hills. I'm hoping you and Ma were listening to the radio and can tell Pap when he comes in from the fields for dinner. The Germans surrendered and they declared 'Victory in Europe Day' so that's got to mean it can't be much longer before this whole war is over and we can come home.

Love and hope to see you soon,
Roy

May 13, 1945
Happy Mother's Day my sweetheart,

I been doing a pretty good job reading and answering your letters all the while wondering if you're ever going to answer the one about the Hull. I know it takes a long time for my letters to get to you and then your answer to get back to me so a month probably hadn't been long enough, but since that last one I got came from April 2 and you still hadn't mentioned it I thought that maybe it got lost and I was glad in a way.

But then you moved back to Georgia and I was still sending your letters to Tennessee so I don't rightly know when you would have got a letter I wrote on March 13. It's all so confusing sometimes. But we got mail today and I only got one letter. I'll probably get more now that we're in port. Maybe they'll catch up with me faster. But this is the one I been waiting for.

You wrote it on April 13 because you just got my letter about me being the reason Mildred's husband died.

You said you had to read it more than one time and had to think on it a while before you answered seeing as how you love me so much but Mildred loved her husband too and you know how bad she's hurting without him. You went to visit her right before you left Tennessee. She lost a lot of weight from worry and trying to keep up with taking care of the baby and finding a job because she needs the money. She had to move back in with her folks and she's not happy there because they're fighting all the time. Not a good place to bring up a baby that she wants to be happy and hear only good things every day.

I'm real sorry about all that. I know you want to make it better for your friend and now you are so far away you can't see her like you used to do. After the babies come and you can travel better maybe you can take the train up to visit her. It's really not all that far away. You just can't do that kind of traveling now because of the babies being so big and your headaches and blood pressure and Doc Taylor needing you close by to keep an eye on you.

And then you find out your husbands the reason for your friend hurting so bad. I can see how you have to think on it a bit and didn't write me for a couple days after that. But I'm sure glad you still love me and don't blame me for it. I carry about the blame bad enough for the both of us.

It's alright with me whatever you decide to tell Mildred. You say you hadn't decided yet. But after I get home, I want us to go visit her and the baby if you don't mind.

We can take our babies and go up to Tennessee for a little trip. Maybe you can show me where you were working for so long. And maybe we can figure a way to help her out so she don't have to live where she doesn't think it's good for her baby girl. Maybe she would want to come to Georgia and live close to us. I'm sure we'll have some secretary work needs doing at our horse ranch and maybe we could build a little cabin somewhere on the land where she and her baby girl can live.

I love you more than all the drops of water in the ocean. If you ever been out here you would know how big that is. I sure am glad you still love me too. I don't know how I coulda lived if you ever stopped loving me. You're my whole life and now the babies are part of it too. We are going to have such a long happy life together and I can't wait to get home and get started on it.

Forever yours,

Roy

May 15, 1945

My darling Evelyn,

I mailed your Mother's Day present today. I know it will be way late, but at least you'll get it sometime. I hope you and Ma got the cards I mailed but I didn't get them off too early either. But I was waiting until I could find the right present for you. I never thought it would be so hard a job to do. I won't tell you in this letter what's in the package because the letter might get there first and that would spoil the surprise.

This Hawaii is a pretty place. I want to bring you here sometime for a real honeymoon. We could come to the island where Pearl Harbor is just so you could see it, but there's other islands too and we could go there so we're not reminded every day about the war. There are not so many people there on the other islands either. Least ways that's what I hear. I think that would be best but you would love the color of the ocean and all the flowers. It just smells good in the air all the time if you get far enough away from where all the ships are in the harbor. It looks better here now than it did the first time I saw it back in '42. It was still bad back then from the Japanese attack, but it's better now.

You hadn't told me before about seeing that movie 'The Fighting Lady.' That must have been a while back. I hadn't seen it but heard some of the fellas talking about it. The shots in there of the fighting might have been real pictures and we probably are in it. They can't fake that kind of stuff like they can the movies with the trench scenes and everything. We're just too big. In movie pictures like that the ships are hard to pick out which one is which but they don't all look alike even if you say they do. Some do but the only other one that looks exactly like us is the Washington.

Lyle got some letters from Mary pretty regular. In case you hadn't heard from her in a while she's doing good. She don't tell him nothing about the job or that place yall lived either and it seems to bother him more than it bothered me. But they're still

273

planning on getting married soon as we can get back home. He asked me to be his best man and he said Mary asked you to stand up with her too. That will be a fun time. Maybe Ma and Pap can keep the babies for us and we can spend a night away by ourselves. We'll be newlyweds just like them, only we have two babies to get back home to so we won't stay away more than one night.

I didn't know there was a show called 'Dear John' cause it ain't a good thing. I know more than one fella here got a 'Dear John' letter from back home and it was like the person writing it didn't care about their feelings one bit even though they were out here fighting for the very person who wrote it. It don't set right by me. I'm glad I hadn't got to worry about nothing like that.

Ok, so I got another joke to tell you then I got to go do some work. Here it is – Jack and Jill went up the hill. They both had a buck and a quarter. Jill came down with two and a half. Do you think they went up for water?'

So it's a bit raunchy but I bet it made you smile. We'll find some hills to climb when I get home but there won't be no money needed.

Loving you more every day,

Roy

May 30, 1945

Darling Evelyn,

I suppose you can tell that it's easier to write and mail letters since we're in port. You should be getting them pretty regular because I been writing and mailing them every day. Not like when we were out to sea and it could be days or weeks between mail going out.

From what I hear, that Victory in Europe hadn't done one thing to make it better for fighting the Japanese. So all the people celebrating better be thinking about the sailors and Marines and Army still fighting to get it over with in the Pacific. If that sounds like a bad mood I'm sorry but I was just hoping it would make a difference and we would be coming home instead of going back out there. This war is not over yet and I'm wishing more than anything in the world that it would be.

I got another letter from you today. They're getting here quicker than when we were out to sea. It had some swell pictures of you and Ma and Pap. They look younger than the last time I saw them at the wedding. All the war years had put some sad looks and lines on their faces but now they're looking better. Must be having you there with them.

The best picture was of you standing sideways holding your dress over your belly. I got about four like that now and I line them up on the bunk and couldn't believe how those babies have grown. Not just from the first one where I could hardly even see a bump but from the one before this last one to this one I can't hardly believe it. And the rest of you looks so little still.

Let's see. You took this one the end of April so you about seven months along. Only two more to go. I guess only one month by now. But those babies better slow down on the growing or you are not going to be able to keep them inside you.

I know you got to be tired carrying them babies around all day. I'm glad you're spending most of the time in the bed listening to the radio and reading and writing to me. You been doing some hand sewing too and some embroidery. My Ma taught you how to knit and you been doing some baby blankets, caps and booties. You are a busy little Mama. What color you doing?

How did you like the way that sounded? Mama instead of Ma. I been thinking maybe we could be Mama and Daddy instead of Ma and Pap. What do you think about that?

I know you are tired, but at least when the babies are born, Ma can help you carry them around. You can share so you're only carrying one at a time. And when I get back home it will be a lot easier on everybody because we'll have another set of hands to help take care of them.

I got to go now, but I'll write again tomorrow. We hadn't done much talking about baby names and we need to be deciding on that real soon.

> Loving you more than life,
> Roy

JUNE

June 1, 1945

My darling Evelyn,

Before I start answering your letter, I heard this joke I got to tell you because you will like this one. So here goes.

There was this young couple just got married. They were staying at his folks house in the bedroom right next to his Ma and Pap. Well, the next day they were leaving on a honeymoon trip. When it was time to go to bed the folks could hear them talking kinda loud through the wall. The husband said, 'I'll get on top and you put it in.' Then the wife said, 'No, I'll get on top and you put it in.' After a few minutes the Pap heard the husband say, 'Oh hell, let's both get on top and both put it in.' Now the Pap told his wife, 'I don't know about you but I got to see this.' So he snuck up the outside of the door and peeped through the keyhole. They was both standing on top of the trunk trying to close it and put the lock in.

Yeah, I thought you'd like that one. Hope it don't make you laugh so hard you laugh them babies right out of you.

I hope you're getting letters from Mary but if you hadn't had one lately Lyle's been getting them regular and she is doing good. She says she misses you something awful. That new girl living in the apartment with her now isn't as nice as you and they hadn't become good friends like you did. But she still doesn't tell Lyle a thing about the work either except that they're doing something to help end the war. I hope it's soon.

Dear Johns are really coming in now. We hear of one or two every mail call. I reckon us being away so long is too hard on some girls back home that don't love their fella enough to wait on him coming home. I feel real bad for the fellas that get them Dear Johns. Ernie - another fella in my division - got one today. He was tore up about it. I'm glad I hadn't ever got to worry about that.

In this letter you were talking about baby names. We got to pick two boy names in case they're both boys, and two girl names in case they're both girls, and choose the one boy name and one girl name we like best if we get one of each. That sure is harder than just picking one name. You had some good ideas. I'm writing them down to see how they look then I'll read them back to myself and see how they sound. I like that some of them have our names mixed in. We got to think about what the nicknames might be too.

Betty Jean – this one wouldn't have a nickname cause its already short. We could call her Betty or Jean or Betty Jean. Or we could call her Bet. I reckon that is a nickname after all.

Ruth Ann – this one don't have any nicknames but we could call her Ruth or Ann or Ruth Ann

Rose Evelyn – we could call her Rose or call her Evelyn or call her Ellie or Lyn

Rebecca Marie – we could call her Rebecca or Bekki or Marie or Becca

Roy Stuart – we could call him Roy or Stuart or Stu

Gregory Daniel – we could call him Gregory or Daniel or Greg or Dan or Danny

Anthony Eugene – Anthony or Tony or Eugene or Gene

Richard Lawrence – Richard or Ricky or Lawrence or Larry or Rick

I been doing a lot of thinking on it and here's my favorites.

If it's two boys I want to name them Gregory Daniel and Anthony Eugene and call them Tony and Danny.

If it's two girls, I think I like Ruth Ann and Betty Jean and call em by both names.

But if it's a boy and a girl (and secretly that's what I hope it is) let's name them Rose Evelyn and Richard Lawrence. And they both got our names in them, your first one and my middle one. I think those names sound grand and proud. Rose Evelyn Harrison and Richard Lawrence Harrison. So when they go out in the world people will really respect them. But back home we can just call them Ellie and Larry. That sounds like mighty fine names for a little boy and a little girl growing up on a horse ranch. Don't you think?

Now that I think about it, I reckon that don't make sense why I don't just choose those two names and add two more, does it? Oh well, we got a little bit of time to think. But not much seeing as how it's already the first day of the month they supposed to be born at the end. You didn't say your favorite ones.

Well I got work duty coming up so I better go. We're still in Pearl Harbor and will be here for a while. If there's a hole or black mark there it's because I said something I shouldn't say but since we can send the post cards I don't see why it matters. I wished my Ma and Pap had a telephone and I could find one here to call you. I wouldn't be able to afford much but just to hear your voice one time sure would be swell. But I know you can't go into town and try to find one and I wouldn't know how to call you if you could, so we'll just have to make do with the letters.

I love you and our little family more than all the water in all the oceans in all the world. I can't wait until I get back home and we start our long life together.

All my love,
Roy

June 3, 1945

My darling wife,

I hope you're doing good. I know you gotta be tireder and tireder every day with the babies growing fast now. The last letter I got you wrote May 26 so the letters are not taking too long to get to me. I hope mine are getting back to you just as fast. It had a swell new picture. Don't take this the bad way cause I mean it the best way ever but you sure do have a great big ole belly!

I lay awake at night sometimes wondering what those babies are going to look like. If they're going to have your firey red hair and emerald green eyes or are they going to have my dull ole brown hair and eyes that ain't neither brown nor green but somewhere in between. I hope they take after their Mama. If not, then maybe they could have those chocolate brown eyes like my Ma.

I can't hardly wait for em to be born and get to hold em in my arms and kiss the little soft chubby cheeks and just smell em. I know babies smell good cause I seen my cousins baby before I left for the war. I reckon that little Bobby is close to five years old by now.

I wrote home to my Pap and talked to him about some acreage. I know he told me a long time ago there was a hundred or so I could have if we decided to stay there for sure. I can't never sell it outside the family though so we got to be sure it's what we want. Some of it's already pasture. He wants to slow down some and not do so many cows so he said we could have some of what he's already using since he won't be needing as much. Some of it's what he inherited from Uncle Joe when he up and died without no family to leave it to. It hadn't been worked in years and the cabin ain't worth nothing but there's a good strong stream coming off the river that runs right through the middle and there's some fine looking trees. There's ash and birch and hickory and boxelder. I believe there's a dogwood or two where the cabins falling down and that would be a mighty fine place to build us our own house.

But the best one I remember is the oak down by the river. Yep that oak where we used to use that rope swing to go out and drop over the water. I believe that's right on the edge of the property, maybe even part of it. Even if it weren't ours to own it would be close enough to the house that our younguns could enjoy the same things we did when we were little. I think that would be a fine thing but I best put up a new rope. I expect that one might be frayed and rotten by now.

I been having a harder time getting to sleep at night since we been in port getting fixed up. It's a different kind of feeling than expecting to be called to GQ at any time and not knowing whether a bomb or kamikaze is nearby. It's a feeling of wishing I could be home so bad that it eats at me and gnaws at my mind like a rat on cheese that keeps me from sleeping. I'm thinking about you all the time and how I wished I was there to help you and just be with you. I miss looking in your eyes and seeing your smile and just the way you started leaning into me when we was walking anywhere.

I miss all the more serious and good stuff we did on our honeymoon too, but I never thought I'd miss the regular stuff so much. And now I'm missing the babies I don't even know yet. I didn't get to see none of their growing except by the pictures you sent me. And I didn't get to see the kicking and moving around. I can't hardly believe you said they really get hickups inside you and you can see and feel it. I hope I don't have to miss all that miracle stuff the next time.

I reckon I'm feeling a might sorry for myself when I should be thinking about how you're feeling. But I just love you so much I can't hardly hold it all inside me and if I was there I wouldn't have to. We could just share it all for the rest of our lives. That day I get home can't come none too soon for me.

Missing you a mighty lot,

Roy

June 7, 1945

My darling Evelyn,

I received your letter of May 31 today. It is very short because you said you are tired, but it has the best news ever. I can't tell you how happy and excited it makes me to be a Daddy. I like that we decided we wanted to be Mama and Daddy instead of Ma and Pap. The names sound a bit younger like us.

TWINS! Born on May 30, 1945. One boy and one girl. Now you're waiting to hear back from me about names before you name them. I hope my letter got there by now. They're not taking but about a week since we're in port.

Our baby boy was the first born and he was the biggest but they were early so they were still little. My son weighed 4 lbs and 14 oz and our baby girl didn't weigh nothing but 4 lbs and 3 oz. But they're fine. The doctor says they're healthy even if they're little. They got all ten fingers and toes – you know because you counted and kissed every one.

They cry real loud and are already hungry. That's good. You done a real good job taking care of them before they were born. I wished I could have been there to help you. But I'll be home soon to help take care of them now. I'm glad you say my Ma is doing a good job and your Ma is coming over to help too. That's good. I reckon you can't have too many hands when you got more than one baby.

I gotta go now. I get some liberty today and I'm going to buy a whole bunch of cigars for the fellas. I hope you're taking good care of yourself and feeling alright. You didn't really say much about that. But I know my Ma and your Ma and both our Paps are going to take good care of you til I get home.

Love and miss you more every day.

A proud Daddy,

Roy

June 12, 1945

My darling Evelyn,

How are you and the babies doing? I hadn't got a letter at all since the last one you wrote right after they were born. I reckon you're so busy taking care of the babies and taking care of yourself that it's hard to find time to write. I expect by the end of the day you might be planning on writing but you fall into the bed dead tired. I can't hardly think how hard it would be and with you just not long ago birthing them and you needing to rest just to get your strength back.

I hadn't had letters from Ma either and that's not so different. She usually was writing one a week or so and sometimes not that many when the farming was at a real busy time. She's got to write to Billy at Fort Bragg and to Sally Jane still up there in Tennessee doing whatever it is she's doing, so my Ma don't have the time to write to me as much as you did. I reckon you're not gonna have the time anymore either even after you're not so tired. I understand.

But not hearing from neither of you and it don't seem like from nobody else either makes me feel a bit worried. I reckon it ain't nothing but what I just said. Everybody's busy and tired at the end of the day.

Well, we got word we should be shipping out in about three weeks. I'm hoping to get some pictures of you and the babies before then because they're ain't no telling when we'll get mail after we leave. We'll be in and out of port doing some training to check the ship out and make sure she's tiptop again and to get us back in shape since we haven't been doing nothing much with shooting and stuff while she was in dry dock. Just weren't no way to do that. But we got to be the best we can be when we go back after Japan. It's about time we get this war over so we can come home.

Since I don't have letters to answer and don't have more news of my own, I'll close for now. I got work duty coming up first thing in the morning, so I gotta be rested up. I'm going to try to put your picture under my pillow again tonight and see if I can dream of you.

All my love forever,

Roy

PS - The fellas loved getting the cigars. They all said to tell you they said you are a fine woman to be putting up with me. And now to give me two babies and not just one. I reckon I got the best girl back home waiting for me as any of them I know.

June 16, 1945

My dearest Evelyn,

I've been writing every day, but it's been a long time now since I got your last letter about the babies being born. I hadn't had no more letters from anybody and that just don't feel right. Even if everybody's busy and tired somebody's got to take a minute to let me know what's going on back home. I hadn't never been this long without a letter except when we were slap dab in the middle of battle and they couldn't get them to us. Then I would get a whole passel of them at one time. But I don't think that's going to happen this time.

We're right here in port where the mail call comes nearly every day, and I hadn't got a letter since the one that was wrote on May 31 the day after the babies were born. I got that one June 7 and this here's June 16 so that makes nine days. Something just ain't right about that.

We'll be leaving tomorrow for a few days training out in the ocean and I won't be getting letters until I get back to port. Won't have a chance to write either. So I have no letters to answer and nothing else to talk about. I'm having a hard time making this letter much longer.

I hope I get a letter and some pictures soon. I want to know what you decided to name the babies and I want to see what they look like and see in a picture that you're alright. Or even just words to at least let me hear whether they got your red curls and green eyes or they got no hair at all like a lot of babies. More than anything I want to know that you're okay and that you still love me. I sure do love you and I'm getting to be worried about you and everybody so somebody please write me soon.

All my love,

Roy

WESTERN UNION

WU9 2 TOUR = PEARL HARBOR HAWAII JUNE 16 1945 716P

MRS ALICE MAY HARRISON=

ROCKY STONE LANE SIMMS HOLLOW GEOR=

NO LETTERS WORRIED SOMEBODY WRITE SOON = ROY

Pearl Harbor: June 16, 1945

I don't know what's going on but I hadn't been so scared even when we were fighting off the kamikazes coming in from every direction. I don't even know how to put it in words but something just ain't right. I can feel it all the way in my bones. But we're going out for gunnery practice for a few days and there's not one thing I can do about none of it.

I'm hoping that telegram I just sent my Ma don't scare her to death before she gets a chance to read it. Telegrams in war time don't hardly ever bring good news except when we were coming home. Most I hear they send telegrams back home when the soldier or the sailor dies or goes missing or gets taken by the enemy as a prisoner of war. My folks got one when Billy went missing but then I hear the Army gave them a visit too. But I didn't know what else to do. I hadn't heard nothing and I just got to know that Evelyn and the babies are alright. I can't hardly bear the not knowing.

I thought if I could write it down here it might ease my mind a bit. Most times it does. I got to be sharp on the target practice. I can't afford for me nor my crew neither to not be ready when we go back out there. We got to go all the way to Japan next time. Get em right where they live. I just hope I got some kind of news when I get back to port. Those are going to be a long long three days.

June 19, 1945

Dear Ma,

I just got back from being out for training and I got your letter late tonight. I been so worried and didn't know what else to do but send a telegram that you probably got after you wrote this letter. I been out of my mind with worry about Evelyn and the babies. Now I see I was right to be worried. I know you meant well not sending me no telegram cause you wanted to explain it all, but I don't know what was worse. Hearing a little bit and waiting for an explanation in a letter or hearing nothing at all.

I don't know that I understand what you're saying exactly except that Evelyn is just too wore out to even take care of the babies. She sleeps most of the time and her heartbeat is weak. Dr. Taylor's been coming to see her regular at the house but she lost a lot of blood when the twins were born. And something else weren't quite right for a while. That must be why she had to go home and stay in the bed most of the time. She never told me none of that except her blood pressure was a bit high and that she was getting big. She said it was nothing to worry about and she sounded fine in all her letters until that last one that was so short. Her handwriting didn't look right in that one either but I thought it was because she just had the babies she might just be tired like she said.

You're telling me I need to get the Navy to let me come home because it's real bad and she might not make it. I don't rightly understand how that can be when she was a strong healthy woman. But I'll do the best I can do. I don't know where to even start but I'll see what I can do. I'll send you a telegram if I find a way to come home. Other than that, I'm going to keep sending letters home to Evelyn. You say she can't even hold her head up to read nothing so can you please read them to her for me?

I know you got your hands full taking care of everybody so don't worry none about writing letters. If something gets worse or better send me a telegram. I'll send you home some money to take care of it. Other than that you just take care of everybody and don't forget to take care of yourself too. We all need you too much for you to let yourself get down. I know I hadn't never told you enough but you been the best Ma a boy could ever ask for. I love you and Pap more than I ever told you.

I'll do my best to get home if they'll let me. The ships supposed to leave to go back to war the end of the month so I don't know how I'm going to make it happen but I'll try. Please take care of Evelyn and the babies for me until I can get there. And thank you for the pictures of my babies. They are some cute little rascals. I'm sorry I ain't there to help you with them. I'll do my best to get home. I'll go talk to my CO right now and see what I got to do.

Your loving son,

Roy

PS - Thank you for telling me the names of my babies – Larry and Ellie. I'm glad there's nothing wrong with them and that they're healthy and already getting bigger.

June 20, 1945
Dear Evelyn,

I asked my Ma to read these letters to you since you're not quite up to reading them yourself. I been talking to some people and trying to find a way to get home to you soon as I can. I hadn't found out nothing just yet, but I won't give up trying and you can't give up either.

I wanted to tell you what I did with the pictures of Larry and Ellie. I hung them up in my locker next to the pictures I lined up of you showing them growing in your belly. They sure are some cute little things. But they're really tiny. I hope you're feeling better and getting to spend some time with them.

Ellie sure don't have much hair but looks like she might have a little fuzz on top. What color is it? Don't seem right that the boy's got the head full of hair and the girl don't have none. I can't tell from the pictures what color their eyes are yet. Ma forgot to tell that. (Don't worry Ma you can tell me when I get home or I can see for myself). My buddy Eugene that's got two kids back home said you can't really tell too much about their eyes when they're little like that. They all just look dark blue or maybe brown or black and they start changing when the baby starts getting a little bit bigger. I hope they change to green like yours or if brown then they're the dark brown like you Ma, not the can't decide what color brown like mine.

I wanted to tell you that I been praying every night and every morning and sometimes in between that God will take care of whatever it is that's wrong with you and get you all healed up to enjoy the babies while you're waiting for me to come home. We got a long happy life to get started on soon as I get there so don't you forget about that.

I know my Ma and your Ma are going to take good care of the babies while you're getting better and back up on your feet so you just think about how you're going to do that and don't you worry about the babies or me or nothing else but yourself. I know that's not in your nature, but it's the most important thing to do right now.

We got to go back out to do some training for a few days so I probably won't be doing much writing and even if I did they wouldn't get mailed, so don't none of you worry if you don't hear from me for a few days. I'm just fine and I'm going to get home soon as I can.

All my love to every one of you. I think about home and that house full of the most important people in my life. I'll be glad when I can walk in that front door and soak in all that love and give all I got to give right back to all of yall.

Loving you with all my heart,
Roy

June 25, 1945
Dearest Evelyn (and Ma too),

How are the two prettiest and best ladies in my life doing? I hope this letter finds you both doing good and Evelyn's getting stronger every day. Ma, I hope you're not doing so much as to wear yourself out. Let Ms. Ruth help out because you know she wants to since Evelyn is her daughter. Between the two of you maybe it won't be so hard taking care of the babies.

I been thinking every day about how it must be to hear them cry when they get hungry or messed up their diapers. Most people might think that's a bad thing, but I'd give anything right now to be close enough to hear it. I know it ain't a man's job to do that part but I want you to teach me how to change the diapers when I get home and how to make the bottles and everything. I want to be a Daddy that knows how to take care of my babies much as I can. I told that to Ernie the other day and he said I was talking about being henpecked and that was woman's work.

But it wasn't much later he said he wouldn't mind knowing how to do those things next baby they have when he gets home. He said sometimes he wished he had knowed how to do it before he left home. There were times he was holding his baby and had to give it up to his wife or his ma cause they knew what the baby needed and how to take care of it. Me and him done both decided we want to be able to do whatever our baby needs us to do. We've been getting pretty close lately now that I got kids and he does too.

I'm still working on getting hold of somebody who can tell me something about coming home. Sometimes when you get transferred to another ship you get to take a leave in between. That might be my best shot at getting home so I asked for two different things. I asked can I come home and just take some time to be there while you get better. And I asked can I get a transfer to another ship or maybe a desk job like Billy got. I know that's the Army and this is the Navy and it ain't the same what happened to him and the reason I need to come home. But I'm working on it. I can only asked my CO and it's got to move up the ranks from there, but I'm trying real hard.

Give the babies a hug for me and tell them their Daddy loves them. Evelyn, I love you more than I ever knew I could love somebody. My Ma told me it would be like that one day when I met the right person so I don't think it's going to hurt her feelings for me to say it. I didn't think she knew what she was talking about when she said that way back a long time ago, but she was right.

Now I hear tell that babies give you a whole different kind of love and they keep filling up your heart til you think there ain't room for no more love but the more love you got the more room there is. That's a funny thing to me but I can't wait to come home and find it out. Those pictures are something that make me love them already but I know it don't compare to what's going to happen when I get to see them and touch them. I thank you for being the best Mama you could be even before they was born.

We're going to have a long happy life together so keep that in your mind and maybe it will help you get better real soon. I bet Ma's putting the babies in the bed with you when she can so you can at least touch them and smell them and they know how much you love them too.

All my love forever,

Roy

PS (Ma – keep this part a secret but I thought you ought to know. The ship is set to get underway in a couple of days. You got to understand that if there's any holes or black marks on my letters I said something I shouldn't say. But if I don't get a transfer or some leave or something by the time the ship gets underway, there ain't no telling when I'll be home. I need you to do some powerful praying that something will happen before we pull out. There ain't nothing more I can do. I got to wait for other people to make the decision for me.)

Pearl Harbor: June 26, 1945

Well, I got bad news today and I don't rightly know how to write home and tell my Ma and Evelyn. My request for a transfer got denied because the ship's pulling out again tomorrow and they have nobody to replace me so I can't transfer somewhere else until they do.

And my request to go home because my wife had the twin babies and is real sick got denied because having babies is a natural thing and most women go through a patch of feeling sorry for themselves after having a baby so having two probably makes it worse but it ain't no reason to grant leave. Lots of people having babies and lots of people been sick so if they granted leave to everybody cause of either one of those reasons, there wouldn't be nobody left in the Navy.

Least ways that's the way my CO explained the decision. I signed up for six years and I hadn't even finished four yet. So I still got a ways to go. He said if the war gets over we might be in port somewhere and maybe I can move my family closer to where I am when that happens. But right now, I hadn't got much of a choice but to stay on the ship and go back to finish what we started.

I just got to figure a way to explain that to Ma and Evelyn tonight. We get underway tomorrow.

June 27, 1945

My darling Evelyn and my sweet Ma,

It's 0300 hours and I can't sleep. I came out on deck with my flashlight because I wanted to write this letter to go out before the ship gets underway tomorrow and today will be a busy day. What I got to say you both need to hear so I figured I'd just address this letter to the both of you. It's news I got last night but didn't know how to say it. I hope you both know how much I love you and how hard I tried to come home. I wasn't able to get the answer we wanted for today.

The Navy sees having babies as a normal part of life which I know it is and lots of people have them while the sailors off at sea. So they don't see that as a reason for me to come home. I don't reckon being tired and worn out after having a baby seems to be a good enough reason either. Maybe if I knew more about what the doctor is saying then it would help, but I know you hadn't had time to write.

Seeing as how I hadn't got a telegram saying things are different I'm thinking that they aren't any worse but they're not a whole lot better either. Ma – I ordered some flowers yesterday to be sent home today. She should get them a long time before this letter gets there. I hope they made her smile.

I love you all so much I don't know how to explain it. I'm going to close for now and take this down to the post office. They said the mail would go out but it all had to be censored and at the post office tonight before we depart at 0700 tomorrow. That's not much time.

Please take care of each other and the babies. I'll do my best to get this war over and get back home soon as I can.

With all my love,

Roy

Pearl Harbor: June 28, 1945
I did the best I could but I failed my Ma and Evelyn and the babies. My CO said they told him my wife would have had to be dying or dead for me to get leave and then it might not happen. I'd rather go back to war than for that to be true.

It's 0300 and I can't sleep. Same time I woke up yesterday but this morning I had to pull out my flashlight and write under the covers so as not to disturb anybody. Writing in this diary ain't like writing a letter home. It can't be seen.

I'm not feeling like too good of a man today. I know I made a promise to the Navy and it was a six-year promise but I made a promise to Evelyn and it was for a lifetime. I never thought the sickness part would come before the health part, but now I failed her in that too. She's sick and I ain't there to take care of her.

I don't know how I'm going to keep my mind on the things I got to do but I got to figure out how to do it. If I don't somebody might die that don't have to if I do my job right.

I pray to God he makes her better and helps me do the job I gotta do to get home to her. We get underway at 0715 this morning.

I never thought I'd think so much about going AWOL.

WESTERN UNION
WU9 2 TOUR = PEARL HARBOR HAWAII JUNE 28 1945 1100A
MRS ALICE MAY HARRISON=
ROCKY STONE LANE SIMMS HOLLOW GEOR=

LEAVE GRANTED BE HOME THREE WEEKS DON'T LET HER DIE = ROY

June 29, 1945

Dear Ma,

I wanted to write this one just to you because I got to say things Evelyn don't need to hear. But then I'm going to write letters to Evelyn every day it takes me to get home and I need you to read them to her. Some of them might be embarrassing to you but I'm thinking if I talk about the time we spent together after we got married and remind her how much we got to look forward to then maybe she'll fight harder.

You should have got my telegram by now saying I was coming home. The ship was pulling anchor and ready to get underway when somebody made them put the gangway down and an officer came on board. He had orders for me to leave the ship. Dr. Taylor's telegram got there just in time. I bet you had something to do with it being him that sent it and not you. You always have been a smart woman.

They let me go below decks and get a little bit of my stuff. I had to leave all my pictures and some other important things that Evelyn sent me over the years. Lyle said he'd take care of the rest and put it in his locker so he could bring it home with him. That's my best friend you met at the wedding. He's going to marry Evelyn's best friend Mary when the war's over. We're supposed to both stand up for them at their wedding.

They let me see the telegram that said my wife is dying and I need to come home immediately. I'm begging you not to let that happen. I know she's got to be fighting best she can to stay alive for the babies but maybe if she knows I'm coming home that will help too. I've just got to see her and tell her how much I love her. I just got to.

We're supposed to have a long happy life together. If somebody died it was supposed to be me. I'm the one in the war for so many years. Babies need their Mama even more than they need their Daddy. You reckon I could make a deal with God that if he lets her live just long enough for me to get home and see her then he could take me instead?

My first chance to leave is on a transport ship pulling out tomorrow morning. It's going to Norfolk but might make a stop in Charleston. If it does, I'll get off there. I been told there might be a military plane that can take me down to Atlanta then I can catch the train from there or I might have to take the train all the way from Charleston to Atlanta to Simms Hollow. It takes almost two weeks just to get to Panama and cross over to the Atlantic Ocean. The ship'll probably stop there for provisions so I'm thinking it may be three weeks before I get home.

Please help her stay alive that long. I don't know much about what's wrong but maybe she can still hear and know what you're saying so keep telling her I'm coming home. Tell her I love her more than life itself. Take the babies in there when they're crying so she can hear them and know they need their Mama. Do anything you got to do. Just don't let her die.

I love you Ma.

Your grateful son,
Roy

June 30, 1945

My dearest Evelyn,

Today I started my journey back home to you. It makes me think about the time I left Pearl Harbor almost a year ago. It was on the NORTH CAROLINA and we were headed to Bremerton. You remember the telegram I sent you saying when I'd be there? And then you had to get busy and finish up all the wedding plans. That was a happy time. I didn't think I'd ever get there and this time I'm thinking the same thing.

Remember how it was when you met me at the train station with my Ma and Pap. I was so happy to see everybody but you the most. We had to wait a week to get married and that was some long days but at least we got to spend time together at night down by the creek laying on the blanket in the moonlight talking about all the things we were going to do together after we got married and after the war was over.

You said you wanted a lot of children but you hoped we had a boy first and then a girl. Well that dream came true. You probably thought there might be two years between them though instead of two minutes! We can make our other dreams come true too. But we got to do it together.

Remember that spider web that was up in the branches of that sparkleberry bush down by the water. We watched that spider working in the moonlight and you said she was spinning her dreams just like us. I thought a lot about what you said and I hadn't never torn down a spider web since.

The best parts of those nights was holding you close to me and kissing and thinking about what we were finally going to be able to do with each other after we got married. We been waiting a long time for that. You said you were nervous about it. I was too but I made out like I wasn't because sailors aren't supposed to be nervous about things like that.

But it all turned out just fine and we were happy as we could be with each other those days on our honeymoon in the mountains and then back at Port Orchard in that little house by the sea. We can be even happier than ever when I get home. I'm coming. Don't leave me.

All my love,
Roy

JULY

July 1, 1945

My darling Evelyn,

I hope this letter finds you feeling better every day. I'm keeping pretty much to myself on this ship. I don't have much to do since I'm only being transported but I help where they let me. I had mess duty tonight and it was not like on the BB55 but swell just the same.

It made me think about our first night in Port Orchard. We were tired but wanted to cook dinner anyhow. We walked down to the market and bought some fresh fruit and vegetables and some bacon and eggs and milk for breakfast. We hadn't even took the time to see what kind of cookstove we had or anything else. But we bought a chicken we wanted to bake it cause you had found a recipe with some herbs and spices. We couldn't find all the ones in the recipe so we bought some different ones with names that sounded sort of the same. I can't remember them now.

The fella at the market told us we better buy some wood and we were glad he did. He even let us borrow his wheelbarrow to take it down to the house. You remember that? Well we got in the house and there weren't nothing but a wood cookstove. I had a hard time getting the fire just right but you put them spices on the chicken and put it in the oven. You cut up the green beans and put them in a pot to boil. You remember that? I helped you cut up some apples and some oranges and we had some grapes and nuts and made us a fruit salad.

We were leaning all against each other working in there together because there wasn't much counter but mostly because we couldn't stand to not always be touching and with our hands busy with the knives, the only way we could do that was to lean against each other. But the leaning got to be better than the cooking and we went right to the bedroom. Remember?

The water burned out of the beans and they got scorched. The fire was too hot and the wood shifted over. The chicken didn't bake like it supposed to. It was burnt on one side and not done on the other and the mixes of spices we picked out that was wrong had the whole place stinking up. So we took the beans off the top and set the pot outside and took the chicken out and set it on the counter and opened the windows to air it all out. Then we grabbed a blanket and a fork and our fruit salad and went down to the beach. We sat on the sand and fed each other fruit salad, then laid back on that blanket and finished what got so rudely interrupted by the stinking fire. That was one of the best picnics I ever had.

Think about that. I know we don't live near the ocean and we got kids we want to take with us when we go, but we can go and we can have a good time showing them the ocean and building sandcastles like that one we built the next day.

I love you always and forever,

Roy

July 2, 1945

My darling wife,

The days are passing slower than I ever knew they could. I got up early today and went above deck. I wasn't on watch but it was alright for me to be there. It was early enough there were still stars in the sky and I got to thinking about how we used to look at the stars and try to count them. Remember when you said that there was more stars than could ever be counted and that was just how much you loved me?

I got to thinking about the night we had the party before we got married. Out on the ranch with the horses grazing in the pasture and the moonlight coming up over the mountain. It was a swell time with everybody there – Lyle and Mary happy because he had proposed and she said yes, Ma and Pap so happy cause Billy had surprised them by coming home, your brother talking about what he had done in college, and Sally Jane talking about the newest fella she met at that place where yall were working. That was some of the best roast pig I ever ate and corn on the cob and Ma's peach cobbler for dessert.

Remember how we danced under the moonlight to that song 'Happy in Love' and we were so happy. We are gonna be that happy again. I'm coming home and we're going to be real happy. You just got to wait for me and think about the good times we're going to have.

I don't want to tire you or Ma out so I'm thinking one good memory a day ought to be just about right. I love you more than life itself. Wait for me.

Your loving husband,
Roy

July 3, 1945

My dearest Evelyn,

Well we're out here in the ocean without land in sight anywhere. I should be used to it by now, but I keep thinking how good it's going to be to walk on solid ground through the pasture and the woods and take the kids down to the stream and let them play in the water when they get a bit bigger. I got to teach them how to skip rocks and you can show them how to find wildflowers.

Remember that first night on our honeymoon when we were at the cabin up in the mountains. It was a while before we got out of the house. We kept saying we would go for a walk or something but we'd start out holding hands and then kissing and then it wasn't long before we were back in the bedroom if we made it that far.

But we finally did get out and take a walk. It was late at night but it was a full moon and the old hoot owl was calling. You said he was talking to us. The crickets were chirping and it had rained enough the day before that the frogs were still happy and they were singing their night song. It was so peaceful. I want you to find that peaceful spot in your mind and think about all the good times we got still to come.

We walked all the way down to the river and it didn't matter that we forgot to take a blanket. I spread out my shirt and you spread out your skirt and we lay naked on top of it. The moonlight was shining on your beautiful skin and your red curls were tumbling everywhere looking like copper in the light of that moon. We didn't do nothing but lay there and hold each other for a long time.

Then you said to me that you weren't scared about nothing as long as we had each other everything would be alright. You keep remembering that. We got to have each other for everything to be alright.

Don't leave me.

All my love,
Roy

July 4, 1945
Darling Evelyn,

It's Independence Day today but nobody on this ship wants to hear fireworks. When you been in battle then you heard all the fireworks you ever want to hear. But I'm not anywhere near the battles now, so you don't have to worry about me at all.

Since I been away from you for the last three 4th of Julys and this being the 4th one, I had to think way back to bring up a memory for Independence Day but I did it.

You're going to like the one I remembered. It was the first time I kissed you. My Ma's going to be surprised when she reads this to you but that will have to be alright. It's a good one to think about how long we really loved each other before we was old enough to know what it was.

It was way back when I was in 7th grade and you would have been in 6th. It was a real hot day like they all are in July and we had finished in the fields for the day. A bunch of us fellas went down to the river about dark and were going to go skinny dipping but then there was a bunch of girls coming down the lane and we had to keep our drawers on.

Some of the girls were older and the fellas was looking at them, especially the ones that had started to bloom out in places. But my eyes were only on you. I remember your red hair all braided in pigtails hanging down to your waist. Yall were supposed to be walking to see Sally Jane for what yall called a pajama party but one of the girls – I don't rightly remember her name but her last name was Smith cause her daddy owned the general store. What was her name Edith or Frances or something like one of those. It don't really matter. She had stole some firecrackers from her daddy's store and she was bragging about it and showing em to the fellas.

I remember how Eugene Brantley took them firecrackers and started setting them off. The first one it scared you and you jumped back and bumped right into me. It shot a feeling through me I hadn't never had before. I reached out and took your hand and you didn't pull it away. The lights from them firecrackers was glistening on your hair and when you turned around and looked at me there was something shining in your green eyes too.

I bent down real quick and kissed you. It weren't much of a kiss, just the first one we ever had and at the time it was enough to set my insides to tumbling. I'm glad we're doing it better now that we're older and married. Do you remember that? It was a while before I got to kiss you again but we got better at it each time we did it. And now we got it perfect. I need to kiss you again. Don't leave me.

All my love,
Roy

July 5, 1945

My darling Evelyn,

I'm not doing too much work on this ship so I got a lot of time to think about things we done in the past. The memories just start flooding through my mind like the river after a soaking summer rain. I don't rightly know where to start but I decided that our wedding would be a good place for today and maybe the next couple of days too. There's a lot to think about with the wedding but my favorite thing is the first time I laid eyes on you that day.

It was hard not to see you all that morning but we were not wanting to start off our married life with bad luck so we did it but we almost messed up because we stayed out so late the night before it was just about midnight when I kissed you good night on your front porch. You remember that? You told me not to dare look back because if I had looked back when I was walking away it would have been our wedding day.

I was nervous standing up there with Lyle beside me and Billy and Samuel and my Pap. The flowers were smelling something strong and it felt mighty warm in the church that day. I reckon now it was just my nerves making me feel that way because when I laid eyes on you everything else just disappeared.

You started walking down that aisle and I swear you looked like an angel. You had your hair down so it was curling all over everywhere under that veil and I could just see your face through it with you smiling at me. I never seen such a pretty dress and it fit you so tight on your waist it was so little I figured I could wrap my hands right around it and I wanted to do it right then. There was some little things on your dress that was catching the light and sparkling when you walked and there was a long bunch of your dress trailing behind you.

When your Pap said he was the one who gave you to me and I took your hand I couldn't hardly keep from crying. I know a man ain't supposed to cry but sometimes it can't be helped when you're so happy it don't hardly seem real and there's a real life angel standing in front of you that you're so lucky to be spending the rest of your life with.

Well I could go on for a while with the wedding recollections but I don't want to tire you and Ma out. You remember it don't you? We'll talk about it some more tomorrow. I love you more every day and can't wait to get there and look in your eyes again just like that day.

Loving you forever and always,
Roy

July 6, 1945

My darling wife,

Today I'm going to jump right in talking about the wedding because there's some things I just got to say. I want you to know that when I said them vows I was meaning it right from the bottom of my heart. I'm feeling pretty low right now that I wasn't there when your sickness started but that don't mean I hadn't loved you through it all just like the vows said – in sickness and in health – you are my wife and I will love you through it all and never let you go. Don't you let go neither. Don't leave me. I'm coming home to make it better.

Remember when I started to say my vows and Lou Ann's baby started to cry? I had to talk loud to be heard over the baby til she finally got up and took him out. Then I was yelling for nothing and the preacher whispered I could say it a little quieter. You remember that?

Then when you started saying yours you were talking so soft and sweet that hardly anybody could hear you. But I heard you and it was like you were talking just to me. Those were the sweetest words I ever heard from the prettiest mouth I ever saw. I watched it moving and wanted to kiss it right then and there. I couldn't hardly wait til the preacher said I could kiss my bride.

Here we are talking about kissing again just like the last letter, but I can't rightly get enough of kissing you. You been picking on me about that and the other things I can't get enough of too but it's a special thing we got between us. You remember that and keep fighting til I get there.

Love you in sickness and in health,

Roy

July 7, 1945

My darling wife,

This ship's moving as fast as it will go but it just ain't fast enough for me. I'm counting the days til I can get home to you. It's probably about eleven more but by the time you get this letter I don't know exactly how many it will be. The fuel tanker took some mail out but I don't know when we'll get another opportunity to send some. They told us today that more mail would get sent when we get to the Panama Canal. That's still about five more days from now but maybe you'll get the first batch soon.

I been thinking about our honeymoon up in the mountains. Being with you and loving you was more than I ever could have imagined. But the times in between were just as good. I know we knew each other just about our whole lives but you don't really know somebody til you live with them. And that didn't disappoint me one bit.

Watching you get ready for bed and brushing your hair and the way you didn't hardly walk but almost floated across a room. And how in the morning you would stand at the door looking out at the mountains and the sun would come streaming through your gown. I reckon I didn't tell you how I would stand there and watch you because I could see the curves of your body and your beautiful legs through that soft white fabric and it done something to me from the inside. Not just the normal stuff you expect that makes me want to grab hold of you and take you back to bed but the real special stuff like feeling a part of me I didn't even know was missing had been put back in place just because you were there. Do you know what I mean?

And I loved the times we sat on the porch swing and rocked and talked about the things we were going to do after the war was over. Us getting some land and building our own house and maybe raising some horses and lots of kids. You remember those times and think about the things we did and the things we talked about and don't forget I'm on my way home to you. Wait for me. Don't leave me.

Loving you with all my heart,
Roy

July 8, 1945
My darling Evelyn,

One of the fellas asked me today how I rated going home instead of back to war and I told him a little bit about you being sick. He said I was a lucky man.

I told him I didn't understand what he meant. He said I was a lucky man to have somebody to love that meant more than the world to me and had waited so long for me. He had got a Dear John letter from his wife while he was out at sea. I told him that I was luckier than he knew because you were the prettiest, sweetest, smartest woman I ever knew and on top of that you gave me two beautiful babies that's made out of love. He said I sure was smitten and I said I reckon I was.

I remember the first time anybody said that about me. I was in the 11th grade which made you in the 10th. School just let out and you were walking down the hall to go home. Your hair was in a long ponytail and everything was swishing when you walked – your ponytail and your hips and your skirt.

I was just standing there staring at you and Johnny Smith knocked me up side the head with his biology book. I said 'what did you do that for?' and he said 'cause I been trying to get your attention for five minutes and you so smitten with that Evelyn girl that you hadn't heard a word I said.' I said I reckon I am and then we went to football practice.

I'm still smitten with you and always will be. You remember that. I'm coming home. Wait for me.

Your loving husband,

Roy

July 9, 1945

My darling Evelyn,

I watched the sunset today and it made me think about the last day we were in Port Orchard. I had started liberty and just got home. You wanted to walk to the beach and watch the sunset. We left our shoes at the house and I rolled up my pants legs. You looked so pretty in that blue dress with the white flowers all over it. It fit tight everywhere but the skirt and you would walk a little and twirl a little and you looked so pretty and happy. I been thinking about the way you looked that night. We probably had babies already growing inside you and didn't even know it.

We took a blanket and sat down on the sand as close as we could get to the water without getting wet. We snuggled up close and you leaned your head over on my shoulder. You had your hair pulled back in a ponytail and I asked you could I take it down and you said yes. So I did and I filled my hands full of your hair and breathed in the scent of you. I was trying to burn it into my memory cause the next day you would be gone.

We talked and we laughed for a while until the sun touched the water and we both just got quiet. We sat there without saying another word and watched the sun melt into a big red puddle on the ocean. The whole ocean turned red and it felt like the saddest thing. You started to cry and I couldn't help but cry too. You were leaving on the train the next day and I didn't know when I would get to see you again.

But I'm coming home now. It won't be too many more days. We got a lot of sunsets and sunrises to share and this time they won't make us cry. Believe me and wait for me.

Your loving husband,
Roy

July 10, 1945

My darling Evelyn,

We're getting closer every day. It just seems like an awful long way to get home. I don't remember it being so long when we came out here. Maybe it's just because I'm in a hurry to get back to you.

You remember that song I sent you when I sent your ring and asked you to marry me? It was 'I'm Making Believe.' It says I'm making believe that you're in my arms. I make believe that every night when I go to sleep. I don't put my head on my pillow but hold it in my arms and pretend like I'm snuggling up to you.

Maybe Ma can get you some extra pillows and put them close so you don't feel alone in that bed. It's my bed I slept in all the time I was growing up. You could pretend you're holding me in your arms and maybe you can wake up and it will all be just a dream and you weren't really asleep at all.

I know the babies need you to hold them. And when I get there I'm going to hold you and never let you go. Just make believe I'm there already. Fight for us. Just keep fighting.

Making believe you're in my arms,
Roy

July 11, 1945

My darling wife,

They had the radio playing today down in the mess hall and I heard a song that made me think of you. It was called 'Every Night About This Time.' I think it's an old one but it's good. It says 'every night about this time, I miss you.' That's true for me every night and every day too. I'm missing you all the time.

I was thinking about the day you left on the train. Do you remember that? That was one of the hardest days of my life. We been together every day since we got married more than a month before. We rode the train together to Port Orchard after our honeymoon and I covered you up when you fell asleep with your head on my shoulder. I made sure you were ok. But then I was sending you back home all by yourself. I didn't want to see you go and I was worried about you going all that way all by yourself. I know some of the other wives were on the train too but I wasn't.

I cried some tears that day too. I ain't ashamed to say it. When you really love somebody you'd be a hardhearted person if the leaving didn't make you cry.

But the coming back should be a joyous occasion and I'm coming back right now as fast as I can. Don't give up on me. I'll be there soon I promise.

Your loving husband,
Roy

July 12, 1945

My darling Evelyn (and Ma too),

We arrived in Panama today. We got to stay here tonight while the ship gets provisions loaded onboard. I get liberty so I might see what I can find that you ladies would like as a gift. I might can find something for Ellie and Larry too.

All the rest of the mail is supposed to go out today so you should be getting all my letters together. I wrote dates on the back of the envelope like we always did so we know which one was wrote first. We learned how to do a lot of different things with our letters since I been gone didn't we? The dates worked good cause then you didn't get all confused if you read one first that was written after the other one.

I remember that one special one you wrote me that had 'Read First' written all over it so I would read it soon as it got there and not line it up after all the others. That was the time you told me we were going to have two babies and not just one. I couldn't hardly believe it. All I knew was that I wanted to be home more than ever after you told me that. I was excited about having the babies but also because I wanted to be there with you to help you and to share all the fun things and the hard things.

But I wasn't there for you and I'm real sorry about that. I can't tell you how much. I'm coming home now and I'm closer than ever so don't give up on me.

All my love,
Roy

July 13, 1945
My darling Evelyn,

I just crossed over into the Atlantic Ocean for the first time in more than three years. That means I'm closer to home than I've been since I left after we got married. It's been almost a year but it seems like half a lifetime and more. I been missing you so bad. I know you been missing me too but that's all about to be over. I'm coming home and I'll be there in just a few more days. Please wait for me.

I been thinking about so many memories and couldn't decide which one to write you about today. But when I went on liberty in Panama City I kept seeing kids and their Mas and last night I had a dream so I'm going to tell you about that instead.

Before I went to bed last night, I put your picture and the pictures of Ellie and Larry under my pillow just to see if I could dream of you. It worked. In my dream it was a hot summer day and I been out mending fences. The pastures were full of green grass and black Tennessee Walkers. That's the kind we decided on raising cause nobody else around home does. But people like them because they're a ride good and easy and smart and gentle. But they're strong too. And the sun just glistens off those black coats and makes em shine.

I parked my truck and came to the house but you weren't nowhere to be found. And neither were the twins. So I walked back out on the porch and just stood there and listened. I could hear the robin singing in that biggest dogwood tree right next to the house and figured she probably had some babies up there in a nest hidden somewhere in the branches. But the sound I heard that was the best one I ever heard in my life was our kids laughing. I stood there and just listened for a minute or two, then I followed that sound like it was drawing me in because it was.

When I got over the rise on that hill I could see yall down by the river. You had on that green dress with pink flowers on it. The one that sets off your eyes so good. You were setting on a big ole red and white check tablecloth spread out on the grass. Ellie and Larry were running around squealing and chasing each other then Ellie jumped in that big ole tire swing we hung up in the oak tree on the land side cause they weren't big enough for a rope over the river yet. Her big brother pulled it back high as his little arms could pull then let her go and she squealed the happiest sound.

I started running fast as I could to get there because everything that meant anything in the world to me was right there in front of me. That's what I'm doing now darling. Coming to my everything fast as I can. Don't leave me. I'll be there soon.

All my love,
Roy

July 14, 1945
My darling wife,

Do you remember that night in Port Orchard when we got invited to the surprise birthday party for John Albertson? His new wife had been working on it for days without his knowing a thing about it. You told me we were invited and I kept my mouth shut even with us going back and forth to the ship together every other day on our work days.

I done something to make him have to leave the ship late that day. Told him the OD wanted to see him before he left so he went looking for him but couldn't find him and I said well maybe he changed his mind. He said he didn't care his liberty started and he was going home to his new wife. He was surprised when I kept walking past our house where I usually stopped and just kept walking with him. He said what you doing, walking me home? And I said, Evelyn told me she was going over to see Grace today and to meet her there. That alright with you? I said it kinda harsh like you don't like it I won't go. But he said, sure long as you don't stay too long. I got better things to do with my wife than entertain company. We laughed, but I knew what he meant.

When we got there she had a big table out back behind the house with a tablecloth and presents and all kinds of food spread out. All the couples newly married like us and some been married longer were there and she had the radio playing. Remember us all dancing all that night? We'd do some slow songs and I could hold you tight, then we'd do some fast ones and get out of breath. You'd laugh and the sound of it was better than any of the music.

We can have our own party soon as you get better. We can laugh and dance and hold each other tight. I'm almost home. Don't give up on me.

All my love,
Roy

July 15, 1945
My darling Evelyn,

Well they told us today wouldn't no more mail be going out til we got to port so everything I wrote since Panama will just come home with me. I reckon I'll keep writing though cause it helps me feel closer to you. I'll read them all to you when I get there if you hadn't got better enough to read them yourself.

I been thinking about your hope chest. How you told me all about it when you bought it. It sounds like it's a pretty good size and it's made out of cedar so if you put blankets in it that will keep the moths from eating them up. Sure better than mothballs. They stink like you said.

You been filling it up with gifts people gave us and things you bought waiting for us to be together in our own place to use it. You told me about the blanket your grandma knitted for us. Good thing the chest is cedar. And the silverware that you picked out. I can't remember, did you ever buy that or were you waiting to see if I like it too? If you liked it I'm sure I would.

Then there's the towels with the initial H on them for Harrison. And you got dishtowels too. I'm sorry I don't remember all the other things you told me about so you need to be ready when I get home to pull it all out and show me. Tell me who gave it to us so I can thank them next time I see them. I know you wrote the thank-you notes but I'd like to say a word of thanks myself and I need you to help me know who to thank.

My hope ain't locked up in a chest right now though. It's in my heart and my mind. Hoping you're getting better every day and by the time I get home this will all be just like a bad dream that lasted too long. And maybe before my emergency leave is up they will find a way to end the war and I won't have to ever leave you again. That's what I hope.

Loving you forever and always,
Roy

July 16, 1945
My darling Evelyn,

You don't know it and neither does anybody else at home but the ship dropped me off in Charleston today instead of taking me all the way to Norfolk and I'm on my way home to you across the land not the sea. I didn't take time to send a telegram or I might have missed the last train going towards home. I got to make one switchover in Atlanta, and then I'll be headed into the Simms Hollow station.

I decided I wasn't going to worry about sending home a telegram. If there ain't somebody I know in Simms Hollow when I get there that'll give me a ride out to the farm, I'll just walk. It ain't but about ten miles and that's nothing at all when I been so far away for so long.

All my love,
Roy

July 17, 1945
My darling Evelyn,

I know this will be a letter I don't read to you. I got home today and I didn't know what to say. You are still so very beautiful but I'm scared. You tried to open your eyes but they wouldn't quite work. I could see you trying. You looked like you tried to smile but your lips hardly moved. I held your hand but you couldn't hold mine back.

I don't hardly know how to talk to you. The words just wouldn't come out but saying I'm sorry over and over again. So I'm thinking I might just write a letter every night and read it to you every day. That way I can take the time to write the words I need to say and make them come out right.

I can bring the babies in to see you and I can feed you and anything else in the whole world that you want or need. My Ma said you can't take care of nothing for yourself. She's been doing it for you. But I asked her to show me how and she asked me was I sure. I said that I wanted to do that for you too.

You been asleep for a while now. Doc Taylor came to see me late today and told me he didn't know how you were still living.

That it won't be long now. Maybe even tonight or tomorrow. That maybe you were just waiting to see me one more time.

He said to be prepared but I don't know how.

All my love,

Roy

July 24, 1945

My darling Evelyn,

I been back for a week now. I hope you like the letters I been writing and reading to you. I think I saw you smile yesterday when I was reminding you about the night in Port Orchard when we was laying on the blanket by the water and got brave or crazy enough to go swimming in the dark. We didn't have our suits but we figured it didn't matter much. Our underclothes worked alright. And I was glad we had two blankets when we got out of the water. One to lay on and one to cover up with. I don't think neither one of us could have waited any longer. Your eyes crinkled a little at the edge when I talked about it. Maybe I should talk about that kind of stuff more.

I can't tell you how smitten I am with our babies. I never knew how full your heart could get with love. They sure are a handful to take care of eating and changing and holding much as I can. I like it best when they just ate and they're happy and I bring them in to put them on the bed with you. Our whole family together like it should be. We need you.

I'm hoping you don't mind that I'm snuggling up so tight at night. I know you're tired and weak but I want to give you my strength. I want to give you everything I got. I would give you my life if that's what you need to get better.

Your loving husband,

Roy

AUGUST

Aug 2, 1945

Dearest Evelyn,

It's been two weeks now since I been home. More than two months since the babies were born. You're surprising Doc Taylor that you're still hanging on. I tell him every day you're going to get better. He tells me not to get my hopes up.

Your Ma and my Ma ganged up on me yesterday. They told me to get out of the house or they were going to beat me with the broom. Said I needed some fresh air to clear my head or I would be no good to you or Ellie and Larry neither. I reckon they were right, but it's just so hard to walk away. My Pap and me rode over to where Uncle Joe's cabin used to be and we stepped off the size of the house we need what with two babies already and us maybe adding some more when you're all well and ready for it. I know you said you wanted at least five or six but we hadn't got to have that many. I'm so full up with love for the two we got that will be enough for me for a lifetime and more if it is for you too.

Ain't much left to the old cabin no more but it had some fine oak wood inside that we dug out. Pap said it would make some strong high chairs. So we gathered up some and threw it in the back of the truck. Seeing as how the babies can't even sit up yet, we figure we got some time to get them built before they need em. But they're growing fast and getting strong. Larry laughed out loud today. Ma said that was real young to do that. And beautiful little Ellie can hold her head up so good.

We took the wood into the barn and Pap and me are going to work on it at night after everybody's settled in. Ma can listen out for you and the babies in case you need anything. I know you like me snuggling in at night and I'll still be doing it but it might be an hour or so later than usual. But if you need me you just let my Ma know some way or some how and I'll come running right back in.

I reckon there's a little bit of truth in saying I need to be making some progress on something and it would sure be a mighty fine surprise for you when you're up and feeling better. Except I just spoiled the surprise I reckon.

But if that ain't alright for me to be out after you go to sleep then you just let me know. You can blink your eyes or squeeze my hand or anything at all right now and tell me so. You just let me know when I ain't doing what you want me to do.

I love you and can't wait til you're feeling better so we can start the rest of our lives together for real. Me and the babies need you something fierce. Please come back to us.

All my love,

Roy

Aug 7, 1945

Dearest Evelyn,

I think the war may be over soon. I heard it on the news that the USA dropped what they're calling an atomic bomb yesterday on Hiroshima, Japan. Seems President Truman told them about the last of July they needed to surrender but they didn't listen. Maybe now they will.

But the thing you got to know is that place where you were working - where Sally Jane is working too - that's where they built it. That's why they were telling you that what yall were doing was going to help end the war and that's why nobody who worked there could say nothing at all about it. It had to be a surprise attack like Pearl Harbor.

Sally Jane went into town there in Tennessee away from work and called the drug store when she heard the news. That's the place she knew there was a telephone. Old man Tibbs drove all the way out here to get Pap back to the phone. Sally Jane weren't even supposed to know and she could be in big trouble for telling, but she thought it might make you better and she wanted to do anything she could.

Ellie laughed today. She couldn't let her brother get too far ahead of her. Her eyes are turning green just like yours. Larry's still look a bit dark kinda like Ma's and all that hair he had on his head is starting to fall out. He looks like my Pap with hair around the sides and none on top. An old man head on a bitty little baby.

You did a good job eating your chicken broth today. Ma cooked a big ole fat hen to give it lots of good taste and to give you something to help you put on a bit of weight. You're getting a bit too skinny and you need your strength when you're feeling better. The twins are getting heavier every day.

When you get to feeling a bit stronger we'll go outside. The sunshine's so pretty this time of year even though it's a bit hot out there. I think it would make you feel better just to see the flowers and the green everywhere. Maybe tomorrow I'll just pick you up and carry you out for a little while. Would you like that?

We'll be having picnics again soon. I just know we will.

I love you so much,

Roy

Aug 10, 1945

Dearest Evelyn,

You're looking a bit tireder today though you got a little more color in your cheeks. Maybe taking you outside was too fast. I'll wait to do it again until you tell me. But the babies sure did love laying on that blanket in the shade of the oak tree with you and I did too. I reckon maybe you just weren't quite ready for it so I'll wait until you tell me to do it again. Weren't no trouble picking you up. You're light as a feather.

Seems one bomb wasn't enough for those Japs. They kept fighting and the US let em have it again yesterday. This time in a place called Nagasaki. I wonder how many of those bombs they built where you were working. I wonder how many it will take to make them give up and surrender.

The high chairs are starting to come along pretty good. We got a good design and got the wood cut into pieces like we want them. We just got to sand the splinters out then we'll be ready to start putting them together. There's a lot of pieces. When you get to feeling better I can take you out to the barn to see them or I can bring them in the house if that's what you want me to do.

I'm getting better at the diapering. My Ma said I was learning faster than she expected. My Pap hadn't never changed a diaper in his life she said. But I want to do it. I want to do anything you and the babies need. It don't matter to me whatever it is.

Please get better soon. I need you and the babies do too.

All my love,

Roy

August 12, 1945

My darling wife,

Well today is a very important day. Do you know what it is? Today is August 12 so that means we been married one year today.

I walked out this morning before I started writing this letter and I watched the sun rise up over the mountain. It was a pretty one today. I know how much you like the sunrise and I almost came back in and picked you up and took you out to see it.

You could see the sky starting to turn a little bit pink like it does when it's still dark outside and then that pink spreads across the hills and the tops of the trees and the sky started getting the yellow and the reds and then that big ole ball of fire just appeared like it was saying here I am. Look at me. And I did cause it was a mighty fine sight to see.

It's a new beginning every day and every day I'm hoping will be the day you start feeling better. Today would be a good day for that too. We started our life together a year ago but then I had to leave.

I'm back now and we can start our life together again. That's what I want more than anything in the world right now.

Doc Taylor says you're just waiting for something but he can't rightly figure out what it is. I wished that you could tell me. I want us to have 70 more anniversaries and be sitting in our rocking chairs on the porch watching the sunrise together when we're a hundred years old. Even that won't be long enough for me.

Happy Anniversary my love,

Roy

August 13, 1945

My darling,

I don't know if you can hear me or not. Today has been a long day. I been trying and trying but you wouldn't wake up. Doc Taylor says you're just too weak to wake up but that you might still be able to hear me so I want to tell you how much I love you. I won't never get tired of saying it and I hope you never get tired of hearing it. More than all the stars in the sky and the water in the ocean and more than all the leaves on all the trees.

Forever and always,

Roy

Aug 15, 1945

My sleeping beauty,

We got the best news ever today. Heard it on the radio and Pap rode into town just to make sure it was true. The Japanese finally surrendered and the war is over. So you can wake up now.

Doc Taylor said you were waiting on something. I got to thinking that maybe you weren't getting better because you didn't want me to go back to war. If they let me come home because you were so sick then you got better I might have to go back.

But now you don't have to worry about that. You don't have to stay sick or asleep cause you think I got to leave again when you get better. The war is over. We made it happen. Me overseas and you back home. We did it together. I won't ever have to go there again. I need you here with me. We got two beautiful babies to raise and a house to build.

Just think how much fun Ellie and Larry are going to have growing up on our horse farm. They need their Mama and I need my beautiful wife. You need us too. We worked too hard to get me home for us not to celebrate together and enjoy living together for lots of years to come.

So please wake up. It's time for celebration. We got to celebrate the end of the war and celebrate the beginning of living.

I will love only you forever,

Roy

August 18, 1945
My Angel Evelyn,

It seemed fitting that I say goodbye in a letter cause that's the only way we had to talk to each other the whole time we been married and for almost three years before that. But this letter ain't as much <u>to</u> you as it is <u>about</u> you.

I want all our friends and neighbors and family gathered here today to understand how special a person every one of us lost when you left me the day the war ended.

Dr. Taylor said you shouldn't have lived that long cause your heart gave out the day you gave us the precious gift of Ellie and Larry. He believes you held on and made your heart keep beating out of sheer will just to make sure I got home and they would have their Daddy here when their Mama left em.

But you were maybe worried I would have to go back to war, so you waited just a bit longer until I told you the war was over and I wouldn't have to leave no more. I wished I could take those words back.

You were the sweetest, prettiest girl anybody could ever know.

319

And the best wife a sailor away from home could hope for. You wrote me all the time and kept my spirits up. You gave me something to come home to – a loving wife and two beautiful perfect babies. And all that time you were working in your own job that was helping end the war. You helped bring us all back home. People talk about heroes when they talk about a war. You are my hero.

You said things that make life really special about the way the spider was spinning dreams just like us. And how the stars you saw at night were the same ones I saw no matter how far away I was and that made us closer together.

You helped your friends when they were in need and you cared about my family like it was your own.

I promise I will take good care of Ellie and Larry and teach them just how special their Mama was. I'll teach them the things you woulda wanted them to know and do. I know I can't never raise them as good as you would've done but I'll do my best. That is my promise to you.

And I promise to love you forever and always for the rest of my life til I see you again in heaven.

Goodbye for now,

Roy

1994

EPILOGUE

August 12, 1994

My darling wife,

Happy anniversary my love. This is what they call the golden one. I been writing you a letter every year on this day since we got married way back in 1944. I sure hope you been hearing them when I read them to you. God's blessed me every year with the prettiest weather you ever seen so I can come out to visit you right at 3 p.m.

You remember way back after we first got married and I was back on the ship? I told you there wasn't ever going to be a next time for either one of us. That was true. I thought it would be true because we would live a long happy life together but God didn't see fit to grant us that.

But what he did give me was the strength to carry on after you left me. He gave me the wisdom and the patience to raise two of the cutest little redheads ever stepped on the face of the earth other than their Mama.

And now our family has grown so big. Got to be close to 40 of us now and a couple more on the way. I been telling you every year about what's been happening that year with the horse ranch and about Ellie and Larry and their families and all that's gone on without you. I had to take to writing stuff down when it happened so I wouldn't forget nothing. But there wasn't a single day we didn't miss you.

And there was no one in the world to take your place. So I'm glad God gave me the peace of being alone at night, of it being enough to watch the twins grow up and raise the horses and be happy. The only way my life could have been better was if you were here to share it with me. And in my heart you always were.

This year we got four more great-grandchildren and three great-great grands. Three more of those on the way. Ellie's knee-baby Marie had a little girl last fall. She's already got long red curls just like you so I know she's going to be a handful. And she got your emerald green eyes. She's a pretty one for sure.

Ellie's oldest boy Roy and his wife had a boy. He was a surprise God saw fit to bless them with. If you been keeping up, you know that was number seven for them and he's younger than their grandkids. Kind of history repeating itself like with Ellie.

Larry's middle girl Sarah Jane had twins. She done fine and the babies are fine too so don't worry none about them. It was two girls.

Larry's youngest son Richard is getting married. He's quite the horseman, and I promised him and his new bride a little piece of the ranch as a wedding present. It's the 50 acre plot at the bottom of Whippoorwill Mountain.

I believe Richard will be the one to keep the ranch going when the rest of us are gone. But the whole things grown to nearly a thousand acres so there's enough to go around for them that's interested in staying. Most of em went to the city and got fancy computer jobs.

We got five in the Navy – four boys and the one girl. They're all on ships. It ain't like it used to be when the girls couldn't be the same place as the boys. I reckon it's a good thing I was born when I was.

We got one in the Air Force and one in the Army and one in the Marines. They every one of them came to me before joining up and asked me did I mind that they weren't going to be Navy. I told them I was proud no matter where they served their country. But I probably already told you that when I told you about the ones who went away but came home safe from Desert Storm. God sure blessed us there.

I hadn't never let the younguns read the letters I wrote home to you but Ellie's youngest Mary Sue loves to count everything she can get her hands on. She was one of those surprise blessings if you remember. She's just turned 12 and like her cousins before her that's the day I introduced them to the cedar chest. They all seen it of course, but on their 12th birthdays I figure they're old enough to learn about the special things. Not those things, that's up to their own Mama and Daddy, but about me and you.

So I open up the hope chest and I show them the things you saved there and told them about how I was away at war but it didn't matter cause we stayed together in our hearts. And I show them the pictures and the things you saved while I was away waiting for us to start our lives together. Then I tell them how I couldn't quite bring myself to use them after you were gone.

You been knowing that every year on our anniversary I go through the chest just before I sit and write to you. After all these years, my favorite thing in there is still the crystal vase with the letter 'H' and our wedding date cut in the glass. That might be a funny thing for a mountain man like me to like but somehow it reminds me most of you, delicate and beautiful.

When Ellie and Larry were little, my Ma just sort of knew that was a day I needed to be by myself so she would always plan a special trip for the twins never saying why. When the kids got old enough to be on their own they just somehow knew I needed the time to be alone with you.

Well the little one Mary Sue was real interested in the letters when I was going through the chest with her. That was just two days ago. I told her maybe one day after I was gone and she got big enough to understand, her Mama might let her read them. She asked me how many was there and I said I didn't rightly know. She said can I count them and I told her she could. She laid them all out on the bed divided up by years. She counted a total of 599, the last one being last year on our 49th Anniversary. I'm still putting the dates on the outside the envelope the way we used to do.

So this one is number 600 and it will be my last. Not because I would ever stop writing you in my lifetime. It's kept me close to you all these years. But I went to the doctor last month and he found some cancer in my stomach. I probably won't see the first snow fall on the mountain tops this year. I won't be writing no more letters home. Won't be needing to. Be watching out for me cause I'm coming home instead.

I been waiting a long time to say this – I'll see you soon.

Loving you for all eternity,

Roy

Also by Cindy Horrell Ramsey
Boys of the Battleship NORTH CAROLINA
John F. Blair, Publisher

ABOUT THE AUTHOR

Cindy Horrell Ramsey lives with her husband in Southeastern North Carolina where they grew up, married, and raised a family. After all their children were grown, Cindy attended the University of North Carolina Wilmington where she earned a BA in English and a Master of Fine Arts in Creative Writing. She is published in fiction, non-fiction, and poetry, and continues to write for local and regional magazines. In addition to being a published author, Cindy has worked in publishing and education. She now spends her time writing, enjoying retirement, and being Mimi to four beautiful granddaughters.

Made in the USA
Lexington, KY
17 February 2018